THE VENGEANCE
OF MERLIN

by

Steven A. McKay

Book 6 in the

WARRIOR DRUID OF BRITAIN
CHRONICLES

KINDLE EDITION

This book is dedicated to my wife, Yvonne, for supporting me through all our years together. I love you.

PLACES in *The Vengeance of Merlin*

Alt Clota – Strathclyde
Cardden Ros – Cardross, Argyll and Bute
Dun Breatann – Dumbarton Castle, West Dunbartonshire
Dun Buic – Dumbuck/Milton, West Dunbartonshire
Dun Edin - Edinburgh
River Aerfen - River Dee, Chester
Caer Legion/Deva - Chester
Garrianum – Burgh Castle
Hanging Stones – Stonehenge
Iova - Iona
Isca - Caerleon
Luguvalium - Carlisle
Mucrois - St. Andrews, Fife
Portus Setantiorum/Twyni Tywod) - Meols, Wirral
River Leamnha – Leven
Shirva – Twechar, East Dunbartonshire

CHAPTER ONE

"Won't be long until that big Damnonii druid, Bellicus, will be screaming for mercy at my feet." The Saxon warrior stood at the prow of his longship and grinned at the images his mind was conjuring. It was a pleasant spring morning and the oars of his warband were powering him towards his destiny; of course he was happy and filled with ambition. "I've waited a long time to meet him again, Sigarr. It will be a happy meeting — for me at least!"

He laughed and his cousin smiled too. "Aye," Sigarr agreed, nodding as he stared out at the coastline to their left. "The druid has been a thorn in all our sides. I'm looking forward to seeing his end, Horsa."

Sigarr was a small man who wheezed and coughed when he physically exerted himself, but Horsa was tall, broad, and as bloodthirsty as any Saxon warrior. He and his brother, Hengist, had come to Britain with their warbands not to settle, as some of their kinsmen had, but to conquer, and to rule. So far, they had been thwarted in their quest, taking control of the old Roman forts like Garrianum on the east coast collectively known as the 'Saxon Shore', but finding it harder than expected to expand outwards. The native kings might not have been an issue, for they were disparate and worked separately for the most part, but the warlord Arthur, the so-called 'Bear of Britain', had grown in prominence and influence in recent years, bringing together enough of the Britons to push back the advancing Saxon tide.

Arthur would need to be dealt with one day if Horsa and Hengist were to fulfil their ambitions, but, for now, the other troublesome Briton, Bellicus of Dun Breatann, would meet his end just as soon as Horsa's warband found him.

"Mucrois is just ahead, my lord."

Horsa nodded to his helmsman and stretched up to his full height of over six feet, drawing in a great chestful of bracing, sea air and letting it out in a bark of laughter.

"By Thunor, I feel good, Sigarr," he said, and it was obvious he was in a fine mood for he usually had little time for his cousin whom he saw as a weakling.

It was true, compared to Horsa or any of the other warriors manning the long, shallow-hulled ship carrying them across the whale road towards Pictland, Sigarr was weak, physically. The smaller jarl had a sharp mind and a quick wit, however; and, although Horsa cared little for those qualities, Hengist was the man in overall command of the Saxons in Britain, being older and wiser than Horsa. Hengist had commanded Sigarr to go on this mission, and so it was, no matter how Horsa felt about it.

"I'd have felt happier if we had Thorbjorg along with us though," Sigarr murmured as they coursed through the white-foamed waves towards the harbour town of Mucrois. "Bellicus isn't just a powerful fighter — his connection to the gods of these lands is well known." He shook his head, frowning as he remembered his own meeting with the warrior-druid in a town not far from where they were now. Bellicus and his companions had attacked Sigarr's men, forcing them to run for their ship and sail off with shameful haste. The memory of the giant druid, who was much taller than even Horsa, still made Sigarr shudder. Never, before or since, had the little jarl came up against a foe as terrifying as Bellicus of Dun Breatann. He'd asked Hengist if they could take Thorbjorg, the wise-woman or *volva* as her kind was known, along on this mission but the *bretwalda* valued her counsel too much to let her leave his side. There was another *volva* that might have come with them, but she'd been with Sigarr on that earlier visit to these lands and had disappeared without trace, coincidentally after a confrontation with Bellicus and his companions.

Sigarr thought of her now – Yngvildr was her name, and she'd been slim and pretty with large breasts. The memory roused a stirring in his breeches and, although she'd been even crazier than Thorbjorg, Sigarr had long fantasised about bedding her.

Horsa broke his train of thought, spitting into the waves and sneering at Sigarr with his usual disdain. "Pah, we don't need any of the *volur* to kill Bellicus. He may be a druid, but he's a man, and he can be hurt. I had him beat, Sigarr, I had him on his knees and I would have ended his life if that Roman friend of his hadn't turned up to save him."

Sigarr knew better than to argue with his cousin, but he'd heard that story a dozen times on the journey and, although it was impressive and painted Horsa's martial prowess in a good light, ultimately, Bellicus of Dun Breatann had *not* been killed. Not then

2

Their approach had been noted by those in Mucrois too, and a hard-eyed Pict stood watching them. Clean shaven and fairly tall, the man was not particularly impressive but he wore an expensive coat of chain-mail and a red and blue checked cloak that was probably worth as much as Sigarr's sword. Flanking him was a number of hardy warriors, some of whom wore no armour or even a cloak, showing off pale skin with blue-inked designs.

"Bloody maniacs," Horsa grumbled, eyeing them with disdain. "It might be sunny, but it's still cold, and there they stand showing off how tough they are." Then he noticed a tall figure with long brown hair and gave a low whistle. "Who's that? Is that the Princess Aife you mentioned? I wouldn't mind her stripping off to show me her tattoos!"

"King Drest," Sigarr called, ignoring Horsa's muttering as he waved and bowed respectfully to the watcher on the beach, who nodded gravely in turn.

"That's Drest?" Horsa asked, looking up at the Pictish king. "Not very impressive is he?"

Horsa judged people on looks, a shallow way to navigate one's world, but Sigarr merely shrugged. "He's no fool. And besides, he's the one paying us to be here and fight for him, so I'd suggest you show him respect." Horsa shot him an angry look, but he forged on regardless. "Drest is in charge here, cousin, don't forget that."

"There's a hundred of us," Horsa retorted, lip curling in a sneer again. "And Drest, as you pointed out, is paying us to fight for him. If anyone deserves respect, I do not think it's him."

"Maybe not," Sigarr replied irritably. Sometimes his cousin was so dense! "But he *is* the one paying us. So, whether you think him worthy of it or not, at least pretend to respect him, Horsa. Once the Damnonii are defeated and Dun Breatann is taken, *then* you can kill Drest and we'll make the fortress ours. Until then, the Picts are in charge, so do your best to be civil."

Horsa bristled at his cousin's tone but they were walking up the beach and had come to the Pictish king now. Both Saxon jarls bowed, Sigarr's being deeper and more respectful, but Drest looked at them both with about as much pleasure as if he'd just trod on dog shit.

4

"Jarl Sigarr," he said. "I remember you from your prior visit here." He gave a very shallow bow, thankfully not going into any more detail about that previous encounter which had been unpleasant in more ways than one for them all. "And you must be Horsa."

The big jarl grunted. "You have our payment?" he demanded with very little of the respect Sigarr had pleaded for.

Drest did not seem bothered by Horsa's rude tone, pointing to a ship a short distance along the beach that was stacked with goods. "There," he said. "All yours to take now, or when we return, victorious, from Dun Breatann."

Horsa eyed the ship greedily. There were furs, fine wines, glassware, and fabrics imported from far off lands piled within that vessel and, when the Damnonii fortress was captured another two ships stocked with as much wealth would be provided to Horsa's warband along with slaves and horses of the best lineage. It was a good deal the Saxons were getting.

Especially since Horsa planned to keep Dun Breatann for himself once the fighting was over. Drest had already lost an earlier war with Queen Narina – to seal the peace, many Pictish nobles had been taken as prisoners of war after it. Instead of being treated respectfully though, those nobles were hanged by Narina's husband, Ysfael. Only Drest's daughter, Aife, escaped the executions and the whole terrible business so enraged the king that he had formed this alliance with the Saxons in hopes of getting his revenge on the Damnonii people and making Narina's lands his own.

"How many men have you brought?" Sigarr asked the king.

"Two hundred," Drest replied. He puffed out his chest as he said it, as though those warriors were all he cared to bring, but Sigarr knew very well it was all the man could spare, for the Pictish army had been decimated not so long ago by the army of Dun Breatann. A generation of young Picts had been slaughtered which was why Drest was forced to hire Saxon mercenaries for this new war.

"Two hundred?" Horsa growled, not even attempting to mask his disdain.

"Aye," Drest replied coldly. "With your hundred that should be enough to take the Damnonii fortress.

"Really?" Sigarr wondered. "Three hundred men doesn't seem that many. I must admit I thought you'd bring more, my lord."

Drest shook his head, lips pursed as he turned away and stared at the land behind him. "Maybe in the southern lands you need more soldiers to take a town, but here in the north our settlements are smaller. Less densely populated." He turned back, staring at them as if expecting more arguments. "Three hundred men will be plenty, assuming your warriors are as skilled as you claim."

Sigarr glanced up at his cousin, fearing Horsa would take umbrage at Drest's words, but the big jarl merely snorted with laughter.

"We are skilled enough, Pict," Horsa said levelly. "And we will do what you are paying us to do. Make sure you and your people do the same."

Drest gave a wry smile and nodded without a word as Sigarr breathed a sigh of relief. It seemed these two noblemen would accept one another's foibles as long as Dun Breatann was subjugated come the end of the campaign.

"Oh, and Drest," Horsa said, making another thrill of tension tighten Sigarr's gut just as the Pictish king turned to walk away.

"What?" Drest demanded irritably.

"I have one demand."

"You make no demands," the king retorted. "I am paying you, remember? But what would you ask of me, Saxon? If it suits me, I'll grant you it."

Horsa snorted with bitter laughter at that. "Bellicus," he said. "The druid. He is mine."

It was Drest's turn to chuckle then, and to Sigarr it was a genuine sound, full of pleasure and even hope. "Now that," said the King of the Picts, "I'm happy to grant you. Come on, my Saxon allies – let's kill ourselves a druid!"

"I couldn't ignore the Merlin's summons," said the druid, shrugging again as the road sloped downwards, taking them beneath the spreading bows of two great chestnut trees and then opening out to reveal sunlit fields bursting with spring flowers and birdsong. "Every so often he calls a Moot, and we druids must answer."

"All of you?" Duro asked.

"Aye," Bellicus nodded. "All who are fit for the journey at least."

"Even Qunavo," said Duro, naming the Pictish druid who'd trained Bellicus as a youth, but then caused much trouble for the Damnonii in recent years. "And Ria?"

Bellicus glanced at the centurion, seeing his friend smiling lasciviously back at him. Ria had caused them bother too, becoming Bellicus's lover for a short time before betraying him and almost causing Dun Breatann to be sacked by Drest's army of Picts. It was a source of embarrassment for the big druid who was ashamed to have been played so easily by the woman, but he couldn't resist smiling back at Duro as he thought of Ria. The dark-haired druidess might have used him, but by the gods she was a beauty, and there were worse ways to be used in this life…

His smile faded as he thought then of Narina, Queen of Alt Clota, left behind to rule from the mighty fortress of Dun Breatann. She loved him, he knew that, and he believed he loved her too but the planets had never aligned just right to really allow them to make anything of their feelings. Maybe one day her husband, Ysfael, would have a nasty accident and Bellicus could marry Narina but, until then, they would never be together.

Maybe Ria would want another night with him at the Moot, he thought, with a stirring in his blood that brought the smile back to his face.

"You take care with that one," Duro growled, like a father giving important life advice to his wayward son. "She's already got you into trouble once. Don't give her the chance to do it again."

Bellicus merely chuckled in reply as their horses carried them onwards to the meeting Merlin had called.

"We must be about halfway there, eh?" Duro asked after a time. He was looking around, trying to figure out where they were although he wasn't familiar with the lands they were passing through.

"Aye," Bellicus agreed, taking some dried pork from his pack and tearing a piece off which he tossed on the ground for his great mastiff, Cai. The dog accompanied him everywhere and had saved the druid's life, and Duro's, more times than they could count, for it was a vicious beast when called upon, although quite friendly and docile normally.

"Another three or four days?" Duro asked, trying to coax more of an answer from his friend.

Bellicus pictured Britain in his mind, following their route and gauging the distance to the meeting point. For some reason, Nemias — better known by his title of Merlin — had chosen Caer Legion as the place for the druids to come together. Bellicus didn't think he'd ever been to Caer Legion, once a Roman fortress called Deva and garrisoned by the Legio XX *Valeria Victrix,* but he was looking forward to seeing it. There would be ruined buildings and, hopefully, some of them might still contain interesting old artifacts including religious items — a literal treasure trove for a druid to explore.

Of course, the Romans had not been kind to the druids, but they were long gone from Caer Legion now while the Old Ways remained — Bellicus assumed that was one reason for the Merlin's choice of meeting place. It was also fairly central for everyone to travel to — the likes of Qunavo and Ria would need to come all the way from Dunnottar far to the northeast of Britain after all.

"I reckon the journey should take two weeks in total," Duro said, answering his own question as Bellicus remained lost in thought. "We've already done ten days, so…"

"You're right," the druid agreed, grinning apologetically. "Another few days and we'll be there. I think we'll have to find a ship to take us back to Dun Breatann though. It's been a long journey for poor Cai."

Neither man was particularly keen on sailing and Duro pursed his lips, watching the huge dog as it trotted along easily beside them, stopping now and again to piss or sniff some interesting bush.

"He looks fine to me," the centurion opined.

9

Bellicus could only agree. Cai was as tough as nails and seemed to thrive on these journeys, but the druid didn't think it could be very healthy for the dog to travel so far in such a short space of time.

"We'll see when we get to Caer Legion," he said. "There might be a trading ship heading right to Dun Breatann — if so we'd be daft not to take it."

"The horses won't like it," Duro noted, and they left it at that, a question for another day, perhaps when the weather wasn't so fine and the road didn't seem so inviting. "What's this Moot about anyway?" he asked instead, changing the subject.

"I've no idea," Bellicus admitted, gazing up as a carrion crow flew by cawing angrily at something. "Perhaps he wants to ask us to work together, instead of being at one another's throats as we have been."

"Have other druids been fighting with one another?" Duro wondered. "Like you have with Qunavo and Ria?"

Bellicus shook his head. "I don't know, but this has long been our problem on this island — we find it hard to pull together, even when we have a common enemy like the Romans or, as now, the Saxons and, perhaps worse, the Christians."

"You don't sound too sure. Have you never been to one of these things before?"

"No," the druid admitted. "It's a long time since a Moot was called like this and, well, I'm not that old compared to the likes of Nemias and Qunavo. They might have been to one before, but I haven't." In truth, he was slightly apprehensive, having no idea what would happen at such a meeting of so many powerful folk, but he was also looking forward to the experience. There would be druids he'd never met before there, and it would be good to get to know them. Who knew when a druid would need help from another? Certainly, Bel and Duro had been glad of assistance when rescuing Catia from the Saxons — the raiders had planned to sacrifice her to their twisted gods at the great stone circle known as the Giant's Dance. Fortunately, the local druid, Lugotorix had helped them, using his carnyx to create a diversion, the instrument's otherworldly, eerie sound terrifying the Saxons while Bel and Duro made off with Catia.

10

It was always useful to make friends with the likes of Lugotorix.

"You didn't have to come, you know?"

Duro gaped at Bellicus as if the druid had just told him to eat his own breastplate. "Not come?" he demanded. "Then who would take care of you? You know you like to get into bother when you go wandering about the lands, Bel."

Laughing, the druid agreed that had been true in recent years. "Still, I think you only came along because you believe the Merlin will put on a grand feast. Always thinking about your belly, even if you're not as fat as you were when we first met at Luguvalium."

"Not fat at all, boy," Duro returned with an arched brow. "All muscle now," and he patted his lean midriff to prove it. "But aye, I do expect there will be a feast worthy of the gods at this Moot of yours. I wouldn't miss it!"

"You and me both," Bellicus agreed with a broad smile, his heart soaring at the sight of the sun-dappled road ahead and his loyal friends by his side. "You and me both, Duro."

CHAPTER THREE

Horsa enjoyed riding, and he was having a pleasant time as they travelled west from Mucrois towards Alt Clota and the lands of the Damnonii. The weather was as good as one could expect in the lands of the Picts, which is to say it remained chilly and rained often, but the sun came out enough to save clothing from being soaked completely through or for the wagons of supplies to become bogged down in the roads.

The Saxon jarl had never been in these lands before and he was struck by how similar they were to his own home in Jutland. The trees were different, and it seemed a little warmer, but the land was sparsely populated with settlements set far apart unlike further south near the Saxon Shore which boasted more people, towns, and even Roman ruins. There seemed to be none of the latter here.

Sigarr had tried to educate him on the history of the place, telling him that the legions had come to these lands but never fully conquered them, and that the road to Dun Breatann would soon bring Drest's army to the earthen wall of Emperor Antoninus. Horsa had cut him off at that point, rudely informing his cousin that he didn't give a shit about the Romans or anyone else, and Sigarr had sighed and taken his horse off to look for more agreeable company.

Now and again it bothered Horsa that hardly anyone liked him — even the other Saxons didn't care for his company much. Where Hengist was confident, outgoing, and friendly to his followers, Horsa was sullen, overloud, and sneered more than he smiled. But he had not come to Britain to make friends — he was there for battle-glory and all that would bring. Hengist was the older of the brothers and everything had been handed to him on a plate when they were growing up, whereas Horsa had been forced to work for what he wanted. So his reputation as a brash, even cruel, young man sat just fine with Horsa — people feared him, and so they should.

Yet, sometimes he thought it would be nice to have a friend other than Hengist. Maybe he should be more pleasant to Sigarr. The little runt might not be much of a warrior, but some of the men seemed to like him.

His eyes roved about the countryside, taking in the hills and glens as they rode, the babbling burns with water that glistened over brown rocks, and the great birds of prey that appeared quite plentiful in that area, hovering and watching for food until screeching crows and gulls tried to chase them off. His gaze fell on the king then - Drest, lord of those lands still, for they had not yet passed into Alt Clota.

Drest was a bland man, Horsa thought. Average in height, average in stature, neither ugly nor handsome — how did such a man come to lead the warlike Picts? Deciding he should really make some attempt to ingratiate himself with the powerful king, Horsa guided his mare closer to Drest, staring at him until their eyes met and the Pict nodded brusquely at him.

"These are barren lands," the Saxon said with characteristic bluntness. "I like them."

Drest's eyes flickered with amusement as he turned and eyed the young jarl. "I'm glad to hear it," he said.

"Where are your druids?" Horsa asked. "Sigarr told me one of them is quite beautiful. I'd been looking forward to meeting her."

"Ah, Ria," Drest said, nodding thoughtfully. "She is indeed an attractive woman, and normally she would ride with us to war. But she, and my other druid, Qunavo, have been summoned south by the Merlin." He shrugged. "The Merlin is High Druid of Britain — when he calls, all must go to him."

"Even if you command them otherwise?" Horsa asked with a frown.

"Aye," the Pict admitted. "The gods take precedence over any earthly king."

Horsa digested that for a moment, and then a dark thought struck him. "Wait," he barked, staring at Drest. "Does that mean Bellicus won't be at Dun Breatann when we attack it?"

The king gave a grim nod. "Don't sound so upset, friend," he said. "Bellicus is a brutal big bastard. Him being away gives us an advantage."

"I know what he's like," Horsa retorted irritably. "I lost two toes to his blade! He's caused me, and my brother Hengist, a lot of trouble. I'd been looking forward to sending him to his gods as painfully as possible."

13

Drest snorted, genuinely pleased to have such a vicious ally along for the coming battle. "You'll get your wish, my lord," he said in a tone designed to mollify the angry Saxon. "Once we take the Damnonii fortress Bellicus will hear of it and come with all haste to rescue his people. That's what he does."

Horsa's head bobbed up and down slowly as he stared at a blasted heath to the north of their position on the road. "Yes," he muttered. "That is what he will do."

"So cheer up," Drest smiled. "But remember — you can do what you like to the people of Dun Breatann, apart from the noblemen and women. Those we keep alive if possible, all right?"

"Why?" Horsa demanded.

"For ransom," Drest replied as if speaking with a child. "And, if that's not enough for you, to entice Bellicus into doing something rash, like trying to rescue them. There's rumours that he's in love with Queen Narina, and he's certainly friends with many of the other nobles so…If they aren't killed during the fighting, let them live until I say otherwise. Yes?"

He stared at Horsa with an intensity that surprised the jarl. Still, Drest was a king — was it really surprising that the man could speak forcefully when required? "Fine," Horsa growled. "I'm sure I'll find plenty of sport with the rest of the fort's inhabitants."

"That's the spirit," Drest said. "There'll be plenty of men to kill, women to hump, and wealth enough for us all, be sure of it." His face darkened and he spat on the side of the road. "Those Damnonii bastards murdered my people. Prisoners they swore to treat with the respect their rank deserved. For that, Narina and her people will pay, and I will become King not only of the Picts, but of the Damnonii as well."

They rode on in silence for a while, both men imagining the trophies and glory they'd claim in the coming days and weeks as they subjugated Alt Clota.

"You spoke of the druids," Drest said at length, as the sun began to peer out from behind the wispy white clouds. "But your companion, Sigarr, had a witch with him the last time he visited my lands, or so I heard."

Horsa grunted.

"Well, where is she?" Drest asked. "Or another of her kind? You Saxons place as much stock in the *volur* as we do in our druids."

"I have no idea where Yngvildr is," Horsa said. "And neither does Sigarr. She was probably killed by that big whoreson Bellicus. As for another witch — my brother refused to send his *volva* with us. Says he needs her with him." The jarl gave a shrug. "They wield great power, the *volur*, but they also make me nervous."

Drest laughed at that. "Oh, I know what you mean, my Saxon friend! Our druids make me feel the same, always talking in riddles and acting as if they were moon-touched. Perhaps it's best we travel without their kind."

"Perhaps," Horsa murmured. "Still, these are not Saxon lands. I would be happy to have the protection of a *volva* if we could have found one."

"Fear not," Drest said, not noticing the angry look Horsa turned on him at the suggestion he might be afraid of anything. "The gods have always been good to me — that's why I'm still alive, and still king in these lands. Without Bellicus to protect Dun Breatann, we will make short work of the Damnonii."

As if in response to his words the clouds swept across from the east, covering the sun and immediately lowering the temperature. Horsa looked up and cursed for the sky overhead was now grey with thunderheads and, as he watched, fat, heavy raindrops began to fall on them. To make matters worse, a carrion crow stood watching them pass and it gave a harsh squawk directly at Horsa.

The jarl was not well-versed in the ways of the gods, but he knew bad omens when he saw them and, as he pulled up his hood and shrugged himself deeper into his cloak he thought again of Thorbjorg and Yngvildr and wished one of those wise-women travelled with the army.

Dun Breatann would fall, Horsa was sure of that, but he'd like to be alive to enjoy it when it happened, and he'd breathe easier if he knew Wotan, Tyr, and Thunor were on his side.

"Where are we, my lord?" Sigarr rode up next to them as the rain began to jump and dance noisily on the land all around. "Are we far from our destination?"

15

Drest wiped water from the front of his hood and squinted into the middle-distance. "Up there is one of the old Roman forts," he said. "And there" – he pointed and the Saxons saw a settlement low down in the grey gloom – "is Shivra. So, in answer to your question, no, we're not far from Dun Breatann now."

Sigarr took in the information with a thoughtful nod, as if storing it for future reference, while Horsa's gaze was drawn to the ruined fort that Drest had pointed out on the hillside to their right. Although there wasn't much left of the place, and what there was lay wreathed in cloud, it still sent a chill through Horsa. There was something deeply unsettling about the old Roman places, he thought, wishing Drest would pick up the pace and lead them on as quickly as possible.

"By Thunor," Sigarr gasped, staring fixedly at the road ahead. "What is *that* apparition waiting to meet us?"

Horsa had bowed his head as a gust of wind blew sheets of rain into their faces but when he raised his eyes again he saw what had caused Sigarr's alarm.

There, on the middle of the road stood a lone figure, arms raised to the sky as if they had personally called down the storm. The riders in the vanguard slowed, and some even brought their mounts to a complete stop, so incongruous was the vision before them. Drest shouted angrily at them to continue, mocking their cowardice, although Horsa could see the Pict was as anxious as any of them.

"Is that...a woman?" Sigarr wondered as they closed on the figure who remained in the road, as if unafraid of the army bearing down upon it.

Horsa could see better now that they were closer, and he nodded. It was indeed a young woman in a faded, filthy blue dress, with once-white sleeves and red cuffs. She wore no shoes and there were murmurs of surprise as the warriors saw silver rings glinting on her toes. Those marked her as a woman of wealth and power, despite her impoverished appearance. Horsa stared at her as the rain ran in rivulets down her body, the blue dress clinging to her skin, revealing a slim waist and large, heavy breasts that fired his blood and made him want to dismount and take her right there in the road.

He noticed then the strange staff in her hand and, as she let out a bizarre, blood-curdling screech he realised just what she was: a "wand carrier" — a *volva.*

"By Wotan's beard," Sigarr gasped, turning to look at Drest and Horsa in amazement. "That must be Yngvildr. She's alive!"

CHAPTER FOUR

Caer Legion was much as Bellicus had expected, and hoped, it would be. There were ruins of old Roman buildings — not just a temple to their gods, but the town that had gone along with it. Houses, workshops, military structures, even baths were still standing in various states of decrepitude. Most had been cannibalised for their materials, and time had done its work on them too, collapsing roofs and walls while ivy and other greenery sprouted from every available crevice.

Bellicus spent some time exploring the ruins on the outskirts of the settlement, noting that anything of value — such as utensils, wall hangings, or pottery, as well as more permanent fittings like mosaics — were long gone, and probably adorning the hall of the local warlord or king. Still, simply standing in those ancient buildings was enough to fire the druid's imagination and make him feel as if he had somehow walked through a portal to the past and was taking part in the lives of the long-departed inhabitants of Roman Deva. Cai lay on the ground next to him as he closed his eyes and felt the spirits flitting around him, even through him, and the sounds and smells of present-day Caer Legion faded into the background.

"What the hell are you doing?" Duro demanded, thrusting his broad frame noisily through the doorway, dislodging clinging ivy and rubble and coughing as the dust suddenly filled his throat.

"I was trying to commune with the souls in the Otherlands," Bellicus replied irritably, but was soon smiling wryly as he looked at his choking friend. "Come on, let's get into town. You've disturbed the peace of this place enough with your coughing."

"That's nice," Duro spluttered, resting his hand on the wall as he tried to regain his breath. "I'm dying here and you're worried about disturbing some invisible spirit. Look, even Cai is sneezing!"

Bellicus patted him, hard, on the back and walked outside, ducking to avoid the low branches of the bushes that had already sprung up around the house. "Come on, we'll get you some ale in town. That'll clear your cough no doubt."

18

"No...doubt," Duro agreed, hacking and spluttering even louder as he followed the druid back to the road and the horses that awaited them there.

By the time they rode into Caer Legion the centurion's face had regained its usual pallor and he was breathing normally. That didn't stop the locals eyeing them suspiciously though. The townsfolk knew the Merlin had called a druid's Moot near their settlement, but Bellicus and Duro did not look like any of the other visitors that had come to answer Nemias's call. Still, despite their wary glances and even superstitious hand signals warding off evil as the travellers moved past, none of the locals were foolish enough to challenge them. Only an idiot would challenge heavily armed men, especially when they travelled with a war-dog like Cai.

"What's wrong with these people?" Duro demanded as silence followed them along the town's main thoroughfare. "Have they never seen a druid before?"

"Be fair," Bellicus laughed. "Nemias, Qunavo, Ria, Lugotorix — none of them look anything like I do."

"You've got the eagle-topped staff," Duro groused, throwing a fierce look at a man who scurried off as they went by. "Isn't that enough?"

"Maybe, on my own," Bellicus said, still laughing at his friend's bemusement. "But with you at my side? No wonder the people here think trouble must be brewing. They probably think you're the ghost of some legionary that was part of the garrison here."

The centurion opened his mouth to make an angry retort, then he realised he was being made fun of and broke off, shaking his head and sharing in the druid's amusement.

"Look," Bellicus said, pointing at an old tombstone that was just lying on the ground, abandoned. "See what I mean?"

The stone had been carved to show a Roman optio, with the inscription beneath naming him as Caecilius Avitus of the Twentieth Legion Valeria Victrix.

Duro paused, reading, and then grunted. "Fifteen years service. Died when he was thirty-four. Mithras protect him."

A stocky, middle-aged man with sun-browned skin appeared on the road before them then, and he did not appear frightened by their presence, although he did peer warily at Cai.

"You a druid?" he asked, pointing at Bellicus's staff, his eyes moving smoothly across Duro and the mastiff before returning to the shaven-headed giant atop the great black horse.

"I am. Bellicus of Dun Breatann. You must be the headman."

The fellow nodded, his stance and demeanour telling of a history as a soldier, either in the local militia or perhaps even, like Duro, as a legionary.

"Your friends are at the old shrine of Minerva," the headman informed them, gesturing along the road. "It's not far along this way. Just keep following the road and you'll see it to the south, across the bridge." He paused and it seemed he wanted to ask them more about their business in Caer Legion, but respect for the druid's office kept him silent and the riders moved on, saluting him and receiving the same gesture in return.

"He looked like he was expecting trouble," Duro muttered when they were some distance away from the headman, who still stood watching them ride on.

Bellicus snorted with laughter. "Duro," he said, "you have the exact same look about you. You always do. It's just something old soldiers have."

The centurion harrumphed but looked abashed, as if he hadn't realised he was so similar to the headman, who'd seemed a grumpy old goat to him. "Well, it's the best way to be. At least we know the town's in good hands."

"True," Bellicus agreed. "Saxon or Irish raiders will find Caer Legion no pushover if they come here looking for easy plunder, I'd think."

On they went, the road opening out as they left the main town behind them, spring greenery and blooms taking its place, leaves and flowers swaying in the warm westerly breeze and the sweet scents of nature filling the air. The River Aerfen wasn't far ahead and they were pleased to see that the bridge the headman had mentioned was in good repair.

"Roman," said Bellicus admiringly. "Still in use decades after it was constructed."

"Of course it is." Duro looked at the stone structure proudly. "We built things to last in those days. Not like now, when bridges are made from wood and rot away within a few years."

There was some traffic making the crossing, a narrow wagon being pulled by a bored old ox, its owner looking similarly aged and unbothered by the people stuck behind it. Druid and centurion reined in their mounts and waited for the creaking wagon to roll past, watching in amused silence as a couple of hunters berated the wagoner for his snail's pace. The old man winked at Duro as if he thought it a great joke to impede his fellow travellers and then the bridge was clear and the horses trotted over the river.

The Aerfen sparkled beneath them and a man in a tiny fishing coracle bobbed along with the current, his catch's scales glittering like treasure in the sun.

"Nice place this," Duro commented cheerily. "My kind of town."

Bellicus nodded, pleased to see his friend back to his usual bluff but contented self. The centurion had suffered a lot of hardships since meeting Bellicus four years before: losing his wife to the Saxon jarl, Horsa; losing two fingers being tortured by the Pictish king, Drest; and, more recently, their friend Eburus was killed by the *volva*, Yngvildr. Eburus had been a brash, loud young Votadini warrior whom Bellicus and Duro both disliked intensely when they first met, but they'd come to value his companionship and bravery greatly — it had been a terrible loss when the witch's blade took him from them.

Still, losing friends and family was part of life, especially for a soldier, and Duro seemed at last to have come to terms with all that had happened.

An image of Eburus, fiery haired and smiling, filled Bellicus's mind then and he felt a pang of deep sorrow. Maybe Duro was over the Votadini warrior's death, but the druid still missed his boyish humour and overloud laughter. Friends like that did not come along often in life.

"Ah," cried Duro as they cleared the bridge and saw the tents that had been setup by the druids summoned to Caer Legion. "Look, Bel. A friendly face has come to greet us!"

Bellicus pushed aside his melancholia and grinned as he spotted the youthful figure in a white robe waving at them.

"Koriosis!" he called, guiding Darac towards the lean young man. "It's good to see you again."

"Likewise," the white-robed youth called back, embracing Bellicus when he dismounted and then repeating the gesture with Duro. "I don't know many people here, so its nice to see some familiar faces."

Koriosis had been Bellicus's student for a time in Alt Clota, learning how to be a working druid within the Damnonii community. He'd proved a fast learner and a pleasant young man whose hobby was keeping bees, and he'd helped hold things together when Bellicus was away fighting battles and travelling around Britain. Over winter, though, a druid had died in Isca and Koriosis had been summoned to take his place there with the Silures tribe.

Another friend gone from Dun Breatann, but Bellicus was proud to see his student looking healthy and confident in his white garb. He even had a circlet of mistletoe around his head, like a crown.

"You look well," the big druid told him, receiving a glowing smile in return. "I like the beard."

"Thank you," Koriosis beamed, self-consciously touching the goatee he'd recently grown. "I wasn't your student for as long as I'd have liked, but I learned a lot from you and it's helped me grow into, I hope, a useful resident of Isca."

"I'm sure of it," Bellicus nodded.

"Where can we pitch our tent?" Duro asked, gazing around at the various leather structures and their inhabitants who were mingling with one another and enjoying the warm sunshine.

"Over here," said Koriosis. "There's space beside mine."

He took them up the slope that led to the old shrine to Minerva which was situated close to the river.

"That's it, eh?" Bellicus said as they approached the mystical site and he sensed the familiar thrumming in the air that marked a place of power. "I can feel it."

"Feel what?" Duro asked, looking around, bewildered.

"The magic," Bellicus replied with a smile. "This site has seen much over the aeons."

"He's right," Koriosis agreed. "The very air thrums with energy here."

22

They paused to take in the view. The shrine itself was small, only really comprising a statue of the goddess, Minerva, which was so weathered that none of the fine detail remained. The figure was about the size of a child and had been carved into a huge, grass-topped sandstone block, which also boasted a small cave to the right of the statue. The three men examined it all with interest and then Bellicus walked around to the back of the sandstone block, intrigued by the strange swirling pattern of oranges and whites within the rock.

"No wonder the Romans chose this site for their shrine," Bellicus murmured, running his hand along the orange seam which felt oddly warm despite being in the shade. "Incredible…"

They moved on, leading the horses with them, until they reached Koriosis's small, one-man tent. It was beneath a tree and there was enough space to setup Bel and Duro's larger shelter so they set about their task with enthusiasm.

Once the horses had been rubbed down and settled, the tent was erected and the companions sat for a well-earned rest. Koriosis had warmed some pottage on a tripod over his fire and he shared it with the newcomers, while Duro passed around some ale and Bellicus slathered butter on the bread they'd brought. It was simple fare, but their location, and the company, meant they enjoyed it as much as any king's feast. All three men, and Cai, ate with gusto and then went for a short walk on the grass as the sun soothed muscles that ached from their long journey to Caer Legion.

Other druids — mainly middle-aged or older men with long beards — called out greetings to them and the gathering was an interesting sight for Bellicus. His first druid Moot! It promised to be quite an experience.

"Am I allowed to be here?" Duro asked. "I feel out of place."

"I don't see why not," Bellicus replied and Koriosis nodded.

"You're fine, centurion," the younger druid said. "Many of our fellows have journeyed here with guards. Only a fool would travel alone."

"Like you?" Duro asked with a twinkle in his eye. "I don't see any guards with you."

Sheepishly, Koriosis shrugged. "I made it here safely didn't I? Besides, I was trained by Bellicus — I can look after myself. Some of the older druids can't."

"Fair enough," Duro laughed. "I doubt us soldiers will be allowed to join you when the real business starts though. I'll take myself off to town for a few ales then."

"No rush," Bellicus assured him. "We'll need to wait for everyone arriving and that could take a couple of days or more." He turned to Koriosis then, asking, "What's this Moot all about anyway? Have you heard anything?"

His fellow druid pursed his lips and shook his head. "No-one I've spoken to has any idea. Most just think the Merlin called it because there hasn't been one for years and it's long overdue. Especially with what's been happening lately, with the Christians growing in power and the Saxons causing all sorts of trouble."

Bellicus was nodding thoughtfully as he listened. "That's true," he agreed. "We really need to stick together going forward, if we can."

Beside him there was a low growl and the druid looked at Cai. "What's wrong, lad?" he asked, ruffling the huge dog's ears. "What's bothered you?"

"Not what," Duro rumbled in a tone similar to the mastiff's. "Who. Look."

Bellicus's eyes followed the direction his friend was pointing and his heart seemed to stop beating for a moment as he saw two people riding across the bridge towards the shrine.

One was an elderly, white-bearded man who looked much like all the other druids at the Moot, but it was the other who'd drawn Cai's attention. Small, raven-haired, and, even at that distance strikingly beautiful. Cai had never liked her, undoubtedly sensing her bad intentions, but Bellicus couldn't take his gaze from her as they approached.

"Ria," Duro muttered, and he rolled his eyes as he noticed the effect the druidess's appearance had on Bellicus. "Keep it in your breeches this time, boy," the centurion warned, shaking his head and standing to meet the Pictish mystics as they dismounted and came up the slope directly towards them.

24

CHAPTER FIVE

Yngvildr was given dry clothes to wear by some of the women who followed Drest's army and, soon the column slowed to a halt and set up camp for the night, rain still lashing the troops as they went about their business.

Sigarr and Horsa, who didn't even attempt to conceal his lust for the *volva,* spoke alone with her. Sigarr had met her before, briefly, during their ill-fated attempt to capture Catia, Aife, and Lancelot, who'd been a slave of another Saxon jarl at the time. He spoke kindly to the young *volva* although he wasn't quite sure if she knew what was going on.

She seemed to be in a trance of some kind — magical, or perhaps from imbibing some strange witch's elixir — and it took quite some time for Sigarr and Horsa to get her story from her. By the time they were dry and warm inside Horsa's large command tent, furnished with food and drink, and seated on folding chairs, the excitement that surrounded the girl's sudden appearance had faded and an air of normality settled over the camp.

The eldritch shrieks that had accompanied their meeting on the road had long since faded and, as the three sat in the tent with the rain drumming on the roof it was a strangely calm scene.

"How did you come to be here, Yngvildr?" Sigarr had asked and, over time, he drew the full story from her. How she'd managed to get the people of Shirva to follow her commands, how they'd then captured the three fugitive Britons, how she'd been so close to sacrificing them to the gods only to be thwarted by Bellicus of Dun Breatann and his companions, then losing a magical battle with the druid before stabbing his red-haired friend to death and making her escape into the wilderness where she'd been living for the past few months.

"That's…quite a story," Sigarr said, letting out a long, amazed breath once they finally had the full tale from her. "Incredible that you managed to survive out here alone for so long."

"The gods took care of me," Yngvildr stated matter-of-factly and the way her gaze penetrated right to his soul suggested her trance had passed and she was back to her normal self. Whatever 'normal' might mean in the case of one plainly touched by the gods as she was.

"Why didn't you seek passage on a ship," Sigarr wondered. "Sail back south to rejoin us at Garrianum? There's port towns not too far from this place."

She shrugged. "I felt as though my work here was not yet done. It seems the gods guided me well, for here you are, and now I will help you in your task."

"Wait," Horsa broke in, brow deeply furrowed as he digested the *volva*'s fantastical account of her months in the lands of the Picts and Damnonii. "You were going to sacrifice the child, Catia, along with Arthur's friend Lancelot, and the girl called Aife? Aife, the Pict?"

"Yes," Yngvildr nodded slowly.

"Drest's daughter?" said Horsa. "*That* Aife?"

Sigarr turned to him with a look of surprise on his face, as if shocked that Horsa had understood what kind of trouble this could mean, and, perhaps, also irritated that he hadn't realised it immediately himself.

"What of it?" Yngvildr demanded, her docile demeanour instantly giving way to a more aggressive one.

"What of it?" Horsa retorted. "We are here with Drest! He's paying us to serve him and, guess what, *wise-woman*, Aife is part of the army too. She's here! We were just lucky she wasn't riding in the vanguard when we met you, or you'd probably be dead already."

"He's right," Sigarr conceded, although his tone was far less confrontational than his cousin's. "Aife is well regarded among the Picts and, despite her youth, is one of their commanders." He looked at Horsa worriedly. "I wouldn't want to get on the wrong side of her. It could make for a very uncomfortable time here in these lands."

Horsa sneered at him. "Hide behind me if you must, cousin," he said. "We go to war, not to plant flowers. We're in for an uncomfortable time no matter what happens!"

Sigarr refused to rise to his bait. "It's one thing to fight with the enemy," he said coolly. "Quite another to fear attack from your own allies." He turned back to the *volva*, wondering if she might offer some advice but her gaze was as hard and unflinching as

Horsa's. "Either we hide you from Aife," Sigarr muttered. "Or we tell her you've joined us, and make it clear why it will be beneficial to us all to have you with us."

"Always so sensible," Horsa said in disgust. "Remember, we are more skilled than Drest's warriors, Sigarr, and they need us more than we need them. If the Pictish bitch has a problem, she can come and see us about it."

There was a commotion outside the tent, the pounding rain doing little to mask the sound of angry voices, and then one of the jarls' guards poked his head into the tent and opened his mouth to say something. Before he could get the words out he was roughly shoved inside, almost falling into Sigarr's lap, and a lithe, muscular figure followed him inside.

"Oh, I do have a problem with her being here, Horsa," Aife growled, glaring at him and Yngvildr in turn, then raising her hands to beckon forward the furious guard she'd shoved, clearly prepared to punch his teeth out.

"Leave," Sigarr said to the guard, flustered, his usual calm demeanour momentarily lost. "Your job was to keep her out, and you've failed. Leave us, by Wotan, before she embarrasses you even more."

The guard's expression was murderous and his hand was on the handle of his seax but, when he looked at Horsa, he received an even darker look than the one Sigarr had given him. He left, growling at Aife as he went, the Pictish princess hardly deigning to return his look.

"Make sure no more of her people come in here," Sigarr shouted as the guard disappeared through the tent flaps. "Not even Drest!"

If his words were meant to frighten Aife, it didn't work. She stood proudly before them, tall and strong and clearly ready to take on all three if that's how things progressed.

"Look, my lady," said Sigarr, doing his best to calm the situation. "We had no idea Yngvildr was even in these lands — this was not planned. But," he held up a hand to stall the outburst that would plainly be forthcoming, "her presence is a good thing."

"Good?" Aife demanded. "That crazy bitch would have slit my throat, and that of a child, if Bellicus hadn't come along in time to rescue us. And you think her presence is a 'good thing'?"

"She is a representative of the gods," Sigarr said reasonably. "She will help us to take Dun Breatann, and you want that as much as any of us, don't you? Think about it," he insisted, spreading his hands wide and smiling as if to encourage her to see his point. "You have no druids to call on the power of the gods, and neither do the Damnonii folk in Dun Breatann. But now…" He gestured at Yngvildr who was staring coldly at Aife. "We have a *volva* to wield the power of the gods on our behalf. It was fated that we should meet Yngvildr on the road, my lady. You must see that."

"I must, eh?" Aife retorted caustically. "Well, let's get one thing straight, you little prick."

Horsa sniggered at that, and his smile only grew wider and even lecherous as the warrior-princess turned her fiery stare on him.

"I am here because my father commanded it. As a soldier in his army I must do my duty and follow his orders. But I have friends — good friends — living in Dun Breatann from the time I spent there as a prisoner and afterwards. Princess Catia for a start, the little girl whose throat your witch wanted to cut, and Bellicus and Duro who rescued us from Yngvildr's sacrificial blade that day."

"So what," Horsa said. "How many lives have you taken, princess?"

"Of children? None!" Eyes blazing she went on. "I will take no pleasure in attacking the Damnonii, and I certainly feel nothing but disgust at being allied with Saxon scum."

Horsa's smile disappeared and he stood up, head scraping the roof of the tent, a menacing, threatening presence.

Aife did not back down. "We are in charge here," she hissed. "Do not ever forget that. My father requires your warriors, but we do not need the help of your twisted gods. If you wish to keep your witch alive" – lip curling she drew her knife from its sheath and pointed it at Yngvildr – "keep her well away from me, or I'll do everyone a favour and finish the job Bellicus started back in Shivra when he tried to kill her."

She turned and ducked out of the tent, hoarsely ordering someone to get out of her way, and then her angry footsteps faded to leave the three Saxons in silence.

"Well," snorted Horsa. "That was fun."

Sigarr didn't reply, merely chewed one of his nails and stared at the tent flap as if he feared Aife would come back and do more than simply threaten violence.

"Fun?" Yngvildr breathed. "It will be fun when we storm the Damnonii fortress and I finally spill that girl Catia's royal blood as an offering to Wotan. It will be fun to see the blood of their men and women streaming into the river that flows beside their rock. And it will be fun when I drag my stone dagger across the pale neck of that Pictish slut."

Horsa was nodding along in amusement as she spoke. "That *does* sound like a lot of fun," he agreed. "Eh, cousin?"

Sigarr remained silent, wondering if it was he who was insane, or everyone else around him.

CHAPTER SIX

Qunavo was an old man now. He'd trained both Bellicus and Ria on the island of Iova when they were youths, teaching them everything a druid needed to know, but he'd been middle-aged even then. Now, as he walked slowly up the gentle slope towards Sulis Minerva's shrine, Bellicus marked the deep lines on his face and the predominance of white in his hair and long beard. Still, despite his advancing years, Qunavo remained as mentally sharp as ever and needed to be viewed with respect for he was a dangerous man to cross.

Ria, on the other hand, seemed to be overflowing with vitality and life. Her shapely legs carried her easily towards the shrine, tight breeches emphasising the muscles in her calves and thighs, a strand of dark hair falling across one dark eye and being blown aside every so often by red-stained lips...

She met Bellicus's hungry stare and broke into a smile, running her tongue along her upper teeth and sending a shiver of overwhelming desire through the giant druid. As so often when he was near Ria, he felt embarrassed by the feelings she invoked in him, and the fact that he could not seem to suppress them, despite his years of rigorous training and the terrible things she'd done not so long ago. He looked at Duro and reminded himself that his friend had been tortured and mutilated for life, and Ria had played a part in that. She'd been an integral part of the plan to fool Bellicus and Duro into bringing her into Dun Breatann.

Those memories overcame his lust and he stared angrily at the druidess and her elderly companion as they stopped in front of them.

"So, this is Sulis Minerva's shrine," Qunavo said in a friendly tone. "Looks just as it did the last time I saw it thirty years or more ago. Good to see you again, Bel."

Bellicus did not reply and Qunavo simply shrugged and handed the reins of his horse to Ria, wandering over to run his hand along the statue of Sulis Minerva, murmuring soft, respectful words to the goddess.

"Pleased to see me?" Ria asked Bellicus.

The big druid couldn't bring himself to reply, instead turning to Koriosis and Duro and saying, "I'm going to sit by our fire and drink ale while we wait for the Merlin to appear."

"I'll join you," Duro said, and Koriosis agreed too. All three walked away from Ria, leaving her standing alone with the two horses. Even Cai didn't give her a backward glance as he trotted along behind Bellicus.

"Well, I'm pleased to see you, Bel," Ria called happily. "Maybe we can share a few drinks together over the next few days, eh? Or perhaps even something more?"

"She's beautiful," Koriosis said quietly when they had returned to the little fire beside their tents. "But more dangerous than an aleskin full of belladonna."

Bellicus grunted and filled their cups, handing one to each friend before downing half of his own in a long pull. He had always liked Ria, even when they were children, and she'd always toyed with his affections, just as she would do now if he let her. He shoved her image aside in his mind and thought instead of Queen Narina. She would make a far better partner for him — she cared deeply for Bellicus, and Princess Catia was actually the result of a night when Narina had come secretly to the druid and lain with him. It had been Beltaine and, while overseeing the rituals, he'd taken strong drink and sacred herbs so when the masked woman came to him he had no idea it was Narina. He'd planted the child in her belly that her husband, Coroticus, was unable to give her, only finding out years later that he was the girl's true father.

Aye, the druid thought, feeling his ale pleasantly warming him from the inside out, Narina would be the ideal wife for him. If she weren't married to that Votadini waster Ysfael.

Duro and Koriosis chatted pleasantly with one another, asking what each had been doing in the months since they'd last met, and Bellicus's frosty reception seemed to have done the trick for Qunavo and Ria moved away to pitch their tent somewhere on the far side of the shrine. One tent, thought Bellicus in disgust as he saw it stowed on Qunavo's horse and guessed what that probably meant.

He put the Picts out of his thoughts, his conscious thoughts at least, and was soon mildly and pleasantly inebriated. Cai sat by his side, allowing him to stroke his smooth coat while the men talked

31

and joked with one another and watched as druids came and went, setting up tents, lighting fires to roast meat or fish over, and sharing herbs and other magical items with one another. It was sunny and warm and Bellicus felt quite content.

"The Merlin!" someone called, and everyone looked at the bridge for, sure enough, Nemias was walking across it, staff in hand, white beard practically glowing in the bright spring sunshine.

"And Bedwyr!" Duro cried, grinning as he recognised one of Arthur's highest-ranking warriors, a man the centurion had come to know well as they'd once gone off on a quest together to find a decurion to train Arthur's cavalry. That had been a rewarding, even healing experience for Duro, and he'd always spoken fondly of Bedwyr ever since.

"And there's Lancelot," Bellicus added, smiling himself now for these men — bodyguards for Merlin undoubtedly — would be fine companions during their time at the druid Moot.

They hurried down to meet the newcomers, although many of the other druids had the same idea, clamouring to chat with the Merlin, asking what this was all about and what news he had from Arthur and of the Saxon incursion into the Britons' lands.

"This is pointless," Bellicus laughed, grasping Cai and waving his two companions back towards their tent. "We can talk with them later, when the excitement dies down."

Duro and Koriosis were happy to follow him, but, as they walked back up the slope, they heard footsteps hurrying after them and turned to see Bedwyr and Lancelot.

There were grins all round as the friends embraced or grasped wrists in welcome. Koriosis had never met either of Arthur's captains but they greeted him warmly, proclaiming any friend of Bel and Duro a friend of theirs.

"Merlin will be busy for a while," Lancelot told them. "We should grab an ale and catch up, lads."

Bellicus nodded, looking at the handsome warrior, pleased to see he'd filled out since they'd last been in one another's company. Lancelot had just been freed from months as a slave to the Saxon jarl, Leofdaeg, and had practically been skin and bone at the time. Now, he was still slim, but his muscle definition had returned and he appeared wiry and strong. "It's good to see you looking healthy, my friend," the druid told him.

Lancelot flashed the smile that had helped him bed many women and clapped Bellicus on the bicep. "You too, big man," he said. "Have you grown even more since our last meeting? I'd swear you're even taller now."

"Maybe you've shrunk," Duro said and the men laughed.

They found their way to the tents and settled down with food and drink to fill each other in on what had been happening throughout their lands.

As always, Bedwyr recounted, the Saxons continued to seek expansion, with Hengist's forces attacking settlements around Garrianum while Arthur did his best to hold them back. Some of the Saxons were less warlike than their fellows though, and were assimilating quite well with the Britons, living and working amongst them in peace.

"Just shows that we can all get along," Duro noted. "If people make the effort not to stab one other to death."

"True," Bellicus agreed. "And at least the Saxons follow gods as old as ours, even if theirs are more bloodthirsty. I'd rather share the island with followers of Wotan and Thunor than the Christians."

"Really?" Bedwyr asked. "You think the Christians so bad? They teach love and peace."

"I know what they teach," Bellicus growled. "And it's all very admirable. But their priests will not co-exist peacefully with those they call heathens — us. They won't be happy until all the old gods are forgotten and their Christ is the only one remaining."

Koriosis sipped his ale, eyes hard, and voiced his agreement with the bigger druid. "I've seen it myself down in Isca," he told them. "The Christ-followers grow in number with every passing month. Their priests speak honeyed words to the people, filling their heads with promises of bliss, if not in this life but in the next. The simple folk seem quite content to believe their lies for it does not take much effort to follow the Christ."

Bellicus sighed. "That's true. Learn a few simple prayers, repeat them when required, and give 'donations' to the priests to earn a place in a glorious afterlife." He brightened a little and laughed, saying to Koriosis, "If only we'd known it was all so easy, eh? We'd not have spent years of our lives studying and learning how to commune with the gods!"

"Years well spent," Koriosis replied with a broad smile, lifting his cup in the air in toast to a childhood filled with work and study. "Years well spent, brother."

They basked in the sun as Merlin moved around the shrine talking to the druids and druidesses that had answered his call. Merchants had come from the nearby town with sacks filled with their wares — sweet cakes, salted meat, fish, wine and ale, freshly baked bread, and spring berries. The druids bartered for the goods and it was clear the Moot would dine well for the next few days.

"I'll certainly have put on even more weight by the time we head homewards after this," Lancelot said, smiling as a portly druid hurried past, beard practically trailing in the air behind him in his haste to buy some of the sweet cakes.

"Indeed," Bellicus replied happily. "If I'd known these Moots were so much fun I'd have begged the Merlin to call one long before now!"

CHAPTER SEVEN

Queen Narina strode along the wooden walkway set high upon Dun Breatann's south-western face, contentedly breathing in the fresh air and looking out at the sparkling clean water of the River Clota. She made this walk every day, watching as trading ships and smaller fishing boats moved along the river, always alert for danger approaching along the Clota. When she reached the end of the walkway, for it did not encircle the entire bulk of the great rock her fortress sat upon, she turned and walked back. Reaching the central gatehouse, she moved upwards, taking the many steep steps in her stride before coming at last to Dun Breatann's great hall.

The commander of Narina's army, and of her personal guards, Gavo, was inside the hall breaking his fast and listening to the reports from the previous night's watch sergeant.

"All well?" the queen asked as she stepped lightly to the table and sat down on a bench opposite Gavo.

He stood and bowed respectfully to her before dismissing the sergeant who went off to get some sleep as Gavo and the queen set about the bread and eggs that had been placed there by the servants.

"All well, my lady," the guard captain said, contentedly shelling one of the eggs and biting into it. It was hard-boiled and he chewed happily before putting a little salt on the remainder. "The Dalriadans are still too busy fighting with one another to be much of a threat, and our patrols on the border with them seem to be working well."

"The Votadini appear to be holding to our alliance too," Narina put in, daintily nibbling a piece of bread. "Even though their prince, Ysfael is no longer sharing my bed, or anything else. King Cunedda seems happy enough with the arrangements after his son tried to start a war between us and the Picts."

Gavo frowned to think about that dark time when Ysfael had wormed his way into the highest echelons of power within Alt Clota and almost destroyed them all by hanging Pictish prisoners of war. Still, things seemed to have settled down now and Ysfael, while still legally married to Narina, wielded no influence at all anymore. Instead, he spent his days with one or two lackeys, gambling, drinking, hunting, and whoring. Truth be told, that life seemed to please the Votadini prince, and Narina was quite happy not to have to deal with him for their marriage had been one of politics rather than love.

Inevitably, her thoughts turned to Bellicus and she wished — again — that she might marry the giant druid. Wasn't wealth and power supposed to lead to happiness? So why did she feel so empty and unfulfilled?

"You were up early this morning."

Narina's melancholia faded when she looked up and saw her twelve-year-old daughter, Catia stepping into the hall. The servants hurried to bring her food and drink, eager to please the princess for she was well liked in Dun Breatann.

"I'm always up early," Narina replied as the girl sat with them and thanked a servant for her breakfast.

"Even earlier today," Catia said, biting off a piece of bread and chewing as she eyed her mother perceptively. Narina shared much with the princess so she suspected Catia had guessed how much she was missing Bellicus's presence in the fortress.

"Or perhaps you were just up too late last night," Narina said archly. "Sparring again."

"She's getting very, very good," Gavo noted. "Beating opponents much older than herself with ease."

Catia beamed at the captain's praise — he wasn't the easiest man to impress — and he smiled back fondly at her.

"Well, remember you have other things to study," Narina said, somewhat mollified. "Don't be up too late with those practice swords."

"Study what, Mother?" Catia said with a heavy sigh. "With Koriosis and Bellicus both gone, I've no one to teach me."

"Bel will be back soon," Narina said. "Until then, I'm sure I can give you some lessons. Gavo too."

The captain's face fell at that — the only things he liked teaching were fighting and battle tactics. He murmured agreement though, for it was not his place to argue with a queen. Gavo had been in charge of the Damnonii army for many years now, since the time when Narina's first husband, Coroticus, had been king. He knew when to argue and when to simply do as he was told.

36

Narina recognised his displeasure though, and winked so he'd know she didn't really expect him to give Catia lessons. The classroom was no place for Gavo.

The trio enjoyed their breakfasts, appreciating the warmth from the firepit for although it was sunny outside the shadowy interior of the hall would be cold if not for the low-burning fire.

"Yes," Narina said softly, more to herself than her companions. "Bel will be back soon." *And maybe then we should just do as we please, and damn what anyone thinks*, she thought. It was high time they stopped worrying about pleasing everyone else and saw to their own happiness.

The sound of running came to them and Gavo instinctively got to his feet, hand falling to the pommel of his sword as he stepped in front of the queen and the princess. Catia moved to stand with him, and she too was ready for she also carried a short sword at her waist, having vowed never to be captured by raiders ever again, like she had been by Horsa and his Saxons four years before.

A soldier appeared at the door, breathless and gasping for air having run up the stairs from the lower gatehouse. From the look on his face Narina knew something terrible had happened.

Or was about to happen.

"What is it?" she demanded, fear making her snap at the messenger, not caring that he was out of breath. "Spit it out, man! What's happening?"

"Scouts, my lady," the soldier gasped, finally catching his breath and straightening up into a position more suited to talking with royalty. "Our scouts have just come back from patrolling our eastern borders. Bad news I'm afraid. Very bad."

"Go on," Gavo said and his calm demeanour made everyone else feel a little more at ease.

"An army has been sighted, my lord," the soldier said to his commander before turning to Narina. "My lady, the scouts report King Drest at the head of the column, and they seem to be coming this way."

"Drest!" Narina hissed. Hadn't that bastard caused them enough trouble in recent years? "But we decimated their army not so long ago. They don't have the numbers to trouble us, surely, Gavo?"

The captain's lips were pursed as he tried to make sense of the messenger's report. "We'll need to go down and speak with the scouts," he said. "But aye, there's no way the Picts can have mustered enough young men to rebuild an army big enough to attack us. Something else must he going on."

"I fear you may be right, lord," the messenger said grimly, nodding at Gavo. "One of the scouts spoke with some people in Shirva, a town the army had just passed. The locals claim a Saxon *volva* has been camping in the area for months, and she joined up with the army."

"A Saxon witch joined an army of Picts?" Narina asked, turning to Gavo in confusion. "What the hell is going on?"

"I know that *volva*," Catia said through gritted teeth, fingers drumming restlessly on her sword hilt. "Yngvildr. The one who tried to sacrifice me, and Aife, and Lancelot. She's crazy, Mother, but there's only one way she'd have joined that army, and this is how Drest has managed to muster an army big enough to attack us."

"It's not just Picts marching into our lands," Gavo said, finally understanding the peril Dun Breatann, and all of Alt Clota, was in. "There's Saxons with them."

"Indeed," murmured Narina, walking to the doors to look out on her fortress and the squat, low house that belonged to Bellicus. "An army of Picts and Saxons, and they have a *volva,* while we are without our druid." She turned back to face them, jaw set in determination. "Gods below, but this is bad. Still, Dun Breatann has never fallen to an enemy, and I'm not about to let it happen now. Gavo — muster the army. If Drest wants another fight, by Taranis we'll give it to the bastard, and this time he won't escape alive!"

CHAPTER EIGHT

For six days the druids shared their news and their knowledge, discussing strategies to deal with the threats from the Saxons and the Christians. They conducted intense rituals during the daytime and also at night, calling down the power of the moon which was nearing its fullest point by then. More of their Order arrived during those days, complaining of the roads and the weather affecting travelling conditions and delaying them.

At last, Merlin announced on the sixth night that the following day would see the culmination of the Moot, where he would reveal the purpose for calling them together from every corner of Britain.

While the ceremonies were taking place, the guards — even Lancelot and Bedwyr who were there on behalf of Merlin himself — had not been allowed to be present. Instead, they'd spent their time in town, playing games of dice or tafl, or competing against one another in archery, running, wrestling, or swordplay. Duro found himself thoroughly enjoying the week, the sense of camaraderie reminding him of his days as an optio and later a young centurion in the Roman legions. The board games kept him mentally alert, the physical competitions worked his body to its limit, and, when all was done, a few ales in Caer Legion's cosy alehouse with good company helped him relax.

"We'll be leaving soon," Bellicus told him on that sixth evening, after Merlin's announcement. "Tomorrow will be the culmination of the Moot, with a great ritual and then… Home, to Dun Breatann."

Duro belched, having downed rather more ale than he was used to. There had been an arm-wrestling competition in town earlier and that always worked up a thirst in the centurion. "I'll be sad to leave," he admitted, lying on his back and staring at the roof of their tent as it slowly seemed to revolve. He shut his eyes and swallowed the bile that was forming in his throat. "It's been good to see our friends again, and to make new ones."

Bellicus watched the centurion, recognising his discomfort and smiling wryly as he lay down himself and blew out the candle. Cai gave a low growl of irritation as the druid nudged him over a little, trying to get comfortable beneath his blanket.

"Aye, it's been a good few days," Bellicus agreed. "We've been telling Merlin he should call another Moot next year, like they used to do before the Romans came."

"Every year?" Duro wondered, breathing deeply, as if fresh air would ease his drunken nausea.

"Yes," the druid said. "Of course, there were a lot more druids back then. Even if only a fraction turned up to a Moot it would be a large gathering in those days."

"Well, you get in Merlin's ear," Duro mumbled tiredly. "And let him know we all want to come back and do it again soon."

A short time later the centurion's soft snores filled the tent and Bellicus shook his head in the darkness. A fine guard Duro would make, sleeping off too much ale, if some enemy attacked during the night. He reached out and stroked Cai's smooth coat, reassured by the dog's great bulk. Ach, who needed a centurion to guard them, he thought, when they had a war-dog as brave and fierce as Cai?

* * *

The next day was fine and dry again, which greatly pleased the druids, for, if it remained like that the moon would be clearly visible when night fell and their final ceremony would be all the more powerful for it.

The mystics spent the day in quiet contemplation for the most part, meditating and communing with the gods. The guards, as usual, took themselves off to the nearby town once the druids came together to begin the week's final, Grand Working.

"Save some of that meat for us," Lancelot called, as two huge white bulls were brought up the slope towards the shrine, for sacrifice at the height of the night's ritual.

"It's magic meat," a druid called out with a grin. "Not for the uninitiated!"

"Pah, you can eat my 'magic meat'!" Lancelot retorted, crudely grabbing his crotch amidst a chorus of indignant, but good-natured boos from the guards as they crossed over the bridge into town. The druids cheered and waved them off with sarcastic farewells, assuring the guards that they'd enjoy every bite of the succulent beef on their behalf.

It was not just the bulls that wore white that day — all the druids did. Indeed, Duro had ribbed Bellicus about it that morning when he awoke with a terrible hangover. The sight of his friend in the unusual white garb had greatly amused Duro for it was a rare sight indeed, and really didn't suit the druid who was as built more like a warrior than a mystic. The white robe had also been made for Bellicus a few years earlier and he'd filled out since then, growing more muscular, so the chest and sleeves of the outfit were uncomfortably and, to Duro, amusingly tight.

When they went out of the tent and Ria walked past she gave Bellicus a lascivious look, admiring his figure within the clinging robe, and Duro's amusement had faded.

"Remember," he muttered to Bellicus as they watched the beautiful druidess disappear behind the shrine in the direction of her and Qunavo's tent, "keep away from that one. I know you druids get up to some strange stuff during your rituals. If you must lie with some woman as part of the ceremony — find one of the other druidesses, or maybe one of the local prostitutes, eh?"

Bellicus laughed loudly at that. "This won't be that kind of ritual," he assured his friend, and Koriosis joined them, looking up at Bellicus in bemusement as the bigger man wiped tears from his eyes.

"You'd better get going, Duro," Koriosis said to the centurion. "Your friends have all gone, look." He pointed and the centurion muttered an oath as he realised it was true, the long, golden hair of Lancelot disappearing behind the buildings on the far side of the bridge.

"Remember, Bel," he called as he buckled his sword belt around his waist, making sure his spatha was secure within. "Keep away from Ria."

"I will," the druid retorted with a wave. "As long as you promise to keep away from the ale. I don't want you drunk when you return from Caer Legion, and snoring again all night!"

"Friends!"

All eyes turned to see Nemias, the Merlin, standing atop the large mound that Minerva's shrine was set into. He too wore a white robe, he had a circlet of ivy in his pale hair, and his long beard was shaped into a point as always. He held his oaken staff of office in his right hand and appeared resplendent in the spring

41

sunshine as he gazed out over them and the River Aerfen flowing behind.

"Friends," he repeated. "We have gathered here to praise and honour the gods, and we have done so over the past seven-day, with offerings, and sacrifices, and music, and poetry, and stories." He paused, looking at each druid, a fatherly smile on his face.

Bellicus found himself smiling in return — he truly liked Nemias, and had done since they'd first met. They'd not spent a great deal of time together over the years but, in the few days and weeks they had been in one another's company they had done great things. Things that people now sang songs about. As far as Bellicus was concerned, Nemias embodied what a druid should be, more than earning his title of Merlin. On top of that, he was a fine companion and friend, and so it was every druid gathered there looked back happily as their leader continued.

"You must all be wondering why I called you to Caer Legion. Why now, after so many years without a Moot?" He waited for the murmurs of agreement to fade away, gazing out at the curious faces looking back at him. "The Saxons," he said at last.

"What about them?" a man asked, and he wasn't the only one with a question on his lips as Bellicus noted more than a few bemused faces.

"What have the Saxons got to do with us?" Qunavo asked. "Wouldn't we be better dealing with the Christians first?"

There were murmurs of agreement with his question and Bellicus looked around at those taking Qunavo's side. He did not know them all, but he was sure they hailed from the western side of the island, where the Saxons did not raid often, if at all. No wonder those druids had failed to recognise the threat of the sea-wolves.

"The Christians are a problem too," Merlin called, nodding and holding out his hands, palms up. "You're right, old friend."

Qunavo looked quite pleased but his face turned dark again as the Merlin went on.

"But the followers of the nailed God are not an immediate danger to us. They will not come to our groves and shrines with blades and hammers, to destroy our bodies as well as our sacred places." He let that sink in for a moment. "The Christians are insidious, and they will one day be the greatest threat to our continued existence. If unchecked, they will brush aside the Old Ways and bury them forever. But!" He stared at Qunavo, who stared balefully back, making Bellicus wonder why exactly the Pict was so annoyed by the Merlin's words.

"The Saxons will kill us all, today if they have the chance," Bellicus cried in his powerful, deep voice, drawing not only Qunavo's gaze but that of everyone else gathered by the shrine. "Merlin is right. The Christian's are a problem for the future — the Saxons must be dealt with now, before they slaughter us all and Taranis, Lug the Light-Bringer, and Sulis Minerva are replaced by Thunor, Wotan, and Tyr."

Most of his fellows shouted agreement with Bellicus and Merlin, but still Qunavo protested.

"The Saxons are like us," he argued. "Much more so than the Christians. The Saxons follow Old Ways, as we do. Old gods, very similar to ours. And they will not forbid us from revering them, the way the Christians will."

His points made sense to many of the druids and Bellicus judged about half agreed with Qunavo, fearing the threat of the Christians more than the Saxons.

Fools! Bellicus thought to himself, but growing angry would not sway people to his cause so he held his tongue, allowing the Merlin to take control of the Moot once more.

"You elected me as High Druid," Nemias reminded them somewhat haughtily. "I live and work at the centre of Britain. I see and hear all that goes on in our lands. I accompany Arthur, Bear of Britain, as he strives to push against the Saxon tide that threatens to soon overwhelm our way of life."

This was all true, and the more provincial druids could not argue with him. They did not have Merlin's contacts or see the things he did. Most lived in out-of-the-way little settlements that saw few visitors and took part in no momentous, epoch-defining events the way Nemias did. And they were no fools — they had all heard the stories of the Merlin fighting beside Arthur. The songs of mighty Bellicus of Dun Breatann brutally dispatching Saxons on the battlefield as part of the warlord's army, and of the Princess Catia being abducted by Saxon raiders who sought to offer her as a sacrifice to the sea-wolves' bloodthirsty gods.

Still, the rapid spread of Christianity — although more peaceful, and less murderous, thus far — engendered fear in the hearts of many druids.

"I am the Merlin," Nemias said firmly, his tone clearly marking the discussion as being at an end. "And I say we will put all our resources towards defeating the Saxons led by the barbarous brothers, Horsa and Hengist. So mote it be!"

"So mote it be," came the standard reply, and it was clear many of the druids were not at all convinced but would not argue the point any further. Nemias was High Druid — that was what the title, Merlin, meant after all — and his word would be obeyed.

Bellicus watched Qunavo and Ria, noting their rather agitated body language, and wondered again what was bothering them so much. Had their King Drest grown friendly with the Saxons who plied the eastern sea, trading with Drest's people? Had the Pictish king even, gods forbid, formed an alliance with the sea-wolves?

A feeling of dread filled the massive druid, a sense of foreboding that made him wish he could stride over and wring Qunavo's neck until the man admitted the truth. Such behaviour would not go down well though, so Bellicus forced himself to remain calm and put his fears aside for now. The Moot was almost at an end and he would return soon to Dun Breatann. Qunavo and Ria could do their worst then — Bellicus would make sure Narina and the Damnonii people were ready for it.

"Well then, my friends," Merlin cried, breaking into a broad smile now that he'd said his piece. "Tomorrow we will discuss the future. Now, bring forward the white bulls, and let us praise the gods in prayer and feasting!"

CHAPTER NINE

The bulls were brought forward, surprisingly docile given the noise. The druids in the procession carried strange staffs with stems made from wood while the leaves were of gilded bronze. Others in the group carried long poles with bronze, leaf-shaped heads, almost spear like, that had bells or rattles hanging from them so they made a musical sound as their bearers shook them. The Merlin remained atop the shrine and the metal top of his own staff was decorated with images of a wheel, an eagle, a dancing god, and a bull's head with three horns. On his own head he now wore a bronze diadem with silver plaques and roundels depicting various divinities.

The white bulls' throats were cut, the blood being caught in great troughs as the druids begged the gods to accept the sacrifice.

Bellicus, despite his relative youth, was one of the most senior druids there, one of the Merlin's favoured ones, and so he was at the very front as the sacrifices were made, his rich voice raised in chanting and in song.

The sun had gone down by now and the moon was overhead, heavy and fat and casting her ethereal brilliance over proceedings. In the pale light the white robes of the druids and the gold torcs many of them wore seemed to shine from within.

Bellicus was called forward by the Merlin and he moved without question to the largest of the dead bulls. The massive carcass had been cut open and Bellicus drew out the steaming entrails, trying not to gag from the stench.

"What do you see brother?" the druids called out to him as he gazed at the entrails, shining in the moonlight. "What do the gods have in store for us?"

For a time Bellicus stared at the stinking offal, occasionally moving them with his hand as he tried to divine the future, and then, frowning, he stood up. "I see great danger ahead," he intoned loudly. This was not what the druids expected to hear and they fell silent, staring at him as he continued. "The Old Ways are in more immediate danger than even the Merlin foresaw," he said, gazing around at his fellows.

"How so?" Qunavo demanded irritably, no doubt put out at not being one of the two chosen to read the entrails.

"I cannot tell," Bellicus admitted, kneeling to gaze at the bull's innards once again. "But, whatever measures we are going to put in place to deal with the Saxons, I would suggest we move forward with them as quickly as possible." He shook his head, wishing he could say more, but that was all the gods had put into his mind and he stood up almost in a daze, oblivious to the gore coating his hands.

The other druids accepted his words with anxious looks at one another, but now the second white bull had been cut open and one of the other men — a squat, red-haired southerner with a pointed crown on his head — set about decoding that one's entrails.

In contrast to Bellicus's gloomy prediction, the flame-haired druid laughed loudly as he prodded at the bull's innards, and raised his hands to the moon happily. "Good news!" he bellowed. "We may well be in danger, as my brother there says." He gestured to Bellicus and went on in a strong, melodious voice that seemed at odds with his physical characteristics. "We may well be in danger right enough, but good news: It won't happen tonight! So let's make the most of the feast, friends, and praise the gods as best we can."

Much merriment accompanied his pronouncement and even Bellicus joined in. It had not been his intention to depress the gathering after all, and he was pleased to see the smiles return to his peers' faces.

The main part of the ritual was almost over. One last thing remained, and the Merlin pointed first to Ria, resplendent in her white robe, and then to an oak tree that grew not far from the shrine. Bellicus noticed now that Ria was barefoot and, clearly primed in advance for this important duty, took out a small hand sickle with what looked like a golden blade. Bellicus had seen such an implement before, while training on Iova in fact, and he guessed this must be same tool. It glistened in the moonlight as Ria walked purposefully towards the oak tree, but Bellicus knew it was not really gold, which would not be strong enough for a blade, but gilded bronze.

The druidess came to the tree and bowed her head in silent prayer. Everyone looked on as she communed with whatever god she'd chosen to guide her in this task, and then with incredible grace she jumped up and grasped the lowest branch of the oak tree. Swiftly, she climbed, seemingly without fear or hesitation, and Bellicus wondered if she'd practised climbing this very trunk, for it appeared she knew exactly where to place her hands and bare feet to progress quickly upwards. Reaching just over the halfway point, she stopped and examined the leaves and branches around her before her teeth flashed in a smile and she began to hack away at something with the sickle.

Beneath, four other druids held a white blanket and they positioned themselves to stand directly beneath Ria who gave a little shout of triumph and then something tumbled downwards, landing with a soft thump on the blanket.

Merlin appeared then, the druids around the oak tree parting to let him pass. He walked to the blanket and reached down, lifting what lay within and raising it triumphantly over his diademed head. It was a large sprig of greenery and Bellicus recognised it immediately from its white berries — that most sacred of plants: mistletoe.

To find mistletoe growing anywhere was a rare thing, but to find it growing upon an oak tree was…The magical significance was incredibly powerful and Bellicus grinned in approval while also wondering if Ria and the Merlin had placed the fallen branch there in advance…

The druidess climbed nimbly down from the oak, bare feet never slipping even once, and then she was standing on the ground and the Merlin had somehow fashioned a headdress from the mistletoe sprig which he placed on Ria's head.

Bellicus gazed at her and swallowed. He was not the only man struck be her beauty for there was an awed, almost hungry silence, as the druids looked upon her, and then Merlin cried out, "Now! Let the feasting begin!" and the spell was broken.

Barrels were broached and mugs filled with foaming ale, while the white bulls were already being butchered, their meat taken to be roasted over spits at the far side of Sulis Minerva's shrine. Within what seemed like just a few moments those druids of a more musical bent — bards — had struck up a tune on drums, pipes, and lutes, and voices were raised to the moon in song.

Bellicus found Koriosis and the pair collected mugs of ale, standing to enjoy the rich, dark drink and discuss the ritual they'd just been part of. As they chatted, Bellicus felt a hand on his arm and he turned to see Merlin looking up at him.

"Nemias," the big druid smiled. "That was wonderful! I've never seen anything like it. No wonder the Romans spoke so wondrously of the old druid Moots. Congratulations on an amazing spectacle." He raised his mug in salute and the Merlin grinned proudly.

"Thank you, Bel," he said. "For your kind words, but also for your…" He paused and looked around to make sure none but they two and Koriosis would hear him. "'Prediction'."

He winked conspiratorially, but Bellicus frowned. "I didn't make it up," he told the High Druid. "Or even exaggerate. That's what I divined in the entrails. I wish I could have given a cheerier prediction, but that's what was there, Nemias."

The Merlin's brows drew together and his pleased expression turned to one of anxiety for just a moment before he brightened again. "Oh well," he chuckled. "I must admit I assumed you'd made the prediction to back-up my call for action against the Saxons. I know how you hate the bastards."

"That's true," Bellicus granted. "But no. I really did foresee terrible danger for us, High Druid."

The Merlin nodded and clapped the big man on the arm again. "Well, that just proves I was right to name them as our greatest threat. Let's not dwell on it tonight though, eh? Enjoy yourselves, my brothers. Drink up, in the name of Lug the Light-Bringer, drink up!"

With a final, broad smile, he spun and wandered away to mingle with the other celebrants. Bellicus watched him go, sipping his ale but feeling as if the whole ceremony had been tainted by his dire prediction. He looked at the happy faces of his fellows, singing, dancing and making merry after what had been a truly powerful ritual, and tried to cheer himself.

It didn't work, and the more ale he downed the more he feared something was terribly wrong.

Or would be soon.

"I'm going to my tent," he said to Koriosis.

"Are you well, my friend?" the younger druid asked, concerned.

Bellicus shrugged. "Well enough," he said. "Just not in the mood to make merry."

"Very well," said Koriosis. "I'll see you later then, perhaps, or are you going to sleep?"

"No," Bellicus replied, shaking his head. "I'll remain awake at least until Duro comes back from Caer Legion with Cai. You enjoy yourself but..." He trailed off, feeling slightly ashamed to be putting his own fears onto his one-time student.

"What?" Koriosis asked. "Go on, Bel. Whatever's bothering you, share it with me."

Bel sighed and looked out towards the river and the surrounding lands. "Just keep your eyes and ears open for the rest of the night, eh?" he said. "I have a terrible feeling we're all in danger."

CHAPTER TEN

Hengist watched the capering druids from his hiding place behind a thick row of bushes. His face, and anything that might catch the light on his armour, was blackened with ashes so, even if one knew he was there, they might not have noticed him. Beside him, the *volva,* Thorbjorg looked on, engrossed by what they were seeing. Never before had either of them seen such a sight and, although she would never admit it, even the *volva* seemed to have no idea what was going on, or what the significance of most of the ritual actions might be.

It did not matter. They were not there that night to appreciate the magic of the Britons — they were there for a much darker purpose.

"Are you absolutely certain this will go as planned?" Hengist asked Thorbjorg for the fifth time that night. "That your magic will protect us as we go to work? There's a lot more of them than there is of you after all."

The *volva* shrugged in the darkness. "They are all drunk, or flying with the gods after swallowing their herbal concoctions. They also have their guard down, thinking themselves safe. Have no fears, *bretwalda,*" she murmured, giving him the title of 'war-leader' that he favoured. "We will strike a mortal blow against the people of this island tonight. One they shall never recover from."

Hengist's mouth twitched in a bitter smile, but his humour faded as he peered through the branches at the druids. Middle-aged, or elderly men mostly. Some younger, and even a few women…This would not be a battle — it would be a massacre. He thought of the story Thorbjorg had told him when she suggested this plan — the story of Ynys Mon, when the Roman legionaries had stormed an island filled with druids. Back in those days there had been many more druids than there were now — *many* more. They had been wiped out by the terrible slashing *gladii* and *spathae* of the Roman war machine, with only a few druids escaping the butchery, forming up later with others of their ilk that lived in the northern parts of the island in places like Alt Clota.

That thought reminded Hengist of the one druid he feared might be a problem for the Saxons that night: Bellicus. He'd never faced the big bastard in a fight himself, not personally, but his brother, Horsa, had, and he'd told Hengist all about the infamous druid's skill in battle. Thinking of his beloved brother made Hengist wish he was there with them, for Horsa was brave and fierce and a good man to have beside you in a fight against the likes of Bellicus of Dun Breatann. Still, one druid would not be enough to cause Hengist's warband trouble that night and Horsa had important matters to attend to far to the north.

The Saxons waiting to attack the Moot numbered thirty men and it looked like the gathered druids had about double that number. Hengist and his warriors were armed with swords and axes though — no spears or shields for this as they had wanted to move across the country as quickly as possible, and without attracting too much attention. There would be no need for a shieldwall anyway, thought the *bretwalda* — the fighting would be over almost as quickly as it began.

"What are we waiting for?" he asked Thorbjorg. "We should attack now, and get it over with."

The *volva* looked up at the moon, as if calculating its position relative to...what? Hengist had no idea how the wise-woman worked. Magic was her domain, as war was his, and he bowed to her wishes where possible with that in mind.

"It's almost time," she murmured, idly fingering the wand she held in her hand. "Not long now, just be patient for a little longer."

Hengist let out a long, irritable breath and wished she would hurry up and give them the command. He thought back to what had set this whole thing into motion, remembering how one of his old shipmates had visited them with some interesting news. The man had originally been a warrior, and had fought beside Hengist more than once, but he'd grown old and disillusioned with raiding and decided to settle down, becoming a farmer in one of the villages near Garrianum. He was a good farmer and was, eventually, welcomed by the natives living there. It had been one of those local Britons who'd mentioned in passing that their druid had been called away by the Merlin, to a great meeting of seers and mystics on the eastern edge of the island. Hengist's old comrade had thought it an interesting piece of news and, thinking the *bretwalda* might find it useful, travelled to tell him.

Hengist hadn't thought it very interesting, but Thorbjorg had. She it was who'd told Hengist this was their chance to destroy the druids forever. Where the Romans had failed, Hengist's sea-wolves would succeed and, with the passing of the Britons priests, there would be no gods to stand in the way of Thunor, Wotan, Tyr and the others that the Saxons venerated. On top of that, the Britons would be disheartened — devastated! — with the loss of their spiritual shepherds. Without their druids to bolster them before battle, even Alfred, the so-called Bear of Britain, would not be able to lead them to victory over the Saxons!

Sometimes, Hengist thought Thorbjorg was a madwoman whose connection with the gods was tenuous at best. But there were other moments when he was awed by her, and now, he had to admit her idea to wipe out all the druids of Britain was an inspired one. It would not only be a devastating blow to the native tribes, but it would also be very easy to carry out. Thirty well-trained warriors who'd been forged in icy, northern lands like Jutland, against sixty or seventy weak old men and women who capered about collecting mistletoe on soft blankets and shaking bells?

Hengist almost felt sorry for the white robed holy men as he pictured the savage end they would soon face. Almost. He might have sent Horsa on this mission but the young jarl was sailing to join Drest so the *bretwalda* led his warband to Caer Legion himself, and he was glad he had now.

"Are you ready?" he asked the man next to him, a slim young warrior who was nothing to look at but had proved himself an absolutely ferocious fighter during recent engagements with the Britons. Hengist had noticed him in action and actually laughed as he looked on, the clean-shaven, lean soldier wielding his sword with the finesse of a dancer rather than one of the brutes that made up most of the Saxon army.

"Oh, I'm ready," the man, who was named Saksnot, replied softly. "May Wotan guide my blade."

A great cheer went up from the druids then, and Hengist looked on, wondering what had happened to please them so much. As with Thorbjorg, their reasoning was beyond him, and he stared, bemused, as they called out strange words and bowed to…Was that a tree they were bowing to? The Saxon warlord shook his head and stroked the handle of his axe, desperately wishing his *volva* would unleash them upon the moon-touched mystics. His stomach rumbled as the smell of roasting bull drifted past and he huffed, turning to regard Thorbjorg with a bleak glance.

"Go," the woman said. "Let their blood soak the ground as a sacrifice not to their gods, but to ours. Go, Hengist, and finish the druids forever!"

* * *

Duro had not downed as much ale that night, having learned his lesson from the day before. Even when he was young he'd not been the type to get drunk day after day — he liked to keep his wits about him, usually. And it seemed he wasn't the only one of the group he was with to feel that way, for Bedwyr was taking it easy and Lancelot, well, that one seemed too self-conscious to end up in the kind of state where he couldn't walk in a straight line.

They were all enjoying themselves though, and the people of Caer Legion had grown to accept the druids' guards as generally well-behaved visitors. More importantly, visitors who would buy their wares, something which always made townsfolk welcoming.

There were thirty of them including Duro, Bedwyr, and Lancelot and most of them had struck up at least a passing friendship. As usual, in a gathering of hard men, there were simmering rivalries, mostly based on nothing more than a look or a word said in passing, but there had been no outright violence so far, something Duro was very pleased about, for he would no doubt have to be the wise, experienced old head who'd need to sort things if a fight erupted.

"You still content to live in Alt Clota with Bel?" Bedwyr asked as night fell and it began to grow rather chilly within the alehouse. The shutters were closed by the barkeep and another log thrown on the fire, crackling and spitting nicely and brightening the gloom.

"Aye," Duro nodded. "Bel and Cai are good friends. I'm happy for now." He reached down and stroked the big dog that was lying at his feet, sleepy but always alert for danger.

"Well, don't forget, there's always a place in Arthur's army for you, centurion," Bedwyr told him, and Lancelot murmured agreement.

53

"Maybe I'll take you up on the offer," Duro said, smiling, pleased to know his companionship and skills were appreciated by these high-ranking soldiers. Their stars were in the ascendancy he knew; maybe one day it would be nice to soar with them. "For now, I'm happy to ride where Bellicus goes. There's never a dull moment with him."

The extra fuel had made the fire burn just a little too warmly for the three men and they went to stand outside the alehouse door, looking up at the sky and the heavy white moon.

"Gods, listen to them over there," Lancelot chuckled, shaking his head at the singing and chanting that carried across the river to the town.

"Sounds like they're making the most of their final night together," Bedwyr agreed. "What d'you think they're getting up to?"

Duro had no idea and admitted as much. "Probably sacrificing those white bulls we saw the other day. Powerful magic in the blood of a beast as majestic as that."

"May their magic work then," Lancelot said softly, staring towards the river. "Well, as long as its good magic."

"What other kind would it be?" Duro asked with a laugh.

Lancelot shrugged, uncharacteristically gloomy. "What's good for one man isn't always good for another."

Bedwyr eyed him as if he'd gone mad. "What's got into you this night?" he asked.

"I don't know," Lancelot admitted, lifting his mug to his lips and swallowing a long draught. "I think druids make me a little nervous now. Maybe because of the Saxon *volva* that wanted to sacrifice me to the gods not so long ago."

"The *volur* are not the same as the druids," Duro averred. "Maybe they were, once. Caesar told of human sacrifice, and of the great wicker men that were used to burn criminals alive as offerings to the gods." He shuddered at the image that conjured in his head. "Those days are long gone though, the druids aren't like that now, if they ever were. Could you see Merlin doing anything evil?"

Lancelot smiled at that, but he shrugged nonetheless. "I like Nemias," he said. "But I'm sure the Saxons would think him evil. It depends which side you view something from."

"You've had too much ale again," Bedwyr said, reaching out as if he'd take Lancelot's mug away from him. "You're getting all philosophical."

Lancelot smiled and pulled away his mug, taking another sip, eyes twinkling in the pale light of the full moon.

They stood in companionable silence for a while, enjoying the night air, trying to make out words in the songs that carried across from Sulis Minerva's shrine.

Then there was a sudden, jarring sound that made all three men look at one another in alarm.

"By Dis, what's that?" Lancelot hissed, hand grasping his sword's pommel.

Duro felt a thrill of fear at the memories the sound dredged up within him. It was a loud, metallic braying note that was so utterly out of place, so unnatural, that it brought the other warriors out of the alehouse to see what was happening.

"It's a carnyx," Duro told those who'd never heard the thing before. "An old musical instrument like a trumpet. We used them in the legions." The fearful braying came again and Duro remembered hearing it the night at the stone circle called the Giant's Dance, when the *volva,* Thorbjorg was just about to cut Princess Catia's throat. The druid, Lugotorix had blown a carnyx to distract the Saxons, while Bellicus and Duro made off with the girl. It had been a daring escape from a truly terrifying situation, and the note of the carnyx would forever put Duro on edge as a result.

That was on top of the fact the sound was eerie anyway, regardless of any other connotations it might hold for a listener.

The centurion thought of the witch, Thorbjorg, and realised Lancelot was right. She seemed evil to Duro, and, he would have thought, to any right-thinking person. But the Saxons viewed her with awe — venerated and almost worshipped by the likes of Hengist who hung on her every pronouncement. Even when she suggested slaughtering innocents in order to appease her strange gods...

The carnyx was blown again and Duro frowned. Although the sound was inherently alarming, there was something truly out of place with it at that moment. The druids had been singing a song with a very distinct, pleasant melody, and the blaring carnyx

55

simply didn't seem to fit. Was it supposed to be bring a dissonant quality to the druids' song? Possibly — maybe it signified something in the ritual that was being conducted? The bulls being sacrificed perhaps?

The centurion looked at Bedwyr and Lancelot, and then at the other warriors who'd come to Caer Legion as guards for the druids. He was not the only one who appeared worried and, when Cai gave a low whine, that was enough for Duro.

"Fuck it," he said. "Something's wrong. I know it." He began walking quickly towards the bridge over the Aerfen, calling over his shoulder to any who cared to listen, "I'm going to check everything's all right. Anyone coming?"

Everyone followed.

As they hurried towards the river another sound came over the blaring of the carnyx, one which frightened Duro even more: the ringing clash of weapons. "Come on!" he roared, and broke into a run, drawing his spatha as he went, its oiled steel blade glinting in the moonshine.

CHAPTER ELEVEN

Bellicus heard the sound of running and instantly awoke from the light sleep he'd fallen into. He was seated on a camp stool and holding his staff which he used to push himself onto his feet. Staring up at the shadowed ridge that ran along behind Minerva's shrine he tried to see what — who — was making the running sounds. Was this some strange part of the Merlin's ritual? Planned in advance to impress his fellow druids?

And then Bellicus saw the soot-blackened faces of dozens of armed men charging down the hill towards the singing druids and he too began running. He had no idea who these newcomers were, but it was clear they were not there to spread peace and love.

As he ran he saw Lugotorix with a small group of their peers and, desperately hoping, Bellicus shouted to him, "If you have your carnyx with you, blow it now, as hard as you can!" and then he was past and sprinting towards a snarling man whose only features Bellicus could see were the whites of his eyes and his teeth.

"Die!" the enemy screamed and Bellicus knew then that they were under attack by Saxons for he recognised the accent and now he thought the man leading them had looked somehow familiar...

Before he could make any more sense of the situation Bellicus was forced to bring up his staff and parry a sword thrust that would certainly have killed him. Time slowed and the druid could see every line and detail of his opponent's features just before the bronze eagle on the top of his staff smashed into the man's mouth. The face crumpled as the white teeth shattered into pieces and Bellicus brought the staff around, clattering the heavy shaft into the enemy's temple and dropping him senseless, or more likely dead, on the ground.

There was a braying, metallic cry from behind him and Bellicus nodded in relief. Lugotorix had brought his carnyx to the Moot. Hopefully Duro and the other guards would hear it and recognise it as the call for help it was.

Bellicus turned as he heard a terrible scream and saw a Saxon slamming his axe into the forehead of an elderly druid. The blow was so violent that the blade of the axe stuck fast in the dead man's skull and, as the spindly body fell, shuddering on the grass, the Saxon pressed his foot down on the druid's face, trying to dislodge the stuck weapon. Just as the blade tore free, the butt of Bellicus's staff smashed into the back of his head. The Saxon fell soundlessly on top of the druid he'd murdered and Bellicus brought the staff down again and again until the sea-wolf's head was a ruined mess.

"Form up!"

The command came from the Merlin and Bellicus moved to protect the older man. The Saxons had already killed or badly injured a number of druids, but things were not quite going to plan for the attackers.

"The bastards thought we'd be an easy target," the Merlin was shouting, nimbly wielding his staff as Bellicus had done, parrying attacks from a swordsman seemingly with ease. "Let's show them we don't just spend our youth learning how to make poetry and potions!"

Bellicus stood beside him, noticing Ria a short distance away, black hair flying as she spun around a massive sea-wolf, somehow avoiding the great axe he wielded. She lunged and the Saxon roared, falling over as his knee gave way. Bellicus grinned, seeing the bloodstained knife in Ria's hand. Her expert cut had severed the tendons in the Saxon's knee and now, as he lay bawling on the ground, she knelt on top of his back and stabbed him repeatedly until he stopped moving.

More druids had come to stand with Bellicus and the Merlin and then they heard pounding footsteps again, this time from the direction of the bridge to Caer Legion.

Bellicus was forced to step back as the tip of a sword punctured the air where his head had just been. His attacker stepped forward, thrusting his blade at the big druid but then a dark shape streaked past Bellicus and thundered into the Saxon's groin. The man shrieked in agony and doubled over as Cai's teeth locked around his manhood, squeezing and tearing into the sensitive, soft flesh.

Bellicus did the man a favour then, bringing his staff down on the Saxon's head with so much force it rang through the druid's forearms.

"You all right, Bel?"

"Aye, Duro, I'm fine. Help the other druids fight off the sea-wolf scum!"

The Saxons plainly knew their sneak attack had gone wrong. They were no longer the aggressors — many of the druids were skilled warriors who wielded their staffs with deadly force, and, now that Duro and the rest of the Briton soldiers were there, the battle had been turned on its head.

Bellicus paused to catch his breath, holding Cai back for fear a rogue blade would slice through the hound's unarmoured fur.

The Saxons were not all cowards, or perhaps they were simply too crazed with battle-fever, for some chose not to run away, instead continuing to hack and slash at the druids and their guards. Duro, Lancelot, and Bedwyr worked together as a team, commanding those around them to fight with their backs to one another while others moved forward in a line.

Screams and roared imprecations to a multitude of gods filled the night sky along with the smoke that glowed red like blood from the bonfire. Bellicus grunted as an axe was thrown at him by a beardless young Saxon, and only the blade glinting as it came towards him allowed him to notice it in time to avoid it caving in his face. He lost his balance and fell, one of the Saxons taking advantage of his slip to thrust a sword at him. There was no real pain at first, but Bellicus felt warm blood quickly soak his sleeve and he knew he'd been injured.

At his side, the Merlin clattered his staff against the Saxon's neck and the warrior let out a strange, strangled squawk as he stumbled to the side, Cai snapping at his bicep. Bellicus roared a battle cry and kicked the man in the knee and, when he fell, the druid jumped on him, punching him in the face until he knew the man was no longer a threat.

"Come, Cai," he called as he levered himself back to his feet with his staff, eyeing the great tear in his white robe that was already saturated with blood. The mastiff, growling, came to his side immediately and Bellicus looked about, praying that the fight would be over soon so he could see to his injury.

"Are you all right?" Ria asked, appearing at his side, staring up at him with a worried expression.

"I'm fine," he replied, but he felt terribly weak and stumbled backwards.

"You're not," Ria said in a firm voice, grasping his uninjured arm and guiding him backwards. "Sit down, before you fall down. Cai will guard you until I can look at your wound."

Bellicus did not argue, he could not, for his knees were trembling and he was glad to sit before he collapsed. He watched as Ria ducked beneath another attack from a screeching Saxon then plunged her knife into the man's guts. The tip struck the enemy's chainmail and skidded to the side without piercing the armour, but it was a hard enough blow that the Saxon was winded. He paused, trying to catch a breath, but Ria brought the knife up and frenziedly hacked at his neck and face.

Watching, Bellicus admired her savagery and he could see that the Saxons were running away now, if they could, back in the direction they'd come from. A few of the druids and their guards chased after them, but it was so dark away from the crackling bonfire that to continue too far would be dangerous. A Saxon could hide in the woods and pick off any who came after them so, before long, the pursuers made their way back to the shrine.

"Where's Bel?" Duro called to Ria. "Have you seen him?"

The druidess was breathing heavily after her exertions but she looked over her shoulder and gestured towards Bellicus. "He's there. He's been wounded. Find a bandage and some clean water and I'll tend to him."

The centurion might not like Ria, or trust her, but he knew from personal experience that she could work miracles with injuries. She'd looked after his hand after King Drest had severed his fingers, doing a much cleaner job of bandaging the bloody, cauterized stumps than Bellicus had done. Without hesitation Duro hurried away to where he could see some of the druids helping other casualties, asking them if they had bandages he could use.

"Bastards," Bellicus muttered as Ria came to him and sliced open his sleeve, gingerly peeling back the cloth where it had stuck to the gash in his arm. "Attacking us in a sacred place. Attacking druids!"

Ria grunted agreement and took the cup of water that Duro brought over, using it to clean Bellicus's wound.

"Is it bad?" the centurion asked with an anxious frown.

Ria dipped her head to get a closer look, brow furrowed in concentration as she tried to see in the dim light. "It's quite deep," she said. "But it's a clean cut, so it should heal well enough if it's kept clean."

"I can't believe they attacked us here," Bellicus said, wincing slightly as Ria wound a bandage tightly around his forearm.

"They thought you'd be easy targets," Duro replied, looking around at the Saxon corpses scattered about the ground.

There were no enemy wounded and Bellicus guessed his brothers had already slit the throats of any survivors. Good.

"They got a shock, didn't they?" Ria smiled. "They lost more men than we did from the looks of it. Their mission was a failure."

Bellicus nodded, glad to feel his earlier shakiness had passed and the dressing on his wound was not red, suggesting the bleeding had stopped. He would be fine in a little while. And then his gaze fell on one of the murdered druids nearby and he stared in horror at the white-bearded face that looked back at him from dead, sightless eyes.

The Saxons' mission had not been a complete failure after all he thought in despair, as Ria followed the direction he was looking and cried out when she too recognised the fallen mystic.

"The Merlin!" she cried in a high, keening voice, standing up and running across to kneel by the old man's side. "The sea-wolves have killed the Merlin!"

CHAPTER TWELVE

"This is bad," said Narina as she looked out from the highest point of Dun Breatann's eastern peak. From there she had a fine view of the fortress's main gatehouse as well as the road leading there, and the River Clota. Well, normally it was a fine view but today Narina found it utterly depressing. "Gods, this is bad," she repeated and the fear was evident in her voice.

Gerallt, the other captain of Alt Clota's military, stood beside her and nodded at her gloomy pronouncement. Truly, things looked bad for the men and women within Dun Breatann, for camped outside the walls was the combined army of Picts and Saxons that had come from the east.

"We'll see them off, my lady," the captain said in a firm tone. He was ten years older than Gavo and not as broad, but his long silver hair and beard were immaculate, as were his clothing and armour. He was an unimaginative man, much less impulsive than Gavo, but that made him a fine commander and Narina felt he was a good man to have at her side in a situation like this.

When the reports had first come in of Drest's approach the Damnonii army had been mustered, or at least as many of the warriors as possible at short notice, and Gavo had planned to meet the enemy force before they could reach the fortress. He'd ridden out with some of the scouts and found higher ground near Litana where he could observe the column marching past. What Gavo had seen shocked him, for Drest had somehow joined forces with so many Saxons that it would be folly to meet them in battle. Messengers had gone out with all haste to command all available Damnonii warriors to muster at Dun Breatann, but Gavo knew the enemy would be at the fortress's gates long before his own army was fully formed.

The Damnonii would be outnumbered within their own lands and not just by the inexperienced farmers and labourers that had formed the backbone of Drest's previous army — this time he commanded dozens of Saxons. Gavo had not fought the sea-wolves before, but he'd heard enough about them from Catia, Bellicus, and Duro, to know they were vicious, brutal warriors who made killing their trade.

The guard captain had taken his news back to Narina and discussed their options which both were forced to admit were severely limited. In the end, knowing Drest was moving quickly, it had been decided that Gerallt would remain with Narina to command the main body of the Damnonii army. Gavo would take twenty horsemen and they would do their best to gather more warriors to their banner. Eventually, depending on what Drest did when he reached Dun Breatann, Narina hoped Gavo would bring an army of his own to attack the enemy from behind while she and Gerallt led the warriors out from the fortress to join in the battle.

That was the ideal scenario, and Narina prayed to the gods that things would turn out like that, but she was no fool. Drest was about as impulsive as Gerallt, or he'd have tried to conquer the Damnonii years before, but now that he was in league with the Saxons, who knew how the siege would go?

She stared down at a copse of trees, tiny from her lofty vantage point, and noticed movement within the lush, green foliage; violent movement, as the branches of one of the trees shook and then disappeared. No, it seemed like that from this distance, but Narina realised the tree had been felled, and now others within the copse were shaking and falling. She could hear shouts and thumps as the enemy warriors hacked at the trees with axes and saws and anxiety clutched at her.

Perhaps Drest merely needed wood for his camp-fires? The queen knew that was blindly optimistic — those great trunks would be far too much for firewood. The Picts and Saxons were building ladders and, undoubtedly, a battering ram.

Could Dun Breatann withstand a concerted assault from so many determined warriors? Narina did not know, but she wished Gavo and Bellicus were with her at that moment. Gerallt was a good commander — steady, loyal, and reliable — but Narina would have liked a more inspirational presence beside her for the inevitable siege.

It will have to be me, she realised, looking at Gerallt and seeing only bland indifference on his lined face as the tiny figures beneath them began dragging trees out into a clearing and hacking the branches from them. *I will need to be the inspirational figurehead for my people until this is over.*

So be it, she'd been queen for long enough now to know she was more than capable. Still, it would be nice to have Bellicus beside her — Narina always felt safe when the giant druid was with her.

"Do you think Ysfael's father will send us reinforcements?" Gerallt asked, oblivious to the turmoil within his queen.

Narina snorted, only realising then that her husband had not even crossed her mind while she'd stood there contemplating the oncoming siege. What a waster that man was.

Of the Votadini tribe on the eastern coast of Britain, Ysfael had married Narina to form an alliance between their two tribes. It made sense, for the Votadini had attacked Dun Breatann in partnership with Drest not too long ago. The Damnonii had won that war and, to save future troubles, marrying the queen to one of the Votadini princes had seemed like a good idea. And it might well have been, but for the fact Ysfael had proved to be a duplicitous, arrogant young man who conspired with his men to start a war between the Damnonii and the Picts. Narina had thought that disaster had been averted but it clearly had not, given the army at her very door.

Ysfael was still her husband, but in name only now. They shared nothing together — not a house, a bed, or even meals. Narina would have liked to send him back to his father, King Cunedda, in disgrace, no longer wed to the useless oaf, but that would have broken their alliance and, as she saw now, Dun Breatann needed no more enemies.

She remembered speaking with Ysfael when the scouts reported the Pictish/Saxon army's approach, asking him to send word to Cunedda. Even thirty or forty Votadini warriors would be a massive help to Narina but Ysfael had sneered at her and told her to send a message herself. He was a proud man and hated that he'd been stripped of all power and influence within Alt Clota, despite being married to its queen. He would not lift a finger to help her. Of course, he was not a fool either and, when it dawned on him that he would also be sealed within the fortress when the invading army arrived at Dun Breatann, he tried to take a horse and ride back to the Votadini stronghold in Dun Edin.

Narina's soldiers had been ordered not to let Ysfael leave without permission so his escape plan was quickly thwarted and he was returned to his quarters on the top of the fortress. It had been another embarrassing episode in their marriage and left both Ysfael and Narina disliking one another even more than they already had.

Do you think Ysfael's father will send reinforcements, Gerallt had asked. Narina gave her captain a bleak laugh and shrugged her shoulders. "Maybe," she said. "But I'm not pinning my hopes on it. I don't think Cunedda is very fond, or proud, of his son. It would probably be no great loss to him if Ysfael was killed during this siege. Especially if Drest wins and takes Alt Clota for himself — my alliance with Cunedda will be over in that case anyway."

Gerallt grunted in agreement. "I suppose so," he said. "Cunedda will likely just leave us to it and befriend whoever comes out of this war on top."

"Which may seem sensible," Narina said. "But if the Saxons help Drest, there'll be nothing to stop them moving on to attack the Votadini. Dun Edin will fall if Dun Breatann does, of that I'm sure."

Narina pondered the futility of it all. They fought, and won, a war, only for another to erupt soon after. And then another after that. And another, and so on, until what? What would unite all the tribes as one? The queen sighed, feeling sorrow not just for herself and those trapped within Dun Breatann, but for all the people of Northern Britain. She had won a war against the other tribes and some had hoped that would see the end of all hostilities, perhaps with Narina even becoming High Queen. A golden age of friendship, inter-tribe co-operation, and wealth for all was forecast by those of a positive bent but Narina had never truly thought it possible. Even if it had been, raiders would come from elsewhere to bring blood, fire, and death to the lands.

The Saxons, for example. She wondered what they were like — were they *all* violent monsters? They couldn't be. In fact, at least one of them had been kind to Catia when she was abducted by the Saxon warband some years before. He had even saved Bellicus from being killed so that proved some of them were good people. Unfortunately, she doubted the ones laying siege to Dun Breatann at that moment would prove to be particularly nice.

She turned her gaze away from the trees being destroyed below and looked out at the sparkling waters of the Clota, breathing in the clean, fresh air with its familiar spring scents. Gods, how she loved these lands.

"My lady."

Narina spun to see one of her guards striding towards them. He halted and bowed respectfully.

"King Drest would speak with you, lady," said the soldier, a slim, young man with a thick beard. "And he has others with him. Saxons."

She glanced at Gerallt and received a stony look in return. He would not show fear, she thought, taking heart from his grim countenance and resolving to put on her bravest face for this meeting with the men who sought to kill her and steal her lands from her.

"Was his daughter, Aife, with them?" Narina asked.

"I never saw any women, my lady," the soldier replied.

Narina felt oddly anxious at that. She had never got on very well with the Pictish princess, but she hoped Aife would keep Catia safe if Dun Breatann eventually fell. It would have been reassuring to see her somewhere amongst the enemy leaders, but perhaps Drest knew that, and that was why he had not brought his daughter along to speak with Narina just now.

"We had best go and talk with them then," Narina said to the guard, who bowed and moved to lead the way down the many steps to the outer gatehouse. "Come, Gerallt. And have someone fetch Catia. It'll do her good to see how these things are done."

The queen felt a momentary pang of guilt at asking for Catia. Was she simply looking for moral support from a child? Was that unfair of her? Perhaps yes, to both those questions, but Catia would be a noblewoman herself one day, and this would stand her in good stead for her own future dealings with men like Drest.

Assuming, of course, that the girl survived the coming battles.

That thought was enough to galvanise Narina and she gritted her teeth, striding ahead of the young guardsman. Drest had tried to take Dun Breatann twice before, and both times he had failed miserably. She would make sure it was not third time lucky for the Pictish bastard!

CHAPTER THIRTEEN

Bellicus gaped at the body of the white-bearded druid lying on the grass just a few paces away from him. In the flickering light of the bonfire it almost seemed as if Merlin's face was twitching with small movements — with life! But the blank, unseeing stare gave the lie to such notions.

The Merlin was dead, that much was clear from the size of the bloody stain on his white robe and the pool that was saturating the grass beneath him.

How could this be? Bellicus felt like he'd fallen into the ocean and was desperately seeking for which way the surface lay so he could swim towards it before he drowned. The big druid had never felt a sensation like this before, that he could remember, and that was a mark of just how shocking the night's events had been.

It was bad enough that someone had attacked, killed, druids. They were a protected class after all, representatives of the gods on earth. Holy men! But to murder the High Druid himself, Merlin? As far as omens went, this was the most dire Bellicus had ever heard of, never mind witnessed himself. The Saxons had meant to kill not just the Merlin, but all the druids gathered there at Caer Legion — it was a bold plan and there were clear parallels to the Romans' attack on Ynys Mon nearly four hundred years before, when the druids had almost been wiped out forever.

Undoubtedly that had been Hengist's plan.

"It was just a boy," Bedwyr was saying. "I saw him stabbing his blade into Nemias. It was a skinny, beardless youth!"

"Wake up." Duro's voice came then, stern and commanding. "Bel, snap out of it."

Bellicus blinked and took a deep breath, his massive chest expanding as he stretched up to his full height and gripped his staff as if he might squeeze the wood into splinters. "We must go after the raiders," he said. "This can't go unpunished."

"Damn right," Lancelot said, his usually immaculate blond hair unkempt and streaked with soot.

Without thinking of who held the greatest rank amongst the company now that the Merlin was dead, Bellicus turned to Bedwyr. "You remain here with a couple of the other guards. Keep an eye out for any more Saxons lingering nearby, in case they attack again. Help tend to the injured as best you can. The folk of Caer Legion are coming across the bridge now, they'll assist you as well." He looked then at Duro, Lancelot and those of the druids who seemed of a mind to hunt Saxons. "The rest of you, come with me."

Lancelot, as Arthur's right-hand man, was probably the highest ranking of everyone there and he would have been within his rights to insist on taking command. Arthur was not a king, but he was a powerful warlord with probably more influence over the tribes of Britain than any other man — but Lancelot knew Bellicus well and he was happy to follow the druid's lead.

Cai was shown a piece of tunic ripped from one of the escaped Saxons in the fighting and immediately loped off into the darkness. Bellicus jogged behind the mastiff and the others ran with him, leaving behind those who were more suited to healing than hunting.

"What if they have horses?" someone panted as they reached the top of the slope the Saxons had concealed themselves behind.

"Then they're long gone," Duro replied dourly. "So pray to Sulis Minerva that they're on foot, at least long enough for us to catch up with them."

Bellicus was focused on following Cai. The mastiff was not the greatest hunting dog in the world — once, the druid had another dog named Eolas and that one had been able to follow any scent with uncanny precision, but Cai seemed to be doing well. Perhaps there was a trail of blood dripping from wounds the Saxons had suffered, in that case Cai might lead them directly to their quarry without any trouble.

As they left behind the glow of the bonfire their eyes grew accustomed to the lower level of light cast by the full moon and they were able to run faster.

"There!" Lancelot said, pointing as he jumped over a dip in the ground. "I see figures ahead of us. That has to be them. Who are they anyway, by Dis?"

"It's Hengist," Bellicus replied, suddenly remembering the man who'd led the enemy charge at the start of the battle. The Saxon's face had been blackened with ashes but the druid now realised it was the *bretwalda*.

"I might have known that piece of shit would be behind it," the blond swordsman spat. "Sending men to do his dirty work as usual. Was it Horsa that commanded them then?"

"No," Bellicus replied shortly, trying to conserve his breath for the chase, and for the fight he hoped would soon come. "Hengist is with them himself. I saw him."

"He's there?" Lancelot shouted breathlessly. "Gods, we *have* to catch up with them then, Bel. If we can capture, or kill, Hengist himself…" He did not finish the sentence — everyone knew what such an outcome could mean. Hengist's death would send just as powerful a message to the Saxons as the killing of the Merlin would to the Britons.

There was a noticeable speeding up as the hunters spotted their prey ahead and foresaw the glory that would be theirs if they could kill the *bretwalda*. Bellicus called on Cai to slow down and stay beside him now, the mastiff's long, loping stride easily covering the ground.

"They're not moving fast," Duro said as they pounded across the grass.

"Some must be injured," Lancelot noted. "They won't be able to outrun us!"

As if hearing his words and recognising the truth of them, some of the Saxons turned back, faces pale in the moonlight, and stopped running.

"Bastards want a fight," one of the other druids laughed. "Let's give it to 'em."

Bellicus could see now that there were around ten men standing in a line, waiting for their pursuers to reach them.

"Steady," he said, slowing his pace and grasping Cai by his collar. "They're not farmers remember. Even injured, they're dangerous. I don't want any more of us falling to their swords and axes."

"At least they don't have spears and shields," Duro said, drawing in great lungfuls of air as they marched in a line of their own towards the waiting enemy formation.

"Neither do we," Bellicus noted. "So be careful. Look out for the men either side of you. If you see an opening, take it, but don't act rashly."

69

"We need to deal with these shit-eaters as quickly as possible, Bel," Lancelot said, drawing his sword and pointing the shining blade at the land behind the wall of Saxons. "Some of them are still running and I'll wager you my prized bronze mirror that Hengist is among those ones."

Bellicus didn't argue the point. He would rather not lose any of their men, but Lancelot was right, and letting Hengist escape would be a crushing blow after coming so close to catching him.

"Ready, lads?" he asked, taking up a position at the centre of their line, Duro on his right, Lancelot on his left.

"Ready," the others cried, brandishing their weapons and calling out imprecations to the gods.

"Dis Pater take their souls!" the druid cried and the line of Britons broke into a run again, charging at the hated sea-wolves.

Cai had fought beside his master many times over the years and knew instinctively how best to aid him. When Bellicus knocked aside a Saxon sword thrust, the dog crouched low and clamped his teeth around the enemy's ankle. The man screamed but, caught off balance, fell sideways into one of his own comrades. Bellicus's staff smashed into his face just as Duro's spatha skewered the second Saxon who'd been knocked sideways.

Wincing, the big druid looked down and saw scarlet on his bandage and knew he'd opened the wound on his arm. Ria would be angry at him, he thought, then laughed at how ludicrous that thought was, spinning his staff around two-handed and smashing it into the head of another Saxon.

Although Bellicus had noted that these were no mere farmers they faced, it was clear their opponents had been injured during the earlier fighting, some quite badly. As such, they were no match for the Britons who fought with a righteous, gods-given savagery.

"Right," said Lancelot, running a hand through his hair and staring down at the corpses littering the ground with grave satisfaction. "I don't see Hengist amongst that lot. Let's get after the rest of 'em."

One of the druids had knelt beside the fallen Saxons and, eyes closed, was mouthing some silent prayer, or more likely a curse, sending the souls of the dead, screaming, to some terrible doom.

Lancelot was already moving, running, as Duro and the others hurried after him, not even stopping to clean the blood from their weapons. There would be time for that later — for now, Hengist had to be found, and made to pay for the crimes he'd committed against not only the druids, but all the Britons. Horsa might be the one people knew as the cruel one, the raper, the merciless face of the Saxon invasion forces, but Hengist was the man behind Horsa. Stop Hengist, and there was a good chance the sea-wolves would disintegrate, or at least become far less of a unified threat.

It was growing much lighter now though, and, as they continued on their way — without suffering a single loss in the last skirmish — Bellicus felt dismay threaten to overwhelm him.

"No…!" Lancelot drew up, bending over to catch his breath, palms on his thighs as he gazed ahead at the men they'd desperately been hoping to catch up with.

"Bastards," Duro gasped, gazing up at the lightening sky despairingly.

On the horizon ahead of them were a dozen or so figures, silhouetted against the dawn sky.

"They did have horses waiting for them," said Bellicus, catching sight of the Saxon *bretwalda* and, beside him, the lean, beardless warrior that had taken the Merlin's life.

It was a cruel end to the chase that had taken so much out of the Britons and left ten or more Saxons dead at their backs, but it was over now, and Hengist had escaped. As if to hammer that fact home, one of the distant riders raised a fist in the air in triumph and the sound of laughter carried on the morning breeze to Bellicus and his companions.

One of the other druids screamed a terrible curse into the air, arms stretched wide as he stared at the escaping enemy *bretwalda.* If he hoped his hateful imprecation would have an immediate effect, he was disappointed.

They all watched, druids and their guards, utterly spent mentally and physically, as the horsemen disappeared into the distance. Hengist was gone, the Merlin was dead, and this had been one of the worst nights of Bellicus's entire life.

"Come on," he said, turning away and forcing himself to stride back towards Caer Legion and the desecrated shrine of Sulis Minerva. "The Saxons have won for now, but by Taranis this is not over."

CHAPTER FOURTEEN

"We've been here before, Drest, and things did not turn out well for you, or for the men you had allied yourself with."

The Pictish king smiled up at Narina with genuine, if bitter, humour. "True," he admitted. "I stood here once with Cunedda and Loarn mac Eirc and asked you to surrender. You refused—"

"And where is Loarn mac Eirc now?" Narina demanded, eyes blazing. Loarn had been king of the Dalriadans at the time, and he had made disgusting comments about Catia who'd been abducted by the Saxons. Narina had never forgotten those words and, eventually, Bellicus and Duro killed King Loarn after wounding him in a fight. "Where is Cunedda?" she continued. "Allied to me, after his army was defeated as well."

Her speech did not seem to impress Drest overmuch for his smile never faded and he turned to the huge, long-haired, handsome man that stood beside him, silent thus far. "We were unprepared for a war with you back then, Narina," the Pict called, massaging his neck as if it was starting to ache from gazing up at her on the outer gatehouse of Dun Breatann. "But this time, as you can see, we have new allies. And these will not be so easily beaten as the Dalriadans or Votadini were."

Narina opened her mouth to dispute that assertion but the warrior with Drest stepped forward, stretching up to his full height and folding his muscular arms across his chest. She guessed this was Horsa and that was confirmed by Catia who stood next to her mother, jaw clenched as she looked down upon one of the Saxons who'd abducted her four years before.

The man was not as tall as Bellicus, but he was bigger than most of the warriors in either Drest's or Narina's armies. He wore a coat of mail over a green tunic with red trim on the neck and cuffs, brown trousers with blue bindings around the ankles, and a leather belt with a sword and a seax attached to it. Even from that distance Narina could see the buckles on his gear were inlaid with glittering gemstones, marking him very clearly as someone of high status, as if his arrogant demeanour and confident stance hadn't already done so.

"Will you surrender to us, woman?" the Saxon demanded without preamble, his eyes boring into the queen who shuddered involuntarily at the force of that stare. This was the worst of the men who'd stolen Catia from her, as the princess had made clear when she recounted the story of her abduction upon her safe return. Where his brother Hengist was said to be a thoughtful, even calm, man, Horsa was well-known as a cruel, vicious brute who embodied everything Narina feared about the sea-wolves.

"How's your foot?" she asked, hoping to shake Horsa who still walked with a slight limp even now, so many years after Bellicus had sliced off two of his toes.

He was used to such jibes now though, and merely eyed her with a sneer before replying. "I've given you one chance to surrender to us, Damnonii whore," he called in a loud, clear voice that carried to the defenders on Dun Breatann's outer wall and even to some of those deeper within the fortress. "Will you do so? Or would you like us to start killing your people now?"

"These walls have never — never! — been breached by any invading army, you Saxon piece of filth," Narina retorted. "You will not fare any better than those who tried before you. So, do your worst. I will take great satisfaction from seeing you, and that bastard Drest, cut down, and then your heads will be hacked off and displayed upon these walls for all to see and for the crows to feast upon." She wished that there were some such heads hanging from the walls at that moment — her dead former husband, Coroticus, had often displayed those gruesome trophies, taken in battle from vanquished enemies, but there were none there now, rendering Narina's threat rather less potent than it might have been.

"You will not be taking my head," Horsa replied, slowly, so his unusual accent could be understood. He spoke the language of the Britons quite well, the queen was forced to admit. "But if that is what impresses you, let me give you a demonstration of what fate has in store for you and the craven dogs that hide with you behind those walls." He raised a hand and waved as if calling someone forward.

From among the ranks of warriors behind him came another man who was clearly a Saxon from his dress, and he was dragging a woman by the arm. This Saxon was much smaller than Horsa, nowhere near as physically impressive, and yet he wore similarly rich clothing and there was even a resemblance to Horsa in his features. Narina had heard the stories from Bellicus, Catia, and others about these raiders and she knew immediately that this must be Sigarr, Horsa's cousin. He did not seem overly happy with the task he was performing, but he did it in silence, forcibly pulling the woman forward until she was beside Horsa, where Sigarr shoved her onto the ground.

She fell without even raising her hands to protect herself, her face thumping into the hard earth. Narina could see there were already bruises there, and her clothing had been torn open to reveal her breasts and her pale legs. Whoever this was, she had not been treated well by her captors.

"This is one of your people," Horsa called up, kicking the prone woman in the side. She squealed in agony but Horsa ignored it, returning his stony gaze to Narina. "We captured her, and more like her, when we passed the village not far back that way."

From his pointing finger Narina knew he was talking about Dun Buic and she felt a chill run down her spine. Dun Buic was a small settlement, totally unequipped to withstand an army of the size Horsa and Drest commanded — if Drest had allowed his men to do as their base instincts dictated the place would be nothing but a smoking ruin by now, its people scattered or, worse, slaughtered or captured.

Like the sobbing woman that lay at Horsa's feet now. She turned her battered face to look up at Narina, and shouted, "Help me!"

Horsa laughed and Narina felt like she might be sick, bile rising in her throat at the thought of what might be about to happen and the knowledge that there was absolutely nothing she could do to stop it. The enemy jarl was too far away for her archers to hit and, to lead her garrison out from the safety of Dun Breatann's walls would mean annihilation for them since they were outnumbered.

"Catia," she murmured, swallowing the bitter taste in her throat. "Go back and stand over there. You should not see this."

The princess's face was pale but she gritted her teeth and stared murderously out at Horsa. "I should see it, Mother," she argued. "I should know what these monsters are capable of."

"You already know what they're capable of!" Narina shouted, angry that she was allowing her emotions to show so openly to the Saxon and his Pictish allies. "Please, Catia, do not watch this."

"Look!" Horsa roared gleefully, bending down to grasp the beaten woman by the hair. She tried to hit his hands, to break his grip, but he simply slapped her brutally on the ear and the fight went out of her. Horsa pulled her hair back, exposing her throat, and Narina saw the glint of sharpened iron and, without another word, the Saxon bent down and dragged his seax across the Damnonii woman's throat.

Narina turned away, eyes screwed firmly shut as she desperately tried to block out what was happening to one of her own people. A woman who expected Narina to protect her, but now lay gasping to draw in a breath through the gaping, bloody slash in her windpipe.

"I told you not to watch," the queen said through tears, forcibly turning Catia who had seen the woman's murder and was as pale now as Narina knew she must be herself.

"Are you alright, my lady?" Gerallt asked in a cool, detached voice. He, at least, seemed able to stoically accept the butchery going on outside the gatehouse.

"No, of course I'm not," she snapped, then immediately regretted her words. It wasn't the captain's fault that the Saxons were so cruel. "Gods, is he still yammering on out there?" she asked as Horsa's thickly accented tones carried up to them relentlessly.

They turned and looked over the wall again and Narina immediately wished she hadn't for Sigarr was dragging another half-naked person to Horsa. It was a man this time — a young man, and the queen recognised him. "By Taranis, that's the blacksmith's apprentice," she said to Gerallt who nodded.

"His jaw's been broken, poor lad," the captain noted, but Narina knew a broken jaw would soon be the least of the apprentice's worries.

"You sure you don't want to surrender?" Horsa bellowed, ending with a nasty laugh.

Narina could feel the eyes of everyone within Dun Breatann boring into her and she felt trapped and alone. What did they expect her to do? Gods below, what *could* she do! She felt like her

75

throat was constricting and, desperately, she wondered if surrendering would save the life of the young smith's apprentice. Of all her followers within the fortress.

As despair washed over her she felt something grasp her hand and looked down. It was Catia, taking her mother's hand in hers. The girl met her gaze and there was strength and reassurance in the twelve-year-old's eyes.

"Be strong," Catia said softly, hand on her sword. "There's nothing we can do for those captives, other than pray that the gods ease their passage to the Otherlands."

Narina's despair was immediately replaced by shame. She was the adult — the queen of Alt Clota! — yet here she was being comforted by her own daughter. It was humiliating, yet, at the same time, deeply moving. The hatred, terror, and pain outside the fortress wall was countered within by the love of a child, and Narina felt blessed to know she was not alone after all. Not while she had Catia with her.

She took a deep, steadying breath and smiled at the princess. "Wait here," she said, then stepped back to gaze out proudly over the crenelated timber wall at Horsa and Sigarr who had now been joined by a woman with a strangely shaped wand in her hand. The *volva,* undoubtedly.

"May Dis Pater curse you," Narina called to the Saxons, her voice surprisingly steady as she saw the crimson wounds in the blacksmith's apprentice's chest. They'd killed him too. "May Dis Pater take you, and all who are with you!" she cried.

The *volva* laughed at Narina's curse and shrieked something back but the words came out in an insane jumble and the queen had no idea what was being said. Before she could make any reply another captured Damnonii man was dragged roughly out from the enemy army. He tried to fight off his tormentors but they rained down blows on his head and body and pulled him inexorably towards the *volva* who had a broken stone dagger in her right hand and a malevolent smile on her face.

"We can do this all day!" Horsa laughed. "I can think of worse ways to spend an afternoon."

Narina bit back a retort, knowing it was futile. She turned to Gerallt and said, "Leave a handful of guards here, and on the walls, to make sure the enemy army doesn't try to break in. Everyone else should move back to the inner gatehouse — watching our own people being slaughtered will not be good for morale."

Gerallt raised his eyebrows but offered no opinion on her orders and she walked past him, gesturing for Catia to follow her down from the walkway to the inner courtyard.

"This is where we killed so many of Drest's Picts the last time they came here to attack us," Narina said, mostly to herself as she remembered the shattered bodies that had been strewn about there on that momentous day. "We will do it again, of that I'm sure."

"I hope so," said Catia as they walked to the inner gatehouse. "But what do we do until then?"

"Now," the queen replied. "We stay alert and wait. And pray Gavo can muster enough men to attack Drest's army from outside Dun Breatann."

CHAPTER FIFTEEN

Gavo could hardly take in what he was seeing. "It's gone," he said in shock. "They've destroyed the entire village."

"They never did this the last time they came to Alt Clota," said Sentica, a wiry soldier in his late twenties who'd served Queen Narina for years and had been trusted to act now as Gavo's second-in-command while they were outside Dun Breatann's protective walls.

"No, they did not," Gavo replied, still staring bleakly at the smouldering remains of Dun Buic. "Drest wanted a kingdom to rule. He knew there was no point in destroying settlements and slaughtering the people — who would work the fields, the mines, the quarries…" He trailed off as his eyes fell on the body of an old man. The enemy warriors had stabbed him in the back numerous times, despite the fact it was clear the elderly Damnonii must have been unable to hobble away from them.

"Look at that," Sentica snarled, pointing at the corpse of the greybeard. "He would have been no threat to them! Why cut down someone like that? What honour, what glory, is there in such murder?"

Gavo let out a slow breath, steadying himself, for he guessed there would be more dead littering what remained of Dun Buic.

"We're fighting a new enemy here," he said to Sentica and to the other Damnonii soldiers he'd taken with him from Dun Breatann before it was sealed shut by Drest's army. "This is not like the war we fought before with Drest, and Loarn mac Eirc, and Cunedda. The Saxons are like nothing we've ever seen before, just like Bellicus was always saying. Well," he held out his palms towards the smoking shells of Dun Buic's once cosy buildings. "This is what happens when the Saxons come to a place."

"What are we going to do, lord?" Sentica asked and there was a note of despair in his voice. They were so few, and the enemy so many and so…brutal! How could anyone stand against such a foe?

"We're not going to lose heart," Gavo said sternly, patting the shaft of his spear. "We still have our weapons, and we know these lands. So, we will do our best to gather an army of our own from the settlements hereabouts but, for now, we need to scour Dun

Buic for survivors, and for supplies, if anything's left. Sentica, you take half the men and search the eastern side of the village, I'll take the west. Be careful, there may be Picts or Saxons still lingering, looting the dead or sleeping off drunken stupors."

"If we find any?"

Gavo's mouth curled in a bleak smile. "Give them the same kind of death they gave to the innocent folk of Dun Buic."

The two groups went about their business quickly and efficiently. It was not a large village so it did not take too long. They found a dozen more bodies and they were not all old people; there were younger men and women, and even a child.

Gavo found the corpse of the settlement's headman, Nectovelius, sprawled right in the centre of the village. He must have come to speak with Drest and his raiders and been killed for his trouble. There was a single wound in his belly that had been inflicted with such force that the blade had torn right through Nectovelius, leaving a second bloody hole in his back. Four more bodies lay nearby and Gavo could picture what must have transpired there.

"Nectovelius and the people of Dun Buic didn't expect to be attacked," he said, eyes scanning the scene as he put it all together in his mind. "They just expected Drest to demand supplies — that's what happened when the Picts came before. But this time the Saxons, I imagine, had other ideas. One put his blade right through the headman and others started killing anyone standing nearby."

"Where's everyone else then?" one of his men asked, looking about in consternation. "There should be more bodies, shouldn't there?"

Gavo nodded slowly. "When the killing began the people probably ran away." He jerked his head towards the hills that surrounded Dun Buic on three sides. "Hopefully there's survivors scattered up there." He was hopeful, but, at the same time, he expected the Saxons would have taken captives. Slaves were a valuable commodity after all. Gavo shuddered inwardly as he imagined the fate those poor wretches would suffer. A quick death would be preferable to a life spent in thrall to a sea-wolf!

They met up with Sentica and his detachment and reported their findings to one another.

"There were no survivors, no supplies," Gavo said bleakly. "And any animals have been taken by Drest to feed his army."

It was the same story on Sentica's side of the village. "More bodies, men, women, children, even dogs," he said in a hollow tone and Gavo hoped the man would be able to hold himself together. Sentica, and the other Damnonii warriors with them, had fought battles before — they had seen what sword and spear did to a man's body. They had seen the mangled, bloodied remnants of soldiers — friend and foe — hacked to pieces, torn asunder, decapitated and the myriad other results of a fight to the death.

But none of them had ever seen the aftermath of a Saxon raid upon an unsuspecting, peaceful settlement. It had shaken them all, particularly Sentica who must have also been feeling the pressure of command for he'd only been promoted to his new rank when Drest's approaching army was reported by the Damnonii scouts.

"Why?" the sergeant asked dazedly. "Why kill innocents? What's the point in conquering a kingdom if there's no-one left to work it?"

"To send a message to Queen Narina," one of the older warriors suggested. "Surrender Dun Breatann, or see your people and your lands turned to ash."

Gavo laid a hand reassuringly on his sergeant's shoulder. "Don't worry, Sentica," he said. "We'll pay the bastards back for what they've done here."

The thought of revenge gave Sentica something to focus on other than the horror that was all around them in the burnt out husks of homes and workshops. "I'll look forward to it," he growled, knuckles white as he gripped his spear and stared towards the imposing bulk of Dun Breatann less than an hour's march to the west.

"We all will," Gavo said, and the rest of the men murmured agreement.

"What now though?" Sentica asked, and his voice was stronger already. "We should look for anyone who escaped this carnage."

"Indeed. There's nothing else to be done here anyway." Gavo took a last look at the remnants of a once proud village and cursed the monsters that had wiped it from the earth. "One day," he said, "we'll rebuild Dun Buic. For now, let's head up the hill towards the stables at Ard Sabhal. We have to hope Drest didn't command his men to chase Dun Buic's refugees into the hills. They were in a hurry after all."

Sentica nodded vigorously. "Aye," he said. "The stables are well known around here, everyone knows old Boduoc and his wife. They helped Bellicus and Duro before — I'm sure they'll help any survivors from this."

The atmosphere, sorrowful and grim, rose now as Gavo and his men marched away from Dun Buic and started up the hill that led to the stables. Of course, if some of the enemy army had done the same thing, and gone after those who'd fled their butchery, the little steading at Ard Sabhal, along with the farmer and his wife, might also be nothing but a memory, but Gavo prayed that was not the case. Ideally, they would find the stables intact and survivors from Dun Buic alive and well. With any luck, a few of them would be men of fighting age that could join Gavo's warband. Queen Narina had ordered him to try and build an army after all, or at least a warband big enough to cause Drest's raiders trouble.

Gavo meant to carry out that mission, and see the Pictish king where he belonged — in the ground, or swinging from a rope over the Dun Breatann's walls!

CHAPTER SIXTEEN

The day after the attack on the druid Moot was sunny but somewhat overcast. The smell of spring was in the air and a cool breeze seemed to freshen things, blowing away the lingering smells of roasting beef, bonfires, and blood.

Bellicus's arm had been freshly bandaged again by Ria who'd done her best to help the wounded left in the Saxons' wake. Even with her expert help, many of the druids were dead, their bodies lying beside the Merlin's as preparations were made for a great funeral.

Despite the fact that many of them were, like Bellicus, warriors as well as druids, the gathering remained in shock after the past night's events.

"This was supposed to be a happy occasion," Lancelot said, looking around at the glum faces milling about beside the river, almost as if the murder of their leader had left them without a purpose in life.

"A happy occasion," Bellicus repeated. "And one attended by the gods. We did not expect the blood sacrifice to be Nemias though." He chewed his lip, gazing across at the dead Merlin whose body was being prepared for the funeral by two elderly druids. "You know, Nemias really wasn't as old as he looked. That long, white beard made him seem ancient, but I doubt he was much older than sixty."

Lancelot and Bedwyr nodded, having known the High Druid better than anyone at the Moot, spending a fair bit of time with him over recent years as they all did their best to make Arthur's army as potent, and feared, as possible. Merlin was much-loved by Arthur and his warriors for, although he could be as enigmatic as any druid, he was a humorous and entertaining companion who boosted the morale of all who came into contact with him.

"Arthur is going to be devastated," said Bedwyr. "Those two were the best of friends. And the Merlin was his closest advisor." He shook his head and Bellicus saw tears in the young man's eyes.

"It's a terrible blow for us all," Duro stated. The attack had hit the centurion hard too, for he felt like he'd failed in his job as guard for the druids. Of course, he had been there with Bellicus, not the Merlin, but, even so, Duro believed he could have done more to stop the Saxon attack. But if even druids — who were said to have the gift of precognition — could not foresee the doom that lay in wait for them at the height of last night's ceremony, how could a former legionary?

"It is indeed a blow," Bellicus agreed. "And it just shows how brazen the Saxons have become. If ever we needed a strong Arthur, now is the time. He may well be upset at the loss of his friend, but he'll need to act quickly and decisively to put an end to Hengist's plans once and for all."

Bedwyr and Lancelot shared unhappy looks, apparently not too pleased by Bellicus's dire pronouncement. They did not argue, however. Today was not the day to fall out with one another. Word was already on the way to Arthur regarding the attack on Sulis's shrine — it would be up to the warlord to decide himself what to do about it, no matter what Bellicus said.

"What are you all going to do?" Lancelot asked, nodding at the other druids who were standing or sitting around singly or in small groups, chattering in either sorrowful or outraged, angry tones.

Bellicus shrugged. "I'd like to ride to Arthur and ask him to attack Hengist with all haste, but that will have to wait. First, we must have the funeral for our fallen brothers, and then, if we can concentrate properly, a new Merlin must be elected."

"So soon?" Duro wondered.

Bellicus nodded. "I think so. We're all gathered here, so it's the ideal time to do it. Besides, the sooner the better, even if it does seem a little disrespectful to replace Nemias almost before his body has grown cold." He sighed. "In more peaceful times perhaps the decision could wait, but the Saxons' attack has shown how imperative it is that we druids have strong leadership, and can offer the people of Britain the same strong leadership."

"Another funeral, by Mithras," muttered Duro. "I'm not sure I can deal with that. I'd rather face another attack by Hengist's scum than watch people grieving."

Bellicus reached out and grasped his friend by the shoulder. "Don't worry," he said. "Our funerals are not such gloomy affairs. We know Nemias and the others who fell will be reborn; this is not the end for them."

"How long will preparations take?" Lancelot asked. "We were supposed to be on the road to rejoin Arthur." He shook his head in exasperation. "Gods, this whole situation is horrendous! I have no idea what we should do."

"The preparations are already well underway," Bellicus told him. "All you need to do is wait a while longer, remain alert in case Hengist returns with another warband, and then we'll see what's to be done after that. A day or two at most, then you and Bedwyr can return to Arthur, probably with me and Duro at your side."

The suggestion that he, and the other guards, stay vigilant, was exactly what Lancelot and his comrades needed. Patrolling the shrine, and scouting the lands around Caer Legion, would give them something to do while the druids made ready for the funerary rites.

"Come on, lads," said Lancelot to Duro and Bedwyr. "We'll round up the other guards and make sure the druids can deal with the funeral in peace."

After a nod from Bellicus, Duro gladly went with the others and they moved away, leaving the big druid standing with Cai.

"Would you like to say a few words for Nemias?" asked a wizened old fellow in a soot-stained white robe. "At the funeral, I mean."

Bellicus thought about it and nodded. "Of course," he said to the older druid whose face crinkled as he smiled and made a note on the wax tablet he was carrying.

"Good," the man said. "Keep it short though, eh? There's a lot of people wanting to say their piece and we don't want to be here until the next solstice."

Qunavo strode across to gaze up at Bellicus then. Of everyone at the Moot, Bellicus suspected Qunavo had known Nemias for the longest, although he had no idea if they were actually friends or simply acquaintances. Perhaps they'd been close in their youth, but it was hard to maintain a friendship when you lived at the other end of the island from one another.

"What d'you want?" Bellicus asked his childhood tutor, in no mood for a conversation with the man who'd been behind Duro's torture and mutilation in Drest's fortress at Dunnottar.

Qunavo shook his head sorrowfully. "Can we not be civil at least, Bel? We were once friends."

"Before you tried to kill the people of Alt Clota," Bellicus retorted coldly. "And had Drest hack the fingers from my closest friend's hand. Say your piece, old man, then be silent."

Qunavo's eyes widened at his former student's angry words. "We will need to elect a new High Druid," he said. "Someone with the experience, knowledge, and gravitas to act as the Merlin, drawing together all the tribes of Britain."

Bellicus stared at him, knowing where the conversation was going and feeling laughter bubbling up within him. "You?" he asked in disbelief. "You want me to support you? Are you mad?"

"You know I fit the criteria, Bel," Qunavo said, spreading his arms almost in supplication. "You might not think much of me nowadays thanks to our opposing loyalties, but you must know I'm the best man to be Merlin."

Bellicus's smile faded and he thought about what the Pictish druid was proposing. It was true, Qunavo had a breadth of knowledge and learning that surpassed most of his fellow druids and druidesses gathered at the moot, and he had been a fine mentor to Bellicus in his youth. Indeed, had been a mentor to many young aspirants, including Ria and probably many others at the Moot. He was, at times, a sly, duplicitous old shit, but even that could be a strength in certain situations.

Was he the best candidate to replace Nemias? Bellicus looked around at the other druids and felt a chill for he could not see anyone that might challenge Qunavo and, if the Pict did become High Druid, what would that mean for the people of Alt Clota? King Drest would have power to wield that had never been his before, and that could not be good for the Damnonii, or, probably, the other tribes of Northern Britain.

True, the druids were not as powerful as they'd been five hundred years ago, their numbers having dwindled greatly ever since that near-genocide on Ynys Mon, but still, the Merlin wielded great influence. If Qunavo took over from Nemias it would surely bring trouble to Bellicus's people.

"Who else can do it?" the older man demanded. "You said yourself the Saxon threat needs to be met robustly. I promise you, I'll make sure the Saxons do not cause any more trouble."

"That's a huge thing to promise," Bellicus replied. "How can you guarantee something like that?"

"The sea-wolves trade with us," Qunavo said matter-of-factly. "Their ships come to Dunnottar often. I have made connections with them."

Bellicus's lip curled. "I can imagine the conversations you've had with them," he said.

"Your view of me is clouded, Bel, thanks to the troubles between your people and the Picts lately. But it's a druid's place to support the king whose lands he is given to look after. I only do for Drest what you do for Narina, and Coroticus before her." He paused, allowing Bellicus to absorb his argument, then went on. "The new Merlin must be someone with decades of experience. Not just a druid, but a teacher, a mentor, a warrior — I am all of these things. Think about it, and think back dispassionately on your time as my student on the island of Iova." He smiled and patted Bellicus's great bicep. "When it comes time to cast your vote, you must do what you think is right. But if you want to see the druids grow in power and influence, you will see me as the only choice."

He turned and strode off, his gait purposeful in stark contrast to the listless other druids that populated the shrine's environs at that moment.

Qunavo as the Merlin? And with Ria at his side. They would be a potent pair, but would they do what was best for all the druids, or just what was best for themselves, and for Drest?

Sadly, Bellicus feared the latter, but he did not see anyone other than Qunavo being elected — there was simply no one better suited to be High Druid at the Moot. They were all too old, too inexperienced, or, like Bellicus, too young.

He sighed for what felt like the hundredth time that day and turned his gaze to the sky. The earlier glints of sunshine were no more, for pale grey clouds completely covered its yellow face and there was a hint of moisture in the air that suggested rain was on the way.

There was no point in worrying about things, Bellicus thought, forcing himself to put thoughts of what Qunavo might do if elected as Merlin out of his head. The gods would guide them, as they always did. If Qunavo had earned the respect of the others at the Moot, perhaps it was for the best that he replace Nemias.

"Taranis help us," he murmured as the first drops of rain fell on his shaved head. "All of this could not have come at a worse time."

CHAPTER SEVENTEEN

Nemias's body had been washed and wrapped in a shroud the night before, and then it had been watched over. For one of such high status there really should have been days of such watching, and then days of feasting to celebrate the dead one's life and coming rebirth. There simply wasn't time for that just now, and the funeral rites were carried out the day after the Saxons' attack. Nemias was placed on a bier, and then the druids chanted, and sang the Lamentation of Sorrow, and told tales of their fallen Merlin's life and deeds, before asking the gods to take care of his soul.

A grave had been dug near to Sulis Minerva's shrine, a deep one so no animals could disturb it, and the shrouded body was carried there on its bier, draped in green birch branches. Nemias was interred along with his staff of office, his sacrificial knife, and a spherical piece of greenstone, carved with spirals and known as a druid's egg, which was believed to have magical properties.

The grave was filled in and then the bier that Nemias's body had rested upon in death was destroyed so it could not be used by evil spirits.

When the funeral was over the feast began, as usual. Ale and wine were served, and roast beef and pork too, along with poultry, and fish caught in the nearby river. The people of Caer Legion had sent another delivery that morning which included freshly baked bread, spring vegetables and berries.

It should have been a most joyous occasion — the end of the first druid Moot in years, and a ceremony witnessed by the full moon. It would be remembered for generations undoubtedly, but for the wrong reasons.

Duro and the other guards had found no trace of Saxons, or any other enemies, despite scouring the land for miles around. Even so, they were dotted about the perimeter of Sulis Minerva's shrine, heavily armed and alert for danger. There would be no repeat of the previous attack, that was certain. And somewhat unfortunate, Bellicus thought, for he'd have loved the chance to slaughter a few more of the Saxon whoresons. Sea-wolf blood would nourish the earth even better than the mighty pair of bulls that had been sacrificed.

There was hardly a delay between the end of the funeral rites and the start of the next piece of business. The longer the day went on, the more intoxicated the druids would get, so the task of electing the new High Druid got underway without much preamble.

"You all know what we have to do now," said Qunavo, who'd taken it upon himself to speak first. He was in his sixties now and, like Nemias, wore a long white beard which he kept neatly trimmed and combed. That, along with his pale, occasionally watery, blue eyes, made him seem even older, more venerable he'd have suggested, than he really was. If the druids wished to elect a new Merlin who at least looked rather like the old one, Qunavo would be an easy choice.

He climbed to the top of the mound that housed Sulis Minerva's shrine and Ria — small and dark by comparison, as well as young and quite beautiful — stood just behind him, smiling and nodding as he spoke.

"I knew Nemias for many, many years," Qunavo began in a loud, powerful voice that echoed out across the River Aerfen. "We spent much time together back when we were just starting out as druids, helping one another find the path that suited them, and traversing the obstacles we all face before hard-earned experience makes things easier. Later, Nemias became Merlin, and I did my part for the Order by teaching students, mainly on Iova but in other places as well. Some of my students are here today, distinguished, revered members of not only our Order, but also of the communities they serve." He glanced over his shoulder and gestured at Ria, whose dazzling smile seemed to light up the ill-fated shrine. "Ria, of course, and Bellicus of Dun Breatann being just two you will all know."

Bellicus scowled, not wanting anyone to think he endorsed Qunavo's claim to the title of Merlin. Unfortunately, Bellicus was very familiar to all the druids thanks to the stories and songs of his exciting adventures. The fact that Qunavo had taught such an impressive figure would most certainly go in the older man's favour.

"I am well into middle-age, I must admit," Qunavo chuckled self-deprecatingly. "But with years come knowledge, experience and wisdom, as we all know. I've dedicated my life to strengthening our Order, brothers and sisters, and I know what it takes to lead from the very front. Besides that, you may have noticed that when the Saxons attacked us the other night I was more than capable of standing toe-to-toe with them, even managing to kill one and badly injure another." He thumped his staff on the ground, dust falling from the hillock onto the shrine beneath. "We need the Merlin to be someone who can hold their own in a fight, and I believe even Hengist will fear Qunavo of the Picts now!"

Some of the druids laughed grimly at his pronouncement, swayed by the arguments he was making and impressed by his confidence. Outsiders — Duro for example, had he been standing with Bellicus — might have been disgusted by what he would see as arrogance but it was a druid's job to be full of confidence in oneself. Their very existence hinged upon persuading people they were a conduit to the gods after all; self-belief was perhaps the most important trait for a druid.

And Qunavo was not short of self-belief.

"What about the Saxons?" one of the other druids called up. "Nemias wanted us to focus on dealing with them as a priority. You argued against it, but it's pretty damn obvious now that he was right!"

Qunavo peered gravely down at the man and nodded, accepting the accusation. "You're right, Diseta." Clearly the would-be Merlin had made sure to memorise the names of those he aspired to lead, thought Bellicus. "I did argue that we should seek to make friends rather than enemies of the Saxons." He clenched his fist and held it out before him, gritting his teeth as he went on. "But you're right. The attack here cannot go without reply, and it's shown me that Hengist is a threat that must be met head on, as soon as possible."

Diseta, a bald man with a great, grizzled beard, frowned and rubbed his shining scalp. From the look on his face he was not convinced Qunavo meant what he said, and, as Bellicus eyed the rest of the Moot, he could tell many of the other druids felt the same way. Qunavo was telling them what they wanted to hear, but whether he actually meant any of it was another matter.

"What would you have us do, if you become the new High Druid?" a small, stout druidess demanded, pointing her finger up at Qunavo. "About the Saxons I mean."

"What can we do, realistically? We are far, far too few to mount an attack ourselves." Qunavo shook his head. "No, we must be clever, my friends. We must use our influence with the great kings and warlords of these lands, with the ultimate aim of uniting them. At least for long enough to sweep the sea-wolves back into the ocean that washed them up here on our shores."

That brought some murmurs of agreement from the more pragmatic of the druids, but it wasn't enough for others.

"We must do more than that," Diseta cried. "My home lands are on the east coast — the raiders attack us constantly, their ships bringing more and more across their whale road every month."

"I agree," Qunavo replied, attempting to mollify the outspoken man. "And we shall move with as much haste as possible to stop them, I swear it by Taranis and Dis Pater."

Still, many of those gathered did not quite accept that Qunavo was feeding them anything more than empty platitudes, and the druidess spoke up again.

"Are there no more candidates?" she demanded, looking around at her fellows almost threateningly. "Does no-one else seek to become the Merlin?"

Three more men did, and they climbed atop the shrine to deliver their reasons to be granted the title but none were as impressive as Qunavo, and Bellicus felt a seed of despair growing within him. Qunavo would be hailed as High Druid, and the Picts would become an even bigger threat to the Damnonii than they already were. It was not quite a disaster, but it was beginning to feel like it.

"Would you be willing to leave your own lands," a new voice called out, a voice that was crisp and clear and carried an easy air of command. Bellicus looked around and realised Bedwyr, Duro, and Lancelot were behind him, and it was the golden-haired swordsman who was speaking. "Arthur, Bear of Britain, must have the Merlin by his side if he is to defeat the Saxons. A task that was given to him, I should remind you all, by Nemias. Any who seek to replace him, must be prepared to serve the gods at Arthur's side."

Normally there would not be anyone allowed at a gathering such as this who was not a member of the Druid Order, and Lancelot would certainly would not be allowed to speak — but the butchery of the previous night had meant the guards were allowed to remain with their charges.

"Who are you to set out demands for us?" Qunavo demanded.

"He's Lancelot," Diseta shouted back. "And he, at least, is committed to killing Saxons, as you'd know if you ever left those gods forsaken northern lands of yours, Qunavo."

"I am no druid," Lancelot admitted. "But I speak for Arthur, who is the most powerful and influential warlord in Britain just now. I tell you, if you would have Arthur's support, the Merlin must live and serve beside him." He shrugged. "I have no authority over you — you are free to disregard my words. But Nemias saw Arthur as the greatest hope Britain has, and he would want his successor to work with the warlord, as he did."

Everyone there knew of Arthur. They knew he was not a king, but they knew his star was in the ascendancy. And, if the druids truly wanted to smash the Saxons, working in tandem with the warlord made complete sense.

"Well?" the stout druidess demanded, glaring up at Qunavo. "Would you swear to leave King Drest and your home in Dunnottar, and come south to serve beside Arthur?"

Qunavo, it was obvious, did not want to agree to that. He turned and looked at Ria, as if he hoped she might offer some clever way of side-stepping this issue. Ria, however, was ambitious in her own right Bellicus knew, and she did not look too unhappy at how things were going. She simply nodded, silently encouraging her mentor to agree to the deal that would see him become Merlin, and her take his place as Drest's sole druid.

"Pah, this is nonsense," another new voice cried and Bellicus smiled inwardly as he recognised Duro's parade-ground bellow. "Qunavo is a sly old fool, and he's likely to betray you all if the Saxons offer him wealth and power. You can't trust a word he says. He probably had a hand in the attack the other night! We all know the Picts trade with Hengist's sea-wolves."

"Silence!" Qunavo shrieked, glaring murderously at the centurion who was dressed in his full legionary armour and helmet. "The profane may not speak at a gathering such as this."

92

"Shut up yourself," Duro retorted, his dislike for the white-bearded old druid making his eyes blaze as he turned away from Qunavo and pointed at Bellicus. "There's only one person you should be looking at to succeed Nemias. Him!"

There was a stunned silence then. Many of the druids had been grinning at the exchange between Duro and Qunavo, enjoying the entertainment, but their faces became thoughtful as they followed the centurion's finger and contemplated the man he'd nominated.

Bellicus was much younger than Qunavo at just thirty summers, and, as far as looks went, he did not quite fit the stereotype the way the older man did. Bellicus had no beard, just stubble, and his head was shaved. He also towered over everyone there at more than six and a half feet and looked more like a mighty warrior than a mystic or a scholar. Those who actually knew him knew that he was all of those things though, and more.

"Why haven't any of you put Bellicus forward as Nemias's replacement?" Duro demanded.

"Bellicus is too young," Ria called down dismissively. "He's the same age as me," and she gave a childlike smile that made some of the men laugh.

"He's a fine soldier," Qunavo said. "I know that well, for it was me who trained him. And one day, aye, he could be the Merlin. But, as Ria says, he's too young, too inexperienced, and, frankly, too aggressive."

"Maybe that's what we need," Diseta argued. "Take a look around, old man. The Saxons don't fear us — aggression and force is the one thing they do respect. If Bel can bring that, he has my vote."

There was a loud chorus of agreement and Diseta seemed to grow in stature as he noticed his peers were actually taking his arguments on board.

"And is Bellicus willing to do as Lancelot demands?" Ria asked sourly. "Will you leave Dun Breatann behind, Bel? Leave behind your beloved Queen Narina to live in the south, far from the Damnonii tribe?"

All eyes turned to Bellicus and his mind was racing for he had never even contemplated putting himself forward for High Druid. Did he even want to be Merlin? He liked Arthur and his captains a great deal, but Ria's question was insightful: did he want to leave Narina, Catia, and the lands that had become his home?

"It's not about what he wants," Diseta shouted, waving his hand as if to dismiss Ria's issues. "We druids swear to serve our Order, and the people of Britain. If we vote for Bellicus to take up Nemias's mantle and become Merlin, then he surely must do so."

Still, Bellicus did not reply, for he truly did not know what to say, or what he wanted to do.

"You can't refuse, Bel," said Duro, coming to stand right next to him. "You cannot let Qunavo become even more powerful. This is your chance to guide things as you see fit. Take it!"

It was obvious the majority of the druids supported Bellicus now, and would vote for him over Qunavo or anyone else, if he agreed to put himself forward.

As if sensing this power shift, Qunavo pointed his staff at Bellicus and cried out, "What if there was a raid on Dun Breatann? Would you remain by Arthur's side, Bel? If you knew a Saxon warband had besieged Narina's fortress? Or would you renounce your sacred oath and leave your duties behind to ride north with all haste to save the life of your mistress?"

Bellicus felt the aggression Qunavo had mentioned building within him and he knew if he'd been standing closer to his old tutor he'd have reached out and throttled him. He forced himself to look deeper though, to imagine if Qunavo's words were more than a fantasy scenario he'd cooked up to make Bel seem weak and unfit to be High Druid.

"*Has* there been a raid on Dun Breatann?" he demanded, walking forward and climbing up the front of the mound, his huge arms easily hauling himself up until he stood facing a visibly nervous Qunavo. "Have you been working with the Saxons, you old bastard?" With an effort, he restrained himself from grabbing Qunavo and forcing him to give up the truth — this was supposed to be a civilised gathering of learned men and women after all.

"Of course not." It was Ria who replied with a disdainful sneer. "Qunavo is merely imagining a hypothetical scenario. What *would* you do, Bellicus of Dun Breatann, if sea-wolves were at Narina's gates now, ready to overwhelm her fortress and make her their thrall?"

The way she looked directly at him and said the words made Bellicus shiver. She, and Qunavo knew something, and they revelled in their knowledge.

As Bellicus gazed at them, reading their amused, cunning expressions, he knew they were not making up an imaginary scenario; Dun Breatann was under attack and, most likely by Drest's Picts as well as Saxons.

Hengist had led the raid on Sulis Minerva's shrine, he thought. That was unusual — Horsa was always the one to carry out such missions. Yet there had been no sign of the *bretwalda's* younger brother either during the fighting or as the attackers were chased away.

"By Dis Pater," said Bellicus quietly, towering over Qunavo and Ria. "If what you say turns out to be true, you will wish the gods had not shat you out into this world."

Qunavo blanched but smiled sweetly. "You had better return to Narina and make sure all is well then," he said, matching Bellicus's soft tones so none of the other druids gathered about the base of the mound could hear. "Return home now, Bel, before it's too late, and your lover is dead."

CHAPTER EIGHTEEN

Emotions warred within Bellicus as he stared at Qunavo and Ria. These two had already caused him, and the good people of Alt Clota so much trouble over recent years. Many warriors — Picts as well as Damnonii — had been cut down in their prime as a result of their actions, and that of their king, Drest. On top of that, Ria had toyed with Bellicus's emotions, playing him like a lovestruck fool. Not only did it hurt to know she had not cared for him but had merely been using him, but it embarrassed him to know he'd been manipulated so easily. Him, the mighty Bellicus of Dun Breatann!

And he was now being touted as High Druid! It was ludicrous.

He realised at that moment that he did not want to become the Merlin — not yet at least. One day in the future, aye, it would be good to lead the Order, to shape it as he saw fit and perhaps even return them to the prominence they'd once enjoyed before the Romans effectively neutered them.

But now, when he'd just turned thirty and had so many other things going on? No, he did not want to take over from Nemias. He wanted to go home, remove Ysfael from Alt Clota no matter how, and marry Narina himself. If an army of Picts, or Saxons — or both! — stood in his way, he would find a way through, somehow.

Yet, as Qunavo returned his gaze, Bellicus knew that to leave the Moot now would mean Qunavo would be named High Druid. He would be handing his enemies the power they craved, and doing irreparable damage to the other tribes in northern Britain. Perhaps *all* Britain, if the Picts had indeed thrown their lot in with the Saxons as Qunavo and Ria had hinted.

"Bellicus! Bel!"

He finally noticed his name being called and forced himself to break out of his thoughtful stupor, turning to look down at Diseta on the ground below. "What?" he asked.

"Will you return to Dun Breatann, as Qunavo says, or will you vow to join Arthur and become the Merlin? Speak now, and let us cast our votes for you, or for Qunavo."

Looking over his shoulder at Ria, Bellicus said harshly, "Is it true there's an army besieging Dun Breatann right now?"

The druidess laughed sweetly and tilted her head to one side, a strand of dark hair falling over one eye. This time though, her beauty failed to move Bellicus, and she perhaps read as much in his expression for her smile faded and she replied, "If not today, they will be soon."

For a moment longer Bellicus eyed them, and then he turned and looked once more at Diseta. "My brothers and sisters," he cried, "I will join Arthur, if you will name me as High Druid."

Cheers erupted at his words and Diseta, Lancelot, Bedwyr, and Duro laughed and threw their hands in the air. It was terrible that their friend Nemias was dead, but, if someone had to take his place, they'd hoped it would be Bellicus.

"You big fool," Qunavo hissed behind him. "Drest and Horsa will lay waste to your precious Alt Clota while you play at being Merlin here. The cries of despair will haunt your dreams, Bel, and you shall never know a moment's peace. The bodies of young Damnonii warriors will litter the fields and walls of Dun Breatann, while your Queen Narina finds herself the plaything of Horsa and a hundred Saxon warriors. Catia—"

Bellicus spun, eyes blazing and gripped Qunavo by the throat, lifting him from the mound and holding him in the air as he squeezed, choking the breath from the older druid.

"Catia *what?*" Bellicus growled. "Tell me, you twisted old rat. Tell me what you were about to say. It will be the last words you ever speak, by Dis Pater I swear it!"

"Put him down!" Ria commanded, although she did not come too close to Bellicus. "Aife is with the army," she hissed. "She will make sure nothing happens to Catia, you can be sure of that, Bel. She loves the girl! Now, put him down, before you kill him."

There could be no doubt any more — the Picts had marched on Alt Clota and were laying siege to Dun Breatann. Bellicus saw the truth of it in Ria's eyes, and in Qunavo's desperate, pleading gasps. He opened his hand and let the white-bearded older man fall heavily to the ground, spluttering and mewling and desperately trying to fill his lungs before he passed out.

"I am one man," Bellicus said, addressing Ria now, as if Qunavo was not even worth bothering with. "Returning to Dun Breatann would not end the war you people have set in motion. But my remaining here shall, gods willing, make sure you can do no more mischief, and, if I am elected Merlin, you can be sure I'll use the power that brings to make an end of you two." So saying, he turned and slipped easily, nimbly down from the mound before walking to join Duro and the others who welcomed him back with more cheers and laughter.

* * *

The voting went exactly as predicted. Each druid or druidess was given a small piece from a fallen yew branch and that was dropped on the ground before either Qunavo or Bellicus to mark which candidate they favoured. It did not take long before there was a large pile around the younger druid's feet and Cai was sniffing at them curiously as Duro smiled triumphantly at the Picts he despised so much.

"I think it's clear," Diseta cried, even before the yew twigs had all been set down, "that we have a winner."

Qunavo refused to give in however, and demanded all votes be cast. This only made him look worse, as almost every other vote that came afterwards went to Bellicus.

"People have had enough," Bedwyr said as two of the highest ranking members of the Order carefully counted the votes. "They want leaders like Arthur, who will protect them from the Saxons. Who will protect their way of life. It seems your fellow druids think you, Bel, will do a better job of that than Qunavo."

"We have a clear winner!" one of the men counting the yew twigs called out. "In the name of the gods, Bellicus of Dun Breatann shall be High Druid. May he follow in the exalted footsteps of Nemias, and all those who held the title of Merlin before him."

Bellicus couldn't help smiling as the results were announced. Despite everything that was happening in Britain at that time, and the knowledge that Narina and Catia were in mortal danger, he felt enormous pride at the faith the druids had placed in him. What an honour, to be named High Druid at such a young age!

"Would you like to congratulate Bellicus?" Duro shouted to Qunavo, who'd turned away and was walking with Ria back to their tent on the far side of the shrine. "Maybe wish him well in his new role?"

Lancelot was chuckling away as Duro heckled the beaten Pict. "I've never seen the centurion act like this before," he told Bellicus. "What's got into him?"

"The Picts tortured him and cut off two of his fingers," the druid replied gravely. "Not Qunavo or Ria personally, but they were the ones behind it, we believe. Duro hates them, and Drest, more than anyone other than Horsa, and I don't blame him."

"You don't hate the druidess," Lancelot said, nudging the bigger man suggestively. "I can see that much every time you look at her."

Bellicus shrugged. "She's beautiful, but I've never met a more dangerous woman."

"And that," Lancelot murmured as he watched her lithe figure move behind the shrine, "is part of the attraction."

Bedwyr came and grasped Bellicus by the wrist. He was smiling although there was a tinge of sadness to it. "Congratulations, big man," he said. "You would have been my choice to replace Nemias too, if I had a vote."

"Indeed," Lancelot agreed. "Mine too. Wait," he grinned then as a thought struck him. "This means that we're now *your* guards, Bel!"

"So it does," Bedwyr nodded happily. "When are we leaving then? It looks like the rest of the druids are packing their things up already. Is that the Moot over?"

"I'm not sure," Bellicus admitted, casting his gaze about the place.

"Not sure?" Duro demanded as he came back to join them. "You're in charge now, Bel. The Moot's over if you say it is!"

"I suppose so. Well, we better get our things packed up too then, eh?"

Lancelot and Bedwyr agreed and went off to collect their things, and those of Nemias's as well, although the deceased man's belongings would pass automatically to his successor.

Duro led the way to their tents, Cai staying close to Bellicus as if the dog was still wary of another Saxon attack.

"I must admit," Duro said over his shoulder as they neared the tents and saw Koriosis there breaking down his own small campsite. "I'm surprised you agreed to join Arthur's retinue. Never thought you'd want to leave Alt Clota, Narina, Catia…All of it."

"I'm not," the new Merlin replied, and Duro spun to face him, astonished.

"What d'ye mean?" the centurion demanded. "You agreed—"

"I know what happened," Bellicus hissed. "I was there. Keep your voice down."

Two druids, and the portly druidess who'd spoken up in support of Bellicus wandered past them, eyeing them with interest for it was clear they were having some kind of disagreement. When the people were past Duro asked again in a lower tones, "What d'ye mean, you're not? What's going on?"

"Qunavo and Ria let me know that Dun Breatann is being attacked right now by an army of Picts and Saxons."

"Not again," Duro sighed, then he shook his head, bemused. "But you still agreed to go and join Arthur. It was a condition of being named High Druid. You can't just go back on your word, Bel."

"I will join Arthur's retinue," Bellicus said. "Just not yet."

"So what are you going to do?"

"We'll let the Moot disband, then, when my brothers and sisters are on the road back to their homes, they won't know, or care, what I'm doing." He started walking again towards their tents. "I was elected as Merlin because my fellow druids want me to do what I can to stop the Saxons from taking over our lands. If I start by returning to Alt Clota and defeating Horsa's army, surely that fits my remit?"

Duro seemed unsure as he hurried after his friend, whose long stride was eating up the ground much quicker than the centurion's. "But what about Arthur? He has no druid now that Nemias is dead. He'll need one — the Saxons have that witch Thorbjorg!"

"I'll join Arthur once Alt Clota is safe," Bellicus assured him. "So the sooner we get moving the better."

"Lancelot and Bedwyr won't like this," Duro muttered, and it seemed to Bellicus like the centurion had been looking forward to joining Arthur's army. This new development was not at all to his liking.

"Won't like what?" Koriosis asked, overhearing them as they reached the tents.

"Well done, big mouth," Bellicus said, shooting a dark look at Duro, who returned it with some annoyance.

"Like what?" Koriosis repeated. "What's going on?"

"I'm not going to join Arthur yet," Bellicus told him, glancing about to make sure no-one else could discover his secret. "Alt Clota is in danger of being conquered by the Picts. I can't just bugger off to the south and forsake my people, can I?"

Koriosis didn't seem certain himself, and admitted as much. "I'm not sure. I would hate anything to happen to Narina and the Damnonii people. Would you fulfil your oath to serve beside Arthur once you knew Alt Clota was safe?"

"Of course."

"Well, I suppose it's all right then."

"See?" Bellicus said triumphantly to Duro.

"Oh, you're taking advice from your own student now, are you? Bellicus, the new Merlin, looking to a novice for guidance!"

"He's a druid as much as any of them here," Bellicus said, still smiling, refusing to take the centurion's bait. "Keep it to yourself though, Koriosis. If word gets out before the Moot has fully disbanded they might decide to make Qunavo High Druid instead."

The young man smiled conspiratorially and even winked at Bellicus. "Your secret's safe with me. Qunavo and Ria are no friends of mine."

Koriosis helped them tear down their tent and pack away their cooking utensils and bedrolls and other belongings while Cai decided to take a nap nearby. It took longer than expected to break camp for the druids at the Moot wanted to wish Bellicus well in his new position and to say farewell before setting off on the road home.

Lancelot and Bedwyr came to join them and, at last, a little while after midday, the last of the druids had departed.

"Did Qunavo say goodbye?" Lancelot asked, running a hand through his hair and smiling at Duro, who returned his look as if they were a pair of naughty boys out to steal apples.

"No, he never," replied the centurion. "Unless he's not left yet. Come on, we'll check."

"Don't be attacking him or anything silly like that," Bellicus warned as they wandered off.

"Why not? If the Picts *have* attacked Dun Breatann, doesn't that mean we're at war with Qunavo?"

The new Merlin thought about that for a moment and then snorted with amusement. "I suppose it does. Fair enough, do what you like."

He, Bedwyr and Koriosis continued to stow their goods on their horses but it wasn't long before Lancelot and Duro came back, looking rather disappointed.

"Nah, they've gone," said the centurion. "Everyone's gone, except us."

"Good," said Bellicus, then he drew in a deep breath and looked at Arthur's captains. "I know I said I'd take the road south with you two, and I will join Arthur eventually but, for now, I must return to Alt Clota."

The two men didn't seem all that surprised. Lancelot simply asked, "Why?" and, when the druid explained, they actually agreed it was the right thing to do.

"See?" Bellicus said to Duro. "I told you."

The centurion shrugged. "Well, if this is what you want, we'd better get moving, or Dun Breatann will have fallen by the time we get back."

"Are you riding again?" Bedwyr asked.

"Aye," said Duro, and "No," said Bellicus at the same time.

"We need to take a ship," the druid argued. "It's so much faster, and time is of the essence. There's an old Roman port not twenty miles from here."

The centurion nodded. He did not want to see Dun Breatann in the hands of Drest and Horsa any more than Bellicus did.

"If Horsa has a warband there," said Bedwyr, "your people may be outnumbered."

"Probably," Bellicus agreed. "That's why I want you to ask Arthur to send reinforcements. If they also come by ship they might just reach us in time to defeat the enemy."

"All right," Lancelot agreed. "We'll speak with Arthur, and hopefully he'll agree to your request. He'll be upset though — Nemias was like a father to him."

"Come on then, let's get moving," Bedwyr said. "There's no time to waste. Are you riding south too, Koriosis? You can travel with us until our roads split."

To everyone's surprise, the young druid shook his head. "No, I'm going with the Merlin and the centurion, back to Alt Clota."

"Eh? Why?"

"Think about it, Bel," Koriosis said seriously. "Drest will have two druids to help him to victory. The Damnonii will only have one — you, when you make it back there. High Druid or not, two against one is never good odds. So, I'll come with you and we'll send the raiders back where they came from. Don't worry, the people of Isca won't miss me for a while."

With that, and with a final blessing on their missions by the new Merlin, the two groups went their separate ways. Before the sun was even beginning to set Bellicus's party had reached Portus Setantiorum, once a major Roman trade and military centre, known nowadays as Twyni Tywod. There they found a ship large enough to take them and their horses to Dun Breatann and were on their way home, praying Taranis would see them there with all haste.

CHAPTER NINETEEN

"When are we going to raid more of the settlements nearby?" Horsa demanded, striding into Drest's command tent as if it was his own. The guards did not even attempt to stop him now, for the Saxon had started fighting with them the first time they tried and it had not ended well for one of the Picts. Drest had told them to let Horsa in if he came in the future, unless specifically commanded not to.

"What do you mean?" Drest asked, jerking upright at the sudden intrusion.

"Are you sleeping?" Horsa asked, glaring at the king with obvious disdain. "By the gods, how old are you anyway, Drest? Napping in the daytime?"

The Pict scowled. He was in his early forties now, but he was not about to admit that to the irritating big Saxon. "What else would you have me do? Have you never laid siege to a fortress before, Horsa? It's bloody boring."

"What else would I have you do?" the Saxon repeated. "Get off your arse and raid more of the Damnonii settlements! I thought we were here to wage war on these people, but I don't see much evidence of it."

"We are here," the king replied icily, "to kill Queen Narina and take control of Dun Breatann. Once we do that, Alt Clota will be mine. I allowed you to make an example of the settlement at Dun Buic, but by Herne's balls, man, I have no interest in ruling over a barren wasteland!"

"So your plan is to just sit here until, what? The Damnonii bitch surrenders? Or starves to death? How long will that take? Look at the size of that fucking rock her fortress is built upon — there could be a months worth of food stored in there. More! I have better things to do with my summer than sit around here picking lice from my beard, Drest. You're paying me and my warriors to fight, not to grow fat and lazy."

"I'm paying you to help me conquer Alt Clota," Drest replied irritably. "If that means fighting, so be it. But slaughtering innocent villagers — women and children! — is not my idea of 'fighting'."

104

"Nor is it mine," Horsa replied with a dangerous glint in his eye that unsettled the Pictish king. "But if you want to force the Damnonii to come out from that rock and fight us, we need to show them what will happen if they don't. Besides, there must be more men of fighting age living in the towns and villages around here — they will have been summoned when news of our approach reached Queen Narina."

Drest sighed and stood up, walking to the tent's entrance and looking out at the imposing volcanic rock that Dun Breatann was built upon. He knew Horsa was right of course; it was simply not possible that the entire Damnonii army was cooped up within the fortress. Most of Narina's warriors lived and worked elsewhere, only mustering when called upon.

"It's true," he said, flinching as he turned back to find the big Saxon standing right behind him. Annoyed by his nervous reaction, he pushed past Horsa and returned to his seat, drumming his fingers on the table before him. "An army will be gathering, but they will have no real leadership."

"How do you know that?" Horsa demanded.

"I saw her captain, Gerallt, on the wall beside Narina," Drest said. "I know him. And, on top of that, the druid, Bellicus is far to the south attending some gathering of mystics. My own druids are there too." What he did not tell the Saxon was that Narina had another, more senior military commander, a bear of a man named Gavo, who had not been spotted by Drest. For all the king knew though, Gavo might have died or be unwell — that he was somewhere outside the walls of Dun Breatann, organising a burgeoning army of Damnonii troops, was unlikely.

"Whatever," Horsa said angrily. His default mood seemed to be anger Drest thought, wishing he could deal with the other Saxon Jarl, the little one with the wheeze, Sigarr. "I don't really care whether you rule Alt Clota, or the whore does. But me and my men want battle, and glory, and plunder — either you somehow make Narina come out and fight, or I will start bringing people here from nearby settlements and make an example of them, as I did before."

"It never worked before, damn it," Drest retorted.

"Maybe we didn't kill enough victims," Horsa said with a nasty smile. "Narina didn't get the message. I'll see to it that she does next time."

"No, you'll do nothing for now. Sieges sometimes take a while, and I planned for that before I even set off from Dunnottar. We have plenty of supplies, and my own warriors are ready to wait until battle can be joined." He waved a hand over his shoulder, where the Clota flowed past their camp. "If your men are so desperate for something to do, tell them to catch us some fish. There's plenty in the river back there. Or to hunt in the woods to the north — more meat is always welcome."

"I am not a damn fisherman," Horsa returned venomously. "And neither are the men who march with me. They won't be happy sitting around playing hnefatafl and humping the camp whores for long, and then things will get ugly."

"Then keep them under control, by the gods!" Drest shouted. "Or you can take them, and yourself, back to Hengist and tell him he can forget any alliance between us."

Horsa's fists clenched and he took a step towards the king. The Saxon was still young, and his temper was legendary — people simply didn't speak to him the way Drest was doing. Not without getting a sore face, or worse, for it at least.

Before a blow could be struck, probably ending their partnership for good, a shout came from outside. It was the kind of shout a man lets out when he's in great danger or pain and Horsa immediately turned away from Drest and hurried out of the tent. By the time the king had come after him the Saxon was already holding his sword in his hand and was staring at the northeastern edge of the camp.

"What's happening?" Drest asked him. He was a good bit shorter than the Saxon and couldn't make out who had let out the shout, or why. "Can you see anything?"

Horsa didn't need to reply, for it suddenly became very plain what was happening, as a small portion of the sky turned black for a moment, before clearing again. The sound of heavy thumping reached Drest and he winced as more cries went up. Cries of fear and agony.

"We're under attack!" Horsa bellowed, charging like the animal he was named after right towards the spot where the throwing spears had done their damage. "The bastards are within the perimeter. To arms!"

Drest's mind spun and he found himself following the Saxon at a trot rather than a gallop. What was going on? Panic filled him as he realised this could be a ruse — one small force would attack them at the northeastern edge of their camp, then, while they were distracted, Narina's warriors would flood out of Dun Breatann and take them by surprise from the rear.

"You men!" he shrieked, pointing to twenty confused Picts who were standing waiting for orders. Drest was happy to give them. "Spread the word. I want all our men — all the Picts, that is — to form up over there, in front of the fortress. Move!" He waited until the ten warriors had moved to do his bidding and then he walked to the position he'd indicated, shouting at everyone else he saw to form a shieldwall beside him.

Horsa and his sea-wolves could deal with the attack to the northeast, and Drest would wait with his shieldwall for the gates of Dun Breatann to open. He thought back to the last time he'd led an army here — something very similar had happened and Drest had fallen into the Damnonii trap. That had resulted in the almost total destruction of his army and he'd been captured himself alongside his daughter.

"Aife!" he saw the princess now, striding towards him, tall and powerfully built, emanating confidence and competence. She carried spear and shield and wore a helmet on her head, dark brown hair spilling out from beneath it.

"What's happening, my lord?" she asked, coming to stand beside him. She was taller than him too, although not as big as Horsa.

"Taranis knows," he admitted. "But I fear a ruse by Queen Narina. Get the men lined up, ready for an attack from this side."

Aife gave a quick salute and then began shouting at the troops around them, marshalling them into position, her voice rich and as loud as any of the men's. Drest watched her with pride, and with some relief. He had never felt totally comfortable commanding armies — he was simply not aggressive enough to enjoy war the way someone like Horsa did. At least Aife seemed ideally suited to lead, and Drest was glad to have her with him. He might have fathered her on a slave-woman, but she had proved herself more than capable of standing in a shieldwall.

An utterly bizarre, ululating screech filled the air and Drest spun, eyes searching out the source, focusing at last on the Saxon *volva*, Yngvildr. She was looking up at the sky, arms outstretched, eyes unfocused, and calling out to her gods in the Saxon tongue. It was a harsh, guttural chant, and it sent a shiver down Drest's spine although he could not understand a word of it.

"Someone shut that crazy sow up!" Aife shouted, staring hatefully at the *volva*.

"No," Drest called before anyone could move to carry out the princess's command. "Let the witch call to the gods. Without our druids, Yngvildr is all we have to bring us their favour."

Aife met his gaze and opened her mouth to object, but thought better of undermining her own father and turned away, face flushing with anger, clearly hating the fact that she was forced to serve in an army with the likes of Horsa and Yngvildr.

When he was content that the shieldwall, three ranks deep and growing, was solidly in position Drest walked quickly to the far edge of the encampment to see what was happening there. Whatever had gone on seemed to be over now, for Horsa's Saxons were lined up, chattering excitedly amongst themselves.

Horsa appeared before the king, scowling and pointing at the ground behind him. "Look. This is what happens when the Damnonii do not fear us enough."

Eight corpses were scattered about, each with a javelin through their torso or, in one case, lodged right into the dead man's forehead.

Drest winced at the sight but shrugged. "It's only a handful of men," he said. "It's unfortunate, but men die in war."

"This is not war!" Horsa roared, spreading his great arms wide and nodding to the bodies littering the ground.

"Look, Jarl Horsa," said Drest calmly, understanding the other's anger at losing so many warriors without even striking a blow against the enemy who'd clearly disappeared as fast as they came. "A handful of Damnonii riders came and threw a few spears before scurrying away again with their tails between their legs. It's not really that much to worry about." He held up a hand to stem the Saxon's furious retort. "But I agree, this is not good for morale. So, why don't you take a few of your men and hunt down those responsible for this? You have my permission to do whatever you like to them if you catch them. Bring them here alive and sacrifice them to Thunor if you want. Narina would enjoy that, I'm sure."

Horsa's emotions warred within him, Drest could see it clearly on his face. Anger at taking orders from a king he believed was weaker than himself, but also pleasure at the thought of finally getting a chance to use his blade against an opponent who would fight back.

"All right," he said. "I'll do that. But while I'm gone, *King* Drest, I expect you to do more than just sit on your arse drinking and eating." He pointed at the towering fortress that dominated the skyline. "Find a way to get inside there. You must have some climbers among your army. All we need is a couple of men to get up to the top and throw ropes down for the rest of us to climb up."

Drest opened his mouth to protest — that had been tried before. Indeed, it had even been successful, once, when some raiders from Dalriada managed to scale the walls and get inside Dun Breatann before they were discovered. After that, the only way to make it into the fortress by climbing had been sealed shut with a wall that was always patrolled. Still, it would do no harm to try and find another way in, even if Drest knew fine well it was impossible.

"Fine," he said, nodding and tapping Horsa fraternally on the arm. "I'll do that, and you find the scum that did that." He jerked his chin at the fallen Saxons. "But take care, my lord. If there's an army of leaderless Damnonii soldiers gathering out there, you may find yourself badly outnumbered."

"Good," Horsa replied with characteristic arrogance. "That will at least give the enemy a chance."

CHAPTER TWENTY

"I wish I was out there with Gavo."

Narina sighed in exasperation and shook her head, frowning at her daughter. "Don't be silly, Catia. In the name of Lug, girl, you're only twelve summers old!"

"It would be better than sitting here waiting to starve."

"We won't starve," Narina said firmly. "We've plenty of food and, if it came to it, you escaped Dun Breatann once before by climbing down a rope and running off. You can do it again if needs be."

Catia winced at the memory. She'd been utterly terrified during that nighttime climb down the face of the rock, accompanying Aife who was now, ironically, outside trying to get in. "I wouldn't want to make that climb again," the girl admitted. "And I know it will be dangerous with Gavo but at least he can go where he will, and fight if he wants."

Narina allowed herself a broad smile at that, picturing the hit-and-run attack that her bold captain had pulled off earlier. They'd been alerted to the commotion in the enemy camp by one of the sentries on the wall and run to see what was happening. They'd been just in time to see the flurry of javelins as they arced out of the sky in the distance, and hear the pained cries of those struck by the missiles. It had brought most of the inhabitants of Dun Breatann hurrying to enjoy the enemy's consternation; a small but most welcome victory for Narina and her people who would take any good news after a few days under siege.

"Gavo will hopefully gather our warriors and come to help us out of this mess before too long," said the queen with a confidence she was not sure she really felt. Gavo was a good commander, but...She looked down once again on the army that had come to destroy her and subjugate her people and felt despair threaten to overwhelm her. She almost wished Catia was out there with Gavo — the thought of her daughter being inside the fortress if it fell to Drest and Horsa was horrifying to Narina. At least the girl had her sword, and knew how to use it. Aife would protect Catia, the queen felt sure of that, for the two princesses had formed a strong friendship despite the age gap but, then again, what if Aife fell

110

during any fighting? The other Picts would not spare Catia the horrors of war, and the Saxon leader, Horsa, would likely revel in…

Narina forced her churning thoughts to still, focusing on the waters of the Clota and wondering where Bellicus was. Thinking of the druid made her angry as she mentally kicked herself for never marrying the big fool. He loved her, she was sure of it, and Narina loved him too — they even had a child together! — yet they'd never allowed themselves to follow their own hearts and do what would make them happy. Instead, Narina had married Ysfael to cement an alliance that had hardly proved worth it, and Bellicus…Would he ever settle down? The thought of him marrying another woman while Narina was left to grow old in Dun Breatann still tied to that useless Votadini prince was unbearable.

"Why don't you learn to use a sword, mother?"

Narina turned to Catia, glad to think of something other than Picts, Saxons, and her marriage. "Do I look like a warrior?" she asked with a chuckle, raising her right arm and attempting to flex her slim bicep.

"Do I?" Catia countered.

"Of course," Narina said, still smiling. "Very fierce and imposing."

Catia laughed at her mother's praise but went on earnestly attempting to persuade Narina to learn how to fight. "You can spar with me," the girl suggested. "I promise to go easy on you."

Narina reached out and hugged her tightly, thanking the gods for blessing her with such a wonderful child. "I'm no soldier," she said. "I never have been and never will be. That's why I have people like Gavo, and Gerallt, and you around to take care of me." It was said lightly and partly in jest but Narina once again felt sadness at the idea of Catia being forced to fight to protect herself and her mother with the short sword she'd taken to carrying at all times. The child had endured so much in her short life and yet Narina smiled as their gazes met and she realised her daughter was happy and quite content with her place in this life. Perhaps she got that grit from Bellicus, for Narina certainly didn't feel strong — it was incredibly hard being queen even when your lands weren't under siege by vicious invaders!

111

"You're just worried I'll beat you," Catia said with a mischievous smile. "A twelve-year-old beating a queen. Embarrassing. I don't really blame you for not wanting to take me on."

Narina laughed at the effrontery and bent to look her daughter in the eye, although she didn't have to bend very far as Catia was rather taller than most girls her age — another thing she'd clearly taken from her father. "Take you on?" the queen demanded. "Afraid of you? Well, as I said, I'm no warrior, but I was always a fast runner. You think you could beat me in a race?"

Catia sized her up, taking in her mother's lithe legs but nodding confidently. "I'm twenty years younger than you. I could take you, no problem."

Narina laughed again, determined to show the girl she might not be useful with a sword but she was not some weakling. She really was a fast runner, always had been, and as competitive as anyone when it came to winning. "Come on then," she said, leading the way to the clear space that was used for sparring.

Men were being drilled by Gerallt but he must have guessed what was happening, that some contest was about to begin, for he immediately barked at his spearmen to stand aside and leave the ground clear for the queen and her daughter.

"The princess thinks she can run faster than me," Narina called to the captain who responded with a smile and a nod. "So lay your bets, everyone. Who do you think will win?"

She immediately regretted her words as the warriors — even the usually taciturn Gerallt — began chattering excitedly amongst themselves, arguing over who would win, listing each competitor's strengths and weaknesses, and laying bets. It amazed the queen, who watched as one of the men took control of the betting, taking coins and informing the men of his odds.

"See?" Catia said, smiling rather smugly. "Even they think I'll win."

Narina felt uncomfortable to hear herself being spoken of as "too old", or "not as competitive" as her daughter — but more men and women were hurrying to see the entertainment and laying their own bets. It was the first piece of non-violent entertainment Dun Breatann had seen for a while and Narina could see the positive effect it was having on morale.

Part of her still wished she'd never suggested this race, or at least had simply conducted it between the two of them without creating all this fuss. Besides, she wasn't so sure she could win any more, Catia's position as favourite amongst the betting folk denting the queen's confidence.

It did not even cross her mind to let Catia win. Narina might not be quite as competitive as the girl when it came to things like this, but she had brought her daughter up never to expect favours. If you wanted something in this life you had to fight for it, even if you were lucky enough to be born into a noble family.

"Are you all ready?" Narina shouted, laughing to mask her growing irritation. "Can we get this over with before night falls?"

"Do you want to place a bet on yourself, my lady?" the man running the wagers called to her respectfully. "I reckon your daughter is favourite, so you'll get good odds. Double your money if you win."

What a bizarre conversation to be having in the midst of a siege, Narina thought, feeling like the world had somehow turned upside down. She didn't try to fight it, though. "I'll have some of that," she agreed. "Put me down for five denarii."

Roman coins had not been minted in Britain for decades, but they had been imported right up until the legions left the island so they were still used widely. Five denarii was not a massive sum by any means, but it was enough to make a few of those who'd already bet on Catia change their mind. If Narina was sure of herself enough to place five silver coins on her victory, well, maybe they should too.

"Put me down for the same," Catia shouted over the hubbub. "On me winning, of course."

At last, everyone had placed their bets and the two runners stood beside one another on the line that was always used for these foot races which were universally popular.

Gerallt took charge of proceedings now, being the highest ranking officer there. "Are you both ready?" he called.

Narina licked her lips and wiped her palms on her tunic, feeling more nervous than she thought she would. "I am," she said.

Catia was smiling, eager to begin, and she too called out her readiness.

"No cheating," Gerallt warned them. "No pulling one another or anything like that. We want a good, fair race. Are you ready? On your marks."

Narina and Catia both placed their toes on the line and bent their legs. Their smiles had faded and their eyes were focused on the finishing line which Gerallt was striding towards so he could accurately gauge the winner. "Get set," he shouted back over his shoulder, and Narina drew in a deep breath, feeling her nervousness fading as her mind became utterly intent on the task at hand.

"Careful you don't slip, Mother," Catia murmured, but Narina ignored her.

"Go!"

They exploded into motion, feet thumping against the worn grass as they sprinted for all their worth. Catia began to edge in front and Narina felt her left knee tighten. *Should have warmed up*, she thought, gritting her teeth and forcing her legs to pump harder.

The onlookers cheered them on, exhorting their chosen runner to go faster so they could collect their winnings.

The pair were evenly matched but Catia was just in front as they crossed the line at the end of the sparring ground and, as Gerallt pronounced her the winner Narina laughed and hugged her daughter. She might not have won, but the joy she'd felt as she flew across the ground made it hardly matter. Besides, if she had to lose to someone, she was glad it was Catia.

"It was close," she said, gasping to catch her breath. "I didn't get off to a good start or I think I'd have beaten you."

Catia laughed but she'd already got her wind back. "Oh really?" she demanded. "Should we go again then? Best of three?"

Some of the people heard her and those who'd bet on Narina hollered for them to race again, but Narina shook her head. Her knee had not got any more painful but she wanted it to stay that way so, with good grace, she paid over her five denarii to the man arranging the bets, accepted the commiserations from the people, and walked with Catia down to the great hall for a cool drink.

As they walked, she eyed Catia, noting how tall and strong the girl was, and how well she carried herself, shoulders back, head up. It was not arrogance, or any sense of entitlement from the privileged position she'd been born into — it was simple self-confidence and acceptance of who she was.

It was a great relief to the queen for, when the girl had returned with Bellicus after being abducted by Horsa's Saxons she'd been quiet and withdrawn and generally frightened of the world around her. To see her grown into the strong young woman she was now truly lightened Narina's heart.

They walked into the hall, guarded as always by two sentries who nodded respectfully to them, and Narina's good mood faded as she saw her waster of a husband, Ysfael, and remembered what her life was like now.

CHAPTER TWENTY-ONE

"This was a mistake." Duro gripped the side of the ship, staring out at the leaden grey sky, not even caring that his face was slick with sea spray. "A storm's coming, I can feel it," he said, looking up and mouthing a prayer to Mithras, begging the god for protection.

"It'll be fine," Bellicus said, reaching out to stroke his horse's neck reassuringly. The big black stallion, Darac, did not enjoy travelling by ship, but the waters really were not as choppy as Duro was making out. "At least you don't have to stand for the entire journey," the druid said. "The poor horses have it far worse, even if this ship is designed to carry them."

Duro looked up dejectedly at his own steed, Pryderi, a mare that had served him well ever since they'd escaped from Drest's fortress of Dunnottar. "You're right," the centurion admitted, standing and coming across to copy Bellicus in comforting the animals. Both horses were secure but it could not have been very pleasant for them at all, as the ship rose and fell with the waves, a strong north-westerly wind powering them homewards. Koriosis had not brought his mount with him, instead selling it at the port near Caer Legion. If needed he could buy another from one of the stables in Alt Clota, which made travelling by sea easier, but Bellicus and Duro were too attached to Darac and Pryderi to be parted from them, paying extra for this ship with its section specifically designed to carry large animals and a crew experienced in carrying such cargo.

Cai didn't seem too bothered by the journey — not much worried the mastiff.

"At least this is pretty big ship," Koriosis noted, slapping his bench appreciatively. "You don't feel the motion of the sea so much. Nothing worse than being tossed about in a little vessel."

"How d'you think Qunavo and Ria will be travelling?" Duro asked, still absentmindedly petting his horse. "And where will they be going?"

"Oh, to Dun Breatann, that much is certain," Bellicus growled. "And if they are in as much of a hurry as us they'll also have found a ship to take them there."

"So we'll be behind them," Koriosis said.

"Aye, probably," Bellicus nodded. "Not much we can do about that, and I'm not sure it'll matter anyway. I've still got no idea what we'll do when we get to the fortress."

The men lapsed into silence then, all imagining the scene when the ship finally carried them along the Clota to Dun Breatann. If there was an army of Picts and Saxons surrounding the fortress what could the three of them do against it? Even if Bellicus and Koriosis could call down the power of the gods to help them, Drest would have his own druids to do the same. And the gods rarely performed miracles of the type that would be required to dislodge an army, Bellicus mused. Even the Merlin could not wield such tremendous power — calling down fireballs from the heavens was something that only usually took place in stories. Druid magic generally worked slower and in less extreme manifestations such as storms or perhaps with some illness affecting an individual cursed by the mystic.

"Will Arthur send men to help us?" Koriosis asked. He had never met the famous warlord but he'd heard the stories about him from Bellicus and Duro.

"I think so," Bellicus said, grasping Darac's reins as the horse tossed its head nervously, the boat seeming to sink down into a trough before plunging back upwards, spray flying across them all.

"He will," Duro averred. "He might even come himself, if he believes this is a chance to kill Horsa."

"If Horsa is even there." Koriosis ran a hand across his face, rather hopefully attempting to dry it. "We only have the angry threats of Qunavo and Ria to suggest he is, and those were possibly just a ploy to make you give up any claim to be High Druid, Bel."

"Maybe," Bellicus replied thoughtfully. "But whether it's Horsa leading them, or some other jarl, I believe Drest must have a Saxon warband with him. His army was as good as destroyed by us during the last battle — he will need reinforcements from somewhere. The Saxons would be more than willing to help him, I fear."

"It would give them influence on the western side of Britain," Koriosis mused.

"Aye, and when Drest is no longer useful to them, the Saxons will happily betray him, or even just kill him and take his lands for their own." Bellicus chuckled bleakly. "Trusting the likes of Horsa is a mistake, and I've no doubt Drest will discover that for himself at some point."

"Perhaps," said Duro. "But that will be too late for Alt Clota, as Dun Breatann will have fallen before then."

"Dun Breatann has never fallen to an enemy army yet," Bellicus countered. "If Narina and Gavo can hold off Drest for a few weeks, Arthur will hopefully bring us an army of our own." He bared his teeth in a savage, lupine grin. "Killing Drest and Horsa will be very satisfying, eh, Duro?"

The centurion still stroked Pryderi's mane but his other hand, the one with the missing fingers, fell to rest on his spatha's handle and he nodded slowly. "Aye, my friend," he returned in a voice laden with emotion. "The two men I despise most in all the world. It will be a very good day when I see them both dead."

* * *

"Did you find them?" Drest asked as Horsa approached, scowling as usual. Aife stood beside the king, a similarly sour expression on her face at the sight of the jarl.

"No," the Saxon barked. "They disappeared into the woods and when we tried to follow they attacked us with arrows, so we turned back."

Drest frowned. Horsa had been away for a full two days. "Where have you been then?" he asked.

Horsa's lips curled upwards in a smile that Drest found disturbing.

"We visited one of the settlements over in that direction." He pointed to the west, where a village sat on some low cliffs above the Clota.

"I don't see any smoke," Aife said caustically. "So I assume you didn't slaughter everyone there and burn the place to the ground."

"No, your father asked me not to," Horsa smirked. "Besides most of the inhabitants ran off when they saw us coming."

"'Most'?" the warrior-princess demanded.

"A few of the men chose to stay and defend themselves. Fools."

"And?"

Horsa smirked at Drest and the king's blood ran cold. "Some we killed. Those that survived we have brought back with us."

"For what?" Aife asked, eyes boring into the Saxon.

"Another demonstration for Queen Narina." He gestured to his warriors and they walked forward. The Saxons were tall, mostly with blond or red hair and beards, and the broad shoulders of professional soldiers — the prisoners they dragged or shoved ahead of them were a stark contrast. Not only were they generally smaller than the sea-wolves, but they had been beaten almost to the point of death, their faces and bare torsos and limbs bearing the marks of that violence.

"These men are just villagers," Aife cried, unable to hide her dismay.

"These men are Damnonii, are they not?" Horsa asked levelly, staring at Drest, who nodded. "Well then, we are at war with them. *You* are at war with them, girl."

"That is not war," Aife spat.

"It is where I come from," Horsa returned with a dismissive wave, pushing past her and her father and commanding his men to follow him.

Drest was not surprised to see the *volva*, Yngvildr amongst them, eyeing the prisoners hungrily, as though she expected to devour them one by one. He frowned when he noticed a glint of metal at her waist and realised she was carrying the type of hand saw that would be used to cut branches into smaller lengths. He shuddered, imagination running wild as he tried to think what she was planning to do with it.

"Come," Horsa called over his shoulder to the king and his daughter. "See the show! Or don't. I care not. But Narina and her soldiers in Dun Breatann will watch, and see what fate lies in store for those who stand against the Saxons."

"This was a mistake," Aife snarled to her father. "Working with those animals was never going to end well."

Drest bristled at the criticism. "You're too young to understand the horrors of war," he said. "This was all started by the Damnonii, when Narina's last husband, Coroticus, slaughtered our young men and even a druid! You can't blame me for doing something about it."

"These Saxons are not like us," Aife argued, almost pleading.

"Of course they're not!" Drest shouted, drawing uneasy looks from the Picts who were nearby. He noticed the attention and lowered his voice. "From what I hear, most of the Saxons who've come across the sea are decent people. Many have integrated with communities in the south — living and working beside the Britons, and even marrying them. But we needed hardened, experienced warriors, Aife. I want to win this war as quickly as possible, with as little bloodshed as possible, and the only way to do it is by drawing Narina into a fight and defeating her comprehensively." He shook his head, feeling like he wasn't convincing himself never mind his daughter. "Come, we must see what Horsa and the *volva* have in store for those Damnonii prisoners. With any luck, once they start Narina will be too sickened to let Horsa's brutality continue and she'll surrender."

"I'm not going to watch that evil witch torture innocent captives," Aife replied, drawing herself up proudly and glaring at him. "You'll come to regret allying yourself to Horsa," she predicted. "Of all the sea-wolves to hire as a mercenary, he is the worst. I'll see you later, my lord. If you need me, I'll be in my tent, doing my best to ignore the screams of those innocent villagers. May the gods forgive us."

Drest bit back an angry retort, wishing he could go to his own tent and pretend he hadn't thrown his lot in with the Saxons. He did not have that luxury though — he was the king, and this army was his. He had to show Narina that he was the one in command, and he had to show Horsa he was not too squeamish to do what was required to make Alt Clota his.

"Come," he said to his guards who, until then, had stood back at a respectful distance, pretending not to hear the argument between king and princess. "Let's get this over with."

He led the way, forcing his way through the group of Saxons that had formed a semi-circle around Horsa, Yngvildr, and the prisoners. The other jarl, Sigarr, did not seem to be around and Drest suspected he'd followed Aife's lead and taken himself off somewhere he wouldn't need to be a part of the coming barbarity.

"King Drest." It was Yngvildr who called out to him as he was finally allowed through the throng of sea-wolves to stand beside the *volva* and Horsa. "You are served by a druid and a druidess, yet neither are here with us."

"They were summoned south by the Merlin," Drest said with a shrug. What the hell was she getting at?

"Perhaps if they'd been here to seek the help of the gods we would already have taken the fortress."

The Saxons murmured and nodded agreement. Everyone knew it was vitally important to have the gods on your side when it came to war. Without a druid, the Picts were at a disadvantage.

"The Damnonii have no druid either," Drest argued. "Bellicus was also summoned by the Merlin."

"Ja, but the Damnonii have a rock to hide upon," Yngvildr returned as if the king was a simpleton. "You need all the help you can get to make it onto that rock." She raised her arms in the air and Drest noticed now that her pupils were enlarged, as if she was under the influence of some mystical draught or concoction. She also still carried the hand-saw and, again, Drest was forced to suppress a shudder at the sight of it. It was only about a foot and a half long, but its teeth looked wickedly sharp and it would certainly make short work of…

Yngvildr let out a shocking scream, breaking Drest's line of thought, and he stepped back involuntarily, wondering what on earth was wrong with her. Of course he'd attended many magical rituals presided over by Qunavo and Ria but such an alarming noise had never come from either of them.

The Saxon witch was quite clearly moon-touched, and Drest mouthed a soft prayer of thanks that he was not one of the Damnonii prisoners.

He noticed those prisoners now and a chill ran down his back as he saw one of them had been forced onto his belly on the ground near the outer gates of Dun Breatann. The captive's back was bare and his arms and legs were being held down by four burly Saxons. On the walls of the fortress, Damnonii soldiers stared down at them. There was no sign of Narina but Drest was certain she'd be watching.

The *volva* was still screaming words in her own harsh language which Drest couldn't understand and probably didn't want to. She turned slowly in a circle, staring up at the sky which had coincidentally grown dark with clouds, shrieking and shaking that damnable saw which the Pictish king found so terribly sinister.

"Are you ready for this, Drest?" Horsa asked with a leer. "*This* is our magic. Powerful magic. Once, your druids could wield power like this but, like so many of the weaklings on this island, they grew soft. Well, watch, Drest, and witness the power of Thunor, god of thunder."

Yngvildr mercifully ceased her shrill calls and turned her massive pupils on the Saxons holding down the prisoner who had now started begging for his life. "Hold him," the *volva* commanded. "Do not let him move."

There seemed little chance of that to Drest for the man was positioned in such a way that he could not use whatever strength he still had left to raise his hands or feet, not with the crushing weight of a warrior on each appendage.

The king looked on in grim fascination as Yngvildr stepped slowly, almost reverentially towards the prone captive who, although he couldn't see her with his face pressed down into the grass, must have sensed her approach for his cries for mercy grew louder and more desperate. Drest wondered if he'd been told what was about to happen to him, for he became increasingly frenzied as the *volva* drew nearer.

And then, as the witch bent and began the ritual, Drest wished he'd followed Aife's lead and gone off to hide in his tent until this was over.

CHAPTER TWENTY-TWO

"You'll curse us all with this!" Aife had come running as the first of the Damnonii prisoner's screams echoed out across the encampment. It reverberated from the rock of Dun Breatann, mingling with the outraged shouts from the men and women watching from those walls.

Drest felt a tightness in his throat as he watched the *volva* take her saw to the captive's back and begin to cut it apart, severing the ribs from the spine one by one. When Aife came running up to the king, demanding that he put an end to such horrific butchery, he was forced to command his guards to hold her back and, eventually, remove her. Although he agreed with her sentiments, he couldn't allow her to publicly undermine him in such a way.

There's only seven prisoners, he told himself, forcing his feet to remain rooted to the spot. *It'll all be over soon. No man can survive such agony for long. And if this doesn't persuade Narina to surrender or come out fighting, nothing will!*

Much to his horror, however, it was not over soon. The prisoner's screams continued for much longer than Drest would have thought possible, as his back was torn asunder by Yngvildr who wielded her saw with all the skill of a practiced butcher. When she'd cut away most of the ribs she reached in and pulled out the shuddering man's lungs, placing them on his shoulders so he seemed like some monstrous eagle.

Men did vomit then, shocked by the inhuman brutality of the *volva*. Horsa, Drest noticed, had turned pale and his smile had faded, but he still looked on stonily as the second prisoner was forced, begging and sobbing, onto his stomach beside the first man who was, the king guessed, dead now. At least his screams had finally subsided, thank Taranis.

The thought of watching all seven of the Damnonii captives being brutally sacrificed in this slow, drawn-out manner, was horrifying to Drest, but he knew he had to remain there, watching every rasping cut of the saw, hearing every pitiful shriek. He wanted Narina to believe he would continue to brutalise her beloved subjects in this manner until she capitulated. Otherwise, the deaths of these men would be pointless.

The Pictish king was not a squeamish man. He had tortured men himself over the years — such actions were necessary at times when one ruled over others. He'd hacked two fingers from that former centurion the druid Bellicus travelled with, hadn't he? That had never bothered him, and neither had any of the other violence he'd perpetrated on victims yet now, as he endured the horrific wails of the second prisoner, he found he had tears in his eyes.

It was simply too much for him to bear. It was, as Aife had noted, evil.

By the time the seventh man lay torn to bloody shreds, ribs opened to the sky like white wings, his back a gaping ruin, Drest's tears had dried and he found himself feeling oddly bored with the whole disgusting ceremony. The noise of the saw as it scraped across flesh and bone, and the pained cries of the victims, had eventually worn the king down — desensitised him to the savagery — and he was relieved when it was over at last.

He swallowed and blinked, forcing himself to wake from his stupor, and looked up at the walls of Dun Breatann. He still could not see Narina, and he could hardly see anyone else there. Only a handful of sentries remained, forced to gaze upon the barbarians' savagery since it was their duty as lookouts. Everyone else in the fortress had fled deeper into the towering rock's enfolding arms.

"It seems your plan has failed," Drest said to Horsa, licking lips that felt dry and cracked. "Narina has neither surrendered nor come out to meet us in battle."

The Saxon said nothing for a long moment, stretching up and sucking in a huge breath, as if relieved that his own lungs had not been rendered useless by Yngvildr's saw. Then, at last, he shrugged. "The ritual is over, now we see what the gods make of it. They will not ignore the souls of seven victims given in such a powerful ceremony." He looked down at the mangled Damnonii corpses and pursed his lips thoughtfully. "It will count for something, you will see. The *volva's* work will be rewarded, and Dun Breatann will be ours in due course."

Drest stared at him, those ominous words ringing in his ears: 'Dun Breatann will be *ours*.'

Without saying anything else the king turned and stalked away, not even sure where he was going, just knowing he had to get away from the Saxon jarl and his wide-eyed, slavering 'wise woman'.

God help the people of Alt Clota, he thought as he pushed through the stunned soldiers around him. *What have I unleashed upon them?*

* * *

"This... This is just pure evil." Gavo had not wanted to let his feelings show to his men but it was impossible to hide them. The sorrow he'd felt when they picked through the charred remains of Dun Buic had faded, replaced by a white hot fury and need for vengeance. Now, as they combed through this second settlement to the west of Dun Breatann the Damnonii captain felt mostly bemused. He had never experienced warfare like this before — what kind of invader would just destroy the lands they hoped to conquer, and lay waste to the inhabitants that would be working those lands and paying taxes to the new king?

It made no sense to Gavo.

"This," replied Sentica, "is exactly what Drest hired the Saxons to do. He couldn't take Queen Narina's crown himself — not ruthless enough, or skilled enough — so he's paid Horsa to do the dirty work for him, and then he'll take Alt Clota's throne once there's no one left to stand against him."

There were not as many bodies scattered around this settlement as there had been at Dun Buic. The inhabitants here must have had more warning of the enemy's approach and beat a hasty retreat into the hills nearby. They would return to find their homes destroyed, and their possessions and livestock stolen.

"We need to step up our raids on their camp," Gavo mused. "Hit them hard, then run, like we did before."

Sentica frowned uncertainly. "If we do that, Horsa will surely come after us and, when he fails to catch us, do this," he gestured around at the ruined settlement, "to some other poor village."

The ruined settlement lay high above the Clota and Gavo looked out now on what was a peaceful, pleasant view. The river sparkled in the early summer sunshine and the fields on the far bank were green and vibrant. Sea birds wheeled overhead, calling out to one another and harassing a sparrowhawk that hovered nearby, languidly evading the angry gulls' attacks. Gavo could not allow these lands to fall into the hands of the Picts or, worse, the Saxons.

As Narina had hoped, the warriors that had been summoned from across Alt Clota by her messengers had been making their way to Dun Breatann and Gavo's men were intercepting them if they spotted them on the road. Sometimes the enemy scouts noticed them first and chased them off or attacked them. Those who escaped were found wandering by Gavo and assimilated into his burgeoning army, although it was not growing anywhere near as fast as he'd like.

The truth was, the best warriors that the Damnonii could call upon were mostly trapped within Dun Breatann, protecting Queen Narina and the fortress. The men that were doing their best to muster in response to the invasion were farmers, craftsmen, traders, hunters, labourers, fishermen and so on. Aye, most of them had fought in skirmishes or even been part of the army that defeated Drest's Picts not so long ago, but they did not spend every day training for battle. They might have heart, but they weren't skilled enough to go toe-to-toe with Horsa's mercenaries.

The only way to defeat those mercenaries, and ultimately Drest, would be with superior numbers. Thus far, Gavo did not have those numbers — nowhere near it.

Until he did, they would need to find some other way to cause trouble for the raiders.

He took a long, deep breath of the fragrant river air, calmed by its freshness and its familiarity, and turned to Sentica and the others of his warband who acted as his guards and confidants. "What if we mount another sneak attack on Drest's camp," he suggested. "And then, if Horsa comes after us like before, we lay a trap for him?"

Sentica smiled. "I like it. Go on, my lord."

"Horsa only brought what, thirty men with him the last time he chased us? We have about four times that number, with more joining us each day — rather than running away, we lure Horsa somewhere we can trap him, and then we get revenge for what he did here and in Dun Buic."

It was a sound plan. Gavo's warband knew these lands far better than the Saxons ever would, and there were many places around Dun Breatann that would be suitable for such an ambuscade.

"If we can make the most of the terrain, and our numbers, that will offset the Saxons' better training," Sentica said, glancing at the other warriors with them, all of whom nodded and murmured their support for the plan. They were just as fed-up with seeing the aftermath of Horsa's cruelty as Gavo. A chance to finally meet the big sea-wolf and pay him back for his crimes was too good to pass up.

"It's settled then," Gavo said. "Now, do any of you have thoughts on where we can set up the ambush?"

"What about the road to the west of Dun Buic, the one leading up to the old cairn?" one of the men suggested.

"At the Sleeping Giant?" Gavo asked, thinking of the massive rock that, from certain angles, looked rather like a man lying on his back.

"Aye," the man replied.

Gavo knew the road he meant. In fact, the Saxons who'd abducted Princess Catia four years earlier had gone up that very road. When the Damnonii caught up with them it became clear the girl had been taken in the opposite direction by a second group of raiders and the ensuing fighting had been brutal, if over quickly. Steep, and with high rocky walls on either side, the road seemed like a good place to trap Horsa and his men.

"Fair enough," the captain agreed. "We slaughtered another group of sea-wolves there once before, now we'll do it again." He could picture the terrain in his mind, and even saw himself launching rocks down on the despised enemy although the memory of that last encounter on the road came to him and he wished Bellicus was with them. The cairn that road led up to was an ill-omened place that had once been used for human sacrifices, and the protection of a druid would be very welcome. Indeed, Bellicus himself had slowly taken the life of one of those earlier Saxons, torturing him until he told them where Catia was — it was an act of terrible brutality that Gavo had been surprised by, but it was necessary to find the princess, and the sea-wolf was an enemy. Still, the memory was a disturbing one and the thought of returning to that hilly path was not particularly inviting.

Gavo shoved such superstitious fears aside, reminding himself that these were Damnonii lands, watched over by Damnonii gods, and he led the men back to the rest of the warband he'd managed to piece together. Over one hundred men of all ages formed that burgeoning army, some experienced, some too young to ever have stood in a shieldwall, and others too old to do much other than add to their numbers once it came to a fight. It would be up to Gavo to make the most of what they had.

They were not enough to bring Drest's army to battle, but they were enough to give the Pictish bastard a bloody nose.

The promise of another strike at the enemy had bolstered everyone's morale after finding the second immolated settlement and it didn't take long for Gavo to choose twelve men who would accompany him to strike at Drest's encampment. Sentica would take the rest of the army to the road at Ard Sabhal and lay the trap for Horsa. There was no doubt in anyone's mind that the Saxon jarl would come hunting for them — he was not the type of leader to let a sneak attack pass without reply. Drest might be, for he was as cautious a commander and king as Gavo had ever come across, but Horsa was the polar opposite.

He would come after them, and Gavo's warriors would kill him.

"Ready, Sentica?"

"Aye, my lord," his sergeant confirmed, saluting brusquely. "We'll be ready when you come. Just make sure the sea-wolves don't catch you before you can reach us."

"Cernunnos, god of the forest, protect us," Gavo said, looking around at the Damnonii warriors. They were not as well armed or armoured as the Saxons they hoped to slaughter, but they would do.

They would have to.

CHAPTER TWENTY-THREE

Qunavo stepped off the ship and gazed up at Dun Breatann with a smile on his seamed face. It was windy, as it so often was beside the Clota, and he pulled his cloak tighter around himself as he tried to make out any familiar faces on the fortress walls. The higher parts of the rock were just a blur to his ageing eyesight but the men on the outer walls were clear enough; he did not recognise any of them, however. Oh well, he was sure Narina and her brat would be cooped up somewhere inside, a prison as much as a fortress for them until Drest finally decided to use force and break inside.

He turned, remembering his manners, and held out a hand to assist Ria from the ship but she'd already jumped nimbly down and splashed through the shallow water onto the pebbled beach.

"The siege is still in progress then," she noted. "I'd rather hoped it would be over by the time we got here."

"It'll be interesting to see how Drest and the Saxons are getting on," Qunavo said with a chuckle.

"No doubt Aife will have had something to complain about too," said Ria who liked the warrior-princess well enough but had little time for her unusually strict sense of morality.

The captain of the ship had his sailors carry off their belongings, meagre as they were, and, having already received payment from the elderly druid, looked about in confusion.

"Where is everyone?" he asked no one in particular. "Where's the officials looking to tax us? Where's the traders? The labourers to unload the ships? Where," he finished in exasperation, "are all the ships?"

Qunavo gave a bark of laughter and pointed towards the gates of Dun Breatann. "There lies your answer, my lad," he said.

The ship's captain took a moment to understand what was happening, and then he cursed. "Did you know about this, you old trickster?" he demanded. "When I agreed to bring you and the girl here I assumed I'd be able to sell my cargo. It would have made the trip more than worth my while. But…" He trailed off, turning his angry gaze backwards, onto the laden hull of his vessel.

"Take care how you speak to us," Qunavo snapped, brandishing his staff. "Or I'll call on Taranis to snap your ship in half when you're in the middle of the sea!"

The captain blanched at the threat and his attitude noticeably softened, but he was still furious at travelling all that way only to discover he couldn't trade his wares.

"There's plenty of other settlements back along the Clota," Ria said, waving vaguely to the west. "You'll be sailing that way anyhow. Sell your cargo there."

Riders were already thundering towards them, wondering whether they were a threat or not, and, when one of them called out cheerily, recognising Qunavo, the captain knew he was beaten.

Muttering sourly to himself he ordered his men to push off. None of the sailors argued for, although they were tired after the journey and had been greatly looking forward to a night or two enjoying the pleasures of Alt Clota, they could see there would be no warm welcome for them there.

Qunavo and Ria called their thanks to the crew unironically for the ship had carried them to their destination quickly and safely. They did not receive any response however, and gladly walked off with the horsemen who'd come to meet them.

"How's the war going?" Qunavo asked the most senior of the riders, a Pictish nobleman he knew fairly well.

"It's not," the man replied in a bored tone. "Not really. The Damnonii have locked themselves away and refuse to come out to fight us. Even when Horsa—"

"By the breath of Dis Pater," Ria gasped as they walked past Dun Breatann's outer gatehouse. "What happened to those poor bastards?"

The horseman turned away from the sight of the blood-eagled Damnonii prisoners. It had been a horrific display when the corpses had been fresh but now, after days of being pecked by crows and gulls and the inevitable putrefaction of the flesh, it was a truly hideous scene.

"It was Horsa," the rider replied. "Well, him and his *volva*."

"*Volva!*" both druids demanded in unison.

"Aye, we met her on the road here and she joined the Saxons." He spat as they continued heading towards Drest's large command tent. "She's a fucking maniac if you ask me," he told them in a

130

low, confidential voice. "But she insisted on sacrificing those Damnonii prisoners so her gods would help us take the fortress."

"That worked well," Ria snorted, looking back at the mangled bodies in disgust. "What did the witch even *do* to them? It looks like something exploded out from inside their ribcages."

"Something like that," their escort nodded bleakly. "She ripped them apart with a saw while they were still alive. The Saxons call it a 'blood-eagle'." He looked at the bodies momentarily then turned away with a shudder.

"Why did Drest allow this?" Qunavo wondered, and he did his best to keep his voice level, not wishing to be critical of the king before he had the full facts. "We no longer perform human sacrifices to our gods. Executing criminals is one thing, but prisoners of war?"

The horseman reined in his mount and the other riders did the same. "I guess the *volva* doesn't have the same view as you druids do, my lord. Anyway, the king is in his tent there, but he's not in the best of moods." With that he gave a shallow bow from the back of his horse and led his riders away to continue whatever they'd been doing before the ship had deposited Qunavo and Ria at the camp.

The old druid and his younger companion shared a glance and then, with a shrug, Qunavo led the way past the guards and into the command tent.

CHAPTER TWENTY-FOUR

Gavo had picked some good men to ride with him to Dun Breatann. He knew most of them well, and he trusted them to follow his orders and carry out their duties without question. Would it be enough? He hoped so but, as they drew nearer to the towering rock that dominated the skyline he couldn't help feeling a little sliver of doubt.

Horsa and Drest would probably be watching for more sneak attacks like the one Gavo had pulled off before. They might even have laid traps themselves, and be waiting, hidden, watching for the Damnonii warband as it rode ever closer, oblivious to their peril.

The captain shrugged off the fears. They were not unfounded, but there was nothing he could do about it if he was leading his men into a trap — he had to do something to lift the siege and dealing with Horsa seemed the best way. Gavo could not repeat the exact formula that had worked successfully before however, that would be folly. He had to change his approach a little this time around.

Instead of coming from the north, as they had for the previous attack, Gavo's riders approached from the east, along a small, overgrown path that only the locals knew existed. Of course, the enemy army had been camped outside Dun Breatann for a while now so it was quite possible some of them, foraging for food and other supplies, might have discovered the path, but it was an old one that had fallen into disuse in recent years and Gavo prayed the brambles, nettles, and long grass had rendered it completely invisible to those who didn't know it was there.

It was hard going for the horses as they forced a way through the undergrowth, their riders trying to pick out the old track. The thick brambles were the biggest issue, their thorns catching in the animals' coats so the men had to hack the branches off with their swords or axes. They made slow progress but Gavo made sure to clear a path so that they could ride back this way at some speed once their attack was completed.

"What if it's not the Saxons that are at the side of the camp this path will lead us out at?" one of the warriors asked.

"Won't matter," Gavo said with conviction. "Horsa will be the one who comes after us. He's the most bloodthirsty of all Drest's followers, and I'm sure Drest himself will be happy to let the Saxons take risks rather than his own men. But wait, slow down." He pushed himself up on his horse, trying to see as far ahead as possible, then immediately ducked down, sucking breath through his teeth as he spotted an enemy sentry not far ahead. "Dismount," he hissed. "We're almost on top of 'em."

His men did as they were told quickly and quietly, pegging their mounts to the ground so they wouldn't wander off.

"Are we ready, lads?" Gavo asked, making sure his sword was safely in its sheath and he had the two throwing spears he'd brought along for this mission.

The rest of the men were similarly armed and they nodded gravely.

The captain looked at all twelve of his warriors in turn, examining their faces, making sure they were prepared should their lightning strike not go to plan. He saw fear and trepidation on those faces, but he knew his would betray similar emotions. The important thing was the grim determination he sensed in the men.

A smile crept across his lips and he nodded slowly, the familiar excitement of battle beginning to build within him. "Let's go then," he said. "Remember, we follow the path to its end, then stop until we see how the enemy camp is laid out near us."

"I could climb one of these trees," someone offered. "Get a better view of what's ahead."

Gavo shook his head. "You might be spotted. I'm sure there's Picts just ahead of us, camped close together. With nothing to do they'll be sitting bored, talking bollocks, lost in their own little world. They'll be easy targets for our javelins."

Vicious chuckles followed his prediction and then they were moving, gliding along the path like wraiths, gently shoving branches and foliage aside, ignoring the pain if a thorn tore at a patch of bare skin or nettles stung them.

Gavo stopped at a shout ahead, turning to gesture for his men to do the same but they'd all heard it too. Sweating hands gripped javelins, ready to throw them at a moment's notice, and then the shout was repeated, and the familiar sound of a fist striking flesh was followed by more shouts and even cheers.

"The useless sheep-humpers are fighting amongst themselves," Gavo smiled. "All their attention will be on one another, and the fight. Cernunnos is with us, my friends."

They moved on, Gavo reaching the end of the path and the foliage that concealed it. He peered through the leaves of a pussy willow and felt his heart soar. Sure enough, Picts were the enemy troops nearest to the path, but they were not too close to be an immediate threat, and, as hoped, they were focused on the brawl that was going on between four of their own comrades.

"Forward," the captain ordered. "Line up, and release on my mark."

His men moved into position without anyone in the enemy camp noticing them and Gavo's heart was thumping in his chest as he raised the first of his javelins and, smiling, called in a low voice, "Loose!"

The short spears arced up into the air, seemed to hang there, suspended for a moment, and then they came down directly into the throng of bodies enjoying the fist-fight. The cheers and laughter instantly turned to screams and roars of outrage as the sharpened iron heads tore through flesh and bone.

"Loose!" Gavo repeated, grinning maniacally as he drew back his right arm, adjusted his grip, then threw the javelin with all his strength. His eyes traced its flight as it sailed up and then gently turned downwards, gaining speed until it disappeared into the confused mass of enemy soldiers.

All the Damnonii missiles were spent now and the thirteen men of the warband stood for a few heartbeats, gleefully watching the aftermath of their attack.

"Bastards," one of them crowed. "I hope we killed a load of them."

"Good enough for 'em," another agreed.

"Aye," said Gavo, realising they'd been spotted. "But now we have to get the fuck out of here! Come on!"

They ran back into the undergrowth, along the overgrown path, racing past brambles and branches that whipped and tore at them, laughing like misbehaving children until they came to their waiting horses.

"Hurry!" Gavo shouted as the sound of thundering footsteps reached the path behind them. He wasn't as young as he'd once been but he practically flew up onto his mount's back as if Cernunnos himself, lord of the forest, had lifted him there himself. "Hurry!" he repeated, for he couldn't move along the narrow track until those in front of him did.

He glanced over his shoulder, the blood thumping in his ears as he saw the first of their pursuers forcing a way towards them, bearded face twisted with rage and hatred, sword in hand.

At last, the horses in front of him began to move, picking up speed as Gavo's beast followed. He was glad they'd cleared the worst of the foliage away for they were able to canter much quicker than the men behind on foot could run and they soon left the Saxons behind, bellowing curses and threats.

They reached a clearing and, as agreed previously, came to a halt, allowing the horses to rest for a few moments.

"Well done," Gavo said cheerily as he rode up last to join his men. "I think we did what we set out to do, and then some! Now, we wait until we hear riders coming for us." *And pray it's Horsa's sea-wolves*, he added silently to himself.

It was strangely quiet there in the clearing, considering what had just gone on. The trees and undergrowth seemed to muffle the shouts and other noises coming from the direction of Dun Breatann and it was almost peaceful.

Then there were thuds and more cries behind them and Gavo knew riders were coming along the track.

"Time to go," he said and took point once more, urging his horse into a trot until he was sure his men were behind him, and then he allowed his mount to reach a canter. This was a crucial point in the plan — move too fast and their pursuers might give up, move too slowly and they might be caught. Gavo did not think even the dense foliage would be enough to hold back the enraged riders who were coming to kill them.

Dun Breatann was not far from where Sentica and the others waited for them beside Dun Buic. Gavo thought of that place with its cairn that had borne witness to gruesome rites back in the days when the druids' practices were far more...sinister. He looked over his shoulder and prayed that Dun Buic's spirits would use their malevolent energy against the Saxons rather than the Damnonii.

The foliage disappeared and they were racing over open ground, their destination in sight. Gavo could see the horsemen behind them now, twenty or more, grim and silent, determined to catch up to them and spill their blood.

Good, he thought. *Let them come.*

He reached the track that led up the hill towards the cairn and, taking a deep breath and, uttering an impassioned plea for Cernunnos to protect them from both the Saxons and the wraiths that haunted that place, he guided his horse upwards.

The rest of the warband followed him, anxiously casting backward glances but still smiling as the battle-fever coursed through them. Up they went, the horses placing their feet carefully on the rocky, uneven path, their pursuers closing in upon them.

"Where's Sentica and the others?" the rider behind Gavo demanded, a note of panic in his voice. "They should be here, shouldn't they, my lord?"

Gavo was wondering the same thing but his own fears dissipated as his sergeant stuck his head out from behind a boulder and waved.

"There!" Gavo cried in relief, noticing the other men that had been left here to lay the ambush also hidden within the terrain. "We've made it," he said, although he knew they still had the hard part to do.

When they'd rode on another forty or fifty paces, Gavo tugged on his mount's reins, drawing it to a stop. Then he jumped down, shooing the horse away in the opposite direction as the rest of his riders came up behind him and followed suit.

"Form up!" he roared, lifting one of the spears and a shield that had been left lying there for them, and running to stand in the middle of the track. Twelve more spears and shields were lifted, and his warriors came to line up beside him in a wall two men deep.

The Saxons were almost upon them but Gavo and his men held their spears out, pointing back along the road and the enemy horses balked, too clever to impale themselves on the lethal lengths of ash and iron.

One of the Saxon warriors laughed mockingly and jumped easily down from his mount, calling something in his own language so Gavo couldn't make it out. He could guess though — something about being happy to face them man to man, or how easy the sea-wolves would kill them all, or how Gavo's mother was a whore. The usual pre-battle insults, rather wasted when the opposition couldn't even understand them but, Gavo mused, a proud tradition.

"Bring it then, Horsa, you stinking squirrel's turd," he called back, grinning and gesturing the Saxons forward. He examined their foes as they began stepping towards Gavo's shieldwall, noting the chainmail byrnies, heavy axes, and well-made helmets. The leader's helm was a particularly fine example, with protection not just for the head but for the eyes as well. There was no time for the Damnonii captain to inspect its intricacies further though, as the Saxons suddenly, and without any audible command, came charging towards them.

"Brace!" Gavo shouted just as he felt and axe slam into his shield. The shock of the blow ran all the way up his arm and he swore in pain but the man beside him thrust his spear into the Saxon who fell away, reeling back before collapsing on the rocky path.

The Damnonii warriors were outnumbered but with their shields and spears the Saxons found it almost impossible to break through their wall. The axes and swords the enemy soldiers carried were simply not effective enough. Given time, their numbers would surely have carried them to victory, but they were not given that time.

Gavo laughed as he saw Sentica and the rest of their men running up the track also carrying spears and shields to join the fight.

Some of the Saxons noticed the reinforcements coming to join Gavo and they turned to face them, trapped as they were now between to impenetrable walls of Damnonii spearmen. The path was quite narrow so it soon became less about numbers and more about who was armed better, and who could fight with the most savagery. The Saxons were more than capable of the latter and they smashed their axes on the linden boards that Gavo and his men sheltered behind, while those with swords sought for ways to pierce the gaps in the line.

And then a boulder seemed to fall out of the sky as if dropped by one of the gods, its weight crashing down on the helmet of one of the invaders. The man fell without so much as a cry and, when more rocks dropped on them, the Saxons began to panic, wondering what was happening.

"Kill them!" Gavo screamed, and Sentica shouted a similar command on the other side of their foes as missiles continued to rain down, dropped by the Damnonii troops who'd been hiding high up above the path.

The battle did not last long then. The Saxons didn't know whether to look up, or ahead, or behind, or simply to try and escape that terrible killing ground and, in the end, their confusion was their undoing. Gavo's spear was coated in blood by the time the last of the enemy warriors fell and the hail of rocks ceased.

"We did it," said Sentica, chest heaving as he walked to Gavo, trying to get his breath back. "The plan worked perfectly."

"It did," the captain agreed, reaching out to grasp Sentica's wrist, both men grinning in triumph. "It's one thing to face an enemy armed with a spear, you feel like you can win that fight. But when boulders start dropping out the sky and you have no way to defend yourself, ha! That must have been bloody terrifying for the stinking sea-wolves." He looked up at the Damnonii soldiers who'd been hurling the rocks and shook his fist triumphantly, congratulating them, and all his men, on their victory.

"Two of you," he said. "Take your horses and ride back down to make sure no more of the bastards turn up. The rest of you — where are the casks of ale we brought here? Break them open, by Cernunnos, I think we've earned a good drink!"

This was, of course, met with lusty cheers and soon Gavo and Sentica had cups of ale in their hands and were gulping down the dark, heady brew.

"This'll be a huge blow for Drest," predicted Sentica, standing proudly over the bodies of the Saxons. Not all of them had been dead at the end of the battle, but they were all dead now.

"It will," agreed Gavo. "To lose so many of his Saxon mercenaries, and Horsa himself…" He laughed joyfully and raised his cup high, imagining this as the moment where the tide of war turned in favour of Narina's Damnonii.

"That's a fine helmet," said Sentica, bending down and loosening the strap that held it in place on the enemy leader's head. "You want it, my lord?"

"Nah," said Gavo. "I like mine. It's got dents in all the same places as my skull. You can have that one."

Sentica prised the helmet loose and lifted it up. It was indeed a very fine, and undoubtedly a very expensive, piece of craftsmanship — a helmet fit for a nobleman.

Unfortunately, that nobleman was not Horsa.

Gavo's joy evaporated as he took in the face of the dead Saxon, and, after a few moments checking the rest of the fallen sea-wolves, was forced to accept the fact that Horsa was not among the dead.

Somehow the great Damnonii victory no longer seemed like the turning point Gavo had believed it to be.

CHAPTER TWENTY-FIVE

Duro looked at the lands along the Clota and smiled. Bellicus noticed his friend's pleasure and was glad — there had been a time when the centurion planned to leave Alt Clota and go back south to live. To ride with Arthur's army and hunt down the Saxons who were intent on subjugating the Britons. Perhaps one day Duro would do so but, for now, he seemed happy to be returning to Bellicus's home and that was encouraging for the druid.

"Well, Merlin," the centurion said, turning away from the pleasant brown and green lands they were sailing past. "Where are we getting off?"

Bellicus had been thinking about this already — it would not be safe to disembark right at Dun Breatann if the place was surrounded by Drest's army. Of course, it was possible that Qunavo and Ria had made that whole story up, but Bellicus did not think so. He knew Drest coveted the lands of the Damnonii, and still hated Narina for allowing Ysfael to execute the Pictish prisoners who should have been safe, and treated with respect at least by Narina's people. Bellicus also knew the Picts were trading more and more with Hengist's sailors. They both had their main fortresses on the eastern coast so it made perfect sense for them to trade and, through that, become close. With hindsight, an alliance was inevitable, and Bellicus mentally berated himself for not advising Narina to do what she could to prevent it happening.

"Eh? Wake up, big man."

Bellicus came back to himself, seeing Duro grinning lopsidedly at him. "Sorry," he said. "The motion of the ship and the warm weather..."

"High Druid?" Duro snorted. "How can you be in charge of your Order when you can hardly keep awake in the middle of the day? You're getting old, my friend."

"Still about sixteen years younger than you, you old bastard," Bellicus retorted with good humour. "But, to answer your question, I think we should get off the ship at Carden Ros, as we did that time before, when we returned from hunting Loarn mac Eirc in Dalriada."

Duro thought back to that time, nodding slowly. "Fair enough," he agreed. "At least we have horses this time so we won't have to walk everywhere."

"I don't," Koriosis noted.

"We can take turns to ride, if needs be," said Bellicus. "But the last time we were there together we'd been named as outlaws by King Coroticus so we were forced to remain hidden. This time is different — we can buy you a horse, Koriosis. It shouldn't be hard."

"That's assuming Carden Ros hasn't been taken over by Drest's men," Duro noted bleakly, his earlier smile now a worried frown.

Bellicus had no answer for him. They both knew what Horsa was capable of so it was quite possible that some of the settlements near Dun Breatann would have been captured, but there was nothing they could do about it. They had to get off the ship somewhere, and Carden Ros was the most logical place.

The captain of the ship happily put in at the village on the northern bank of the Clota. Unlike his counterpart who'd taken Qunavo and Ria to Dun Breatann this captain carried only a little cargo — Bellicus had paid him very handsomely to bring them here and the man was pleased to have served the new Merlin in such a way. His crew helped them take Darac and Pryderi off the vessel and then, with cheery farewells — mostly for Cai who had made friends with the crew during the voyage — turned the ship and headed off to wherever the wind would carry them.

"Looks like we have a welcoming party," said Koriosis as they made their way up from the beach towards the village. They had not disembarked at the settlement's little docks, not wanting to attract the attention of enemies should they be nearby, but their arrival had not gone unnoticed.

"Friends?" Duro muttered, eyeing the group of twenty or so armed men coming towards them. He and Bellicus were mounted, while Koriosis was on foot.

"They don't look like Saxons at least," said the Bellicus. "And Cai doesn't seem too worried, which is always a good sign."

"Even so," the centurion said, loosening his spatha in its scabbard. "Best be ready for trouble."

They stopped walking, and the two groups eyed one another curiously. Before long one of the men from the village called out, "Bellicus! Is that you, my lord?"

"Aye," the druid returned, shaking his great staff and smiling as he dismounted, Duro following his lead.

"Oh, praise the gods!" the man shouted, bursting into relieved laughter as his fellows joined in and they hurried towards the three travellers.

"This is all seeming very familiar," said Duro sardonically.

"Aye," Bellicus nodded. He was glad the men were not enemies, but it was obvious they were frightened and disturbed and that did not bode well for what had been happening in the druid's absence. "What's been going on here?" he asked as the village militia reached them. Inspecting them up close, Bellicus noted the group were all around middle-age or even older — there were no young men amongst them.

"King Drest has come back," said the man who'd hailed him. "Queen Narina summoned the army to Dun Breatann, but the Picts arrived before most of them could get there."

"Not just Picts either," another man said. He was at least seventy, perhaps older, and most of his muscle tone had wasted away with age. Still, he carried a spear and his eyes were hard. If it came to a fight, Bellicus had stood beside lesser warriors in the shieldwall.

"Saxons," the druid said. "We know."

"Drest might not be so bad on his own," the first man, plainly the leader, noted. "But there's a big brute in charge of the Saxons. He's burned down at least two villages and…" His voice trailed off and his fingers worked convulsively on the shaft of his spear.

"The bastards took prisoners from the village just along the road from here," a small man with a battered old shield and an axe said, voice shaking with emotion. "We heard them being tortured even from here. All the way from Dun Breatann, their screams carried along the Clota." He shuddered and made a sign with his hand to ward off evil. "Dis Pater rest their souls, but they must have suffered terribly."

Bellicus shared a glance with Duro. Both men had feared Horsa might brutalise the Damnonii people if Narina didn't surrender to Drest's army which, of course, she would hardly do.

142

"Have the Saxons come here?" Koriosis asked. He remembered some of these faces from his time as apprentice druid in Alt Clota, Bellicus could tell.

"Not yet," said the little man with the axe. "But it's only a matter of time. Gavo has—"

"Gavo!" Bellicus broke in. "What of him? Is he alive?"

"Oh, aye, my lord, Gavo is as well as ever," the militia leader assured him. "He's been doing his best to gather all the warriors who were on their way to Dun Breatann before the place was besieged. He was here the other day, warning us about what's been happening and telling us to be careful. The survivors from the next village mostly came here so we're taking care of them but we've to run for the hills if the raiders turn up."

"He has command of the warriors from Carden Ros?" Duro asked, then added almost apologetically, "the younger ones I mean."

"Aye," the leader replied. "And hopefully plenty more by now as well." The man shook his head. "It's a right mess."

"Indeed," said Bellicus. "But of all the men in Alt Clota, I would choose Gavo for this task."

"And you, my lord," the most elderly of the militia said. "I've seen you fight. And the centurion there. You'll join Gavo and kick Drest and his filthy rats out of our lands, won't you?"

The men looked up at him, wrinkled faces filled with almost pitiful hope. They had once been proud warriors, now reduced to hiding in their village while younger men did what they could to protect Alt Clota.

"We'll deal with the Saxons," the druid said with much more confidence than he felt. He drew himself up to his full height, dwarfing everyone there, and thumped his eagle-topped staff on the ground. "By Taranis, I swear it."

His words awed the villagers and they took heart.

"We may have need of you men too though," Bellicus added, gazing down upon them sombrely. "For now, remain here and protect the women and children in Carden Ros. But there may come a time when we'll need every experienced warrior we can muster. Will you come when we call?"

"Of course!" the men cried almost in unison, promising to do their part, as they had done in the past when summoned by King Coroticus or even the rulers of Alt Clota before him.

"Where is Gavo now?" Duro asked. "Do you have any idea?"

"The last we heard he was near Dun Buic," the leader said. "Sending out scouts east and west to try and find the Damnonii warriors coming to Dun Breatann before they stumbled into Drest's army."

"Shit," Koriosis muttered. "That's probably already happened to a few of them."

"No doubt," said Bellicus. "But there's nothing we can do about that."

"What *will* you do?" the little axeman wondered.

"Find Gavo," said Bellicus decisively. "And then?" He shrugged and jumped onto Darac's back. "We'll take back our lands and dispatch Drest once and for all. Can any of you men find us a horse for my brother druid here?"

Soon, Koriosis was mounted on a horse that wasn't much more sprightly than the elderly spearman in Carden Ros, on their way east, towards Dun Buic and, gods willing, a reunion with Gavo.

CHAPTER TWENTY-SIX

Drest was furious when Qunavo and Ria joined him in his command tent. He was pacing up and down, or doing his best to within the confines of the tent, and sipping mead that he'd bought from Saxon traders back at Dunnottar. His face was red and his eyes were bloodshot and he did not look well.

"My lord," said Qunavo in greeting.

The king glanced at them and it seemed to take him a long time to recognise who they were. "Oh, by Sulis Minerva's tits," he gasped eventually, halting his pacing and looking at his newcomers with relief. "About time you two joined us." He lowered his voice and eyed the tent's entrance as if he feared someone might overhear him as he went on. "This whole siege has been a nightmare. I should have known it was ill-omened when we met that crazy *volva* on the road and Horsa insisted she come with us."

"Ill-omened?" Qunavo demanded, voice harsh, as if talking to a child having a tantrum. "Have you lost the war with the Damnonii?"

"No," Drest admitted, sipping his mead again.

"Have you even lost a skirmish with Narina's soldiers?"

"Not exactly," said Drest. "But some of them attacked us with javelins not long ago. Of course, the Saxons insisted on being the ones to hunt them down but," the king shook his head and Qunavo wondered if he actually caught the hint of a smile on Drest's face. "The Damnonii somehow killed the lot of them. One of my patrols found their decapitated heads on the road to the north just an hour or so back."

"How many lost?" Ria wondered.

"About twenty or so," Drest replied.

"That's nothing," Qunavo argued. "Not in an army of this size."

"Perhaps. But if we keep losing men at that rate there'll be none of us left." He sighed and flopped onto his camp chair, cradling his mead protectively. "Ach, I know, twenty men is a drop in the ocean. But you must have seen those butchered bodies outside the fortress gates. And those aren't even the first Damnonii prisoners

Horsa and the witch 'sacrificed'. God, it was something I hope never to see again."

Qunavo took a seat across from him and Ria one to his left.

"Human sacrifice is not something we do these days," the older druid said firmly. "Not to innocent people. We cannot let the woman do it again."

"You try stopping them!" Drest cried plaintively.

"Listen to yourself," Qunavo berated him. "You are the king. You lead this army, not Horsa or the *volva*. Take command, Drest!"

The druid had always known Drest was not the strongest leader the Picts might have had. For years the man had been content to sit within his own borders, never seeking to grow his wealth or his lands if it meant conflict. It had taken Qunavo a long time to finally persuade him that being more aggressive was actually the best way to protect his own interests. Still, it was not really in Drest's nature to be as brutal as a warlord needed to be at times like this and he had to be poked and prodded into action, his anger, and his confidence, built up until he felt strong enough to do what must be done.

"All right," the king retorted, skin flushing red as he downed the remainder of his mead in a quick swallow. "I will. Come on, you two can come with me. We'll have a word with Horsa and his *volva*, and let them know there's to be no more unnecessary cruelty towards Damnonii captives." As if eager to complete the task before he lost his nerve, he pushed through the tent flaps and stepped outside, taking a hurried breath of air and looking around. His hearth warriors were nearby, chatting beneath a leather canopy that sheltered them from the rain or, as today, the sunshine. "You men," he barked. "Come with us. Bring your spears, and put on your helmets."

The soldiers didn't hesitate, following Drest's command immediately and falling into step behind and beside the king and the pair of druids. Qunavo examined them, the cream of the Pictish army, tall, powerfully built, intelligent, and armed to the teeth. They made a hugely impressive guard of honour and Horsa would be a fool to argue with Drest when these warriors were there to look after him.

Of course, Horsa *was* said to be something of a fool so this meeting should be interesting if nothing else.

They walked past the tents of the Saxons at the northern edge of the encampment, ignoring the curious looks from the sea-wolves, some of whom did touch their seaxes and axes. It was obvious something big was about to happen.

The other jarl who'd accompanied Horsa appeared, hurrying over to stand before Drest, halting the entire party.

"My lord," said the little Saxon, a slight whistle in his voice as though even that short walk had made him out of breath. "What's happening?"

"I've had enough of your cousin and the *volva* brutalising and murdering the people that will be my own subjects once this war is won. I'm here to make sure it stops, Sigarr, so get out of the way."

Qunavo smiled. The mead had made Drest bold, and Sigarr did not want to stand up to him. That particular jarl might be weak physically, but he was as sharp as Qunavo's sacrificial blade, and he knew how to look after his own skin. He stepped aside with a shallow bow, letting Drest and his grim-faced party walk by, towards the biggest, grandest tent within the Saxon section of the camp.

Horsa's tent was not guarded which Qunavo was surprised about, but the druid took it as a sign of the jarl's arrogance. He did not need protection — no one would dare attack Horsa within his own tent.

Which might even be true, but Drest and his party were not there to spill blood, merely to talk.

Qunavo could see Drest visibly slowing as they neared the large tent, focusing completely on the entrance, ignoring the curious and even sardonic looks from the Saxons around them. The Pictish king practically came to a stop just before the shelter, took a breath so long and deep that his shoulders could be seen rising and falling, and then, with a glance at the druid, Drest pushed through the entrance flaps without calling for Horsa's permission.

It was a bold move, and Qunavo was glad when two of the king's largest hearth-warriors came into the tent with them. Horsa would not enjoy being disturbed so rudely. Ria came inside too and, as their eyes adjusted to the gloomy interior — the leather of

147

the tent's walls and roof letting in little of the sunshine — it was the druidess who spoke first.

"Oh my," she said, lips curling in the familiar smile that Qunavo had seen drive men to distraction so many times. "Are we disturbing you, Horsa?"

The big jarl had, incredibly, not noticed their arrival. He was utterly engrossed in what he was doing and, as Qunavo's older eyes became used to the dim light he noticed two rounded, white shapes at the far end of the tent. His gaze moved to the left, and he finally realised he'd been looking at the Saxon's bare arse — the jarl was in bed, and he was not alone.

"What is this?" Horsa demanded in his heavily accented baritone, glaring at the newcomers.

"We just came to talk to you," Drest replied. "Don't bother to get up."

"Too late," said Ria with obvious amusement. "I don't think he could get any further up."

"You can be next, girl," Horsa said, teeth flashing. "There's more than enough of me to go around."

He did roll off the woman he was on top of now, and Qunavo felt himself becoming aroused at the sight of the slim, large-breasted figure. He had no idea who she was, until Drest spoke.

"You're humping the *volva*? Really, Horsa?"

"Why not?" the jarl replied, standing but not bothering to cover his erect manhood as he looked at the Picts, eyes lingering on Ria who returned his look coolly. "Have you never bedded this one?" he asked Drest. "Who is she anyway?"

"She's a druidess," the king replied irritably, clearly flustered himself at the sight of Yngvildr, naked on the bedroll. "Never mind that," Drest said, tearing his eyes from the *volva* and addressing Horsa. "I've come here to tell you — both of you — that there's to be no more sacrifices of Damnonii prisoners, do you hear me? No more throats being slit, no more blood-eagles, nothing, unless I give the order."

"Why not?" Horsa demanded. "If Narina won't do what we want, we must make her."

"Because we do not sacrifice human victims," Qunavo said firmly. "It is not our way, and has not been for generations."

148

"Another druid?" Horsa sneered, eyeing the older man up and down. "Don't come here moralising — I know you sacrifice people to your gods."

"Criminals," Qunavo said. "Murderers, rapists, people like that. Not prisoners of war!"

"The Damnonii murdered Pictish prisoners of war," said Yngvildr in a low, sultry voice, stretching out so that Qunavo had to avert his gaze. "That's what started all this, is it not?"

"Exactly," Drest replied, eyes fixed on Horsa. "The Damnonii broke the rules of war, and now they must pay for their crime. So I will not stand by and watch while you two do the same — the gods will not reward us for such behaviour, will they, Qunavo?"

"No, they will not," the druid said with conviction. "We have learned this over many hundreds of years, knowledge passed down from druid to druid."

Yngvildr gave a dry chuckle. "You think we *volur* do not have similar knowledge? Similar, old traditions?"

"I don't care for your traditions!" Drest spat. "These are not your lands—"

"They're not yours either," Yngvildr replied, rolling onto her side so her heavy breasts hung down. It might have been gloomy in the tent, but it was light enough to make out every one of her curves, and she knew it. A *volva* at work, thought Qunavo with more than just admiration for her wiles.

"They will be soon," the king said, still clearly forcing himself to stare at Horsa. "Besides, we share the same gods with the Damnonii. Those gods — Taranis, Cernunnos, Lug the Light-Bringer, Sulis, Dis — they have always held sway in this corner of the world. Anyway," he swept his hand down in a cutting motion. "I am the king, and I'm in charge of this army, as I already told you before. That includes you, Horsa, and you will follow my orders or you can march back to Hengist."

"I would be happy to," the Saxon drawled, drawing himself up straight and still naked although thankfully his manhood was no longer standing to attention. "I will remain here for a while longer, Drest. You lead, in your fashion, and I will follow. But if we're still stuck here after another two weeks, chasing shadows or sitting around bored, I will take my payment from you and leave."

"Bored?" asked Ria sarcastically. "You didn't look bored."

149

Horsa laughed but kept his attention on Drest. "Leave me now, king. I want to finish what I had started." He looked at Ria. "You can stay if you wish though, druidess."

"Yes, stay," said Yngvildr. "There's room for three in here. We can work our magic together."

"I don't think so," Ria replied. "That kind of magic *is* rather more to my liking than human sacrifice, but I would not share a bed with the likes of you two," and she led the way out of the tent, the others following at her back.

CHAPTER TWENTY-SEVEN

The story at Dun Buic was much the same as it had been at Carden Ros. When Bellicus, Duro, and Koriosis approached the devastated settlement they became aware of armed men on the road ahead and behind. As at the previous village, Bellicus was very quickly recognised — on his black warhorse the giant druid was easy to spot, even from a distance.

Gavo himself came riding to greet them, and the smile he wore on his face seemed to Bellicus like the first one the captain's face had seen in quite some time.

"Bel!" he called as his horse trotted up to them, a handful of other hard-looking horsemen at his back. "And Duro too, it's good to see you, lads. And wait, who's this? Koriosis, back for more, eh? Well, you're more than welcome here, druid. The more on our side the better. Did you make it here without trouble?"

Bellicus nodded. "We did, thankfully. Our ship let us off at Carden Ros and the road from there was mercifully free of enemies. How's the war going, old friend?"

Gavo shrugged, face impassive, which Bellicus took as a good sign. The taciturn captain could not be expected to look joyful even if things were going his way — the fact he didn't look too dour meant things could be worse, or so the druid hoped.

"It could be better," Gavo replied. "But it could be worse. We've just ambushed some of Horsa's sea-wolves, slaughtered the lot without taking a casualty ourselves."

"That's good," said Duro.

"Aye, but Horsa wasn't with them."

"Oh."

"Exactly," chuckled Gavo dryly. "Like I say: could be worse, could be better. But come on, you three, we better get into cover before another of Drest's patrols comes along. I doubt the loss of twenty of his men will make Horsa any less bloodthirsty."

He turned his horse and led the way up towards Dun Buic Cairn, the warriors who'd been watching their meeting on foot melting back into the undergrowth that grew around the road.

"Your camp is up here?" Bellicus asked in surprise as the horses carried them up the slope towards the site of the sacred old shrine that had been used since before the Romans had even come to Britain. "I'm impressed, Gavo. The last time we came up here you were so afraid of the place I had to give you a stone of protection to get you moving."

The captain nodded, not taking offence to the druid's words for they were true. "Aye, well, this place served us well for the ambush. I figure the gods or spirits that linger about the cairn are *our* gods, not the Saxons' so..." He shrugged. "I'm glad you're here though. Two druids should make sure we're safe."

"Not just two druids," said Duro with a smile that seemed to reflect both pride and amusement, Bellicus thought. "The *Merlin*."

Gavo frowned and turned to look at them as if he was being made fun of. "Where?" he asked. "I only see you three. I thought the Merlin was an old man with a flowing white beard, like druids are supposed to look." He smirked at Bellicus and Koriosis, neither of whom matched his description. "No offence, lads."

"None taken," said Koriosis, returning his smirk. "But, in future, rather than addressing Bellicus as 'lad', you might want to give him his proper title: Merlin, High Druid of Britain!"

Still it was obvious Gavo was not following what was happening, and he made that abundantly clear when he demanded with some annoyance, "What the fuck are you two on about?"

Duro laughed, greatly enjoying the bluff captain's confusion. "Bellicus," he said, slowly as if talking to a child, "is the new Merlin. The old one was killed in a Saxon raid."

Gavo's face was already comical to the centurion and Koriosis, but it was even more so now as he looked at Bellicus as if the big druid had suddenly grown an extra head, or burst into flames. At length the captain smiled and shrugged. "Congratulations, I suppose," he said. "But to me you'll always be the daft, gangly boy that came to us in Dun Breatann years ago, *Merlin*."

"And, to me," Bellicus replied with a shallow nod, accepting the other's insult, "you'll always be a torn-faced old prick."

"Give me something to smile about then, Merlin," Gavo laughed. "I could do with cheering up."

They came to a bend in the road and Gavo led them into the foliage there. It was not dense by any means, allowing the horses to move through it fairly easily, but thick enough to hide the path that Bellicus realised they were following. They continued along in that direction for a short time longer and then the long grass and weeds opened up to reveal a clearing.

"Our camp," said Gavo, sliding down from his mount's back and handing the reins to a young man who came to take the animal for a rub down.

Bellicus looked around with a critical eye but found nothing to complain about. Gavo truly was a marvel, he thought.

The Damnonii rebels' camp had a small cooking fire but it was set beneath a couple of trees so the smoke was dissipated. On top of that, the place was impossible to spot from the road unless one knew what they were looking for, and with the trees and the bulk of the hill at their backs the elements would not be too much of an inconvenience.

"We have sentries posted above," Gavo told them, pointing upwards to the rocky face of the hill that rose over them. "And on the roads leading here." He smiled. "So you can make yourselves at home without fear of being attacked, lads. Oh, sorry, I mean, my lord *Merlin*."

"Piss off, Gavo," Bellicus laughed, allowing Darac to be led away by another man who seemed like he wouldn't be much use in a battle but was more than capable of looking after the horses. Everyone had a part to play, and taking care of the horses, cooking meals, or keeping lookout was every bit as important as standing in the shieldwall.

"Ah, it's good to have you home, Bel. And you two," Gavo said, his usual bluff mask momentarily slipping to reveal an insecurity and even fear that Bellicus had never seen before on the experienced soldier. It was a little unsettling, and even upsetting, for the druid counted Gavo as one of his closest friends. To see him so worried was not pleasant.

"It's good to be home," Bellicus said earnestly, reaching out to grasp Gavo's arm in the timeless, warrior's grip. "Have no fears, old friend. Drest and Horsa will be put in their place soon."

It was as if Gavo had felt the weight of command bearing down on him unbearably, like Atlas with the entire world upon his ageing shoulders, but, now that he had men of his own rank — higher! — to look to, that weight had been shifted. Shared, rather than carried by himself alone.

"I've got some good men with me," the captain told them as they took up positions near the fire, smells of smoke and broth filling the air around them. "Sentica, you remember him? Well, he's been my second-in-command."

"Where is he?" Bellicus asked, accepting a bowl of the broth from another young man who was little more than a beardless boy.

"He's taken the main body of our army further up the hill. This place isn't big enough for everyone but if I keep some men here we can quickly move to protect the main road if any of Drest's patrols come along and try to ride up here."

Once they were all furnished with food and drink they chatted amiably, the newcomers filling in Gavo on everything that had happened at the druid Moot. He spat into the fire in disgust when Koriosis related the tale of Hengist's attack and Nemias's death.

"The sea-wolves are truly a curse on these lands," the captain said, staring morosely into the dancing flames. "Without them to back him up Drest would not be here now, and Alt Clota would be at peace."

"Well, at least our brothers and sisters recognise their threat now," Bellicus said. "They elected me as the new Merlin because I promised to do what I could to remove the Saxons from these shores once and for all."

Gavo looked at him thoughtfully, his earlier jocularity at Bellicus's new title gone, for now. "It's a grand thing that the Merlin of Britain is from the Damnonii tribe," he said. "But what exactly can you do, Bel? I mean, that you couldn't do before?"

"Well, I'm not entirely sure myself," Bellicus admitted with a rueful smile. "I've only been High Druid for a few days and, well, no-one really gave me any training!" He sighed, looking down into his ale cup sorrowfully. "It would have been nice to speak with Nemias about all this. He was a good man, and a good friend."

Koriosis nodded. "I only met Nemias a couple of times. Once, when he visited the novice druids being trained on Iova, and then again at the Moot. He struck me as a very wise man, but strong too. He will be missed."

Duro murmured agreement but he turned to Bellicus and clapped him on the arm. "You'll do a good job too, my friend, I'm certain of it. You just need to learn the ropes."

154

"Oh, I'm sure he'll do a good job too," Gavo put in. "I've been around you long enough to know that. But, I go back to my original question: What kind of power do you wield now that you're Merlin?"

"Well, I can decide when to call a Moot, I can guide the training the novices receive, I can allocate druids to settlements...." He shrugged. "Most importantly I can guide the Order when it comes to what we should be focusing our influence upon. So, for now, I suggested the druids guide the kings and warlords they serve to begin taking the Saxon threat more seriously and, ultimately, to do something about it." He smiled sheepishly. "I guess I'll find out more when I head south to join Arthur and I can summon the druid council to come and help me ease into my new role. We were in such a hurry to get back here to help you fight Drest that I never had time to really ask anyone what my duties, or powers, would be."

Gavo took all this in and then, eventually, his brows drew together and he said, "When you go south? What do you mean, you'll join Arthur?"

"That was a condition placed on whoever became the new Merlin," Koriosis said. "Since the Saxons *are* such a danger to us all, it was agreed that whoever is High Druid should serve beside Arthur, just as Nemias did."

"And you agreed to that?" Gavo demanded, clearly upset.

"I had to," Bellicus said apologetically. "Or Qunavo would have been elected as Merlin, and he has no appetite to defeat the Saxons. Quite the opposite. It would have been a disaster for us here in Alt Clota if that happened, so...I had to agree to join Arthur."

"Shit," Gavo muttered, reaching out and helping himself to a refill from the jug of ale that sat on the ground near the fire. "I don't like this Bel, and neither will Catia, or Narina."

"You won't be left without a druid," Bellicus told him. "I can make sure of that now. Gods, I could even have Koriosis placed back in Alt Clota."

The younger druid's face split in a massive grin at that suggestion.

Gavo's dour expression did not mirror Koriosis's, however. "Nothing against the young man," he said. "But you're part of the land up here now Bel, even though you've just turned, what, thirty? Everyone knows you, including our enemies. Life just won't be the same if you leave."

Bellicus was genuinely touched. Gavo was not normally so forthcoming about his feelings — to know the captain cared about him so much was a pleasant feeling.

"All of that's in the future," the druid told him, smiling in gratitude at the kind words. "No point worrying about it now. We still have an army to dislodge from Dun Breatann, remember? Let's get that sorted, and then we can see what's to be done about the Merlin."

"All right, fine," Gavo said. "I like the sound of that. Now…How the hell do we get rid of Drest's army? Any ideas?"

Bellicus looked from Gavo to his other two companions and shrugged. "Not yet, but something will come to us. Have faith in the gods, my friends — Alt Clota will be free again, I'm sure of it."

"Well, if you say so," said Duro with a glint in his eye. "You are the Merlin after all."

CHAPTER TWENTY-EIGHT

Unfortunately, no good ideas or good news came to Bellicus and the other Damnonii warriors camped out around Dun Buic cairn. Drest's men continued to forage in the area, stealing food, supplies, weapons, and anything else they wanted from Narina's towns and villages. Twice Gavo's scouts spotted enemy patrols and a warband was sent to engage them. Both skirmishes ended in victory for the Damnonii warriors but not without taking casualties of their own.

For the most part, it seemed like Drest was content to simply wait at Dun Breatann until Narina ran out of supplies or decided she had no way to defeat the enemy army and surrendered.

Sentica had been involved in both of the engagements with Drest's patrols and, although happy to have emerged victorious, the sight of his comrades being cut down, along with the earlier experiences in the burnt-out villages, had taken a toll on him. Not just Sentica either, most of the soldiers in Gavo's army were disillusioned, and frightened of what was in store for them. The morale boost that Bellicus's return had provided soon wore off and despair started to wind its thorny tendrils around the Damnonii troops.

"Are there no more soldiers on the way to join us?" Koriosis asked one afternoon. It was extremely hot and humid and most of the men in the camp were lounging around, bored. A thunderstorm seemed to be building, and Bellicus had suggested the two druids perform a ritual to beg for Taranis's aid since a storm was always a time of great power but, for now, even Bellicus was lying on his back on the grass, watching the clouds build.

"I had expected more to come," Gavo admitted. "But they'd have been here by now." He heaved out an exasperated breath. "Either many of our men simply didn't answer Narina's call and have remained in their homes, or they tried to come to Dun Breatann and were attacked on the road by Drest's patrols. Regardless, the numbers we have are all we're going to get, unless the gods themselves send us more."

"We definitely need more?" Koriosis asked somewhat meekly.

"Aye, we do," Gavo replied. "Drest still has us outnumbered, unfortunately."

"Don't forget, Bel sent Lancelot and Bedwyr to ask Arthur for reinforcements," Duro said. "If they turn up with even a hundred men, that will turn the tide in our favour. We'll be able to take the fight to Drest, rather than just hitting his patrols or mounting sneak attacks."

Indeed, the sneak attacks were not proving very successful at this stage of the war. The Picts and the Saxons had grown wary and were placing more guards around their camp, and even on the roads close to Dun Breatann. Indeed, Gavo had been most downhearted two days before when he'd sent out fifteen of his men to launch a missile attack on the northern edge of Drest's encampment. Not one of the fifteen men had returned from the mission and it became abundantly clear what had happened to them when a Damnonii scout discovered fifteen severed heads set up on spears lining the road near Dun Buic.

It had been a shocking discovery — not simply because the Damnonii dead had been so horrifically violated, but because the location of their decapitated heads proved that Drest knew where Gavo's army was encamped. The Pictish king might not have done anything about it yet, probably because he was wary after the Saxons were ambushed on the road there, but an attack might come at any moment. There was more than one way to reach Gavo's camp after all.

That afternoon, a rider from the east did not need to hunt for a hidden way to their camp, though. He was escorted up to the clearing by two of Gavo's men and Bellicus immediately recognised him as the leader of the militia at Carden Ros.

"It's good to see you again," the druid said and then, pleasantries out of the way, asked, "What brings you here, friend?"

The middle-aged villager accepted a cup of ale from Gavo who also knew the man, having served with him more than once over the years.

"A message for you, my lords," the man said. "From down south."

"Sit," Bellicus said, gesturing to one of the logs that lay by the small campfire. It was not cold at all, but still the fire was always the focal point of the camp and the man from Carden Ros gladly dropped onto the log and stretched out his legs, grimacing as he did so.

"I'm not used to riding much these days," he admitted ruefully. "But I knew you'd want to hear this as soon as possible. Or maybe not..."

"Go on," said Gavo. "What's happened?"

"A ship put in at Carden Ros this morning," the messenger said. "On board was a merchant we know well in the village. He brings us things from time to time — glass, furs, spices, trinkets, you know the kind of thing I mean."

Bellicus nodded, masking his impatience and ignoring the urge to tell the man to get on with it.

"Anyway," the messenger said after taking a long pull of his ale. "This merchant carried more than just his usual wares on this voyage. He brought word from Arthur for you, Bellicus."

One of the young cooks came and handed the man a platter with roasted meat and some buttered bread on it and his attention immediately turned to that.

"Will you get on with it?" Gavo demanded in such an imperious tone that the messenger practically jumped off the log.

Sheepishly, the man swallowed the piece of beef he'd started chewing and nodded apologetically. "Of course, my lord," he said, then spoke again to Bellicus. "Arthur sends word that he was devastated to hear of the death of his friend Nem..."

"Nemias," Bellicus broke in.

"That's it," the messenger agreed. "He was devastated to hear of Nemias's death, but he is glad you will be the new Merlin. Is that right?" he asked Bellicus. "Did I remember the message right?"

"Aye," Duro said. "But there must have been more, was there not?"

"I'm afraid so," the messenger nodded, looking around at them glumly. "Arthur also says he's sorry, but he can't send any men to reinforce the Damnonii army."

"Ah, shit," Duro muttered, and Gavo voiced a similar sentiment.

"Why not?" Bellicus asked with a sinking feeling in his guts. He'd been praying Lancelot and Bedwyr would come riding into Alt Clota at the head of a warband that would swing things in their

159

favour. The knowledge that no reinforcements were coming was a crushing blow to Bellicus's plans.

"Arthur has been beset himself by the Saxons this spring," the messenger reported, concentrating hard on what he'd memorised, not wanting to get any of his message wrong. "Hengist's army has grown somehow, and the *bretwalda* has pushed further," he paused, chewing his lip as he recalled the words of the merchant, "west, that's it, Hengist has pushed further west than ever before." He leaned back, obviously relieved to have delivered his message. "So, we're on our own, eh, my lords?"

"Shit," Duro repeated, slapping his leg in disappointment. "This is not good. Not good at all."

"It could be worse," Koriosis said, eyebrows raised, lips pursed.

"Eh?" Duro and Gavo both demanded at the same time. "How?"

"Well, Hengist could be coming here to help Horsa instead of remaining in the south to fight Arthur."

"Oh, let's all praise the gods for that small mercy," Duro muttered, throwing the young druid a black look.

Bellicus couldn't help laughing at their exchange. "He's right though. We're no worse off than we were this morning. And at least we know now that we're on our own."

"Has that useless bastard Ysfael not asked for reinforcements from his da?" Duro demanded. "Surely Cunedda would want to protect his son, even if he is a worthless prick."

Gavo shrugged. "Messengers have been sent, of course, but…" He looked around, and even lifted a branch to peer under it theatrically. "I don't see any sign of Votadini reinforcements."

"Cunedda will be happy to let us fight it out with Drest," Bellicus said. "Weaken us both so we're less of a threat to him, and possibly even susceptible to an invasion attempt by his own forces once it's all over."

"By Mithras, does it never end?" Duro scowled into the fire. "We just seem to lurch from one battle, one war, to the next."

"You'd be bored if we didn't," Bellicus replied with a chuckle. "Admit it."

Duro did smile at his friend's accusation but his frown soon returned. "No, I'm not sure I would be. Not any more. I've just about had enough of fighting."

"What, even if you get a chance to kill Horsa?" Gavo asked. "'Cause there's a very good chance we're going to come up against him sooner or later."

Duro drew his spatha from its scabbard and held it out so the shining, oiled steel reflected the dancing firelight. "No, I'll gladly fight on until that whoreson is dead at least," he vowed, thoughtfully sighting along the blade. "But the way things are going it might be us who end up as food for the worms."

"Have faith," said Koriosis, still attempting to be positive despite his earlier attempt earning only derision. "We have the Merlin with us after all. The gods will provide for us."

"They will indeed," Bellicus proclaimed, getting to his feet and stretching to work out a stiffness that had set into his neck. "To that end, brother, I think we should perform a ritual to win the gods' favour. What d'you think?"

Koriosis stood too, eyes flashing eagerly at the thought. "I think it's a great idea," he said. "At the cairn?"

Bellicus opened his mouth to reject the younger druid's suggestion — the cairn was a place of much death and sacrifices to the darkest of the old gods. A place steeped in aeons of sinister magic and haunted by the shades of those whose bodies had been viciously carved open by the stone knives of Bellicus's predecessors. But then the new Merlin realised that such a place was the ideal setting for their proposed ritual. If he and Koriosis could harness the energy that still swirled around the cairn, the gods could not possibly fail to hear their supplications. It was perfect, although admittedly somewhat daunting as well.

"Let's do it," he said to Koriosis. "We'll go now and make things ready for nightfall. You have an animal we can take with us?" he asked Gavo.

"I'll have one brought to the cairn," said the captain. "A chicken? Sheep?"

"A decent sized fowl will do," Bellicus replied after some thought. "A dark coloured one, if possible."

"You want us to come with you?" Duro asked, ready to follow his friends if required.

Bellicus shook his head. "No, we'll be able to look after ourselves. And keep Cai here with you." He bent and ruffled the mastiff's ears, saying to it, "Don't worry, boy, you'll get some of the meat when we return."

Cai replied by thumping his tail but seemed to understand he was being left behind so didn't bother to stand up. He was well used to spending time with Duro and the pair watched as Bellicus and Koriosis ascended the road up towards the cairn at the top of the hill.

"You think their ceremony will work?" Gavo asked when the druids had disappeared from sight.

Duro bobbed his head gently. "Aye, I do," he said. "Any time I've known Bel to do something like this there's *some* kind of effect not long after."

Gavo could only agree. "Let's hope that effect goes in our favour," he said, and wandered off to find someone to procure the fowl Bellicus had requested.

CHAPTER TWENTY-NINE

Aife swept up her weapon and parried her opponent's. The impact ran along her arm and she grunted but did not stop moving, twisting her body around and lashing out with her shield. The iron boss struck the enemy in the stomach, winding him, and Aife kicked out, sending the man flying across the grass.

"Ow! By the gods, my lady, go easy."

Aife grinned and tossed the wooden practice sword into the little pile that lay at the edge of the area set out for Drest's warriors to train within. She removed her helmet and shook out her long, chestnut brown hair which was damp with sweat after her exertions. "The Damnonii won't go easy," she replied. "Best you learn that now, before it's too late."

"I think I'd rather face one of them than you," the beaten Pict muttered, pushing himself to his feet. He was about the same age as Aife, maybe twenty summers or so, but not quite as tall as her, and certainly not as experienced in the use of sword and shield.

"Stop complaining and join the rest of your warband," Aife said, laughing to offset her harsh words. Drest had ordered her to help keep the men busy during the interminable, boring hours of the siege, and Aife was happy to oblige. They'd not brought practice swords to Alt Clota but crafting them was another task that gave the warriors something to do while they awaited battle.

At first, when Aife had bested some of the younger recruits, they had been mocked for losing to a girl. That mockery had soon faded when it became clear the princess was more than a match for just about anyone in Drest's army. Those who'd served beside her before knew better than to challenge her and now the rest of the men were learning the same lesson.

Of course, she did not win every bout — there was always someone faster, or stronger, or more skilled than any warrior, but Aife was able to beat the majority of her opponents. Some of the men, even those who were classed as the best fighters by their peers, would not even challenge the princess, knowing it would not do their reputation any good if they lost to her.

A tall man walked towards her now and Aife's stomach gave a little lurch as she recognised Horsa. Would he challenge her? The thought thrilled her, for she would dearly love to smack the big bastard about with one of the practice swords, but she knew he was no unskilled novice. Horsa was relatively young, but he had seen plenty of battles, killed countless men, and there would be absolutely no question of him going easy on Aife if they were to spar. He might even actively seek to injure her; that would certainly be his style. By Taranis, how could her father ally himself to such a man?

His smile was disrespectful as he reached her, mocking even, and he did not stop to challenge her.

"Would you like to spar, Saxon?" she asked, riled by his sneering face. "Pick up a sword and let us see if you can best a woman."

"Later," Horsa replied with apparent indifference, as though he thought her so far beneath him that her challenge could not rile him. "I have more important business to deal with just now."

Aife noticed more Saxons marching behind Horsa now, Jarl Sigarr and Yngvildr among them. She gritted her teeth as she saw the sea-wolves were not alone either — they were escorting men with bruised faces. "More Damnonii prisoners," she growled to herself, wondering what evil fate was in store for this lot.

She hurried after Horsa, glaring up at him as they moved towards the gates of Dun Breatann. "Who are they?" she demanded. "You were warned there was to be no more butchery of innocent victims, Saxon."

He turned and flashed his white teeth at her, seemingly enjoying himself. "These are no innocents," he replied. "They are part of the enemy army that is hiding out in the hills to the north. They attacked one of your father's patrols but," his grin became even wider, "I was hiding in the trees with my men. We rescued your people from a massacre, and captured these Damnonii 'warriors'." His voice was filled with scorn, and not just for the prisoners. "I'm sure your father, and his druids, won't mind Yngvildr sacrificing captured enemy soldiers, eh, girl?"

Again, his tone was scornful and Aife felt her ire rising even further. She stopped walking with him and stood back to allow the Saxons to pass with the prisoners. Her mind was whirling — was she simply too young to fully grasp the realities of war? Why did the thought of executing captured prisoners fill her with disgust and even dread? As prisoners, was their killing really classed as execution? Why was it not simple murder? What made this different to killing civilians? In that instant she hated not just Horsa and Yngvildr, but her own father too.

She watched the frightened captives as they were marched roughly past. Most were aged between twenty and thirty summers she guessed — young men, who'd been captured while trying to defend their own lands from invaders, as any soldier would do.

Drest came striding across from his tent with Qunavo and Ria at his back and Aife hurried to meet them.

"That big bastard has more captives," she blurted before recounting Horsa's version of how the Damnonii warriors had come to be captured.

"And he means to sacrifice them?" Drest said when she was finished. "Well, I don't have a problem with that — they are the enemy. We came here to fight the Damnonii, and to kill those who stood in our way." He shrugged, unable to understand why Aife was so upset.

In truth, the princess was not entirely sure herself. Was she only really bothered because she'd spent so much time in Dun Breatann herself? Had grown to like and admire many of the people there so the thought of butchering them now horrified her? Maybe it was the realisation that, if Horsa and her own father were happy to slaughter Damnonii prisoners, they would certainly do the same to Catia when Dun Breatann was finally captured.

"Look, Aife," Drest said to her coldly, unable or unwilling to recognise the emotions warring within his daughter. "You are a Pictish soldier. A commander. We came here to kill the people of Alt Clota. You have killed men yourself — you're a warrior, not a damn nursemaid. Do your duty, and stop bothering me with your moral dilemmas!"

The king shoved past her and the druids followed him although both gave her sympathetic looks. Clearly, they too were wondering what was in store for the prisoners, and none too happy about anything that was happening.

"The gods enjoy variation, just like any of us," Yngvildr was saying when Aife finally caught up with the Saxons. The Damnonii men had their hands and feet bound and were kneeling on the grass, looking up at the walls of Dun Breatann with pleading expressions on their faces.

Aife could see Narina there and wondered what kind of agony the queen must be feeling. Aife had not grown close to the queen during her time as a prisoner-of-war in the fortress, but she could still feel some empathy with the woman. And then she saw Catia, pale-faced yet somehow more composed than her mother as she stared down on the spectacle below.

This is all wrong, thought Aife. *We should not be working with the very sea-wolves who tried to cut my throat just last year.* They *are the enemy we should be seeking to defeat, not the Damnonii!* What could she do though? She may be a princess, but her mother had been a slave and she'd only risen to her present lofty position within the Pictish army as a result of her martial prowess. She could not halt what Horsa was about to do any more than she could stop the war.

"First," Yngvildr shouted again, "we sacrificed our captured thralls by slitting their throats, allowing their blood to nourish the earth and to please the gods with its metallic taste." She appeared to be talking to the sky rather than the people that had crowded around to watch the show. "Then," she went on in a gleeful tone, "we performed the sacred blood-eagle on those wretches there." She pointed at the tattered, rotting remnants of the men that had been so brutally slaughtered in a way that Aife believed would only offend any decent god, not please them.

"Move aside," Horsa commanded, gesturing to a group of men who stood on the southern side of the camp, between the fortress's gates and the River Clota.

Aife turned like everyone else to see four broad-shouldered Saxons carrying a great barrel towards Yngvildr. The princess wondered where the hell such a huge receptacle had been found but her curiosity faded as she quickly came to understand what it was to be used for.

"This time," Yngvildr screeched, "we shall honour the gods by sending them the souls of these captured Damnonii soldiers using a new method: Drowning!"

Aife felt a tightness in her chest as she imagined being plunged headfirst into that monstrous barrel, being held there by her feet as she desperately fought to somehow break free. Such a death was not unheard of amongst the northern tribes — criminals were sometimes executed in such a fashion. Indeed, Aife remembered hearing a story about Bellicus presiding over such an execution. That victim had abused and murdered a child though — drowning had seemed too good for such a piece of filth.

Murdering prisoners-of-war in that manner…The princess could not convince herself that was anything other than wicked. And then Aife actually recognised one of the men who was due to be drowned and her heart sank.

"Sentica!" she breathed.

CHAPTER THIRTY

"You can't kill him," Aife shouted, charging forward and pushing through the Saxons to stand behind Yngvildr. "He is an honourable man. He..." She trailed off realising everyone was staring at her, including her father who did not look pleased at all. "He treated me well when I was a prisoner in Dun Breatann. He should be similarly well treated." She knew her voice had grown high-pitched and whiny and hated herself for it. So much for Aife the Warrior-Princess, begging now for the life of an enemy soldier.

Sentica was watching her in wonder, the gratitude plain on his face. Tears were in his eyes and he nodded to Aife before Horsa stamped across to stand menacingly before her.

"Get out of the way," the jarl commanded, and any earlier jocularity was long gone. He looked like he might explode into violence at any moment. "I've had enough of you Picts getting in the way with your stupid complaints. We are at war with these bastards." He drew back a meaty hand and slapped Sentica a ringing blow across the face. "They tried to kill your people, and mine, and now they will be executed for it."

"He's right," Drest hissed, coming up behind Aife and gripping her roughly by the arm. "Get out of the way, girl, or I will demote you back to the infantry. You can fight alongside the new levies you're supposed to be training!"

"They at least have some honour and don't murder helpless men in the name of cruel, false gods," the princess retorted but did not fight back as the king dragged her away and ordered two of his hearth-warriors to remove her to someplace she couldn't be a nuisance. They respected the girl, and they also knew she could be extremely dangerous if she chose to be, so they grasped her firmly but without any rancour and guided her to the back of the gathering crowd. "This is all wrong," she railed at them. "We should not be allowing those fucking sea-wolves to murder prisoners like this. Narina clearly isn't being swayed by their barbarism, they're just doing it to be cruel at this point."

The men let go of her arms and gave her some space. From the looks on their faces they had sympathy with Aife's complaints, but they were there to follow orders and, like every other soldier in Drest's army, that was what they would do.

Why should she be any different?

Yngvildr was screeching an imprecation to Thunor now, and a man could be heard bellowing and swearing as he fought against the hands that had upended him over the barrel of river water. Aife was taller than most of the people in the crowd and she was able to see the unfortunate Damnonii warrior being plunged face-first into the water, his cries instantly cut off. She could see his legs still struggling as the man slowly expired and, when his movements had stopped, the Saxons holding him stood back, releasing his legs and allowing his corpse to slump against the side of the barrel.

Yngvildr began her supplications to the gods again, capering about like a madwoman — which she quite clearly was — giggling and singing and dancing as though some wonderful event had just taken place. Horsa too was enjoying himself, his eyes straying from the drowned man's feet to the *volva's* lithe, spinning body with obvious, naked lust. As Aife scanned the crowd of Picts and Saxons she realised Horsa was not the only one so smitten by Yngvildr's looks.

Still, not all of the warriors looked like they were pleased by the sacrifices. As the next of the Damnonii were lifted, screaming threats at first only to beg for mercy once they were about to be dropped into the barrel, Aife saw many of her people turn away, muttering amongst one another unhappily. Most of them were simple farmers, labourers, traders, carpenters or the like, and watching helpless captives being suffocated in a barrel was not what they'd come to Dun Breatann to see. The rules of war were clear, and there for a reason. If the Picts did not treat their prisoners with respect, any of the Picts captured in battle could expect to be treated with similar cruelty. And, given how the last battle at Dun Breatann had turned out, many of the Picts thought it unwise to anger Narina and her people in this manner.

Aife could hear such sentiments being murmured around her, mirroring her own feelings, and she wondered how much longer the siege could go on before something major happened. The Picts would not stand by forever while Horsa and Yngvildr continued to behave as if they were accountable to no-one.

Tears of rage and frustration blurred her vision as she saw the Damnonii guard who'd been kind to her during her time as a political prisoner in Dun Breatann: Sentica. The soldier was not much older than Aife, certainly still in his twenties. He had not gone looking for trouble — he had merely been trying to defend his home against an invading force, yet now it was his turn to feed Yngvildr's terrible sacrificial barrel.

As if sensing her despair, Drest's two hearth-warriors stepped closer to her, ready to restrain her if she tried to stop the ritual. She knew it would be pointless so she stood, forcing herself to watch as Sentica was lifted, struggling and pleading for his life just as the previous victims had done, and then, as he cried out for Aife he was plunged down into the water, his sobs cut off in a terrible bubbling. The princess mouthed a silent prayer to her own gods, begging them to ease his suffering and terror as soon as possible, and to guide his soul into the afterlife where he might be reborn at a later date.

Sentica's struggles lasted longer than the two who'd been drowned before him, and Aife felt her rage and despair building until finally, mercifully, the Damnonii guard's convulsions stopped and the Saxons let go of his legs.

Drest did not seem concerned overmuch by the horror he was witnessing. He had obviously convinced himself that his enemies deserved their fate, even if a sizeable number of his own men disagreed.

Aife did not want to watch any more. The terrified cries of the victims would haunt her dreams that night she knew, and, since she could do nothing for them, there seemed little point in watching them expire. "You can return to the king," she told the hearth-warriors, turning and walking towards her own tent. "I've seen enough of this."

If only she could force Drest to fight this war as their people had always done, man to man, woman to woman, without resorting to Saxon rituals. Aife knew there was no chance she could make her father see sense though, and, being only young she had not yet gained the respect of enough of the Pictish warriors to ask them to follow her. That thought shocked her — would she truly rebel against her own father?

It did not matter whether she would or not, for she could never garner enough support to do it. She would surely need others with more influence to do that.

The sound of another prisoner's frightened cries made her turn around and she stopped in her tracks, noticing two more people with expressions just as dark as hers walking towards her, deep in conversation with one another.

"Qunavo," she said as the druid reached her without even noticing she was watching them. "Ria. You two don't approve of this abomination either, I'm guessing."

Qunavo met her gaze and muttered an oath. "Approve of this? A Pictish army sacrificing men to Saxon gods?" He shook his head indignantly.

"Your father's lost his mind," Ria added quietly. "He's always been weak and easily led, but this…This, as you rightly called it, Aife, is an abomination. Our gods will not look on him, or this army, with favour after this."

"Agreed," Aife said, turning and striding towards her tent again, gesturing the mystics to follow her. She pushed through the flaps and poured large cups of ale for them all, handing them to Qunavo and Ria then downing her own. It wasn't just a drink she needed though, she could do with a bath to wash off the taint of Yngvildr, Horsa, and their war crimes. "What can we do about this?" she asked fiercely. "Drest won't listen to me, the bastard daughter of a slave."

"He hasn't listened to us either," said Ria gloomily, sipping at her ale without much relish.

"He's not strong enough to stand against Horsa," Qunavo grumbled. "But if someone doesn't, Alt Clota will end up nothing but a burnt-out shell populated by wraiths, and this entire war will have been for naught. I'm beginning to realise that Bellicus was right about the Saxons all along."

"They still need paid as well," Aife sighed, dropping onto a stool and staring at the bubbles in her ale. "We've emptied our treasury to hire Horsa's warriors, but we'll have no way to refill it for years without men and women to work the land in Alt Clota even if we win the war."

171

"You are assuming Horsa will allow Drest to become king here," Ria said in a low voice. "After what we've seen of the sea-wolf, I'm not so sure."

"You think he'll want Dun Breatann, and Alt Clota, for himself?" Aife asked. "That he'll betray my father?"

"Don't you?" Ria returned.

The three sat in thoughtful silence, nursing their drinks and then, eventually, their eyes met and Qunavo said, "Something has to be done."

"The gods help me," nodded Aife. "It pains me to go against my own father, my own king, but you're right." She swallowed her second cup of ale and, fortified by the drink and her own righteous anger, asked the old druid, "What do you have in mind?"

* * *

Sigarr licked his lips and wished he had a horn of mead or even just water in his hands for his mouth was dry and he feared his voice would crack when he spoke. He stood within Horsa's tent, his cousin seated on a stool while Sigarr stood. The *volva,* Yngvildr, was not there for this was to be a meeting between the two jarls. Sigarr had asked for it, but he was regretting it now, fearing Horsa's vicious temper might see this conversation descending into an argument, or even worse, violence.

Sigarr could not hope to defend himself from his cousin yet, even so, he knew he could not hold his peace any longer. The success of their mission might depend on what was said at this meeting.

"Horsa," he began, swallowing and trying to push aside the anxiety that assailed him. By Wotan, what was he? A thrall? No, he was a jarl, and he shared the same blood as Hengist and Horsa – he must act like it! "Horsa, you need to stop these sacrifices."

It came out in a rush and he stared at his cousin, trying not to cringe away from the blow that he expected might come.

Horsa surprised him for once.

"Why?" he asked simply.

"You saw the effect it had on the princess, Aife. She has influence, Horsa. I do not think it wise to antagonise her."

The big man stood up and poured himself a cup of ale from a jug on a trestle table, not bothering to ask Sigarr if he would like one. He sipped it, staring at the smaller jarl as he did so.

"You are in charge, of course," Sigarr said, frightened by the unexpectedly calm response he was getting to his request. "But Hengist sent me to look at things from a different perspective than you would do. You are a mighty warrior, and you think like one. I think more like a"—

"Like a coward," Horsa broke in, lip curling in a sneer as he drank off the last of his ale and slammed the cup down on the table.

Sigarr stared at him, but he could not deny the accusation for he was feeling terribly frightened at that moment. This campaign against the Damnonii people seemed to have brought out the worst in Horsa. He had always been brutal, treating enemies cruelly, but the past few days seemed to have turned him into something even more frightening. Perhaps it was the baleful influence of the *volva* who was clearly moon-touched. Whatever it was, Horsa did not seem very interested in Sigarr's advice.

"You are a craven, whining cur," Horsa said in a low voice that made the hairs on the back of Sigarr's neck stand on end.

"This has nothing to do with my bravery," the little jarl protested, feeling his breath begin to catch, the old familiar wheeze making it hard for him to think straight. "Besides, if I'm such a coward, why am I here just now? It was obvious you would get angry with me, yet here I am anyway." He gave a sickly smile and even Horsa's mouth twitched as though he grudgingly admitted the truth in his cousin's argument.

"We are waging a war here," Horsa murmured, pouring himself more ale and, surprisingly, even pouring a cup for Sigarr who took it gratefully and drank deeply, swishing the liquid around in his dry mouth.

"We are hated by our enemies," Sigarr said, gesturing in the direction of Dun Breatann's great rock. "The Damnonii despise us, which is only natural. We are an invading army after all." He felt himself relax a little as his cousin sat down again, listening quite intently to him. "But I fear we are turning some of our own allies against us. You've seen Aife railing against you and Yngvildr."

173

"Her own father has put her in her place," Horsa spat, waving a hand dismissively. "She is as weak as you, Sigarr. If anyone is going to cost us the war, it's the likes of you and Aife."

"Armies live and die on their morale," Sigarr argued, growing frustrated. How could Horsa be so dense, when Hengist was wise and clever? "Many of the Picts think like Aife, and they do not like us brutalising the Damnonii prisoners in the name of our Gods. All I'm saying is you should stop the sacrifices. Be as vicious as you like when the fighting finally starts."

Horsa actually seemed to be taking on board Sigarr's points. He might not have accepted them fully, but he had not angrily dismissed them out of hand or simply kicked his cousin out of the tent. They were conversing like rational adults and sharing a drink together, and Sigarr felt buoyed by the way things were going.

"What's he doing here?"

The tent flaps were pushed roughly aside and Yngvildr came striding in as if she were Queen of Alt Clota and all the surrounding lands belonged to her. She stared at Sigarr as she walked past him and bent to kiss Horsa full on the lips. The big jarl returned the kiss forcefully, his right hand reaching up to grasp the *volva's* breast as he dragged her down onto his lap.

Sigarr stared at them, emotions warring within as he felt disgust at their animalistic display, but also lust. Yngvildr's figure would rouse the blood of any man, and jealousy bubbled within Sigarr, wishing he was the tall, commanding cousin instead of the physically weak one, who lost his breath simply climbing into bed.

Horsa growled like a wolf as he took his lips from Yngvildr's and gestured at Sigarr. "He wants us to stop sacrificing people. Says we're turning the Picts against us and ruining the morale of the army."

Yngvildr gave a short bark of laughter and curled her exquisite lip at the smaller jarl. "Why are you even here?" she demanded. "You are no warrior. You serve no purpose. Even the camp whores are more use than you."

"I am a jarl," Sigarr retorted through gritted teeth, incensed at being spoken to in such a way by the crazed *volva*. "You are a madwoman who has bewitched Horsa and use him now to your own ends. You will be the ruin of us all!"

Only when the words had gushed out of him did Sigarr realise his mistake. For once he had allowed himself to be baited and lose his temper and all the good work he'd done during the earlier conversation with Horsa was undone in that moment.

Yngvildr stood up, hand resting on her knife as she eyed Sigarr as though he might be her next sacrifice to Thunor.

Horsa had also stood up and his previous good humour had evaporated. "You think me so weak that I can be manipulated by a mere woman?" he roared, great voice filling the tent and making Sigarr cringe back involuntarily.

"She will be the ruin of us all," the little jarl repeated.

"Send him away," Yngvildr grated. "I am bored listening to his whining. He is worse than the Pictish bitch and will be even less use when we finally meet the enemy army in battle."

Horsa looked at her and then at Sigarr and it was clear he did not want it to seem like he was taking orders from the *volva*. But she reached out and put her hand on his manhood, rubbing gently and begging him to send Sigarr away and take her to bed again.

There could only ever be one outcome in that situation.

"Get out, you little shit," Horsa commanded in a low, dangerous voice. "You have done nothing but complain since we set out from Garrianum and I have had enough of it. Get out of my tent, and leave the camp this very day."

"What?" Sigarr was stunned. "Leave? And go where?"

"I care little for where you crawl to you cowardly bastard. You can take a horse and ride back to Hengist for all I care, or ride for Mucrois and sail the ship with Drest's payment to Garrianum. At least then you would be doing something worthwhile."

Sigarr opened his mouth to protest again but he knew the look he was getting from his cousin. He had seen that look before and it always presaged terrible violence.

Without another word or a backward glance, the jarl left the tent, cringing every step of the way as he half expected his cousin's seax to hammer into his back.

When he was outside he ignored the amused, mocking glances from the Saxons gathered there who'd obviously heard everything that had been said. Face flushing scarlet, Sigarr strode past them and went to his own tent, packing up his clothes, weapons, and enough food and drink to last him a few days at least. Then he went outside to his horse, loaded it up, and without a word to anyone, rode east to Mucrois.

CHAPTER THIRTY-ONE

"There's a warband on the road nearby."

Gavo looked up in consternation at the report from one of the lookouts. He'd not seen or heard from Sentica in two days and he was growing increasingly worried for his second-in-command. Where could he be? The sergeant had engaged some of Drest's men and both sides had suffered losses but Sentica's body had not been amongst the fallen, and some of the others who'd been with him were also unaccounted for. Had they gone hunting some of the enemy, perhaps chasing them off towards the border with Dalriada? If so, they would hopefully return soon, and Sentica would get a furious dressing down from Gavo for such a foolhardy action.

That scenario was far more desirable than anything else that Gavo's imagination had been conjuring up over the past couple of days though...

He heard the lookout shuffling his feet as he waited for Gavo to come out of his daydream and forced himself to come back to the present. "A warband? Whose?"

"Looks like Picts, my lord. There's not many of them, and they don't seem to be doing much."

Bellicus and Duro came to join him and the captain frowned. "What d'you mean? What are they doing?"

"Just riding slowly up and down the road," the lookout reported. "It's almost as if they want to draw us out."

"How many are there?" Duro asked.

"Not many, centurion," the man said. "Only six. And one of them's a woman."

Now all the men were frowning, wondering what was happening.

"A woman?"

"Aye, Merlin," the lookout said, almost stumbling over the unfamiliar title he'd been told belonged to Bellicus now. "A big woman. Dressed like a warrior, and I'd say she knows how to use the sword at her waist just as well as any of us."

The druid's face lit up and he turned to his companions. "A female warrior, and a Pict at that," he said. "Now who might that be?"

"Aife?" Gavo murmured. "Is this some trap of Drest's? Why would he send Aife to ride about near where he knows we're camped?"

"Maybe he wants to draw us out?" Duro said, gazing thoughtfully towards Dun Breatann although even the massive bulk of the fortress could not be seen through the foliage that surrounded their camp. "He'll know we grew friendly with the princess and might expect us to meet her."

"Then he springs his trap," said Gavo, punching his fist into his palm.

"You think Aife would be a part of that?" Bellicus asked uncertainly.

"She's a Pict at the end of the day," Gavo nodded. "And Drest's daughter. So, aye, I don't see why not."

"It's possible she doesn't even realise she's being used as bait for a trap," Duro said. He greatly admired Aife and, it seemed, shared the druid's scepticism over her willingness to ambush the Damnonii commanders.

Bellicus still looked doubtful. He'd travelled with the princess, and he knew she was an honourable warrior — still, it made sense to be careful. "I'll head down there with Duro," he said. "We'll show ourselves to Aife and her warband and we'll see what she has to say. If there's any trouble, we'll come back up here through the trees so the Picts' horses won't be any use to them."

"I'll send a few men with you," Gavo said. "They can hide in the trees and make sure you get back here alive."

Bellicus nodded and looked at Duro who seemed quite happy with the plan and was already strapping on his centurion's breastplate, greaves and crested helmet.

The High Druid glanced down at Cai who was staring back at him with an expression that said, 'don't you dare leave me behind again', and Bellicus laughed. "All right," he said, leaning down and hugging the mastiff's head. "You can come too. I'm sure Aife will be happy to see you."

"What about me?" asked Koriosis, clearly feeling a little left out. He'd been trained to fight during his apprenticeship but he didn't have the experience of the other men and Bellicus didn't want to risk losing the young druid.

"You wait here for now," Duro said, before Bellicus could speak. "The men will have need of a druid if anything happens to Bel."

Koriosis accepted that, for it made perfect sense and allowed him to keep his pride intact, and so Bellicus, Duro, and Cai began making their way down the wooded slope towards the main road. Gavo summoned a handful of men and told them to remain hidden within the trees, doing nothing unless Aife's riders attacked.

It was harder going than they'd expected, for the slope was very steep and they were forced to slip and slide and grab hold of the undergrowth to make sure they weren't injured.

"By Mithras, no wonder the Picts have never tried to sneak up here to attack us," Duro grumbled, rubbing his backside after falling on it for the third time.

"Exactly why Gavo chose this as his campsite," Bellicus said, laughing at his friend's scrabbling and swearing. "At least it'll be easier going back up the way."

"Sod that," the centurion retorted. "Unless we're attacked, I'll just walk back up the path."

Cai seemed to have all the agility of a mountain goat and he at least made the descent without much trouble, tail wagging, mouth open as if he too was grinning at Duro's discomfort.

At last the trio made it to the bottom and the men brushed pieces of broken branches, leaves, and dust from their clothing as Cai relieved himself on a patch of nettles. The road was just visible through the trees but it seemed to be deserted, for now at least, and Bellicus led them forwards warily, senses straining for signs of danger.

It did not take long before they heard the sounds of hooves thumping on the old road and they made sure they were well concealed, hands on staff and spatha as the riders drew closer.

Sure enough, as the lookout reported, there were six people on horseback, and the leader was a woman. She wore a helmet that covered much of her face although hazel eyes could be seen scanning the terrain as they rode towards the hidden watchers. Cai's tail started to wag as he recognised her, either from her appearance or from her scent, but the dog was too well trained to bound out into the road to greet an old friend.

At least they knew exactly who they were dealing with now, though.

Bellicus examined the other riders with Aife, not recognising any of them but agreeing with the lookout's assertion that they were Picts. Their gear, weapons, and even physical appearance told Bellicus they were Drest's people rather than Horsa's and they were all high-ranking men who would be handy in a fight.

The druid glanced at Duro, who nodded, and the pair stepped out into the road just before Aife reached their hiding place. Cai obediently remained where he was behind a tree, alert for any threat to his master or the centurion.

"Ah," said Aife, smiling in satisfaction as she drew her trotting horse to a halt just a few feet from the towering druid. "There you are. I was hoping you'd be back in Alt Clota by now. Well met, Bel. Duro." She appeared genuinely happy to see them but her eyes scanned the terrain all around, searching for danger or, perhaps…. "Cai!" she laughed, and jumped nimbly down from her horse, kneeling in the road as the mastiff came barrelling out of the trees towards her.

The soldiers with her grasped their weapons in alarm at the sight of the enormous war-dog, but Aife had her arms around Cai's neck and the animal's wildly wagging tail proclaimed him emphatically a friend.

At last she stood up, still grinning as if the sight of Cai had brought her more joy than anything else in weeks, and then she turned to the druid again. "It's genuinely good to see you three again," she told them, happiness quickly fading. "But I have some terrible news."

Bellicus and Duro shared worried glances. Terrible news? As if things weren't bad enough already.

"You mean worse news than finding your father had allied himself with the Saxon scum who murdered my wife? Worse news than seeing Alt Clota being ravaged by Picts and Saxons?" Duro might have a lot of time for the princess, but he could not hide his anger at everything that had been happening. As an honorary Damnonii, the state of Narina's kingdom bothered him as much as it did Gavo or Bellicus.

Aife blanched at his ire but bowed her head apologetically. "I had no idea Horsa killed your wife, Duro, I'm sorry to hear it. As for the rest, well, I advised my father not to start another war, and certainly not to trust the Saxons to be useful mercenaries." She shrugged. "You are both warriors. You were in the legions, Duro. You know how it works — the commander gives an order and we follow, whether we like it or not."

Duro grunted but looked at least somewhat mollified.

"What bad news?" Bellicus prompted her. He was terrified that something had happened to Narina or Catia although his training allowed him to mask his fear.

"Sentica," the princess replied.

"Dead?" Duro asked softly.

"Sacrificed," Aife said, looking at the druid. "Drowned by the *volva,* Yngvildr."

"Yngvildr!" Bellicus could well remember the wise-woman from the last time they'd met when she'd stabbed Eburus to death and then run for her life, only just escaping Bellicus's retribution by jumping into a boat, the River Celefyn carrying her to safety.

"That crazy bitch is still in these lands?" Duro asked incredulously.

"Aye. We met her on the road here and Horsa took her into his warband. The pair are lovers now, if you needed any more reason to feel disgusted about things."

"Gods below," Bellicus murmured. "That is truly a match made in the Christians' Hell."

"What happened to Sentica?" Duro asked. "He was a fine young man, a good officer, and a good companion."

"I know," Aife agreed. "He was kind to me when I was imprisoned within Dun Breatann. It sickened me to see him being…murdered by the *volva* and her Saxon lackeys." She sighed and bent to stroke Cai again. "They drowned him in a great barrel, and there was nothing I could do to help him. My father had me removed, forcibly, from the ceremony because I was causing so much trouble. I'm sorry."

"It's not your fault," Bellicus said. "And we thank you for letting us know. Gavo has been worried since Sentica disappeared a couple of days ago. At least now we can stop wondering where he is."

181

"All these people dead," Duro said, his gaze travelling from Aife to the Picts who rode with her. "For what? So Drest can call himself king of Alt Clota? Is it worth all this suffering?"

"To him it is," Aife said defensively. "This all started four years ago when Coroticus—"

"Aye, we know," Bellicus broke in. "No need to go over old ground again. It's not your fault, and we appreciate you bringing us the news about Sentica. I won't ask if he died well — I think we would rather not know the details. But surely you didn't come here just to tell us about our comrade?"

Aife looked around and, for once, her unshakeable confidence seemed to waver before she took a breath and stood up straight. "Many of us in the army are not happy with what's being done," she said. "This is not the first time Yngvildr has sacrificed Damnonii prisoners to her vile gods."

"It's not?" Bellicus had no idea. If Gavo had known about it, he'd not told them.

"It's the third time," Aife said. "The first time the *volva* slit their throats right in front of the gates of Dun Breatann as Narina and Catia stood watching."

Bellicus clenched his fist, remembering what the men at Carden Ros had reported about tortured screams carrying to them along the Clota, but he said nothing.

"Then Horsa brought more captives from one of the nearby villages and blood-eagled them."

Duro and Bellicus both gasped, having heard of this horrific execution method although neither man had ever believed it to more than a myth.

"Gods," Aife added, shaking her head. "Even Horsa's own kinsman, Jarl Sigarr, counselled him to tone down his cruelty, but he listens to no one."

"Are Qunavo and Ria with your army?" the druid demanded, rage twisting his features.

"They are now. And they've argued with my father over the sacrifices, telling him we shouldn't be a part of such barbarism. Qunavo even admitted that you'd been right all along about the Saxons."

Bellicus's fury died down a little at least and he nodded. "I'm glad to hear that. But still, all this sounds horrific and merely kindles my desire to see your army defeated even further. What about that jarl, Sigarr? Could we use him in some way?"

Aife shook her head. "Horsa got fed up with him and sent him away. Shame, of all the Saxons, Sigarr was the most civilized."

Bellicus examined her, noting her slumped shoulders and sorrowful expression. "Why did you come here, Aife," he wondered. "Really?"

Again, the princess looked sheepish, and her youth had never been more apparent to the druid.

"I, we, need your help, Bel. I can't openly revolt against my father but neither can I stand by any more and allow the Saxons to brutalise innocent people. The Saxons are our enemies, far more than your Damnonii, and Qunavo and Ria agree with me."

Duro snorted and Bellicus raised his eyebrows in surprise.

"Oh, they do, do they?" asked the druid. "They didn't seem to hate the Saxons so much at our Moot. They were gloating about Dun Breatann being besieged by your father and Horsa in fact."

Aife laughed humourlessly. "That doesn't surprise me," she admitted. "But I think they've been as shocked as I have at the sights they've seen since joining us. Yngvildr's lunacy has persuaded them that my father's war can't possibly end well. It was Qunavo who suggested I come here today and talk with you." She shook her head bleakly, kicking a pebble across the road. "The Saxons have different beliefs to us, Bel — brutal, barbarous beliefs that are not compatible with ours. And Horsa cannot be trusted."

"Oh, we know that," Bellicus agreed. "But I still don't know what you want me to do?"

"We want you to somehow show Drest that he can't win this war. To show him that the gods of Alt Clota are stronger than the gods of the Saxons. We — Qunavo, Ria, and I — believe that if my father is shown some sign, some omen, he will renounce the alliance with the Saxons. He's on the verge of that already for Horsa is an easy man to hate. Drest just needs a push over the edge."

Bellicus looked baffled by her request. What on earth did she expect him to do — conjure a dragon and burn Yngvildr to cinders with its fiery breath?

"Who are these men with you?" he asked, ignoring his doubts for the moment.

"The most trusted members of my warband," Aife replied, a note of pride in her voice. "They're with us, you can be sure of that."

"So if Bellicus performs some great, impressive magical feat, you and your men — along with Qunavo and Ria — will spread the seeds of doubt throughout the rest of Drest's army?" Duro asked. "Is that about right?"

Aife nodded. "I know it's not going to be easy, but Qunavo says you're now the High Druid of Britain, Bel. The Merlin! If anyone can call down the aid of our gods, according to Qunavo, it's you. What do you say?"

Bellicus looked at Aife, her men, and Duro, and was astonished to see them all watching him with hope in their eyes, as if they fully expected him to perform this miracle the princess had asked for.

He leaned in close to Aife and gestured for her to listen to him. She might trust her men, but Bellicus did not know them and he did not want them to hear his words. He said something to the princess in in a low voice that even Duro could not make out and Aife swallowed when he was finished.

"Will you do that?" Bellicus asked grimly.

For a long moment Aife stared at him, pondering what he'd asked of her and then, at last, she nodded sadly. "I will," she agreed.

"Return to your father's army then," the druid said, nodding in satisfaction. "Go out on patrol tomorrow morning, and bring Drest here, and Horsa too, if you can."

Aife grinned in relief and stood up even straighter, as though a weight had been taken from her broad shoulders. "Is there anything else I can do?"

The druid thought about that, mind working relentlessly for some solution to their problem, and then he leaned in close to her and whispered some instructions.

"Then you think you can do this?" she asked excitedly when he stepped back from her, and she gave Cai one last pat before vaulting onto her horse's back again.

Bellicus spread his arms and bowed to her. "We'll see, my lady. We'll see."

CHAPTER THIRTY-TWO

"Do you really think you can come up with something to persuade Drest to lift his siege and return to his own lands empty-handed?" Duro had great faith in his friend, but, as they watched Aife's riders disappear along the road to Dun Breatann, the centurion couldn't help but think this was a step too far even for Bellicus.

"Maybe," Bellicus said, heading to the east and the road that would carry them back to Gavo's camp without the trouble of retracing their earlier route up the treacherous, overgrown slope.

"How?"

The druid shook his head. "I'm not sure yet, but think about what just happened. Do you think it's a coincidence that Aife came here just after I performed a ritual with Koriosis, asking the thunder god, Taranis, for his help?"

Duro laughed and stared thoughtfully ahead as they began the ascent towards the camp. "That's true," he said. "Your ritual obviously worked — the gods listened to you, and not for the first time since I've known you either."

"We know now that all is not well within Drest's camp. With the gods' help, we can make that unrest even stronger. You know yourself, Duro, an army with morale at rock bottom is much easier to defeat than one that's fully behind their commanders."

"Indeed," the centurion agreed. "I saw it with my legion — even the sight of us, all lined up in formation, was enough to shatter the morale of an enemy army. When that happened our victory was guaranteed, every single time."

"We'll play on the superstitions of our enemies," Bellicus said, becoming lost in thought as they walked up to the camp, Cai happily chasing after a butterfly that somehow kept just out of the mastiff's reach.

"And you believe her about Qunavo and Ria? You really think they've changed their opinion about the Saxons? That they are now ready to bow to your authority over them as Merlin?"

Bellicus pondered that for a long moment before finally nodding. "I know they have been our enemies," he said. "But they are not fools and, if nothing else, they've always been loyal to our Order. I think it quite possible that they've watched the Saxons go

185

about their bloody business and realised that, once Alt Clota falls, Horsa and Hengist will not be finished. The brothers will attack the Picts eventually."

Duro grunted. "Agreed. Whether their motives are noble or not, Qunavo and Ria will want to preserve themselves and the Pictish people. If that means working against Drest," he shrugged, "perhaps that's what they'll do."

That night Koriosis told stories of bravery and loyalty, and the men in Gavo's camp drank and ate double rations. Koriosis and Duro also walked up to the main body of the Damnonii army on the summit of the hill and went among the men, blessing them or offering them words of encouragement. The soldiers had many questions about how the war would progress and the centurion and the young druid did what they could to reassure them that their commanders had things in hand and Dun Breatann would soon be free of the invaders surrounding it. Their reassurances seemed to work, and morale amongst the army was high when the pair returned to the camp further down the slope.

Bellicus could hear Duro and the others talking but he remained on his own in his tent for most of the evening, refusing food and drink and asking to be left alone to commune with the gods. He had as good as promised to find a solution that would help both Aife and the Damnonii people, but, at the moment, he had no idea what form that solution might take.

Cai lay silently, protectively, by his side as night fell and it grew dark inside the tent. Bellicus sat cross-legged on the ground, closed his eyes, and tried to silence the thoughts that were churning like a whirlpool in his head. He had trained for years to go into a trance, learning many of the basic techniques from Qunavo, and he had utilised those skills numerous times since, yet it always amazed him just how *noisy* the inside of one's head was. Random thoughts would pop up out of nowhere and he would push them aside only for another mundane image or word or notion to take its place. It was frustrating but Bellicus knew his mind would fall silent eventually and, after some time breathing slowly and deeply and shutting himself off from the chattering men by the fire outside, Bellicus realised he was standing beside a stream.

He could hear the water bubbling over stones and smell flowers for it was daylight where he was.

The Otherlands. He did not know if the Otherlands were a real place or if it was all within his own imagination — not even Nemias knew that and, now that Bellicus was the Merlin, he still could not tell.

His eyes were open within these daylight lands and he looked around. Trees, some of species that did not grow in Alt Clota, or even Britain, surrounded him, and a smell of roasting meat filled his nostrils, making his mouth water. He could see grey smoke rising up from the other side of the stream and jumped across it, his long legs easily making the leap. When he clambered up the grassy bank he saw the campfire that was the source of the smoke and recognised the man who was seated beside the fire.

"Peredur!"

In his mind, Bellicus knew Peredur was not a living man — if he ever had been he'd died hundreds of years ago, for there were tales of his heroism passed down from druid to druid. Bellicus had 'met' him before during his meditations and counted him a friend and advisor, regardless of whether he was a real man, a god, or something conjured by the druid himself.

"Bel! Come, sit with me, old friend, and share my meat and drink."

Bellicus sat on a log across from Peredur and the mythical hero held out the wooden plate of roast pork that was in his lap. The druid took a piece with thanks and began to chew. It tasted better than anything in the real world, as did the cup of ale that Peredur handed to him.

"What brings you here today?" the man asked. If he wasn't real, he certainly looked it with his large belly and jowly face.

"Dun Breatann is besieged. By both Picts and Saxons."

Peredur scowled. "Damn sea-wolves."

"Exactly," said Bellicus, accepting another piece of meat and chewing with gusto. "I need to find a way to get into Dun Breatann and speak with Narina but…" He shook his head and picked out a piece of the pork from between his teeth. "I've no idea how to go about it. The enemy army has the place sealed up tight according to Gavo's scouts and, as you know, there's no way to climb up the rock. It's too steep."

Peredur nodded slowly, gazing into his campfire, and Bellicus felt a strange sensation, as if his consciousness was expanding, becoming the size of the whole world, the whole universe, and even beyond. It was not unpleasant, but it was disorienting and he was glad it passed when Peredur spoke again.

"Can you fly?" the old hero asked seriously.

"No, of course not," Bellicus replied.

Peredur shrugged and stared directly into the druid's eyes. "Then you must find an ally who can."

They sat together in contemplative silence for a little while longer until Bellicus somehow knew it was time for him to leave the Otherlands for now.

"Thank you, old friend," he said to Peredur. "And give my thanks to the gods. These might be hard times, but there's always something to be grateful for!"

The mythical hero smiled and Bellicus suddenly jerked awake, sucking in a gasping breath, momentarily shocked to find himself no longer in a bright woodland clearing. It was still so dark he couldn't see anything, but he could smell Cai close beside him, and the leather of his tent, and the sounds of his companions murmuring and laughing outside.

He thanked the gods again for their advice, although he had no idea what Peredur's words had meant. It was possible he would never understand them and his meditations would prove fruitless — that happened sometimes — but Bellicus was hopeful a good night's sleep would bring him the understanding he felt was just within reach.

Smiling, he lay down and petted Cai, the big hound turning his head and licking the druid's hand. And then, Bellicus passed from the land of the living once more, but this time it was just into the refreshing dreamscape of natural sleep.

* * *

"What happened to you last night?" Duro asked when Bellicus came out to join him in the morning. The centurion had some bacon and a cup of water, and the druid was handed the same by one of the camp helpers.

"I went into a trance," Bellicus said, taking a drink of the water first for his mouth was dry. When he began eating the bacon he found it tasty and well-cooked, but not as nice as the pork he'd shared with Peredur in the Otherlands.

"What, all night?" Duro asked.

"No. But I fell asleep afterwards." He rolled his neck and fed Cai a piece of the fat from the bacon. "It was a good sleep too! I feel deeply rested this morning."

Koriosis and Gavo came to join them then, eyeing the Merlin with interest.

"That's nice, Bel," Duro said a touch sarcastically. "But did your trance bring you any answers? We still need to find a way to defeat Drest and Horsa, remember?"

Bellicus looked at Duro, and then at the other men around the fire, and at the trees and the hill that surrounded them. There was a smirr of rain in the air and it was not what people usually thought of as a 'nice' day, but, to Bellicus it was wonderful, and bursting with hope. He laughed, drawing raised eyebrows from his companions and the young lad who was serving Koriosis some more fried bacon.

"My trance, or at least the gods, did steer me in a direction that might just bring an end to this war," Bellicus said jovially. "Today, I'll follow my intuition and see what happens."

"Excellent!" Duro said fiercely. "Where are we going?"

"For now, we remain here until Aife brings Drest and Horsa on patrol."

He and Duro had explained to Gavo everything that had been said at their meeting with the Pictish princess and the captain had readied his men on the hillside for trouble again.

"And then?" the centurion asked eagerly.

"And then I must head off alone, I'm afraid," Bellicus replied gravely. "But I should return within a day or two, and then we'll see what happens."

"What?" Gavo demanded irritably. "Come on, druid. None of your riddles and little hints — what are you planning?"

"You'll see," said Bellicus with an enigmatic wink and then beckoned Koriosis over. "I have something I'd like you to do for me."

"Of course," the younger druid said eagerly, bending to take something Bellicus had drawn out from his pocket, and to hear the Merlin's instructions. He was frowning at first, but eventually started to chuckle and, with a happy salute, hurried off to complete the task he'd been given.

Bellicus returned to his breakfast then and, despite repeated promptings from Gavo, refused to say another word as the drizzle continued to moisten the air.

A rider came pounding up the trail towards the camp some time later and the men around the fire jumped to their feet, holding their plates and waiting to find out what had provoked such speed in the horseman.

"Drest!" the scout called as he came into view and saw them watching him. "The enemy king and his riders are on patrol and coming this way."

"Is Princess Aife with them?" Bellicus asked.

"I think so," the scout replied. "It's hard to say, given her size and the armour she wears, but there was someone with long brown hair riding beside Drest, so…"

"Good," the druid murmured to himself and hastened to his tent, lifting his staff of office and saying to the others, "Well, what are you waiting for? Get off your arses and come with me before the enemy patrol passes and we miss our chance! Ah, Koriosis, there you are! Did you manage it?"

The young druid nodded, teeth flashing as he grinned conspiratorially at Bellicus. "I think so."

"Let's move then."

Soon they were running towards a section of the hill that Bellicus had scouted the day before. It was a rocky place, mostly bereft of trees so it was visible from the road and not too high up although if one fell from it they would be badly injured.

"Along there?" Gavo asked unhappily. "Really? It looks dangerous."

"War is dangerous, my friend!" Bellicus returned with wry amusement. "But don't worry, I'll go myself. The rest of you can hide in the trees and watch. I don't think Drest will try and attack, but you'd best all be ready just in case. Our warriors are guarding the road, yes?"

Gavo nodded. "Aye, if any enemy riders come up the hill they'll get a nasty shock. I have men positioned along it ready to form shieldwalls, and more men higher up armed with great bloody boulders." He snickered nastily. "Nothing better than seeing a Pict or a Saxon crushed by a massive rock, I can tell you."

"I'll take your word for it," the druid replied. "Now get into position, and I'll do the same. Remember, when I call out to Taranis, use your hunting bows to make the enemy scatter."

"We'll never hit them through all the foliage, Bel," said Gavo.

"I know, that's not important. I just want a distraction. Do *not* hit Aife!" He spoke then to Koriosis, giving him instructions on where to go and what to do. Finally, giving Cai a last rub behind the ears and leaving the hound in Duro's care Bellicus turned and slowly, carefully, began to make his way across the craggy section of Dun Buic Hill. There were weeds growing from cracks in the rock, affording him handholds although he didn't trust them to hold his considerable weight should he slip. He moved with great care, making sure each foot and each hand was firmly in place before taking another step. His staff was strapped to his back and the butt scraped along the rock as he moved, making him grimace for he hated damaging the staff and knew he would need to polish out the scrapes when this was all over.

At last he reached a flat section of rock that was big enough for him to stand safely upon. Behind it there was a small opening he hoped would offer some cover if Drest's horsemen tried to hit him with arrows or sling shot.

Pressing his back against the hard, grey rock face, Bellicus first looked down, spotting Koriosis hiding behind a tree, and then up at the cloudy sky. Nervous but excited, he mouthed a prayer to the God of Thunder, and waited for Dun Breatann's enemies to ride into view.

CHAPTER THIRTY-THREE

"Drest!"

The High Druid's cry rang out across the hillside and the road, and the Pictish king immediately jerked on his horse, head turning in the direction of the shout. His warband, forty or more men at least, reined in at his back, drawing weapons and forming a protective shield around Drest, Aife, and Horsa who was also in the front rank, head held haughtily aloft as he too looked for the source of the cry.

"You dare ride in these lands as if they were yours?" Bellicus shouted and now everyone on the road below spotted him standing like an enormous, winged beast on the rocky hillside, arms outstretched, staff in hand. "You tempt the wrath of the gods of Alt Clota, Drest? And of me, Merlin of Britain?"

He looked down at Koriosis and the young druid nodded. Within moments red smoke began billowing up, all around Bellicus, framing him on the rock like vapour from some godsforsaken tomb.

Drest scowled up at him and seemed unsure how to reply, or even if he should say anything at all. From the look on his face Qunavo had told him what had happened at the Moot so it was no surprise that Bellicus was now High Druid but, in truth, Drest was already terrified of him. Bellicus needed no grand title for that, and the red smoke that was billowing around him only made the new Merlin seem more otherworldly to the Pictish king.

"Come down, fool, and fight us like men!" It was Horsa who called out first, arrogantly sliding from his mount and holding out his arms in the universal, timeless gesture that meant, 'Come on then'.

"I'll fight you when the time is right, sea-wolf," Bellicus retorted, waving his hand dismissively. "I'll look forward to stabbing your other foot before I dispatch you to serve Taranis in the Otherlands."

"My foot is fine," Horsa roared, but everyone knew he had a permanent limp.

"Drest," Bellicus went on, ignoring Horsa. "Your allies have been performing human sacrifices. You know we do not practise such barbarity in these lands, or in your own. Qunavo and Ria will have told you that, I'm sure. You invite the wrath of our gods by allowing Horsa and his witch to do as they please while you stand and watch like the coward you are."

"Narina can put an end to the sacrifices any time she likes," Drest retorted furiously as his own men muttered behind him, also upset by the actions of the Saxon *volva*. "All she has to do is surrender Dun Breatann and the war will be over, her people can live their lives as normal, and things will go back to as they were before, only with me as king."

"Be silent, Drest, you fucking oaf!" Bellicus bellowed, his trained voice tearing like thunder through the smoky red air and causing some of the horses to shy in alarm. "Dun Breatann is under my protection. I, Merlin of Britain, hereby curse all who seek to set foot inside the fortress without my permission. And, furthermore, I curse you, Horsa, and your woman, Yngvildr. In the name of Taranis, Thunder God, so mote it be!"

At his mention of Taranis there were whipping and whirling sounds as Gavo's men, hidden in the trees beside the road, let fly their arrows and spun slings, loosing stones towards the riders. As predicted very few made it through the smoke and the dense foliage, clattering uselessly against trunks and branches, but it was enough to frighten the enemy riders and they scattered, crying out in alarm.

As Drest and his followers turned their attention away from him, Bellicus dropped down and jumped from the ledge he'd been standing on. There was grass below him and his landing was soft enough, but the slope was still steep and he slid, cursing as quietly as he could, until his torso slammed into a tree.

"Gods, that hurt," he muttered, pushing himself to his knees and breathing deeply. His fingers probed the ribs that had clattered against the tree but there was no sudden, breathless pain to tell him he'd broken any of them.

"Are you all right?" Koriosis asked, hurrying to help him stand.

"Aye, I think so," Bellicus replied through gritted teeth. "Good job with the smoke."

Koriosis smiled proudly. "The saltpetre you gave me was perfect," he said. "The only dye I could find was red, but I think it worked rather well. Interesting little trick."

Bellicus nodded and grinned, the pain in his ribs beginning to ease. "I learned it from Qunavo, funnily enough." Down on the road he could hear Drest leading his warband away, knowing they couldn't head into the trees to find the Damnonii archers and slingers. The sound of thundering hooves soon receded into the distance and Bellicus made his way slowly back up to the camp.

Gavo, Duro, and Koriosis also returned shortly and the captain looked pleased, but more than a little confused.

"That was fun," he conceded. "But I don't understand what the point was. Did you just want to frighten them?"

Bellicus nodded. "That, and also to let them see me here."

"For what purpose?"

"You'll see soon enough, if everything goes to plan."

Gavo rolled his eyes but did not press the druid any further. Being enigmatic was part of a druid's role, as infuriating as it could be at times.

"This morning was just the first part of my plan," Bellicus told him, eyes twinkling. "Now comes the next part." He pushed himself to his feet using his staff, ribs still aching slightly but not enough to worry about. "You men hold the fort here. Be wary of Drest returning — you might want to block the road off with some logs or boulders just in case they try to ride up here."

"Will do," said Gavo.

"But where are you going?" Duro demanded. "And why can't I come?"

"I told you, this will work better if I do it alone." He grinned. "Trust me, I am the Merlin after all."

Duro's reply was not as respectful as Bellicus's title deserved, but it did not surprise him at all. "You help Gavo keep this place, and the men here, secure, old friend. I'll be back soon, all being well."

"Are you at least taking Cai?" the centurion asked.

"I don't think so," Bellicus replied. "Where I'm going, dogs can't follow."

And with that, typically impenetrable line, the High Druid hurried off down the tree-lined slope to put the second phase of his plan into motion.

* * *

194

"You must perform a ritual to ward off that big bastard's curse!" Drest shouted at Qunavo and Ria, neither of whom seemed as if they really knew what they should be doing.

Aife watched the three of them, amazed that this war of her father's had descended to this, with king and druids confused and unhappy and probably wishing they were safely home in Dunnottar.

"There's no need to worry, Drest," said Qunavo, and his voice betrayed the irritation he felt at the king. "Bel's curse was only against those who may try to enter Dun Breatann. You have not done that yet."

"Of course I have!" Drest retorted, wide-eyed. "That's what the siege is for."

"Aye, but until you actively attempt to set foot within the fortress his curse won't come into play. Calm down. We'll perform the necessary rites when the time comes. For now, the only ones who should be worried about his magic are Horsa and Yngvildr."

"Pah, they care little for our gods. Taranis doesn't frighten the *volva*, and Horsa believes himself under her protection." He shook his head dolefully. "That wise woman certainly has a way of bewitching men."

"That's true," Aife agreed sourly. "I saw it last year when she had a whole village ready to sacrifice me to her twisted gods."

Drest winced at that reminder of what the Saxon woman had planned to do to his own daughter, but he'd come too far now, allowed his mercenaries too much leeway, to turn back now.

"Look, you two," the king said to Qunavo and Ria. "Your magic must be at least the equal of Bellicus's." He waved his hand irritably as Qunavo opened his mouth to protest. "I know the big fool is now High Druid, but there are two of you. You taught him all he knows, Qunavo! Surely you can ward him off until we break Narina's spirit and take Dun Breatann. By Lug, I hate this place." He stared up at the towering rock the Damnonii fortress was set upon and made an unintelligible, furious noise. "The damn place is impenetrable!"

"We knew that when we came here," Ria said levelly.

"She's right," said Aife. "You always knew this wouldn't be over quickly, my lord."

They sat in silence, subdued and depressed and wondering how the war would end.

They were outside the command tent for the earlier drizzle had passed, and it was quite warm and pleasant although the sun only made fleeting appearances overhead. They could see the gatehouse of Dun Breatann nearby and the walls that protected the outer entrance. Soldiers guarded those walls as they had done for generations, their helmeted heads and spears clearly visible over the thick timber parapets, watching for any sign that Drest's army was on the offensive.

Aife was a little surprised that her father had not commanded his army to use the ladders they'd fashioned from the trees felled at the very start of the siege. She believed it would be a waste of men's lives to mount such an attack for the outer walls of Dun Breatann would be difficult to breach, but, even if the Picts did get inside them, there was then another set of massive gates and an even higher wall set into the ancient volcanic plug.

As fortresses went, Dun Breatann was not the biggest, but it was, as Drest had noted, essentially impregnable. And, with a spring inside to provide the inhabitants with a ready source of fresh drinking water, it really was no surprise that the place had never been taken by force.

Drest was growing increasingly desperate, Aife could tell, and she feared he would sacrifice dozens of his troops in a pointless assault on the outer walls. She prayed that Bellicus would find some solution to this problem although she could not really see how. It seemed quite hopeless.

Yngvildr and Horsa walked towards the Pictish commanders then, the usual mocking smiles on their faces.

"Do you mean to sit here all year, Drest?" Horsa demanded. Any respect he might once have affected for the king was long gone. "Did the druid's curse frighten you so badly that you can do nothing but sit drinking ale and begging your weak gods to save you from Bellicus?"

Aife watched her father's face, expecting a furious outburst in reply, but he seemed to care little for the Saxon's jibe. "Leave me, Horsa," he said. "And take your whore with you."

Horsa laughed at that. It really did seem like he was thoroughly enjoying this whole war in spite of his continual complaining.

Yngvildr did not share her lover's amusement, though. "You should be careful, King Drest," the *volva* said, making strange, unsettling movements with her hand as she spoke. "Your druids are afraid of their Merlin. My gods, and my magic, are the only thing protecting this camp from his curse."

Drest turned pale at her words but Aife laughed, more loudly than was necessary for she felt the need to put Yngvildr in her place.

"Your gods? Your magic?" the princess demanded with a smile that was easily as mocking as the Saxons'. She stood up, hand on the pommel of her sword and walked to stand directly in front of the witch, staring down at her in disgust. "Where were your gods and your magic when Bellicus defeated you in the magical duel in that shit-hole little village last year when you sought to slit my throat as a sacrifice to your gods? Where were your gods and your magic when you lived in the countryside like a hermit, filthy and stinking of shit, in the months since Bellicus chased you into the river?"

Yngvildr stared at her, the familiar crazed look in her eyes, and Horsa smirked, enjoying the entertainment as always.

"Bellicus has the ear of the gods of these lands," said Aife, still glaring murderously at the *volva*. "And your pitiful magic has proved useless, despite murdering a dozen or more men and women in honour of Wotan and Thunor."

"Aife!" Drest scolded, angered by his daughter's boldness. "That's enough. You sound like you're on Bellicus's side, not ours!"

"I merely state the truth," the warrior-princess returned, fingers still tapping the handle of her sword as though she'd like to draw it and make an end to all of this. "We are in Bellicus's lands, and he is the High Druid of all Britain. No *volva* can match his power, no matter what this pitiful wretch claims. And, Father" – she spun to stare directly into Drest's eyes – "you might want to remember that the witch would have slashed my throat if it hadn't been for Bellicus saving my life."

Drest's face twisted in sheer rage. "I've had enough of this. We're here with our Saxon allies to take Alt Clota, and I don't give a damn what you, or Qunavo, have to say about Bellicus, or druids, or what we *should* be doing! Fuck Bellicus, he is nothing!"

197

"I am the Merlin of Britain!" a voice rang out, clear and powerful and seeming to fill the entire area around the foot of the fortress, echoing back from the rock walls and carrying out across the Clota.

"What?" Drest's face paled and he looked around, trying to see where the voice had come from.

"I am High Druid of these lands, Drest," the voice called again and now everyone looked up at the walls of Dun Breatann for that was where it originated.

Aife gasped, and so did every one of the men who'd been in Drest's patrol that morning for there, larger than life on the walls above them was Bellicus, staring back at them disdainfully from *inside* Dun Breatann.

"How did he get in there?" Horsa demanded. "There is no way in — we sent our best climbers and not one could even get close to making it inside."

Drest was absolutely stunned. Just a few short hours ago he had conversed with Bellicus a mile away — yet there the druid was now, somehow inside Dun Breatann, flanked by the silver-haired guard captain named Gerallt, and Queen Narina who looked like she was rather enjoying herself.

"There used to be a secret tunnel that led within the fortress," Drest muttered, still as white as one of the heavy gulls that cawed overhead.

"It's completely blocked off," Aife said. "We had men check it. Bellicus did not get in using that way."

"Then how did he get in?" Drest demanded furiously. "It's impossible!"

"The gods!" Bellicus roared, raising his arms to the sky. "The gods of these lands are on our side, Drest, and now you and your Saxons will feel their wrath. This is your last chance," and he swept out his staff to take in the entire enemy encampment. "Leave Alt Clota *now*, or feel the full power of Taranis."

CHAPTER THIRTY-FOUR

When Bellicus finished speaking and turned away from the wall he could see Drest's army in uproar. Word of their king's earlier encounter with the druid that morning had filtered through their camp, as had the Saxon's attempts to climb up the steep rock face of Dun Breatann without success. Everyone knew it was utterly impossible that Bellicus could have gone from Dun Buic to inside the fortress yet there he was. And there was no way it could be someone impersonating the druid, for he was unmistakable. There was not another man in Alt Clota who was over six and a half feet tall and built like that.

It was truly Bellicus inside Dun Breatann, and the only way to explain his presence was to take him at his word and accept that the gods had carried him there somehow.

Unless one knew better.

Catia shrieked with laughter once they were away from the wall, and threw her arms around Bellicus for the tenth time since they'd been reunited.

"That was amazing," she cried. "They were absolutely terrified to see you in here."

Narina was similarly excited by the enemy reaction to Bellicus's appearance although she managed to maintain her decorum and, although she too hugged the druid, she did not quite scream like her twelve-year-old daughter even if she might have wanted to.

Even Gerallt's usual stern demeanour had, for a brief time, improved, although his smile soon faded.

"It was a fine performance," the captain said. "But I'm not convinced Drest will simply leave now."

"Probably not," Bellicus agreed. "But their fear of my powers will have sown many a seed of doubt within his soldiers' minds. This was just the beginning, Gerallt. There's more to come, you'll see."

They climbed the steps to the middle portion of the fortress where the great hall was situated and went inside to speak more. Servants brought them drinks and Bellicus proclaimed his immense pleasure at finally being home and tasting ale brewed from the spring within Dun Breatann again. "It has a taste you can't find anywhere else in Britain," he said, taking a long pull and smiling in satisfaction. "Fresher. Cleaner somehow. The ale brewed in Caer Legion was strong, but no match for ours."

"Well, don't be taking too much of it," Narina replied tartly. "You still have to get back outside again."

The thought of that made Bellicus's palms sweat and he put down the ale a touch sheepishly. Only a handful of people within Dun Breatann knew how he'd got inside the fortress, and they were all sworn to keep the secret. It would do Damnonii morale good, just as it would do the opposite for their enemies, to believe Bellicus had managed the feat by using his magical, gods-given powers.

In truth, the explanation was a little more prosaic.

During his earlier ritual Peredur, or one of the gods perhaps, had advised Bellicus to find an ally who could fly, for that would be the key to getting inside Dun Breatann's impenetrable walls. At first, that had seemed like gibberish — a riddle that might never be solved, as so often happened when one looked within and conversed with the gods.

But it had eventually struck the druid that he *did* have an ally who could fly: Uchaf.

Uchaf was the massive raven who made Dun Breatann his home. He could often be seen soaring high over the peaks, particularly the higher, western one, and everyone within the fortress knew the bird by his size and his great squawking cry that was far louder than even those of the gulls that haunted the place.

None knew the corvid as well as Bellicus. Where the druid commanded the earth with his great black stallion, Darac, he realised he might also conquer the skies by way of Uchaf.

The raven was, like all corvids, extremely intelligent. Bellicus discovered it outside his house one day six years or so ago and it had appeared starving to him. It had a malformed leg so it could not walk properly, and it was too timid to stand up to the more aggressive other birds so, when the druid tossed it a piece of bread, a jackdaw or a magpie would swoop down and steal it before the young raven could take it. Over time, druid and raven had built up a friendship, with the raven coming to be fed at certain times when no other birds were around. It had grown stronger, and bigger, and

200

more confident and, eventually, Bellicus had taught it to make a coughing sound, and even to say 'hello'.

Now, after years of feeding the great black bird, Bellicus had called in a favour. He'd walked to Dun Breatann, making sure to skirt Drest's patrols and scouts, his dark robe helping him blend into the undergrowth if danger came too close. He'd made it to the northwestern edge of the fortress which was so overgrown that Drest's army had left it unoccupied, and there he'd waited for the raven to fly overhead.

It always astonished him how clever corvids were, and how incredible their eyesight was, even from a great distance. Uchaf had soared into the sky not long after Bellicus took up a position against Dun Breatann's towering rock and, when the druid stood and lifted his hand in greeting, the raven had cawed once, and come down to meet him.

The druid had brought some cheese with him, the bird's favourite treat, and it was soon devoured. And then, rather hopefully, Bellicus had asked the bird to say, 'hello' a few times and then, pointing upwards, sent it on its way.

He knew it was a long shot, but he also knew Catia enjoyed feeding the bird so it was no massive surprise when, after a short time, faces had peered down over the walls high above, and then a rope had come snaking down to him.

It had all seemed rather easy to Bellicus at the time but he'd later discovered that Uchaf had said his 'hello' to Catia and then perched on the wall far above the druid. The girl had not understood what was happening at first and it had taken the raven four tries, harassing Catia and angrily cawing 'hello' at her before she came and looked down at the ground below. Only then had the raven stopped cawing and flown off, although the princess had not actually spotted Bellicus at that time.

Catia had run to tell her mother Uchaf had been acting strangely but the queen dismissed her report, saying the raven was only a bird, what did it matter? Until Catia reminded her of the bond Bellicus had with the corvid, and then they had gone together to look down over the wall and spotted the dark-robed figure within the foliage.

Gerallt had been summoned and commanded to find a rope long enough to reach the ground. The guards on that section of wall were dismissed and replaced with men Narina knew for certain could keep a secret, and then the rope was passed down to Bellicus.

The druid had never climbed up a rope as long as that before and he'd found it a nerve-racking experience, even though there were knots tied in it to help him keep his hold. He knew Catia and Aife had once escaped Dun Breatann by that method and the thought made him sweat even more than he already was as he hauled himself upwards, forcing himself not to look down. The guards above pulled the rope as he climbed so it didn't take as long as it might have but there were a couple of occasions where his damp palms slipped and he almost lost his grip.

By the time he was being helped over the wall at the top he knew he would rather stand in a shieldwall against a thousand Saxons than repeat that ascent.

He'd tried not to think of his eventual descent until Narina had mentioned it now, and thoughts of enjoying a few ales swiftly fled from his mind.

He ate a meal and spoke with the queen, Catia, and Gerallt. Informing them of his plans and making sure they were on board with them and knew exactly what to do. Gerallt eventually left to patrol the walls and to make sure his warriors were alert for any danger, and Bellicus was able to enjoy a little time with his daughter and Narina.

"You've heard about the disgusting sacrifices that Saxon bitch has been performing?" Narina asked and, when Bellicus admitted he did not know all the details, she filled him in, leaving him even more enraged and determined to see Drest's army defeated than before.

"Catia," Narina said as night drew in. "That big raven will be wanting something to eat about now, won't he? Well, he certainly deserves something special today. Here, take him some of this meat. I would speak with Bel alone for a time."

The princess rolled her eyes as if she knew exactly what her mother meant by 'speak alone', but she gave Bellicus another hug then took a handful of leftover roast pork and chicken and went to find the corvid who would, indeed, be looking for his evening meal about then and certainly deserved his reward.

"Come, Bellicus," said the queen when Catia had left the hall. "We should talk in private. We have much to discuss."

She stood up and held out her hand to the druid, surprising him, for she always hid her affection for him. He normally did the same, but now he took her hand in his and drew her in close as she happily led him out of the great hall and up to her own house on the top of the eastern peak.

CHAPTER THIRTY-FIVE

"How has Ysfael been dealing with all this?" Bellicus asked as they walked. He was smiling, despite the fact they were at war. Liberated, somehow. For so long he and Narina had hidden their feelings, pushed them aside for the good of the kingdom, and where had it got them?

"Honestly, he's kept himself to himself and caused no trouble for weeks," Narina replied as they neared her residence. "I think he's as frightened by this siege as anyone, and probably vexed that his father didn't send us reinforcements to help."

"Can't blame Cunedda for that," Bellicus said as they crested the hill and headed towards the queen's house which had two men guarding the entrance as always. "If he gets involved in this he makes an enemy of both Drest and Horsa."

"Of course," Narina agreed, nodding to her guards who grinned as they saw Bellicus, clearly pleased to have the massive druid back in Dun Breatann. "But I think I can understand why Ysfael would be upset to be left to die by his own father. And Alt Clota is supposed to be an ally of the Votadini, so Cunedda really should be sending us aid."

"Oh, I've no doubt he'll send us aid just as soon as he hears that we've sent Drest packing," Bellicus said with a bitter laugh. "He'll be a good ally once he knows we've won."

"Well, that isn't good enough," said Narina, pushing the door to her house open and stepping inside. Bellicus followed and she closed and bolted the door although there was no chance of anyone daring to enter without permission. Well, maybe Catia.

"What are you saying?" Bellicus asked. "That we break our alliance with the Votadini?"

"What's the point in having an alliance if your allies won't come to your aid when you're attacked?" Narina asked, looking up at him and breaking into a smile. "Besides, I've had a lot of time to think while we've been under siege, and I've realised that Cunedda's refusal to send us aid could be a blessing."

"A blessing?" The druid frowned and then laughed, glancing back over his shoulder at the door as Narina pulled aside his cloak and pushed her hand down inside his breeches. "How can it be a blessing?" he asked again, groaning softly and dipping his head to kiss the queen.

"Because," she replied, pulling him towards her bed. "Cunedda has broken the alliance, and without that alliance, there's no reason for me to remain married to Ysfael." She lay back on the bed and guided the druid inside her. They made love, tenderly and passionately, as if this might be the last time they would ever be together which, if Drest had his way, it might well be.

When they were finished Bellicus lay beside Narina feeling happier than he had in weeks. "This feels right," he told her, stroking her cheek. "Being with you always feels right."

She pushed a strand of hair from her face and returned his smile. "This is how it should be all the time," she agreed. "Us. Together. Every day."

"So, you plan to send Ysfael back to his father in Dun Edin and break off your marriage to him," he said. "Then what?"

"And then," she said firmly, "we do what we should have done a long time ago."

"You want us to be wed?" Bellicus asked. He'd wondered if this was what she'd been leading up to.

"Would you not want to?" Narina asked, still searching his face for some indication of his true feelings. "If we'd done it after Coroticus died it would have saved a lot of trouble, and we would not be at war with the Picts right now. That all happened because I allowed politics to guide me, rather than my own heart. So, I ask again, and this will be the last time, Bel, I warn you: would you want to marry me?"

Bellicus stared at her, his mind churning. He had wished he could be with Narina for a long, long time. Ever since he'd been forced to fight, and kill, his friend and her first husband, King Coroticus in fact. Coroticus had lost his mind when Horsa abducted Catia, starting wars with the neighbouring tribes and accusing Narina of being in love with Bellicus which, at the time, was not true. The king's paranoia saw him arrest Narina, banish Bellicus, and eventually face the druid in a fight to the death right there in Dun Breatann. After all that there was no way Bel and Narina could be together, for the Damnonii people would have believed they'd plotted against Coroticus so they could be together, which was nonsense, as both of them genuinely loved the king until his descent into madness.

Bellicus's dalliance with Ria had been a direct result of Narina's decision to wed Ysfael, and the druid's need for a woman's love and affection.

There had always been something to hold them back, he thought, and even now, there was something other than Ysfael standing in the way of their union.

"I've just been elected High Druid," he told her. "The old Merlin was murdered at our Moot by a Saxon raid led by Hengist himself. The members of my Order voted me as his replacement."

Narina smiled, a hint of pride in her green eyes. "Well, that's wonderful," she said. "Congratulations! So I will be wed to the Merlin and we will rule Dun Breatann together, setting wrongs right and making Britain a better place together." She laughed like a young girl, excited by the prospects she saw opening up before them.

"That won't be possible," Bellicus said, sighing.

"Why not? What do you mean?"

"One of the conditions of becoming High Druid was that whoever was elected must reside with Arthur, in the south. Arthur is the only one really holding back Hengist's Saxons from riding roughshod over the people down there, and if that were to happen, all of Britain would undoubtedly fall to the sea-wolves soon after."

"What are you saying?" Narina asked. "Are you leaving Dun Breatann for ever? Leaving me? And Catia?"

Bellicus stood up from the bed and rearranged his clothes so he looked presentable again. He went to the window at the side of the house and opened the shutters, breathing in the fresh air that blew in from the Clota and looking out at Dun Buic in the middle distance.

"If I hadn't accepted the title of Merlin," he said, still looking out over the land he loved so much. "They would have given it to Qunavo."

"Oh, gods," Narina whispered, standing and fixing her own clothing before coming to join him at the window.

"Exactly," said the druid. "You see why I agreed to the condition of living in the south, beside Arthur? It would have been disastrous for you and the Damnonii people for Drest's own druid to be named Merlin."

"Would it?" Narina asked, putting her arm through his. "If Qunavo had to travel south it would remove one threat from our borders, would it not?"

Bellicus tilted his head to the side thoughtfully. "Maybe eventually," he admitted. "But, like me, he might have simply come here until he saw this siege of Drest's completed. And then, when he did go to join Arthur, he would wield great power and influence over the other druids, and Arthur too. Qunavo is no friend to Alt Clota, Narina, as you well know. I thought it best to become Merlin and take that power for myself."

"Do you truly want the power? If it means leaving us all behind?" She gestured to the crags and sloping fields that surrounded them, the River Clota cutting through it all with its familiar blue waters.

"No," the druid said. "Not really. But Qunavo is not only a friend of Drest's, he also does not see the Saxons as a threat. As Merlin I can make sure the Saxons are dealt with properly." He shook his head angrily. "You can see from Horsa's actions that his people, those who would seek conquest rather than peaceful settlement at least, must be stopped."

Narina sighed heavily. "It's certainly true that the Saxon and the *volva* are far more vicious and cruel than Drest ever was. What will you do then, when this is all over? Will you go to join Arthur, or will you remain here and be my husband?"

She met his gaze and it was quite clear that this would be the last time she ever made him this offer. At that moment, however, he could simply not commit to one path or the other.

"You know what I would like to do, Narina," he said, grasping her hand and kissing her on the head. "But let's deal with this siege first, and then we can decide, together, what we should do. All right?"

For a moment anger flashed in her eyes, but then she accepted that his words were sensible and squeezed his hand. "Fine," she said, and even managed a smile. "Let us go then, and do what we can to end Drest's war."

They went to the door and Bellicus threw back the bolt, allowing Narina to lead the way outside. The guards must have

207

guessed what had been going on within the house for, like all the buildings on Dun Breatann, it was not that large; there was simply not enough room on the twin slopes for ostentatious personal dwellings. Neither of the soldiers made any comment or even allowed a smirk to cross their lips, at least not while the druid and their queen could see them.

People were working, washing clothes, sparring on the practice ground, repairing old timbers on the walls and so on, and all greeted Bellicus with joyful amazement as he passed. Or almost all, at least.

"What's happening here?" an angry voice called to them and they both turned to see Narina's husband, Ysfael, coming up the slope towards them. "I heard you'd somehow spirited yourself inside the walls, Bellicus. What are you planning?"

The druid offered a respectful bow to the prince. "I am planning," he said with a small smile, "to liberate Dun Breatann from its besiegers."

"Well, good!" Ysfael replied. "I should think so too. Do you have a part for me in your scheme?"

Bellicus glanced at Narina who shrugged.

"I have not," he admitted to the haughty young man. "I didn't think you'd be interested."

"Not interested?" Ysfael demanded. "My life is in danger just as much as anyone else's, druid. If you have a way to defeat those bastards outside then I want to be part of it. It's bad enough living here as, essentially, a political prisoner, unloved and feared by everyone, but it's even worse when you know there's an army outside just waiting for their chance to get in and slaughter you like cattle."

"Well," Bellicus almost felt sorry for the prince but reminded himself that Ysfael had brought things upon himself. Still, the man was strong and knew how to wield a sword. "All right," the druid said. "When the time comes, Gerallt will furnish you with weapons and armour, and you can do your bit, if you agree."

Ysfael nodded fiercely. "Damn right I agree," he said, even managing a smile. "When?"

"I haven't decided everything just yet," Bellicus replied cagily, still unwilling to trust a man who'd proved himself duplicitous and cunning before. "But hopefully things will start to move very soon, so speak with Gerallt, and be ready when the time comes, eh?"

Ysfael, to the surprise of both Bellicus and Narina, actually offered them a salute before turning and heading back down the slope. Clearly he was feeling the stress of being under siege just as much as Narina or anyone else and couldn't wait to do something about it.

"What is the next part of your plan then?" Narina asked as Ysfael strode away, and they slowly made their way down towards the great hall and the rope that would take Bellicus back outside the fortress.

"Next," he replied to Narina, and there was obvious excitement in his tone as he thought of what was to come. "We liberate Dun Breatann, defeat the Picts, and gods willing, see an end to Horsa and Yngvildr. Are you ready, my queen?"

Narina stopped at the wall and looked over, wincing at the thought of her lover climbing down such a long, rocky way. "I'm ready," she said, pulling him down and kissing him. "Tell me what we must do."

CHAPTER THIRTY-SIX

The next morning was sunny when dawn came, but by the time Gavo and Duro had roused the camp at Dun Buic and the men were up and prepared for what was to come it was cloudy again.

"Still dry," said the centurion. "Hopefully it stays that way. Nothing worse than standing in a shieldwall when your feet are sliding all over the place in mud. Even the most skilled warrior can lose their life to a bumbling idiot when the conditions are like that."

"A skilled warrior can be killed by an idiot at any time," Bellicus replied with a smile. He'd climbed down from Dun Breatann's walls the previous afternoon and returned to Dun Buic to outline the next part of his plan to his comrades and then to spend another night in quiet meditation, asking the gods for their blessings.

"I know that," said Duro. "Better than most. But dry weather favours a man who knows what he's doing — there's less luck involved."

The druid nodded. He too would much rather fight on dry ground although, if his plan worked, maybe no-one would need to meet in battle that day. He prayed Drest would see sense when the time came but he knew the Pictish king was being heavily influenced by Horsa and a fight might be unavoidable.

There was also the possibility that Aife was double-crossing him. It seemed wholly unlikely, and Bellicus would trust the warrior-princess with his life, but perhaps she'd been fooled by Qunavo and Ria? Those two were masters of manipulation — they had decades of training and experience between them in persuading people to do what they wanted after all. That was what druids did, and if they were unscrupulous it could lead to great abuses of power.

Had the old druid and his druidess protégée tricked Aife into thinking they did not support Drest, in order to flush Bellicus and Gavo out of hiding? It would not be the first time their machinations had reduced Bellicus to a naive fool.

Well, they would find out soon enough, he thought. If he'd had the wool pulled over his eyes again it would be disastrous for the

Damnonii, for they were still greatly outnumbered by Drest's forces and, in a pitched battle, there would only be one winner.

He could not speak with any of the men about this, of course, although he knew Duro could tell he was worried, no matter how he attempted to hide it. The centurion knew him better than anyone now and, truth be told, Duro was likely feeling anxious about things to come as well. He'd been taken in by Ria before as well, if not quite as fully as the druid.

"You really think this will be the day?" Gavo asked him with more enthusiasm than Bellicus had seen from the grizzled captain in many a month. "Will we finally get a chance to avenge the wrongs Horsa in particular has done to our people?"

Bellicus finished the last of his breakfast and licked his fingers clean. "One way or another," he said, washing down the cheese with a little ale. "I think today will be a major turning point in this war and, aye, the gods will probably give us a crack at the Saxons. You think the men are ready?" He lowered his voice so only those closest to the campfire could hear. "This won't be easy, Gavo. Everything is set up for us but if anything goes wrong — even just a little bit — then Drest's superior numbers could mean a crushing defeat for us, especially if our soldiers are not fully prepared for the carnage that may come."

Gavo shook his head emphatically and almost went cross-eyed as he tried to see a crumb of cheese that had become stuck in his beard. He flicked it out and then looked coolly at the druid. "These men have seen the aftermath of Horsa's raids. They are more than ready for Saxon brutality, and more than ready to dish out some of their own. Trust me, Bel, I've never seen an army so ready to fight."

"Ready to fight," Bellicus murmured grimly. "But are they ready to die?"

"As ready as any man can ever be," Gavo returned. "Especially young lads who should have plenty of years left ahead of them. Anyway, you've told us about your speech from the walls of Dun Breatann, and the chaos your appearance there caused. How the hell *did* you get inside anyway?" He held up a hand, shaking his head. "Never mind, I know I'm wasting my breath even asking. I know the secret tunnel is sealed up — I oversaw that myself. No doubt you used some great magic to fly over the walls, eh? Point being, you have some plan and we all have faith in you so...Let's hope there isn't too much fighting."

"Just enough to make sure that arsehole Horsa is dead come the end of the day," Duro put in viciously. "Blood-eagled if possible."

"Aye, and enough to avenge what they did to Sentica and his patrol," Gavo added fiercely.

"The scouts back yet?" Bellicus asked.

"Aye," the captain nodded. "The enemy are still camped around the base of Dun Breatann. We should have no trouble marching there."

"Good," the druid said, taking one last drink to wash down his breakfast and stretching, working the kinks from his neck and shoulders. "Then let's do this."

* * *

Dun Breatann was situated on a rather easily defensible piece of land. Surrounded by the Rivers Clota and Leamnha on three sides, the only way to get to it on foot was to the north and northeast. Furthermore, there was a narrow, but deep stream that cut through the land on the northeastern side, making it difficult for men or horses to travel from that direction.

Essentially, the only way to get to the fortress without using a boat was to come from the north. This is where the Damnonii army was headed to, marching from Dun Buic, and Drest's scouts had informed him of that fact early in the day, riding hard to give him intelligence on numbers and possible unit formations.

In response, and knowing full well that his army outnumbered the force coming towards him, Drest confidently had his men move northwards. He left a few men at Dun Breatann to guard against Narina coming out from the fortress but, in truth, he hoped she would. This was what he'd wanted all along — a chance to use his superior numbers to crush the Damnonii in open battle.

So they marched north, positioning themselves about half a mile from their original position, where the land began to open out. Drest's scouts had told him that the Damnonii army had split into two sections, so one could arrive from the east, the other from the west in a classic pincer movement.

212

"So Gavo thinks to capture us between the hammer and the anvil," the king said to his advisors with a bleak smile. "Well, let him try. He's a fool if he thinks breaking his little army into two even smaller ones will be enough to defeat us."

"What if it's a trap?" asked Aife. "What if there are more men coming from the south?"

Horsa sniggered at the princess's suggestion. "You think these Damnonii fools can walk on water? Have you not seen the big river sitting right there? Pah, you sound as frightened as my fool cousin, Sigarr. If only I could send you home like I did with him."

Aife looked at the big Saxon coldly. "The river is not that deep in certain places, as you'd know if you bothered scouting the terrain rather than humping your witch. And besides, the Damnonii have plenty of boats and ships for fishing and trade. It's far from impossible that a detachment of their warriors might come sailing along the Clota once the battle starts, and come at us from behind."

Drest frowned at his daughter's suggestion. "But we know their numbers," he protested. "They don't have enough men for something like that."

"We don't think they do, but, my lord, we know Prince Ysfael of the Votadini is inside the fortress. He may not be on good terms with Narina, but his father will not want to see his son killed in this war, surely? He may have sent some of his own Votadini troops to join up with the Damnonii." She looked back over her shoulder at the river that lay glistening behind them. It no longer seemed like the impenetrable barrier Drest had been thinking of it as since his siege began.

Ria nodded slowly, thoughtfully. "Aife has a point," she said. "Gavo and Bellicus are in charge of the army that was camped at Dun Buic, and they're no fools. I wouldn't put it past them to come up with some scheme like this — to attack us on three fronts at once when we aren't expecting it."

"Bellicus?" Horsa exploded, eyes boring into Ria. "That bastard is inside Dun Breatann, remember? We all saw him yesterday. He's not in charge of the warbands out here."

"Are you sure about that?" Qunavo asked in astonished tones, pointing towards the road that approached their position from the west.

213

All eyes turned to see a large Damnonii warband marching towards them and, at their head, on a great black horse, was a similarly large man with a shaven head.

"It can't be," Drest whispered, stepping forward two paces as if that might afford him a better view. "How can it be? Qunavo? What evil magic is this?"

"A lookalike," Horsa growled, spitting on the ground in disgust at his allies' superstitions.

When the approaching warband was close enough, however, the rider in the dark robe jumped down, followed by some of his companions. It was clear, even from that distance, that the man towered over those with him.

"Unless that's a normal sized man," Aife said caustically to Horsa, "and the others with him are children or dwarves, I'd say that's Bellicus!"

"Maybe they are children," Horsa retorted. "It's hard to tell from here."

"That's the centurion beside him!" Aife laughed, shaking her head at the Saxon's stupidity. "He's no child. He's nearly as old as me and you combined!"

"How?" Drest repeated, more to himself this time. "How can it be?" He was looking around at random people, wide-eyed and clearly frightened of the Damnonii High Druid's powerful magic. "Did we imagine seeing him on the fortress walls yesterday?"

The sight of Bellicus had a similar effect throughout the ranks of Drest's army. The men shoved one another, demanding how someone could have got in and out of Dun Breatann — an impregnable fortress — while they were camped outside. It beggared belief. Even the Saxons were shaken by this turn of events, turning to Yngvildr for spiritual guidance before the battle commenced.

Bellicus remounted his horse after conferring with his men and, alone, rode ahead to speak with Drest.

"Will you come and talk to me, King of the Picts, lackey of the sea-wolves?" the giant druid demanded, reining in Darac so he was out of range of enemy missiles. "Or are you too terrified? Hide behind Horsa if you must, but your soldiers will see what kind of a man you are, and no-one wants to fight for a coward."

214

Drest's face was ashen but he mastered himself with a visible effort. Clearing his throat, he called out, "I'll talk with you, you big bastard. Why would I fear you? Our numbers are far greater than yours, and I have two druids, *and* a *volva* to call upon the gods for me!" He turned to Aife then and said venomously, "You! Take your warband and guard the river bank. If Bellicus thinks he can surprise us by ferrying men across the Clota to attack us from behind, he'll have to get through you first. Are you up to it, girl?"

"Oh I'm up to it, my lord," the princess replied. "No Damnonii sailors will get past my warband, you can be sure of that."

"Good," Drest said with some relief. "If Narina opens the gates and leads her garrison out, you can deal with them too, all right? Catch them as they try to come out, there's only room for maybe three at a time to march through those gates. Cut them down as they come — even if they have greater numbers it won't matter."

Aife saluted her father and, with a final, dark look at Horsa, she walked away and her powerful voice could be heard moments later, commanding her men to follow her down to the river.

"You will speak with him alone?" Horsa asked, and his tone made it clear he thought Drest mad if he went through with the meeting.

"Aye, why not?"

"Why not? That man is a killer, as I know all too well. Do you think some code of honour, of morality, will stop him from running you through with that sword of his, or spilling your brains across the ground with his staff?"

Drest felt his palms sweating and beads of it ran down his neck. He actually *had* thought Bellicus would speak to him, man-to-man, without offering violence because, well, that was just how things were done. But, with Aife's dark hints at trickery, and now the Saxon's suggestive talk, Drest hardly knew what to think any more.

Things used to be much simpler!

"Take Yngvildr with you at least," Horsa advised. "She may not be a warrior, but she will protect you from the druid's magic."

"I have druids of my own if I wanted that," said Drest.

"Your druids are beholden to Bellicus," Horsa said with a bitter smile. "He is their Merlin. They will not stand against their own High Druid."

Drest looked at Qunavo and Ria. Both seemed furious, but neither rebutted the jarl's claim.

"Besides," Horsa continued condescendingly. "No-one can think you a coward for taking a mere woman with you to meet the Damnonii whoreson."

Again, Drest felt his ire rise at the suggestion he was not man enough to face Bellicus without help. He squashed his anger though, and nodded at Yngvildr. "You come with me," he said, doing his best to sound commanding. "You can deflect any curses the druid might cast upon me?"

"Of course," the *volva* replied. "He has his staff to protect him, but that is crafted from weak wood. I have this." She hefted her wand which was about three feet in length and, Drest now realised, made from iron. "His spells will not work against you when I am there."

Qunavo and Ria said nothing, but Drest could practically feel their hatred radiating from them like a physical force. He knew they didn't approve of his conduct during the siege, and that made up his mind. He could not ask them to accompany him to meet Bellicus, so he would take Yngvildr. If the worst came to the worst and the druid attacked them, Drest felt sure he could run away faster than the *volva* with her long skirts.

"Come on then," the king said, and he straightened his back, sucked in a long breath, and walked forward as confidently as he could manage.

The second Damnonii warband had arrived from the east now, and they stood in a line, shields and spears at the ready, just as their comrades on the western side of the road had done. Insults were hurled at Drest as he approached Bellicus but he ignored them. The sight of another mystic, a younger man but carrying the familiar staff that marked him as a druid, made him even more anxious than he already was.

"We were merciful to you before, Drest," Bellicus shouted once they were close enough to converse. "When the proud warriors of Alt Clota destroyed your army last year, we might have killed you too. But we spared you, and you swore oaths — powerful oaths — to abide by the terms set out by Queen Narina in return for your life. We allowed you to remain as King of the Picts, when we could, perhaps should, have executed you."

"Be silent, you big fool." Yngvildr stepped forward, brandishing her iron wand. She appeared more lucid, less manic, than usual, and Drest wondered if that was a good thing or a bad thing. Her bizarre, wide-eyed behaviour seemed to him to suggest the gods were working through her, but maybe she was just crazy, as Aife and others claimed.

"Your gods have no power in Alt Clota," Bellicus cried, his rich voice rolling out, somehow, on all sides, so the warriors in each army could clearly hear him. "I am the Merlin of Britain, and I call on Taranis to strike you down, witch!"

Yngvildr cackled at that, spinning around in a dance that impressed Drest, mainly thanks to her stunning figure. She was quite the sight.

"My gods have gorged on the blood of multiple Damnonii victims, *druid*," she shrieked happily. "Thunor, Wotan, and Freyja have accepted the sacrifices we have made to them, and they wait now to do my bidding."

Her words, and her exaggerated self-confidence, seemed to have the effect she wanted and Drest looked back to see the men in the front ranks of his army smiling and nodding. They were hopeful smiles and nods, but still, it was far better than the fearful expressions they had worn just a few moments before. Everyone, even the druids, knew that blood sacrifices were incredibly powerful. Yngvildr's victims must have pleased her gods, while Bellicus had nothing to match those sacrifices, as far as Drest's soldiers knew. It was a big boost to morale, and the king was grinning when he turned back to the new Merlin of Britain.

"I defeated you once before in a magical battle," Bellicus called to Yngvildr. "And I would have taken your life if you'd not run away from me like the craven witch you are. Where were your gods then?"

The *volva,* perhaps, like Drest, sensing the growing confidence in her powers from the army gathered behind her, sneered at Bellicus and raised her wand high in the air. "My gods protected me, and brought me here to see your doom," she shouted, spinning around again and laughing joyously. "Now I call on Wotan to strike *you* down, druid, and bring us victory this day!"

With a triumphant cry she swung her wand down, pointing it at Bellicus.

And the wand snapped in half.

CHAPTER THIRTY-SEVEN

The *volva* gaped at her broken wand, utterly astonished. "How…?"

Even Bellicus was surprised — he'd seen that wand before, and he knew it was well constructed. From iron too! Such things didn't just break in half for no reason.

Well, whether that reason was mundane or supernatural, the druid saw an opportunity and he pounced on it.

"See!" he roared, smiling broadly and pointing his own eagle-topped staff at Yngvildr. "The gods of Alt Clota have shown their disapproval of this witch. She holds no sway in these lands, and now, Drest, let us meet in battle, where Taranis and Cernunnos will bring you and your army to their doom."

Drest was gaping open-mouthed at the *volva* who still seemed too amazed to move or reply to Bellicus's taunts. As the dissenting, angry murmurs began to rise in number and volume behind him though, the Pictish king realised he must do something.

"Qunavo!" he shouted, turning to gesture furiously at his own druid. "Ria. Come forward and deal with this big streak of piss. Show him you have the ear of Taranis as well. He's not the only one with the power to speak to the gods!"

Qunavo and Ria looked at one another for a long moment and it seemed like Drest's entire army held their collective breath, waiting for their mystics to counter Bellicus's threats.

"No," Qunavo replied. He did not shout, and his tone was calm, but the word was somehow heard by all gathered there.

"What do you mean, 'no'?" Drest demanded, now seemingly too befuddled by all that was happening to comprehend his druid's reply. "Come here and do as I command, now!"

"You do not command us," Qunavo called. "No king can command a druid. We serve only the gods. For years we have worked beside you, Drest, supporting you, guiding you, counselling you, and acting as your conduit to our gods. But our time serving you has come to an end — your alliance with the sea-wolves, and your acceptance of that"— he pointed at Yngvildr — "*witch's* evil ways cannot be supported any longer."

Ria stepped forward then, and she had her own staff in her hand which she pointed at the *volva*. "Her wand has been ripped asunder, and, with it, her powers have fled. Your war is doomed to failure, Drest, and we shall not stand against the Merlin in this."

So saying, she spun and headed towards Aife's warband at the river, Qunavo nodding agreement and walking beside her.

The stunned army of Picts parted to let them pass, giving them plenty of room, as if they were afraid to even touch or be near the wrathful druids who had forsaken them.

"Get back here, you little bitch!" Drest screeched, face flushing scarlet. "Qunavo, you old bastard, come here, I command you. I am your king!"

Druid and druidess did not even turn their heads to look back at him.

Time seemed to slow and even Horsa was silent for once, a bemused expression on his face as he sought for a solution to their problem. And this certainly was a problem for, although Drest's army outnumbered the two Damnonii warbands — Bellicus's on the left, Gavo leading the one on the right, supported by Koriosis — Pictish morale had been completely shattered. The faces of the troops around them showed fear, anger, and uncertainty, and many were muttering and looking mutinously in Drest's direction.

Again, Bellicus seized on the uncertainty in the enemy camp. "Leave these lands, Drest, now. While you still can." He felt a drop of rain on his shaved scalp and reached his arms up to the sky, calling, "Give them a sign, Taranis, God of Thunder. Show them you are displeased with their treatment of my people, and their vile sacrifices!"

He remained in that position for a few heartbeats, face pointing upwards, arms held wide, and then the rain began to fall, softly at first but quickly growing heavier.

There were some among the Picts, and the Saxons too, who'd also felt the rain coming on before Bellicus had called for a sign, but their protests were lost as the majority of their kinsmen moaned in superstitious fear and demanded Drest protect them from the wrath of the thunder god.

Bellicus was not close enough to hear the enemy king as he muttered to himself, but he could read the man's lips: "What do I do?" he was asking himself, bereft of ideas and perhaps even unfit for command.

Everything was going to plan.

"Gavo!" the druid shouted across the open ground between them. "Are you ready?"

"Aye!" came back the reply, clear and confident.

"Make up your mind, Drest," Bellicus cried, turning again to the shocked Pictish king. "Leave our lands now, or see your army crushed forever. We slaughtered many of your men the last time we met in battle, meaning you had to pay the Saxons to bulk up your numbers. This time there will be no young men, or even middle-aged men, left alive to return home and harvest your fields. Everyone in your lands will starve, Drest, and the Picts will become nothing but a distant memory. You, Drest, will be forever remembered as the architect of Pictish genocide!"

It was clearly too much for the king to take, and he bowed his head, clearly beaten.

"That's it," Bellicus murmured to himself. "Surrender, you weak cretin, and then we can give Horsa and Yngvildr the justice they deserve…"

As if reading the minds of both Drest and Bellicus, Horsa suddenly raised his spear high in the air and roared, "We outnumber these weaklings. Are you with me?"

His Saxons, as ready for a fight as ever, answered his question with throaty shouts of their own.

"Drest! Lead your men, you pitiful sack of shit. It's time for battle!"

* * *

Narina stood on the eastern peak of Dun Breatann staring down at the confrontation   going on half a mile away. She could hear shouts as the leaders of the two sides conversed, but she could not make out a word of it at that distance.

When the enemy army slowly began to move forwards, towards the twin Damnonii armies, Narina knew it was time.

"Gods protect us," she breathed, and turned to Gerallt. "Pass the word," she said. "We're leaving the fortress."

The captain hesitated for just a moment — if he'd been in charge he might well have been too cautious for this move, but he was not, and he was duty bound to obey his queen. He saluted and gestured to a soldier standing in the middle of the twin peaks, at the steps that led down to the main gates.

The soldier had been waiting for this signal and he spun, making the same signal in turn but this time to a man waiting at the bottom of the steps.

"I must go then, my lady," said Gerallt. "And take my place with our garrison as we march out."

"Good luck, my friend," Narina replied, smiling and giving him a quick hug which he did not seem to know how to deal with.

"Thank you, lady," he said and, without another word, hurried off to make his way down to the gates.

Narina watched him go, a heavy weight settling in the pit of her stomach at what was to come. Part of her wished to go with the soldiers but she was no warrior and would only get in the way as they fought to liberate Alt Clota. Gerallt did not need her for this — he may lack Gavo's ingenuity and creativity, but all he was expected to do was lead the soldiers out of Dun Breatann and attack the rear of the enemy army.

Narina turned to see fighting had already started to the north, although the rear ranks of Drest's army had not moved very far and Narina wondered why. She hoped it was because they had no stomach for the fight and were hanging back rather than following their commander's orders to engage Bellicus and Gavo's men.

Catia was beside her and she grabbed Narina by the hand, hauling her away to head for the other side of the peak.

"Come on, Mother," the girl said. "Let's watch Gerallt leave."

The heavy sensation in Narina's guts turned to a churning mass as they ran. They had been watching proceedings since they'd begun, and they'd seen the warband led by Aife — easy to spot even from that lofty vantage point — retreat to the bank of the Clota. Would the Pictish princess keep them there, or would she betray Bellicus and charge to her father's aid?

Everything depended on Aife now. She did not command a huge force, but it was enough to turn the tide of the battle should she decide to attack Gerallt's men.

When they reached the far side of the peak and looked down they could see Aife, long hair flowing behind her as she walked alone towards the rear ranks of Drest's army. She was much closer than the warriors engaged in battle half a mile up the road and Narina could hear what she was shouting.

"We cannot win this!" The princess's voice carried up the rock to the queen and Catia. "Drest has brought us to ruin and would now lead you all to your deaths. Retreat! Retreat back to the river with my warband. I will make sure the Damnonii spare you."

Most of Drest's men ignored her, one or two called her a traitor, but a few did as she asked, their faith in the king completely lost. When others saw those warriors leaving the massed ranks of the shieldwall, even more followed their lead.

"Come!" Aife called, louder and even more forcefully. "The Damnonii are marching out from Dun Breatann! If you don't wish to be slaughtered for no reason, retreat with me to the river, now! I won't be able to help you if you don't."

With that, she turned and walked south, to her warband, and the river, gesturing as she went for all to follow.

The outer gates of Dun Breatann swung open then and Gerallt led his men out.

Narina swallowed the bile that rose in her throat, knowing these moments would be crucial. If Aife suddenly commanded her men to attack the Damnonii soldiers as they came through the gates it could mean disaster.

Yet Gerallt passed out safely and started the march north, passing through the camp that had housed the enemy army since the siege began. His men had been ordered not to waste energy destroying the tents or wagons or anything else belonging to the Picts and Saxons and so they moved quickly, easily covering the ground as, behind them, the gates to Dun Breatann were shut and barred once more.

"This is it," Narina said, feeling utterly sick. "No going back now. All our troops are out there. If Aife betrays us, Alt Clota will fall, and Drest shall take control."

"With Horsa and Yngvildr," Catia muttered, pale-faced at the prospect of being left once more in the grip of the feared Saxons.

CHAPTER THIRTY-EIGHT

Horsa led his Saxons directly towards Bellicus, running as fast as he could while heavily laden with his weapons and armour, and the limp the druid had given him four years before.

"So much for them surrendering," said Duro, locking his shield in place with the druid's and the rest of their warriors lined up beside them, forming a bristling wall of spears.

"That shitbag Drest was just about to," grunted the druid. "Horsa knew it and ordered the attack to make sure things didn't end peacefully."

"Aye," the centurion said, trying to blow a bead of sweat from his upper lip. "These fuckers charging towards us certainly don't look very peaceful."

"Brace!" Bellicus roared, setting his legs firmly in the ground and hunching down behind his shield as the enemy warband drew closer.

The very first clatter of an enemy's weapon on one's shield was always something of a shock to the druid. From a position of security and almost serenity, especially if he'd downed a cup or two of mead, that first blow was a brutal wake-up call to the blood and terror that was about to erupt all around them.

The linden boards of his shield absorbed Horsa's attack, and Bellicus thrust his own spear at the jarl. Somehow, Horsa didn't just dodge the thrust, he managed to disappear.

Either the gods had spirited him away somewhere, or he'd fallen and been hidden amongst the ranks of his men but, whatever had happened, Bellicus had no time to think about it as an axe came thundering down on his shield, sending a horrific jolt of pain lancing through his arm.

Screaming in rage, he leaned back and then, levering himself forward on his back foot, plunged the iron point of his spear into the axeman's neck just as he was winding up for a second attack. Blood sprayed from the terrible gash and the Saxon fell, axe forgotten as he tried to hold his windpipe closed.

"Kill the bastards!" Bellicus roared, bloodlust suddenly filling him. He'd genuinely hoped to avoid battle — had no real appetite for killing a second group of Picts in as many years — but now that the fighting had begun the druid would do his best to slaughter every sheep-humping one of them.

At his side Duro was wielding his spear with skill despite the fact he was far more accustomed to using his spatha. Centurion and Druid stood firm behind their locked shields, dispatching those who sought to slaughter them.

Horsa was still not visible and Bellicus soon stopped looking for him when another Saxon spear whipped past his face. A couple of fingers' width closer and it would have skewered him right through the eye. Duro killed the man but there were more coming and Bellicus focused his full attention on those enemies, forgetting for now about the despised jarl.

An axe hammered down on the druid's shield and this time the wood split. The enemy's weapon also became lodged in it, and Bellicus was forced to drop it, kicking out as the axeman sought to draw his seax. In an instant the druid had let go of his spear as well, and drew his sword which was named Melltgwyn - White Lightning.

"For Wotan!" the enemy soldier screamed, thrusting his seax at Bellicus. The blade was wickedly sharp and managed to slice a long gash in the druid's arm as he tried to deflect the blow. Gritting his teeth against the sudden pain, he brought Melltgwyn down and felt it bite deep into his opponent's collar bone. There was an audible crack, quickly followed by another scream, and then the Saxon dropped to his knees sobbing in shock and Bellicus kicked him brutally in the face.

That was the last the druid saw of that enemy, but still more were coming on and he wondered how the rest of the battle was going. Perhaps it hadn't been such a good idea to lead from the front after all. At least Cai had been kept at the rear of the warband — a shieldwall was no place for a dog. Where was Aife? Had she kept her word and held her detachment of Picts back from the fighting as she'd agreed when she met Bellicus on the road and he whispered that request to her? And what of Gerallt and Ysfael? Were they even now marching to help Bellicus and Gavo?

All these thoughts and more passed through Bellicus's mind as he defended himself from spears and axes, barely registering the fact that his tidy shieldwall had grown ragged and many of the

Damnonii were now fighting with swords or axes rather than spears.

"We need to move back!" Duro shouted, right in the druid's ear. "Let the next row take over."

"All right, no need to shout!" Bellicus retorted, batting aside another seax and reversing his sword to ram the point through a Saxon *brynja,* watching in satisfaction as its wearer spat blood and then collapsed on the Alt Clotan grass, dead.

"No need to shout?" Duro cried, desperately throwing up his shield as an axe came flying through the air towards his face. The weapon, thrown by the gods knew who, smashed into the shield and fell harmless to the ground. "I already asked you three times. You never heard me, you were in one of your trances again."

Bellicus smiled savagely and called out, "Front row, move back!"

Still facing the front, he stepped backwards and the men behind him, fresh and eager for Saxon blood, shuffled forward, locking shields and thrusting spears at the dismayed enemy who were not faring too well, or so it seemed to Bellicus from his vantage point.

"Where is that whoreson, Horsa?" Duro demanded, as if reading Bellicus's mind.

"I don't know. With any luck he fell in the initial fighting."

"I doubt that," Duro replied. "No doubt he'll turn up soon, probably causing more chaos."

Bellicus looked around and saw a yew tree that he reckoned he could climb for a better view. It was not a very tall tree, but it would allow him to see at least more of the battlefield than he could at the moment.

"Give me a leg up," he said to the centurion.

After a moment of grunting, the druid had swung himself up into the branches.

"You're surprisingly nimble for such a big man," Duro said approvingly. "What can you see?"

Bellicus shoved himself up a little further and scanned the combatants through the tree's needles. "Gavo is doing as well as we are. It looks like many of Drest's Picts haven't committed to the battle yet, they seem to be hanging back on the periphery."

"Good news," the centurion nodded, leaning on his spear to catch his breath.

"Aye," Bellicus agreed, then grew more excited, laughing and calling out thanks to Taranis.

"What is it? What's happening?" Duro demanded, standing on his tip-toes and trying to see over the helmeted heads of the warriors fighting for dominance in front of him.

"It's Gerallt," Bellicus reported. "Gerallt is on his way to join us with the garrison of Dun Breatann!"

* * *

"My lady, are we really going through with this? Drest is your father, and our king. We can't just leave him to die, surely?"

Aife looked sharply at the Pictish nobleman who stood beside her. He was a small, wiry man who didn't really look like he wanted to join Drest at all. Especially now that Narina's men had left the fortress to join Gavo and the other Damnonii warriors.

Aife had been agonising over what to do about her father for days and now it came to this. She had barely known Drest growing up, and their relationship in recent years had essentially been that of a king and one of his soldiers. They were not close. Yet, even so, Drest was her blood, as well as her lord, and it was tearing Aife apart to stand there while he fought the Damnonii. *This is the right thing to do*, she told herself firmly. *For me, and for my people.*

"My father led us here on a fool's errand," she said, coolly but loudly, so others could hear her words. "You've all seen what's been happening. The gods are not on our side in this war and when that happens, there is no point in fighting."

"She's right," Qunavo added, lending his own considerable weight to the argument. "Drest chose to seek aid from the Saxons' gods and he's paying the price for it. Any who wish to join him, go now. The rest of us will remain here and pick up the pieces when the battle is done."

"That won't be long now," someone said fretfully. "Look, a load of our men are running away along the road to the east."

"Maybe they want to get behind the Damnonii army at that side," another man suggested.

Time proved him wrong however, as dozens of Drest's men disappeared and did not return.

"This just seems wrong," the nobleman who'd first addressed Aife cried. "Abandoning our own king like this."

"His own actions caused it," Aife replied through gritted teeth. "His leadership would have seen our army crushed and our lands defenceless. Who do you think would have been first to take advantage of that? The Saxons!"

Qunavo had by now fully come around to the thought that the sea-wolves were the biggest threat to the tribes of Britain. Any notion he had of forming an alliance with them had been shattered by the actions of Horsa and Yngvildr and he gladly spoke up against them now.

"Hengist has long coveted Dunnottar," said the druid. "He would have come with his longships and subjugated our people. You could see it here — Horsa was supposed to be under Drest's command, but the arrogant jarl could not bring himself to do anything other than what he thought best."

"Exactly," said Ria. "This war was lost the moment that witch began making human sacrifices, offending the gods of our people. We might have prevailed against the Damnonii warriors, but we cannot fight the gods as well."

"Taranis take the *volva*," Qunavo cried. "Drest should never have allowed her to join his army."

"But he did," said Aife with a sigh. "And this is the result."

* * *

Yngvildr had drunk one of her magical concoctions before the battle started — a mixture of wine, herbs, and henbane. She'd felt as light as a feather when she confronted the big druid, and confidence had flowed through her. Bellicus had defeated her once before in a magical battle, but Yngvildr knew he'd used simple trickery to fool the stupid villagers at that time, resulting in them pronouncing the druid as the victor. The *volva* had not expected this day to turn out the same, not after she'd spilled so much blood in the name of the Saxon gods.

Yet, when her wand had snapped in half at a crucial moment, making it seem like the gods had forsaken her, Yngvildr had felt shock and almost grief. How could Wotan abandon her? How could Thunor snap her wand in twain before so many onlookers, all watching for a sign? How could Tyr allow the Damnonii to be winning the battle?

The effects of her potion made her giddy and unable to properly understand everything that was going on, and it took Horsa to lift her bodily from the field just before battle commenced, otherwise she would have been killed immediately.

The fighting raged before her as she stood, light-headed and half dreaming, seeing shadowy figures moving about the battlefield, and dark, winged shapes flying overhead like the ghosts of long-dead ravens.

Eventually she began to understand what was going on, and she looked around, noticing that the Damnonii forces seemed to be standing their ground and, in places, even pushing the Saxons and the Picts back. Many of Drest's people had already run from the battle, while that big bitch Aife had not brought her warband to reinforce her father's army. Traitorous whore! Yngvildr believed she could see the princess standing before the ranks of her men, long hair flowing about her head like the snakes of Medusa as she watched the fighting impassively.

Yngvildr could see the giant enemy druid climbing a tree now, and she could see him laughing with glee. It was obvious even to the highly intoxicated *volva* that the battle was not going as Drest had hoped.

She looked down and realised she was still clutching the stem of her broken wand. Her eyes took a moment to focus on the end of it and she squinted, wondering if there would be some evidence of Thunor's lightning bolt that had blasted it in two. Bringing it closer to her face, she rubbed a thumb along the tip and sudden understanding flooded her.

It was not the gods that had shattered her wand — someone had sawn through it, just enough to allow it to remain intact until the moment she swung it down, and then it had come apart.

Who could have done such a thing? Yngvildr wondered. It would have to be someone within Drest's camp, and someone with the authority to wander freely around. Someone who hated the Saxons, and particularly Yngvildr herself...

She turned and looked towards Aife, the *volva* still running her thumb across the raised lip of iron that had held her staff together for just long enough to make her look a fool.

"It was you," she hissed, and, feeling as if the gods had lifted her off the ground, she slipped into the undergrowth that flanked the battlefield.

CHAPTER THIRTY-NINE

Gerallt's appearance had prompted more of Drest's men to flee the field of battle without even striking a blow. It must have been obvious to them that things had gone terribly wrong and, with the arrival of the garrison of Dun Breatann at their backs, things could only get worse. So they ran.

Not all of Drest's Picts fled when Gerallt's warband appeared, though. Those who hadn't run off joined the main body of their king's army, turning to face the newcomers fanning out from the fortress.

When the warriors from Dun Breatann attacked, it seemed to rekindle the fighting on the other two fronts and the land north of the fortress became a churning maelstrom of barbarism and slaughter.

The Saxons fought with more skill and ferocity than any of the others, and Horsa was not dead, far from it. Bellicus could see the jarl laying about himself with his mighty axe, shattering helms and skulls as if they were eggs, and woe betide any who fell in front of him, for their limbs, chests, or heads would be smashed to pulp by that heavy iron blade, wielded as if Horsa was chopping wood rather than living men.

So dangerous was the jarl that the Damnonii who faced him started to move back, giving him a wide berth as they sought less deadly targets.

"You!" Horsa roared, pointing at Bellicus and throwing his head back and shaking his head like the animal he was named after. "Face me now, druid, and let us see who is stronger."

Bellicus heard the challenge and immediately moved to accept. He did not fear death for he was a druid and he knew that he would be reborn one day in some other body. He also did not fear Horsa for, although the ground near the jarl was littered with mangled corpses, Bellicus was every bit as dangerous in a fight.

"No!" Duro shouted, hacking off the hand of a fallen Saxon who was trying to claw his way back to his feet by using the centurion's legs and tunic as leverage. "Hold, Bellicus! That bastard is mine!" He shoved his sword down, through the back of the Saxon on the ground, and then moved over to stand in front of the towering druid. "He killed my wife, remember?"

Bellicus did, of course, remember. And he knew Duro was a hardy fighter. But he also knew that Horsa was about twenty years younger than the centurion and barely out of breath despite reaping a bloody harvest of many Damnonii soldiers.

Still, Duro had sworn to avenge Alatucca's death and Bellicus did not think it honourable to refuse the man's request.

Reaching down, the druid picked up the shield of a slaughtered Damnonii warrior, made sure it was still fully intact, and handed it to his friend. "Go, then, but take this, and be careful, Duro. He's dangerous, and he will fight dirty."

"That's fine," the centurion hissed, grasping the shield in his left hand and twirling his spatha expertly. "So will I."

There were pockets of men fighting individual battles all over the road and the field now and it was almost as if they parted to let Duro and Horsa come together. As though some giant hand was moving pieces on a tafl board.

"I don't want you, Roman," the Saxon sneered as Duro strode towards him. "I want the druid. I owe him for my limp."

"And I owe you for murdering my wife, you piece of shit," the centurion retorted, setting his feet and thrusting his sword at the jarl. The spatha had originally been used by the Romans as a cavalry sword, and it had a longer blade than the old infantry gladius, so Horsa was immediately forced to dance backwards to avoid being run through.

"What wife?" Horsa asked, frowning.

"You and your men chased us, me and Bellicus, to my home town of Luguvalium. We weren't there, but my wife and friends were. You slaughtered them all."

A light dawned in the Saxon's eyes as he cast his mind back to that time, not long after Bellicus had injured his foot. "I remember that!" he cried, swinging his axe at Duro who jumped aside and struck out with his sword. Horsa's shield absorbed the blow and he said, "I didn't just kill your wife, you know."

His lewd smile made it very clear what he meant and Duro, even more enraged than before, mounted another attack, slashing and thrusting with terrible ferocity.

"Don't let him rile you," Bellicus called. "Remember your training." The centurion had commanded in the legions, and he had also trained with the druid — he was an expert in not only fighting beside comrades in a shieldwall, but also in one-on-one duels like this.

Horsa was one of the greatest Saxon warriors that had ever come to Britain though. He was not just skilled, and experienced in warfare, he was younger and faster than the centurion. Realising he was at a disadvantage with his heavy axe he tossed it aside and drew his own sword which was very similar in design to Duro's spatha.

"Your wife parted her legs for me, Roman," said the Saxon, still grinning and hardly out of breath whereas Duro was panting heavily after his sustained flurry of blows which had not resulted in so much as a nick to the sea-wolf's skin. "She screamed as I ploughed her. I think she was enjoying it." He laughed nastily as Duro's face twisted in fury. "She was not enjoying it by the time the fifth or sixth of my men took their turn, though."

Bellicus had no idea if any of that was true, and Duro couldn't know it either. Horsa was bound to be exaggerating to make the centurion angry, to goad him into a mistake. And Duro was falling for it, the druid realised with dismay, as the older man came forward again, swinging wildly with his sword, the blade smashing against Horsa's shield, chipping off splinters of wood but doing nothing to injure its bearer. He was bellowing like an animal too, and Bellicus was dismayed — he had known Duro for a while now, fought beside him on many occasions, and the centurion was generally calm and in control.

To see him like this was frightening, and the druid guessed it was the result of the pain that had built up within his friend over the past four years. Even a centurion could only take so much, and Horsa's taunts had obviously opened the floodgates to Duro's long-supressed emotions.

Seeing the effect he was having on his opponent, Horsa grinned, taunting Duro further, telling him what raping Alatucca had been like, what she'd said, how she'd begged for her life. As he spoke, the Saxon defended himself with his shield, only throwing the odd thrust or slash of his own, but seemingly content to let the older man tire himself out.

"Duro, you need to calm down," Bellicus shouted, wondering if he should sneak around behind Horsa and kill him, or at least distract the bastard. But he knew Duro would never forgive him — he wanted revenge, and he would not appreciate being helped, as if he wasn't man enough to take it himself.

"Your wife loved having a young man to spread her legs for," the jarl said with a mocking laugh. "It must have been years since you gave her what she needed."

Duro roared again, and again unleashed a flurry of combinations, but each strike was parried either by Horsa's shield or by his sword.

"You should have seen her after we were finished with her. Panting and sweating. I don't think she really believed I was going to kill her. Not until"— He flinched, holding up his shield, but this time Duro's sword remained held aloft.

Bellicus stared at his friend in shock as he stood, frozen for what seemed like forever, and then, instead of bringing down his spatha in another attack, he pressed his clenched fist against his chest, a terror-stricken look on his face.

Horsa gave a triumphant laugh, understanding filling him at the same time it did Bellicus: Duro was having a seizure of some kind.

The druid had seen men die like this before, generally older men who were physically unfit. Of course, the centurion was as fit as any man his age now, but, when Bellicus had first met him, he'd been hugely overweight. It seemed those middle years of his life, when he'd let himself go, sampling too many of his own wares as a baker in Luguvalium, had come back to haunt him.

Horsa's sword and shield dropped as he saw his opponent was no longer a threat, and he stepped closer to deliver yet another vile taunt about Duro's wife.

Bellicus started moving, knowing he could not let this continue any longer. He couldn't just stand by as Duro was tortured into his grave by this twisted sea-wolf. Melltgwyn was in the druid's hand and he took a step forward, but, as he did, he faltered, wondering if he could believe his own eyes.

As Horsa let his guard down and came closer to Duro the centurion's right foot suddenly came up with all the power of a Roman ballista, slamming directly between Horsa's legs.

Even Bellicus winced at the sight, and Horsa groaned, knees buckling.

"You won't be using that to rape any more women, you gutless Saxon bastard," Duro growled, apparently over the seizure that had incapacitated him. Then, as the jarl bent over, trying to somehow lessen the pain, Duro's spatha licked out, its tip sliding between the mail links of Horsa's *brynja* and on, into his heart.

The big Saxon who had caused so much pain and suffering for Duro, Catia, and countless other Britons, slumped to the ground at the centurion's feet, dead.

"What the hell was that?" Bellicus asked in amazement. He simply could not believe that his friend was still alive after such a one-sided fight.

"I told you I would fight dirty," Duro replied with a twinkle in his eye, and then he sat down on the grass, utterly spent.

CHAPTER FORTY

Any thoughts the Picts beside the Clota might have had of ignoring Aife's command to hang back and stay out of the battle were quickly blown away, as Gerallt's men joined the fray and it became very clear how things were going to play out. Then, possible thoughts of fighting were replaced with thoughts of self-preservation.

"What's to stop the Damnonii falling on us once they're done?" one of the warriors behind her demanded as the battle neared its conclusion. "They'll be filled with battle-fever, looking for more victims to kill."

"I'm here," Aife said, turning to address the man, who was called Maelchon. "Bellicus and the other Damnonii leaders know me, and they will recognise that we remained out of the fighting. They won't harm us, so calm down."

"This is all wrong. Drest's her father, and she's just left him to those Damnonii dogs."

"So did you, Maelchon!" another of the Picts, a noble named Oengus, retorted. "We all did, but we had no choice. At least this way Dunnottar will have a garrison to return home and keep the Saxons from its walls. This way, we Picts will not be erased from Britain forever."

There was silence as the warriors absorbed that. And then Maelchon spoke up again.

"You want Drest's throne for yourself, don't you?"

Aife was stunned. The thought had never crossed her mind — in all honesty she had not really believed her father would be killed. Bellicus and Gavo would recognise him, she'd hoped, and take him hostage, ransoming him back later.

"So what if she does?" the nobleman, Oengus asked. "She couldn't lead us any worse than Drest has done."

"That's not the point," Maelchon returned, and then other voices joined in and a whole discussion got underway.

"Let them squabble," Qunavo said to the princess, touching her arm reassuringly. "It'll give them something to focus on other than that." He jerked his head to the north where the battle was now finished apart from a few isolated pockets where a handful of men,

Saxons, or Picts, refused to give in until their last breath was hacked from their bodies.

"They do have a point though," Aife murmured so only he and Ria could hear her. "What will happen if my father falls to Damnonii blades? Who will take the throne?"

"I rather suspect Narina will have something to say about it," Qunavo replied.

"And Bellicus," added Ria. "They'll want some puppet they can control I imagine."

"That is some way off yet, however," Qunavo said. "Let's just get through today before we start to look to tomorrow's problems. At least, as you noted, there will still be some Pictish warriors left alive to defend our lands after this. We can rebuild."

"As we should have done this year!" Aife said caustically. "Instead of coming here for yet another ill-advised siege."

"Hindsight is wonderful, isn't it, my lady?" Qunavo replied tartly.

"Never mind hindsight," she growled. "You and Ria are supposed to have the gift of foresight. You should have seen this coming."

"Did you?" Ria asked, annoyed by the girl's tone.

"Not exactly, but I knew from the start it was a terrible mistake to try and be friends with the sea-wolves."

Qunavo sighed and gestured with his hand as if to cut off any further discussion on the topic. "We can all see now that we made a mistake there. It won't happen again."

Aife looked up at the walls of the fortress that had witnessed so many deaths over the centuries it had stood there grim, grey, and apparently unconquerable. She saw at the very top, so high and so steep that it almost made Aife dizzy to crane her neck upwards, a small figure standing. No, two small figures, looking out at the battle.

The princess smiled. At least her young friend, and one-time travelling companion, had not been harmed during this latest war. Aife wished she could see Catia at that very moment and a sudden, overwhelming urge to put distance between herself and the bickering Pictish warriors at her back came over her.

"I'll be back," she said to Qunavo and Ria. "I must clear my head."

So saying, she walked forward, trying to silence the thoughts that were whirling about her mind like December snows in coastal Dunnottar. The ground was flat, and churned mostly to mud from the feet of the besiegers over the weeks they'd been camping there. It was a grim, depressing sight, and Aife turned to the east, where some undergrowth remained, and the stream ran down from the hills — near Dun Buic she guessed — into the Clota.

Images of men who might replace her father as King of the Picts filled her head despite her best efforts to think of nothing at all. Would any of those noblemen prove worthy leaders of such a proud, ancient people? Would any of them even survive the fighting today?

And what of Horsa and Yngvildr? Would they continue to live a charmed existence, protected from harm by their cruel northern gods who revelled in the blood of innocents?

Where was the *volva* anyway? Surely she hadn't chosen to stand in the shieldwall with the warriors?

Aife wondered if the iron wand had snapped. It had been the princess who slipped into Horsa's tent when he was out looking for more locals to brutalise, and taken a small handsaw to the *volva's* wand. The little rasping teeth had been just sharp enough to cut halfway into the metal shaft and Aife had imagined what would happen the next time the witch tried to wield it.

She truly wished she had been there to see it if it had snapped off in Yngvildr's hand. What a sight that would have been. If it happened as she imagined, Bellicus and Duro would have got a shock, and a laugh as well, no doubt about it. Aife grinned, picturing the scene.

"Serves her right," she muttered as she reached the undergrowth. "Evil witch."

She started, wondering if she was going mad as she noticed two smouldering blue eyes staring out of the greenery at her. And then a cold chill swept over her as she realised it was Yngvildr, and the *volva* was coming towards her with half an iron wand held in her upraised right hand.

They were so close that Aife did not have time to draw her sword all the way out of its scabbard. She got it halfway before she felt the iron bar smash into her helmet and she fell onto one knee.

"Stop!" she cried, head ringing from the blow, mind racing as she tried desperately to think of something else to say to the *volva* that might halt her attack.

"You did this!" Yngvildr screeched, and brought the bar around again.

Instinctively, Aife threw up her arm to protect her head, and let out a terrible scream as the wand struck her. From the pain she guessed bones had been broken — and in her right arm too. Even if she got to her feet she would not be able to draw her sword using her left arm — there simply wasn't enough room to do so, for it had to be drawn out across the body to let the blade clear its scabbard. And how could she fight left-handed anyway? She was not skilled in using a sword like that.

Reeling, she staggered to her feet as Yngvildr ranted at her, invoking the gods, beseeching them to strike down the warrior-princess who had so humiliated her.

"It wasn't me," Aife heard herself shouting, and she hated herself for showing her fear so clearly to the Saxon woman. The iron wand rose up again, and again it came around in a wild swing but Yngvildr was not a trained warrior. She was highly adept at slitting the throats of men and women who were restrained or placid, but she was not so good at hitting a moving opponent.

Aife cried out in agony as she dodged another blow, pain lancing along her broken arm, and she wondered if she should run away but her head was still ringing from that initial blow she'd suffered. She knew she would not get very far before she vomited or simply collapsed, and the thought of presenting Yngvildr with a prone, immobile target to bring down that fearful sawn-off wand upon, over and over, until Aife was just—

At last, Aife's training kicked in, fuelled by sheer rage at being bested by a woman who had rarely, if ever, swung a weapon in battle before. Throwing herself forward, she grabbed for the *volva*'s throat, good hand squeezing, nails biting deep into flesh. The princess felt the wand jab her in the guts and she almost let go of her enemy, but her mail coat stopped the weapon from doing too much damage.

"I'll kill you!" Yngvildr tried to shout, but Aife's grip was incredibly strong and tightening by the moment, so all that came out was a guttural hiss.

Aife felt herself beginning to black out and knew she had to do as much damage as possible to her would-be murderer before she was incapable. Leaning forward, she bit Yngvildr's nose, feeling her teeth sink into the soft flesh before her mouth filled with blood and screaming filled the princess's ears as everything went black and she fell to the ground.

* * *

Gavo, like all good commanders, stood with his men as they fought, leading by example, his spear and, eventually, his sword, spilling much enemy blood. Like Bellicus and the others in the Damnonii army Gavo had no idea how the battle was progressing. It was, he thought, as scrappy an affair as any skirmish he'd ever been a part of, and he wished he could soar high overhead to get a bird's eye view of things. He looked for the druid, Koriosis, wondering if perhaps the seer might attempt such a magical feat, but the young man was standing off to the side, arms held up, calling on the gods to help Gavo's troops.

Narina would be on the summit of Dun Breatann watching the opposing sides hack at each other as their numbers dwindled, the captain thought. He looked up as there was a momentary lull in the fighting and fancied he could see two tiny, distant figures on top of the rock but his eyes were not what they had once been and he thought it might be his imagination. A massive, black shape caught his attention though, soaring overhead, and, when it let out a loud caw, Gavo knew it was the raven, Uchaf, come to scavenge on whatever flesh it could find.

Well, by the time the sun set, Uchaf would be able to fill his belly with as much meat as he could eat. The raven would likely not be able to fly for days, so full would it be!

A sword flashed past his ear, nicking it, and he came back to the present with a start, realising he was utterly exhausted. He parried the next attack and struck out with his own blade, catching his opponent on the side of the neck. It was not a killing blow, but it had been ferocious enough to send the Pict reeling backwards, stumbling into his own men and disturbing their rhythm. The warriors flanking Gavo took advantage of that and Gavo pressed his hand to his ear. It came away scarlet and the terrible stinging pain told him that a chunk of flesh had been sliced off.

He would not die from the injury though, so he continued to fight on, despite his tiredness.

He was not certain, but it seemed to him that the battle was nearing an end. The combatants on both sides were tiring and, without fresh troops to bring in, there would need to be a rest soon. Drest, if he still lived, would call his men back towards Dun Breatann, and Gavo would order his own temporary retreat. The thought of a momentary respite from the endless hacking and slashing, replaced by a mug of ale and perhaps a chunk of black bread lifted his spirits.

And then he knew Drest *was* still alive, for the King of the Picts was standing right in front of him, and doing his best to split Gavo's head in two.

"That's Drest!" the captain shouted, hoarse from the day's exertions and trying desperately to bring up his shield and absorb the enemy king's attack. "Kill the whoreson!"

Thoughts of tiredness, and even of a well-earned mug of ale, evaporated and Gavo stepped forward half a pace, thrusting his sword out viciously towards Drest. The blade was parried, and the two men began trading blows.

The rest of the world disappeared for Gavo as he focused his entire attention on Drest. Watching his face for slight twitches that would warn of an impending slash, watching the tip of his sword to see which direction it would next lick out, watching the king's movement to determine if a heavy attack, or faster flurry would come next.

"Surrender, Drest!" the captain shouted as he dodged another thrust from the man who'd brought all this trouble to Alt Clota. "You know you can't win. Surrender, and spare the lives of these men."

"And be executed? Fuck off!" Drest redoubled his efforts to hack Gavo to ribbons, catching the Damnonii captain on the arm, his sword tearing open his bicep. With the blood from his wounded ear now running down to mingle with that of his arm, the captain was a mess. Yet he did not feel the pain from either injury now, just tiredness and, worryingly, that was now turning into drowsiness. Whether it was from lack of blood or something less ominous, Gavo could not tell. What he did know was that he should step back and let another man, younger and less exhausted, take his place in the line.

Yet the prospect of killing the filthy rat who'd done so much harm to Alt Clota was too enticing for the experienced captain though and he continued to evade Drest's blade, probing for an opening of his own, for a chance to end the threat this man posed to Gavo's people once and for all.

It finally came when Drest slipped on the blood-soaked grass, falling forward a half-step before he was able to regain his equilibrium. Gavo saw the slip and lunged, putting everything he had into a thrust that took the king low on the left side, the tip of the sword tearing through the mailcoat Drest wore and deep into his guts.

"That'll put an end to all of this," Gavo said, breathing deeply as he stared into his enemy's eyes. "You'll never trouble us again, Drest, you useless lump of horse shit."

The Pictish king swallowed and his mouth worked as if he might speak but couldn't find the strength to force the words out. Blood streamed from the sides of his lips and he looked like he wanted to cry.

"We've won," Gavo said grimly, elation filling him. "The Damnonii have won, and now Narina will take Dunnottar, and all the rest of your lands, Drest. May the gods torment you forever." It was not normally in Gavo's nature to be so vindictive but he could not forget what had been done to Sentica, or the sights he'd seen in Dun Buic and the other villages the invaders had put to sword and torch.

"Step back, lads!" the captain roared, newfound strength filling him as he drew out his blade from Drest's torso and slowly retreated. His command was echoed along the Damnonii line and the men gladly did as they were bade, desperate for a rest. The Picts were just as eager for a momentary respite and they too broke off their attack, shuffling backwards until a gap appeared between the opposing factions.

Gavo bent and huffed in gusting, deep breaths, like a drowning man pulled from the sea. Now that the battle-fury was fading he could feel the pain of his injuries, as well as the aches in his joints that came with middle-age. Someone ran to him and handed him a

242

cup which he emptied in quick, shuddering swallows, and then raised it in the air and turned to face his men with a grin.

"Drest is dead!" he cried. "Their leader is dead, and once they realise it they'll lose heart for the fight. Grab what rest you can, warriors of Alt Clota, for this battle is ours, and soon we'll put an end to the rest of the Pictish and Saxon bastards!"

The Damnonii soldiers heard his words, most of them at least, and a triumphant, relieved shout filled the air. Dun Breatann would soon be free again!

CHAPTER FORTY-ONE

The Saxons did not surrender — it was not in their nature to give in to Britons, especially when they knew they would simply be executed anyway. It was quite obvious Bellicus and his followers despised the raiders thanks to the way they'd torched villages and brutalised their Damnonii occupants. So, when Horsa fell and their conduit to the gods, Yngvildr, was no longer around to influence them, the sea-wolves either continued to fight, hoping for an exalted, hero's place in the afterlife, or they ran, following those of the Picts who'd headed east when it became clear they were losing the battle.

Bellicus did not command his men to chase them — there was little point, for hardly any were left. Those few might make it back to their ships at Mucrois and carry word of their defeat to Hengist. That, the druid hoped, might make the Saxon *bretwalda* think twice about sending men to Alt Clota in future. Of course, word of his brother's death might spur Hengist to come seeking vengeance, but it was a long road to Dun Breatann from Garrianum and the Damnonii would be watching for future attacks. They would not be caught so unprepared again.

"There's Gavo," said Duro, pointing his spatha across the field towards the second warband that had come from Dun Buic Cairn. "He looks happy."

"So he should, the battle is almost won."

"No, he looks *really* happy," the centurion clarified. "I've never seen the dour bastard with such a wide smile."

Bellicus laughed. Duro and Gavo were both rather dour so it was amusing to hear the centurion commenting on the captain's grin. "Maybe he's killed Drest," the druid said.

"Let's hope so," the centurion agreed. "Although I had hoped to kill the prick myself." He held up his hand and grimly eyed the missing fingers. "I owed him."

"Well, you've had your vengeance on Horsa," said Bellicus. "That'll have to be enough if Gavo or one of his men have done for Drest."

They turned to the south then, and the remainder of the Pictish army. There were only a few dozen of them left and they were

244

mostly fighting the troops that had marched out from Dun Breatann with Gerallt.

"Come," said the druid, raising his voice so the rest of his warband could hear him. "Surround them. We'll give them one last chance to surrender."

* * *

Narina and Catia had seen the way the battle was going and, as it neared its conclusion, they ran down the steps from the middle section of the fortress to join the handful of guards who'd remained on the outer walls. From there they could see Aife's warband still standing, taking no part in the battle, and Gerallt's troops engaging the rear of Drest's army. Ysfael was with them too, clad in an unmistakable purple cloak, carrying shield and spear and fighting with as much ferocity as any of Gerallt's other soldiers.

Despite the fact that many of the Picts had run from the field — morale shattered by the ferocity of the Damnonii attacks and everything that had happened leading up to the battle — those who remained were Drest's fiercest supporters and his bravest warriors. They had fought like demons, killing many Damnonii. Even when they saw Gerallt's warband coming towards them they had not faltered, redoubling their efforts for the king.

"Drest is dead!" Narina heard the cry echoing around the battlefield, growing in volume as it was passed from mouth to mouth until Gerallt's men were shouting it.

"Poor Aife," said Catia, turning from the fighting to look at her friend, although she could not see Aife amongst the men beside the river.

"Was she close to her father?" asked the queen. "I didn't think they were."

Catia thought about it for a moment and shrugged. "No, not particularly, but he was still her father. And she'll blame herself for his death. If she hadn't taken her men away the Picts might well have won the battle."

Narina sighed. "Maybe. She'll have to live with that guilt, but if she had joined in with the fighting more men on both sides would have died. I believe she did the right thing, but I'm biased of course."

Catia nodded. "I wonder where she is. She was standing in the centre of that warband during the whole battle near enough."

Narina didn't reply, she'd turned her attention back to the last pockets of fighting on the road that led to the fortress. Gerallt's men were holding their own, all the aggression that had been building up throughout the siege now given free rein, and, even from this lower vantage point the queen could see Bellicus and Gavo's twin warbands converging on the remaining Picts. It would not be long now, she thought, praying desperately that the druid had survived the fighting. And Gavo too, of course.

As the shouts proclaiming the doom of the Pictish king reached those last few enemy warriors they lost heart — most of them anyway. Hemmed in to the north and the south with nowhere to run to, many laid down their weapons in surrender.

"It's over," Catia said in relief. "And we've won."

Narina nodded. They had won, aye, but at what cost? How many of her people had been slaughtered that day? How many of her friends now lay dead, their corpses trampled underfoot on the battlefield? She had wanted Bellicus to marry her, she had such high hopes for a future where they would finally live together in happiness and peace but…what if he'd died out there? He might be the finest warrior in Alt Clota, and favoured by the gods, but that mattered little if a stray javelin dropped out of the sky or a lucky spear thrust took him in the guts.

Narina sucked a breath in through gritted teeth and forced herself not to think such terrible thoughts. Bellicus would be all right — he always was.

"Look, Gerallt is speaking with the leader of the Picts," Catia said, thankfully taking Narina's thoughts in a different direction. "He must be accepting their surrender."

The queen squinted, trying to make out what was happening below. She could see her captain, stiff and erect as ever, his red cloak making him easy to spot even at a distance. Narina felt immense pride as she gazed out over her armies and the men who'd led them to this victory. Gerallt might not be the most spontaneous or even interesting of men, but he was loyal and steadfast and his simple stolidity had been a great inspiration for the queen throughout their time under siege. He was the perfect foil for Gavo, and Narina knew she was lucky to have them both to help her run the kingdom.

The battle was over and Gerallt stood beside Ysfael, hand outstretched to accept the surrender of the Pict who ranked highest now that Drest himself was dead.

Only, as Narina and Catia watched, that enemy nobleman did not drop his sword, or bend the knee to the captain of Dun Breatann's garrison. Instead, the Pict's blade glinted in the light as it came up, and then down again, into Gerallt's shoulder.

The cry of dismay could be heard on the fortress walls as could the next one as that hateful sword came down again on the collapsing captain, then Gerallt was silent and on the ground, unmoving.

Narina stared in shock, but the Pict was not finished. He screamed a battle cry and exhorted his men to fight on. One or two did, but Ysfael and Gerallt's other warriors closed in on them with terrible fury, hacking at them with savage abandon until their torn, dismembered bodies lay beside the fallen Damnonii captain.

The battle was over, but it had been costly for both sides.

"Maybe he's not dead," Narina shouted, stubbornly refusing to believe the evidence of her own eyes. She ran down the stairs from the wall to the ground and shouted at the men manning the gates to open them for her. Catia ran at her back, as did her personal guards, doing their best to keep up with Narina despite their armour and weapons.

When they reached Gerallt it was clear he had not survived the attack. The ground was stained with his blood and he stared silently at the sky. Then, just a few paces away from the captain, Narina noticed another figure, face down on the grass, purple cloak torn through by a number of sword cuts.

Although she had not cared for Ysfael the man had fought here against their enemies and the sight of his torn body made her feel sick.

"Who did it?" the queen asked, voice choked with emotion. "Who was the man who surrendered to Gerallt and then attacked?"

"Him, my lady," said one of the Damnonii warriors, pointing to the mutilated, tattered remnants of a heavily armoured Pict.

Narina stared at the enemy soldier and then turned away, pulling Catia close to her as tears ran down her pale cheeks. "So many good men butchered, and for what?"

No one replied, for these was no satisfactory answer to her question.

CHAPTER FORTY-TWO

Bellicus bent down over the unconscious woman, examining the lump on her head. "It's a big one," he admitted. "But the helmet saved her life. She should be all right in time, I think."

"Agreed," said Ria. "But look at her arm." The druidess huffed in dismay at the sight of Aife's broken limb. It was a bad break, that much was obvious from the bruising.

"She's lucky," Bellicus said.

"Lucky!" Catia burst out, red-rimmed eyes latching furiously on the druid. "How can you say that? She was nearly killed and had her wrist broken by that witch with her iron bar!"

"It's a clean break," Bellicus replied calmly, also anguished by the warrior-princess's injuries but knowing she should make a full recovery from them. "If both the bones in her arm had been snapped and there was an open wound, chances are infection would have set in and she'd die, or lose her arm." He turned to see Qunavo coming with the necessary supplies to fashion a splint for Aife. "As it is, she'll have some pain for a while, and not be able to wield her sword, but, aye, she's lucky compared to many others this day."

Catia swallowed but must have realised the truth of Bellicus's words for she nodded and looked away, abashed.

"Where's the *volva*?" the druid asked, getting to his feet and shuffling back out of the way. Ria and Qunavo were Picts, it was their place to tend to Aife. Besides, Bellicus knew Ria was far better at healing than he was — her dressings were legendary compared to his clumsy efforts. Even Duro could attest to that.

"She's been taken down to the river where the rest of our warband are still waiting to find out what's to happen to them," a Pictish nobleman said.

"You are?" Narina asked.

"Oengus son of Uradech."

"You saved Aife?"

"I did, lady," the man nodded. "I saw the witch sneaking about in the undergrowth and then jumping out and attacking the princess. Luckily I was able to reach them in time to stop Yngvildr from killing her."

Narina looked at the distance Oengus must have had to run and raised her eyebrows. "That was lucky," she agreed. "You must be quite the runner."

He shook his head. "Aife was caught by surprise, but she put up a good fight. She bit the witch's nose off before collapsing. That gave me just enough time to get here before the witch could come to her senses again."

"Bit her nose off?" Catia practically shrieked, looking again at her unconscious friend and noting the blood around her mouth.

"Aye," Oengus replied and there was a strangely grudging admiration in his tone. "She's a wild one, our Aife."

"Quite," said Narina with a slight shudder. "You can return to your warband, Oengus son of Uradech. Thank you, I'm glad you could help your princess. We'll send her to join you once Ria has finished her work."

The man bowed and turned to walk towards the river, occasionally glancing back over his shoulder as if he half expected one of the Damnonii to take him down with a javelin. His anxiety showed how on edge the Picts gathered by the Clota must be feeling and Bellicus decided they deserved to have their minds set at ease. They had done the Damnonii a massive favour that day after all.

When the battle was over — properly this time — the Picts who'd taken part in the fighting were disarmed and shepherded into the outer walls of Dun Breatann where they were placed under heavy guard. The wounded on both sides were given medical attention, with the Damnonii taking precedence, naturally.

Gavo had met up with Bellicus and Duro and they'd embraced, just happy to see they'd all survived. The news of Gerallt's death, along with the sheer number of corpses littering the battlefield, had tempered their joy a great deal, however. Even hearing about Ysfael's untimely fate had saddened the victors, for, according to the Damnonii soldiers who'd fought alongside him, the prince had fought well before his death.

The bodies of Drest and Horsa were also taken into Dun Breatann until it was decided what should be done with them, and then the three men had noticed Narina and Catia standing off to the east with a Pict and another prone figure on the ground, and gone to see what was happening.

With Aife now receiving the care she needed, and hopefully out of danger, it was time to determine what would happen next.

"What?" Narina asked in amazement when Gavo suggested as much. "There'll be plenty of time for that on the morrow or the day after. For now, I think you and your men deserve a rest, and a damn good drink."

The captain nodded, clearly exhausted. "That would be good, my lady. But we must see to the dead first. And what about Aife's men?"

Narina thought about it, then said, "All right, organise some of the people to deal with our dead. Bellicus, I'm sure you'll perform the necessary funeral rites? Good. As for Aife's folk — tell them they can gather their own dead and give them whatever send off their customs demand. Qunavo and Ria will undoubtedly help."

"As victors, it's our right to strip the valuables from the enemy dead," Gavo said, a hint of uncertainty in his voice. Clearly he was wary of upsetting Aife's warriors who, although they'd stayed out of the fight, might take umbrage if they thought they, or their fallen kinfolk, were being treated disrespectfully.

"Leave them," said Bellicus. "The Picts will deal with the Picts; we'll deal with ourselves. Oh, and the Saxons — strip them of anything valuable, then have them piled up on the beach and burned."

"A sacrifice?" Gavo asked, frowning.

"No." Bellicus shook his head. "A cleansing."

Narina nodded and Gavo wandered off, a relieved look on his face.

"Where's Catia gone?" the druid asked, looking around but not seeing the princess.

"With Aife," Duro replied, pointing towards a small group of Picts, including Ria and Qunavo, who were carrying the injured princess towards the river on a makeshift stretcher.

Narina blanched, apparently sharing Gavo's fears about the remaining Picts' intentions.

"Don't worry," said Bellicus. "I'll fetch her, and make sure Qunavo and Ria understand what's happening."

"Be careful," Narina told him softly, touching his sleeve as he passed. "I don't want to lose you after surviving all this."

"I'll be fine. Cai will protect me." The mastiff had been brought forward once the battle was over and happily taken up his usual place at his master's side.

"What about me?" Duro demanded.

"You can come with me," Narina told him. "Help me and Gavo organise the men so we get this place cleared of bodies as soon as possible."

Bellicus nodded. "I'll be fine," he assured his friend. "Those Picts are the ones who most respect our gods — they won't harm the Merlin."

"They better not," Duro grumbled, turning to follow Narina towards the battlefield. "Or I'll kill the bloody lot of them."

Chuckling, pleased to have even a moment of humour after such a dark day, Bellicus walked towards the Clota and the dozens of 'enemy' warriors who stood there, still armed and no doubt wondering if they would be attacked at any moment now that the Damnonii had taken full control of the land around Dun Breatann.

When he was close enough, Bellicus thought it prudent to quickly set Pictish minds at ease.

"My friends," he called, raising his arms in the air as Cai sat down beside him, tongue lolling. His great voice quickly caught the attention of the few men who hadn't noticed his approach, and silence fell over the Picts. The druid could see many emotions reflected in their faces: fear, anger, shame, belligerence, and even relief to be addressed in such warm tones by this famous warrior-sage. "My friends," Bellicus repeated. "I know you must be wondering what will happen to you now that the war is over. Have no fear! You are safe in Alt Clota. You will be given food and drink while you remain here, and treated well. Honoured guests," he smiled, "rather than enemies."

Still, the faces that gazed back at him were uncertain.

"I understand it must have been a difficult thing for you to stand here and watch as your kinsmen fought for King Drest. But you must know the gods had forsaken Drest, as Qunavo and Ria told you. Princess Aife guided you right by taking you away from the battle."

"It doesn't feel like we did right," one of the Picts called sourly.

"I am a warrior, as well as a druid," Bellicus replied, nodding. "I understand. But sometimes it takes more courage to walk away

252

from a fight that your heart isn't in. By allying himself to the Saxons, Drest gave up his right to be king, and now it will be up to you men to rebuild your lands."

"You mean you'll let us go home?" another warrior called out suspiciously. "Just like that?"

"Of course," Bellicus assured him. "Listen to me — you men are like we Damnonii. You are not our enemies. The Saxons are the greatest danger facing these shores, and that is why you must now travel back to your lands and make them strong again. Strengthen your walls, train your youths to be soldiers, build watchtowers and signal towers! If you do not, Hengist's sea-wolves will come, and they will do to your people the same things as Horsa and Yngvildr did to mine here in Alt Clota."

"He's right." Another voice piped up, and Bellicus knew this one well. Qunavo stepped out from the crowd and strode over to stand beside the younger druid. "I had not believed the Saxons were such a threat to our ways until I saw them here, thumbing their noses at our ways and glorying in barbaric practices that our people abandoned many generations ago." He looked up at Bellicus and held out his forearm.

Bellicus accepted it, and they shook as if cementing a newfound friendship.

"We must work together," the Damnonii druid called out, "if Britain is to repel these vicious savages from the frozen lands across the sea."

"This is Bellicus," Qunavo shouted, stepping back and holding out his palm. "He is the new High Druid — the Merlin of Britain. We shall work with him, and his people, to defend our shores. To bring peace and prosperity to our own lands, after years wasted fighting one another."

The Picts were more inclined to take their own druid's words at face value. If they couldn't trust Qunavo, whom could they trust?

Still, questions remained to be answered, and the highest ranking of them spoke up now. "If Drest is dead," Oengus son of Uradech shouted, "who will take his place?" The look on his face suggested that he expected a Damnonii puppet to be placed on their throne, someone Narina would force upon them. There had been talk of that happening after the previous war, when Drest had eventually been allowed to remain in power, and look how that had turned out.

"I don't know," Bellicus admitted, unwilling to lie to Oengus or his men. "That, and more, has still be discussed and decided. But, believe me, we Damnonii shall not forget your actions this day. You will be treated with honour."

Oengus did not seem convinced, but he didn't argue the point further. What would be the point? The Picts beside the river were hemmed in, massively outnumbered, and, should Bellicus decide so, could be hacked to pieces without too much trouble. Whatever the Damnonii rulers decided, Oengus and his folk would simply need to accept it.

"How is the princess?" Bellicus asked, looking around at the wary warriors facing him. Mention of Aife did at least soften some of those expressions — she was evidently much loved by some, perhaps most, of the men. Unsurprising, the druid thought, for she was both attractive and charismatic and at least gave the soldiers a royal focal point to follow now that their king was dead.

"Come and see, my lord," Oengus replied grudgingly, waving for the druid to join him. The other Picts parted to let Bellicus, Cai, and Qunavo pass and, although none said a word against him, it was plain that these men were confused and were holding Bellicus responsible for their mixed emotions. So be it, he could shoulder that burden until they came to terms with it and, if possible, he would show them his earlier words were true. These men were the future of the Picts, and Bellicus would prefer them to be on his side going forward.

Aife had been carried to the riverside where, guarded by her kinfolk and Catia, Ria had set about restoring her to full health. The warrior-princess was awake now, and nodded as she saw the druid coming towards her beside Qunavo and Oengus.

"Bel," she said, grimacing and glancing down at the arm that was now held straight by a splint and a cast which the druid guessed to be made from egg white and flour. "Good to see you survived the fighting, big man."

"You too," Bellicus said with genuine warmth. "The *volva* almost took you from us though, eh?"

"Crazy bitch," Aife muttered, shaking her head ruefully. "Appeared from out of nowhere."

"Second time she's tried to kill you," Bellicus replied grimly. "Yet here you still are."

"Aife is too strong to be beaten by that woman," Catia said, evidently proud of her older friend.

"Too strong," Aife laughed, wincing again. "Or too lucky. Either way, I thank the gods for letting me off lightly. But Oengus?"

"Yes, lady?" the nobleman replied.

"My arm is agony. Could you find me a mug of something to dull the pain?" Her words were spoken lightly but through gritted teeth and Oengus nodded, hurrying off to find some strong drink.

"I'll put something in it when he returns," Ria promised. "I'm amazed you're not sobbing, truth be told. I've seen many a hard man crying after suffering an injury like yours, once the shock wears off."

"Oh, believe me," Aife said with a bleak smile. "I'd be greetin' like a baby if you lot weren't standing around watching over me."

It didn't take long for Oengus to return with a jug and a cup which Ria tipped a few herbs into. Oengus poured some of the liquid and handed the cup to Aife who took it and downed the entire thing in one go.

"Gods, that's strong," she gasped, laughing, gasping, and sobbing all at the same time.

"Aye," Oengus admitted ruefully. "It's mead, from the Saxon camp. Horsa's own stash. Thought it would do you more good than ale, and that big turd won't be needing it now."

"Got any more?" Aife asked, still coughing but holding out the cup for a refill. "No wonder Horsa was so crazy," she said as Oengus poured her more. "This stuff is incredible."

"Don't take too much then," he advised. "You don't want to end up like him."

"Another cup will do you good," said Ria. "But no more than that, for now."

Aife swallowed the second cup just as fast as the first and already her eyes were glazing over. "Where's my father?" she asked as she waited for Oengus to fill her cup again.

"Queen Narina had his body taken into Dun Breatann," Bellicus told her. "He'll be treated with respect, my lady, have no fears."

Aife nodded and smiled blearily at Catia. Her eyes were not just sparkling now, they were filled with tears and beginning to roll. "And what of the *volva?* Where is Yngvildr?"

"Over there," Ria said, jerking her chin along the beach to the east.

"Alive?"

"Oh, aye," the druidess nodded gravely. "You made a mess of her face, but she'll survive. I did what I could to make sure of that."

"Shame," Aife said with a bleak chuckle. The drink, and Ria's herbal additions, were quickly taking effect. "What are we going to do with her, eh, Bellicus?"

The druid straightened, and gazed along the beach in the direction Oengus had indicated Yngvildr was located, although he couldn't see her. He turned to Qunavo and then to Ria, shrugging. "What would you suggest?"

"She can't be allowed to live," Ria said emphatically. "Not after what she's done."

Qunavo nodded in agreement. "The gods of our lands must be appeased," he said. "The witch must die."

Bellicus thought of his friend, Eburus, so cruelly stabbed to death by Yngvildr. The man had been a good soul and a loyal friend and his death had hit both Bellicus and Duro hard. For that act alone Yngvildr should die. When her other crimes were added to that it was clear there could only be one sentence.

"Agreed," he growled. "Make sure she's kept under heavy guard, Oengus. Tomorrow, justice will be done."

CHAPTER FORTY-THREE

The bodies were soon cleared from the battlefield, with the Saxons being tossed on a great pyre and set alight to cleanse their taint from Alt Clota. Bellicus, Koriosis, Qunavo, and Ria worked together, presiding over the ritual which all could tell was an incredibly powerful one. Horsa was not placed in the great bonfire however — instead, his body was hung from the walls of Dun Breatann, a warning to any others who might seek to bring death to the fortress, be they Pict, sea-wolf, or something else.

Mounted scouts were sent out by Gavo to make sure no enemies lingered around Dun Breatann, or any other of the Damnonii villages on the road back to Dunnottar. A few stragglers had been caught by the riders and cut down, so it seemed that was the end of it. Bellicus had a sneaking suspicion one or two of the Saxons were probably still hiding nearby though, wanting to discover the fate of their leader before returning to Hengist. The druid hoped they enjoyed the sight of Horsa swinging from a rope, and he hoped Hengist would appreciate the news even more.

Horsemen were sent out to the nearest large settlements and within just a few hours ships laden with supplies were being unloaded into Dun Breatann, restocking the reserves that had been depleted during the siege.

The remaining, friendly Picts were allowed to return to Drest's camp where they collected their dead comrades' belongings and made themselves comfortable while matters were decided by their leaders and the Damnonii leaders.

The cast on Aife's arm was fully set hard now and her pain was being managed as well as possible by Ria, who was allowed to use some of Bellicus's personal store of herbs now that his house in Dun Breatann was available once more. The rest of the wounded continued to be treated right through the night for there were many, but some simply could not be helped. It might have been a victory for the Damnonii, but Bellicus couldn't help feeling like it was hollow. So many had died for what? Nothing, in the end. Unless one saw Drest's death as a good thing, but who would take his place as Pictish King? Someone even more ambitious and warlike?

That was a distinct possibility, for the type of men who sought such positions of power were by their very nature ambitious. One kingdom was rarely enough for such rulers.

This was discussed by Narina, Bellicus, Gavo, and Duro the night after the battle. Food and drink was available, although none particularly felt like indulging. The soldiers feasted, their drunken singing — laments as well as triumphant battle songs — filling the air above the Clota long after the sun had set, but the leaders were more interested in finding ways to make sure this war was never repeated.

Although it was a chilly night no one felt like being cooped up inside, so they sat on chairs by the north-western wall, outside the great hall, gazing over the peaceful lands and the twin rivers Clota and Leamnha, content in the knowledge that they were safe again and need not fear an attack during the night.

"I have a solution to our problem," Narina told her advisors as they nursed their drinks and breathed in the smells of roasting meat that wafted up to them from below. "Actually, it was suggested to me by Catia."

Bellicus raised an eyebrow. "If this was an idea of our little princess," he mused, "I'd imagine it involves her best friend, Aife."

"Why not," Narina asked a little waspishly. "It's always men that start these wars."

Gavo and Duro looked at one another and, although they offered no comment, their expressions suggested agreement with the queen.

"You think Aife should succeed her father?" Bellicus asked, doing his best to keep his tone neutral.

"Why should she not? She's a princess. She's a warrior too, if that matters — a damn good one."

"All fine points," Gavo admitted. "And she's respected by her people, as we saw during the battle when she held so many of them back from attacking us."

"But she's only young," Bellicus said. "What is she? Twenty?"

"There have been younger rulers before," Koriosis pointed out.

"I think this is actually a very wise suggestion," Duro said, nodding. "Aife is on good terms with us, especially with Catia. She didn't want this war her father started, and she would likely make sure it didn't happen again."

"She'll also need help from us to make sure her lands aren't attacked and overrun by Hengist once he finds out everything that's gone on here," Narina said. "He'll know Dunnottar is woefully undefended — an easy target — and look to capitalise on its vulnerability before moving onto attack other Pictish settlements."

"Their lands would be quickly captured," Gavo said grimly. "And then we'd have Hengist and his bloody sea-wolves on our borders to deal with. Aife would at least put up a good fight to make sure that doesn't come to pass."

"So would other, older candidates for the throne," Bellicus noted.

"Like who?" Narina asked levelly. "Most of their noblemen fell in the battle, or in the previous battle we had with them, or ran away when they saw they were losing. And remember, Bel, we have a chance now to select someone who will be a true ally to us. Let's not make the same mistake we made with Drest."

Bellicus was not truly opposed to Aife becoming Queen of the Picts, he was simply trying to come up with reasons why someone else might be better suited. To be honest, he couldn't think of anyone.

"Oengus?" he wondered, naming the only surviving nobleman he could think of.

"Oengus will never trust you, not completely," Duro said. "You could see it in his eyes when we spoke with him. He's known the Damnonii as his enemies, or rivals at least, for his whole life — making him king will not suddenly make him your friend."

"Aife will need a loyal captain, though," Narina interjected. "Just as I've needed Gavo and Gerallt." She broke off at the mention of the dead man, swallowing before trusting herself to speak again. "Oengus seems to be highly regarded among those men on the beach, and he's an impressive individual. Perhaps he could work as Aife's second-in-command."

"I don't know about all this," Bellicus said, still searching for possible downsides to Narina's plans. "None of us knew this man Oengus before today, I don't think. What if the Pictish people don't accept him, or Aife? What if they don't accept each other? I know Oengus supported Aife when she asked the army not to join Drest in the battle, but he probably resents his decision, like many of those survivors, and blames her for putting them in that position."

"It was the right decision," Narina argued. "By both of them. Oengus will come to accept it when his emotions over losing the war fade and he looks at things rationally. They saved many lives."

"I know, and I completely agree," Bellicus said, nodding slowly. "But Oengus and Aife are warriors. The shame of standing by while their kinsmen fought and died might never leave them."

"That's not my concern," Narina replied dismissively. "They were the aggressors. Bad things happen in war, Bel, as you well know. If some Picts feel guilty about their actions they'll simply need to deal with it. Better that, I would suggest, than dealing with a limb hacked off, or a sword in the guts. They'll accept their lot eventually."

Bellicus almost told her that she would, of course, look at the situation like that, not being a warrior, but he felt it might come out, or at least be interpreted the wrong way, and he had no desire to fall out with the queen. Not now when peace reigned in Alt Clota, and especially when Bellicus saw her point anyway.

Aife and Oengus and all the other surviving Picts might be conflicted over their own actions, but at least they were alive and could return to their homes to rebuild their shattered kingdom.

"We need to ask Aife if she'd even be willing to become queen," the druid said. "We should also seek Qunavo and Ria's counsel on the matter."

Narina frowned at that. She did not like the older Pictish druid simply because he'd been the one mostly goading Drest to attack her lands, and she resented Ria not only for that, amongst other things, but also because she knew Bellicus had been her lover for a short time. "I thought you hated those two," the queen said icily. "Yet you would give them a say in this?"

Bellicus tilted his head to the side and shrugged. "Let's be fair to them," he said. "They played a huge part in getting those Picts to stay out of the battle. And they seem to have come to realise what I've been saying all along — that Hengist's sea-wolves are our biggest threat. I honestly get the impression they are no longer enemies of Alt Clota."

"You do, eh?" Narina asked and, although she was trying to mask her disapproval, Bellicus could read her as easily as he would read an old Roman curse tablet.

"I do," he said levelly. "And we will certainly need them on our side, unless you plan to execute them beside Yngvildr on the morrow."

The queen visibly balked at that suggestion. Bellicus knew she would have no part in killing druids — it brought only evil luck on the perpetrators.

"No," she said. "Of course we can't do that, so I suppose you're right. Very well, summon Aife from the Pictish camp. Oh, and bring Catia here as well."

"You think it wise to involve a girl of twelve summers, my lady?" Gavo asked uncertainly.

"This was her idea, and she's Aife's friend. They have a bond none of us quite understand I think, and Catia may prove instrumental in bringing Aife around to our plan."

It took a while for their messenger to reach the camp by the river and bring the injured Pictish princess up the stairs to the central part of Dun Breatann. Time that Bellicus, Narina, Gavo, and Duro spent in thoughtful silence, some of them fortifying themselves with a little more meat and ale. For some reason this meeting, and the ones that would quickly follow should Aife agree to their request, seemed more daunting than the earlier battle had.

When she was brought to them by a guard Aife seemed in surprisingly good spirits, considering her father had just been killed, and her arm broken. Catia ran to meet her and they hugged one another gingerly. Clearly the age gap, eight years or so, did not hinder their friendship. Both young women had seen much in their lives, far more than most their age, and their experiences had tempered them as well as forming a powerful bond between them. Perhaps one day Aife would rule in Dunnottar while Catia ruled in Dun Breatann. Woe betide any Saxons who tried to attack either of them should that be the case, the druid thought with a wry smile.

Everyone stood to welcome Aife, bowing to her respectfully and smiling at her. She returned their smiles warily, as if suspecting some trick or scheme. She might trust Catia, and like Bellicus and Duro in particular after sharing some adventures with them, but she was still Drest's daughter and had come to Dun

Breatann as part of his would-be conquering army. She was wise enough to know that might be held against her, especially by Narina who had never been close to the warrior-princess.

"Please, take a seat and join us," the queen said, gesturing.

When they were all comfortable more refreshments were offered, and Aife's injured arm enquired after, and then they got down to business.

"We wondered what you would say," Bellicus said gravely, "to becoming queen of the Picts."

Aife's reaction was not what anyone expected. She burst out laughing, staring from one to the other in disbelief before her mirth dissipated and was replaced by suspicion. "Is this a joke?" she demanded. "You must all know that I am a bastard."

"Of course," Narina replied. "So what? Bastards can rule too. I'll bet the druids have a long list of precedents to call upon should anyone object."

"She's right," Bellicus agreed emphatically. "Such things should not matter."

"But my mother was a slave!"

"And your father was a king, and you are a commander in his army." Bellicus waved a hand to dismiss her argument. "I'm sure Qunavo and Ria will be able to come up with a suitably noble backstory for your mother and have it spread about your people. Let's be honest, your parentage will only matter if you do a bad job as queen, and we don't think you will."

Aife swallowed and looked at Catia. "What do you think?" she asked her friend.

"It was my idea," the younger girl replied.

Aife chuckled at that and gingerly touched her broken arm as if it pained her. "I never — never! — expected to take the throne one day. I've not been trained for it, and, honestly, I don't want it."

"I didn't want to take the throne of Alt Clota either," said Narina, "but sometimes in life we must do things that are distasteful to us. And as for your training — your druids will guide you. And Oengus."

"Oengus?"

"You'll need a captain," Narina nodded. "A right-hand man you can rely on to advise you. We thought Oengus son of Uradech would be suitable, but if you have another you would prefer..?"

262

Aife thought about it, clearly overwhelmed by what was happening. "I don't know," she admitted. "I have no one else I would prefer over Oengus so, fair enough, we'll see what he has to say about it."

"Good," Narina nodded, smiling. "Now we just need to get your druid and druidess on side and things can move forward from there."

CHAPTER FORTY-FOUR

"I think it's a superb idea," said Qunavo. "Truth be told, we assumed you would force one of your own Damnonii noblemen upon us."

Ria was looking at Aife, sizing her up perhaps, although she surely must know the young princess's strengths and weaknesses by now. "I agree," she said thoughtfully. "Aife is young, but she has experience commanding men, and she will grow into the role. We will help her along the way."

Qunavo was actually smiling, as if he'd set up this whole thing himself. "The more I think about it, the more I like it," he admitted. "Hengist grows more brazen, and more aggressive, with every passing day. We saw that at the Moot." He looked at Bellicus then. "I know you suspect I had something to do with that, but I did not. The plan for Drest to hire Horsa's mercenaries, aye, I admit that was partially my doing, but Hengist's attack on our Moot I had no part in. That, and the Saxons' behaviour here during the siege have turned me against them. We need a strong ruler to make sure the Picts are not destroyed by Hengist's raiders, I think and," he turned to Aife, offering her a shallow bow and a fatherly smile, "the princess will certainly not let the Saxons take our lands without a fight."

"She has our blessing," Ria said. "We will support her as best we can."

"Excellent!" Narina cried, genuinely enthused by their decision and by the future that stretched out ahead of them now that, hopefully, thoughts of conquest were past for the next generation of Picts and Damnonii at least. "Now, what of Oengus as her captain? Do you approve of that choice too?"

Qunavo frowned. "Oengus? He's not someone I would have chosen myself. He's unambitious and unimaginative, happy as long as he has an ale in his hand, a roof over his head, and a fire to keep him warm in the winter."

"Sounds like he's perfectly suited to the task," Bellicus said. "The Picts need to rebuild and regroup, while preparing for possible attacks by the Saxons along your coastline. From what you say, Oengus will be ideal."

"Perhaps," Qunavo grudgingly admitted. "He is well-liked by the other noblemen — those who are still alive, at least."

"We don't really have anyone else to look to," Ria conceded. "Not after losing two wars in quick succession. Most of our strong leaders, the ones young enough to fight anyway, are dead." She shrugged. "Let Oengus do his best, if he wishes to try."

"What of you two?" Bellicus asked rather sternly. "Will you swear to uphold this peace between our peoples this time? Or will you begin scheming, looking for ways to invade Alt Clota again the minute you're safely back behind Dunnottar's walls?"

Qunavo and Ria looked at one another for a moment, then the older, more senior druid shook his head. "Even if we thought it worthwhile, we would not have a big enough army for many years yet. I'll be long dead by then! No, Merlin," he said, for the first time giving Bellicus his new title and, in doing so, proving he accepted the new High Druid. "We will not try to persuade Aife to make war on Alt Clota."

"Like Qunavo said," Ria added. "We now understand the Saxon threat. All our efforts will be to fortify our coasts, and our borders, against raids by Hengist and any others. We will look to defend our lands, rather than expand them."

"And yes," Qunavo confirmed. "We will gladly swear an oath to that effect."

Narina was visibly happy as cups were refilled and a toast was drunk to celebrate this new alliance between the two factions. Bellicus was pleased too, although in truth he didn't think the Picts had much choice but to accept the conditions Narina had laid out for them. They were being let off lightly with Aife, one of their own, being allowed to rule.

"What do we do now then?" Aife asked, running splayed fingers through her long hair.

"That depends on you," Bellicus said. "Your father must have his funeral rites performed, and you must be crowned queen. We can do both of those things here, or you can return to Dunnottar and attend to them in your own lands."

Aife looked around uncertainly. "I don't know," she admitted. "What do you think?" she asked Qunavo.

"Drest would not want to be buried here in Alt Clota," the old druid said, shaking his head. "We should take him home and have his funeral feast with our own people."

Narina nodded. "I agree with that."

"As for crowning you queen," Qunavo said. "I believe we should do that as soon as possible, before some other upstart tries to make a claim."

"Like who?" Aife asked.

"I've no idea," Qunavo admitted. "But there's always someone that crawls out of the woodwork when a king dies, claiming royal blood or descent from the gods, or some other tenuous reason why they should be the new ruler. Not all of the nobles travelled here with our army — some, mostly those too old or too young for the journey, remained at home."

"And when they hear of Drest's death they'll put forward their claim," Gavo said. "Of course, it's human nature."

Qunavo nodded emphatically. "So we crown Aife as soon as possible, here in Alt Clota. We can have another ceremony in Dunnottar, invite those surviving nobles to the feast, and make sure they swear allegiance to her or..." He shrugged and his meaning was very clear. The war might be over, but violence was still very much an option if needed, even to one's own people.

"All right," said Narina, reaching out and giving Catia a quick hug of thanks for suggesting this whole thing to her. "No point in waiting any longer then, eh? Let's get Oengus in here, make sure he agrees to be Aife's captain, and get her crowned."

Aife opened her mouth to protest, and no wonder, Bellicus thought. Yesterday she was just one of Drest's commanders, and the illegitimate daughter of a slave-woman, and now here were the victorious Damnonii leaders making her a queen. To her credit she did not actually protest, and, when Catia went to her, telling her she could borrow some of Narina's clothes for the ceremony, Aife's reticence was replaced at last and a tentative smile touched the edges of her mouth.

Oengus was already waiting at Dun Breatann's gatehouse and, when he was brought to Narina and the others and the proposal put to him it didn't take long before he agreed. If he was as unambitious as Qunavo had suggested then this was the chance of a lifetime for the warrior to rise far higher than he might otherwise have done. How could he refuse?

"That's everything settled then," Bellicus said, standing and stretching out, stifling a yawn as he did so. "I think I'll take Cai a walk around the walls now, and make sure our guards are alert even if the war is over."

He smiled at everyone and then began walking towards the steps to head down towards the southwestern wall. He had piece of cheese in his pocket and hoped to find Uchaf around there so he could feed the raven the tasty morsel. Before he reached the steps he heard his name being called and turned to see Narina striding quickly towards him.

"You look serious," he said cheerfully, but she did not brighten as she came before him.

"You said everything is settled," she murmured, making sure no one nearby could hear. "It's not though, is it?"

Bellicus gazed down at her, knowing what she meant but unsure how to respond.

"You have a choice to make, Bel," she told him. "Travel south to join Arthur and become Merlin, or remain here with me. If you haven't decided yet then you better do so while you walk with Cai."

And, before he could make any reply, the queen turned on her heel and stalked back to Gavo and the others.

Bellicus hesitated, wondering if he should go back and speak privately with Narina but, in truth, he had not yet been able to decide what his future should hold.

Cai was standing at the steps, eager for his walk, so the druid followed and soon they were moving along the timber walkway the guards used to patrol the southwestern section of the walls. The air was fine and crisp and Bellicus drew it in like a drowning man handed a cup of cool water. How could he leave this place forever? he wondered. The people, the views even from this lower section of the fortress, Narina, Catia, and, overhead, croaking to make Bellicus aware of his presence, Uchaf.

Reaching the end of the walkway the ground opened out just a little onto a small patch of grass and here the druid halted, drawing out the piece of cheese from his cloak. He placed it on the top of the wall and the raven came swooping confidently down, riding the air currents and landing beside the cheese. The bird eyed the food, and Bellicus, and then it croaked again — not a word, just a greeting — and began to peck at the cheese.

"Good lad," the druid said, feeling a little sorry that he hadn't brought anything for Cai for the dog was watching Uchaf eat with obvious jealousy.

A guard appeared then, making his rounds, and Uchaf took to the sky again, quickly disappearing around the towering rock and flying towards the River Leamnha on the far side. The guard saluted the druid, turned and marched back in the direction he'd come.

What awaited Bellicus, High Druid of Britain, when he journeyed southwards to join with Arthur? Was it worth giving up what he had here? What he could have here?

Of course, it was not just about what he wanted. There were other people to think about. His faithful friend, Duro would probably be quite happy to follow Bellicus wherever he went, but Narina had made it clear this was the druid's last chance to make a life with her. What of the people of Britain, though? Bellicus had sworn to serve them when he'd joined the Druid Order, and now that he'd taken on the mantle of Merlin his duty to those people was even more sacred. If he believed he was the only man to guide Arthur in his sworn duty — to wash the sea-wolves back into the sea forever — then there was only one choice Bellicus could really make.

Being elected High Druid was a once in a lifetime opportunity — the office could not just be put aside because its holder wanted to find personal happiness elsewhere.

Looking out once more on the rippling, familiar waters of the Clota, Bellicus sighed, wishing life was not so hard. "Come on, Cai," he said to the dog, moving towards the walkway to take the steps back up to Narina.

His mind raced as he climbed those steps to the centre of the fortress, and he begged the gods for guidance as he walked towards the great hall. No sign came from the sky, or from anywhere else but, as the druid reached the queen he knew there was only one answer he could give her.

He must do his duty.

CHAPTER FORTY-FIVE

"I must admit, you three are decent company." Qunavo said, enjoying the sunshine as the ship carried them from Dun Breatann, southwards once again, to Caer Legion. "Not as pretty as Ria, perhaps, but better than I expected. Especially you, centurion."

Duro eyed the old druid balefully. He had not, and would never, forgive Qunavo for his part in the torture Duro had endured in Dunnottar. The missing fingers on his left hand would always remind him of that terrible time when he'd almost gone mad from the physical and mental torture he'd endured. Drest's death had gone some way to bringing the centurion some peace, however, and he was at least able to share the ship with the white bearded Pict without tossing him overboard.

Bellicus and Koriosis had both been mentored by Qunavo at different points, with Bellicus spending quite a few of his early years studying under the older man. Qunavo did not have as much to do with the apprentice druids these days, and hadn't for some time, but he did sometimes take a few under his wing either on Iova or Dunnottar, passing on the wisdom and learning gathered over a long lifetime. Although Bellicus in particular would not admit it to Duro, he had generally liked Qunavo and greatly respected him — until they'd become enemies, ended up imprisoned in the Pictish fortress, and been forced to fight two wars against the older druid and Drest's armies.

After the dust had settled in Alt Clota the dead on both sides had been sent on their way to the afterlife with the necessary rites: Qunavo and Ria seeing to the Picts; Bellicus and Koriosis presiding over the Damnonii ceremonies, with Ysfael in particular being afforded a hero's funeral and word sent to King Cunedda of his son's bravery. The Saxons were not, of course, afforded such respectful treatment, simply being heaped up and burned without a word to commend them to their fearful gods.

Yngvildr had been hanged, her body left to dangle beside that of her lover, Horsa. By that point Bellicus was heartily sick of all the death and suffering but the embattled people of Alt Clota had demanded the *volva* suffer, just as she had made so many of their kinfolk suffer. So Yngvildr's execution had been another grand affair with crowds of people turning out from nearby settlements to enjoy the grim spectacle with as much joy and enthusiasm as they'd celebrate a wedding or one of the many religious festivals such as Beltaine or Lughnasadh.

Bellicus had presided over the execution as he was expected to as the Merlin, but it left a bitter taste in his mouth and he was glad when it was over. The witch deserved her fate, he agreed, and it was a relief to know she would never turn up in the future to threaten the safety of those Bellicus loved, but he was happy to put the sight of her hanging from the rope over Dun Breatann's walls out of his mind and look to the future.

After that, Bellicus decided he must call another Moot, even though there had just been one. Two such gatherings in such a short space of time was unheard of, and it would possibly not be well received, especially by the druids at the furthest ends of Britain, but the Merlin deemed it necessary. Hengist had already sought to destroy the druids — how would he react when word reached him that his beloved brother, Horsa, had been killed, his rotting body displayed by Bellicus in Dun Breatann? The druids must be made aware that the war against the Saxons had entered a new and even more dangerous phase.

The new Merlin had other reasons for calling the Moot but he kept them to himself for the time being.

Qunavo threw his hands up in the air and cursed loudly. "Lost again," he said, sourly staring at the dice on the deck between him and Duro. "You have the luck of Lug the Light-Bringer himself, centurion!"

"Hand it over," Duro said, lips twitching in amusement as the druid reached into his purse and, with bad grace, counted out some hack silver.

"We should play tafl," Qunavo suggested. "I'll beat you at that. Give me a chance to win back my money."

Duro sniggered and gestured at the water surrounding them. "Have you not noticed you're on a ship, old man?" he asked. "Tafl pieces won't stay on the board. Come on, another game of dice? I'm enjoying myself, it's taken my mind off the constant rocking motion of this damn vessel."

"No thank you," Qunavo replied. "I think I'll stretch my legs for a bit. I've grown stiff, and my mood has soured since I sat down with you."

"You just told me I was good company," Duro objected, still with that sardonic smile on his face. "Oh well, enjoy your walk. Don't go too far." He cackled at the thought, the ship being much too small to take more than a few paces fore or aft. Bellicus also laughed, sensing there was more humour in Qunavo's reaction than the older druid was letting on.

Koriosis did not join in with the amusement, though. He sat before Duro and said, "I'll play you at dice. Your luck can't hold out forever."

Bellicus watched as the centurion's luck did hold out, and Koriosis gave up in a huff too, following Qunavo to stand gazing out at the distant coastline, discussing how long it would take to reach their destination. Bellicus wondered if Duro had found some way to cheat at the game, but, if he had, he must have been incredibly gifted at sleight-of-hand to fool two druids. Especially Qunavo, who was a master of such trickery.

"What?" Duro demanded with a smirk, noticing Bellicus's scrutiny. "I'm just lucky. Maybe you druids should follow Mithras, like me, instead of those other gods. You want a game?"

"No, you're all right," Bellicus laughed. "I'd rather hold onto my hack silver. We'll need it to pay for the food and other supplies when we reach Caer Legion."

They had not brought their own horses for this journey. They'd seen plenty of decent animals when they departed from the port on their previous trip to Caer Legion so, rather than forcing Darac and Pryderi to endure another voyage, they planned to buy mounts at their destination.

"When did you come to the realisation that I'd been right about the Saxons?" Bellicus called to Qunavo. "What finally changed your mind about them?"

The older druid lifted his chin and looked thoughtfully at Bellicus before stepping over to sit across from him again. "Honestly, I think it was when Hengist attacked the Moot and Nemias was killed." He breathed deeply of the sea air, and it was not just the salt spray that made his eyes damp. "I had been friends with Nemias when we were younger. When he was murdered it

271

planted seeds of doubt in my mind. Then, when we sailed to Dun Breatann and I saw those men blood-eagled..."

"A shocking sight for anyone," Bellicus murmured sadly.

"Even a druid," Qunavo agreed. "Those two things told me that the Saxons were not quite the allies I'd assumed they would be. The actions of Horsa and Yngvildr after that just hammered home to me how different they were to us, and, by *us*, I mean we Britons: Picts, Damnonii, Votadini, whatever."

"I warned you," Bellicus nodded, but his words were not scolding, just a statement of fact.

"You were right," Qunavo admitted with a deep sigh. "Still, in saying all that, I believe your outlook is rather too harsh when it comes to the Saxons as a whole."

"Harsh?" Bellicus exclaimed, and Duro gave a bark of astonished laughter.

"Aye, harsh," Qunavo repeated. "Hengist might not be the kind of man we wish to associate with, and Horsa was certainly not. But not all the Saxons are like that, Bel. Many of them – most, perhaps – simply seek to settle here on our pleasant island and live in peace."

"Even if you're right," Bellicus said, shaking his head. "They remain Saxons, while we remain Britons. When Hengist, or another jarl or *bretwalda,* summons them to war against us they will answer the call, for they will always be Saxons."

"I think you're wrong," Qunavo stated. "I think you are simply afraid of change."

"Is that not natural?" Bellicus asked. The discussion reminded him of his days as a student at Qunavo's feet, and he found himself intrigued by his old mentor's thoughts.

"It's natural," Qunavo granted. "But not always sensible or warranted. The Saxons have much to offer – their carpentry skills, for example, are far more advanced than ours. They are fabulously skilled craftsmen not just with wood, but with other materials too. Have you seen their jewellery?"

"I have, it's exquisite," Bellicus admitted grudgingly.

"And their stories!" Qunavo laughed. "What wonderful stories they can tell. Their myths and legends are on a par with any we druids tell."

"The fact remains," Duro interrupted, "that they want to conquer us."

Qunavo looked up at the centurion and said nothing for a long moment. At last, he pursed his lips and nodded. "Hengist does. And that is a problem for us all. But we should not think we must kill every Saxon in Britain. You are looking at things in black and white, and the world is not like that. Did not your Roman legions conquer the tribes of southern Britain?"

Duro rolled his eyes and turned to stare out across the rippling water. Bellicus smiled but he did not argue with Qunavo anymore for he had to admit the older druid made some interesting points.

"We're nearly there," the ship's captain called out. He was a Damnonii sailor named Cistumucus, and his vessel was the *Milwr Môr*. It had made good time from Dun Breatann and Bellicus was glad for he wanted to arrive in Caer Legion early, to get things set up, ready for the Moot to begin as quickly as possible.

"Will the druids come soon?" Duro wondered. "Will your messengers have got word to them in time for them to make the journey to Caer Legion again? We can't hang around for a month waiting for them, surely."

"My messengers will do their jobs, have no fears," Bellicus assured him. "We have ways of sending word out quickly to the members of our Order."

"What ways?" Duro demanded suspiciously.

Bellicus tapped his nose. "Magic ways," he said enigmatically, laughing when the centurion swore at him. Of course, it was not really magic that Bellicus had used to summon the druids to this second Moot — fast horses, fast ships, and other, more exotic methods such as pigeons with messages fixed to their legs. The druids had long made use of the birds, building a network that could be relied upon in times of need.

As always, there might be a few people missing from the Moot, held up by illness, weather, bandits or other mishaps, but Bellicus was confident that the vast majority of those he'd summoned would turn up in good time. Ria would not be there for Aife would need the support of a druid when she returned to Dunnottar to be crowned, so Qunavo had travelled to the Moot with Bellicus while Ria went with the Picts to begin rebuilding their strength under the new regime.

273

When the *Milwr Môr* arrived at the port in Twyni Tywod Bellicus wasted no time in leading his companions, and, of course, Cai, towards the stables where Koriosis had sold his horse on the previous visit. That horse was still there, and Koriosis was pleased to buy it back, while the other druids and Duro bought three other mounts. Soon they were on the road to Caer Legion and, not long after that, they were once more settled at the same campsite Bellicus, Duro, and Koriosis had shared just a few weeks earlier. This time Qunavo set up his tent alongside theirs and, being the first ones there, sat down to enjoy some time eating, drinking, and telling tales as the sun set.

They took turns to keep watch that night, fearing Hengist might return and attack them, but the hours passed quickly and without event and, the very next afternoon more druids began to arrive. The following day brought more again and by the fifth day almost everyone who'd been called had turned up.

Bellicus was pleased to see the bald, portly druid called Diseta had made it. The man greeted him warmly, great grizzled beard chafing the skin on Bellicus's neck as they embraced.

"What's this all about, Merlin?" Diseta asked. "We've just had a Moot. Why another so soon?"

"Events in Alt Clota prompted it," Bellicus told him. It still felt strange to be addressed as 'Merlin'. "We'll wait just a few more hours to let any stragglers get here, and then I'll tell you everything, all right?"

Diseta nodded and, smiling, wandered off to mingle with the others. It was a cheery group, Bellicus thought, considering how their last meeting had turned out, with the disgraceful attack by Hengist's raiders and the death of Nemias. Remembering that event well, most of the druids had brought extra guards with them and those soldiers made regular patrols around the perimeter of Sulis Minerva's shrine. There would be no repeat of that earlier abomination, Bellicus was sure.

"There you are!"

Bellicus turned at the shout, smiling warmly as he saw Lancelot and Bedwyr coming towards him. He had summoned them to this meeting as well, knowing an escort would be needed for the Merlin's journey to join Arthur, wherever the warlord was at that moment.

"Well met, my friends. How goes the war with Hengist?"

"Not too well," Lancelot admitted dejectedly. "The bastards just continue to push further westwards. We're doing our best to contain them, but they must have brought reinforcements across the sea this spring for there seems to be more of them than ever."

"Nemias is sorely missed," Bedwyr put in. "We'll be glad to have you join us, old friend, for an army isn't complete without a druid to call upon the gods' protection."

Bellicus nodded. "That's true," he said. "Well, Duro is…" He scanned the riverbank and the slope above the shrine, finally spotting the centurion who was accompanied by Cai on another patrol. "There. Join him, and get yourselves some refreshments. Duro will keep you right."

"How long will the Moot last this time?" Bedwyr asked, somewhat fretfully. He was ever the organised one, duty first and foremost, and would want to return to Arthur as soon as possible, whereas Lancelot was more relaxed and ready to enjoy another few days of feasting.

"Don't worry," Bellicus smiled, patting the warrior on the arm. "I won't keep you long, I promise. Just you make sure no more of Hengist's raiders turn up to cause trouble again, eh?"

Bedwyr saluted and Lancelot nodded and the pair hurried off to join Duro who'd already spotted them and was coming down to meet them.

"Things are ready, Bel. We can start whenever you want."

Bellicus glanced around and nodded his thanks to Qunavo, who had been organising things, preparing the shrine and its environs for the council of war that was scheduled for that evening. The older druid had truly shown his qualities during the past few days, not just accepting Bellicus as High Druid without fuss, but actively supporting him as he prepared to address their brothers and sisters.

"Thank you, master," Bellicus said, giving Qunavo the title he'd used while training with him on Iova as a youth. "I appreciate your help."

The older druid smiled. "Happy to help, just as I was always happy to help Nemias before you. I always suspected that you, of all the many students I mentored over the years, would go on to do great things. We may have been enemies before, but I'm proud now to serve under you. You are now the master, Bel."

For a moment, Bellicus was taken aback, and a wave of nostalgia rushed over him as he remembered many good times he'd spent with Qunavo all those years past. The older man threw himself body and soul into everything he did, and that was to be applauded, even if his last venture had been to support Drest, and Pictish attempts to conquer Alt Clota.

"Thank you," he said with genuine pleasure. "I appreciate that. And now, come with me, Qunavo, it's time for me to address the Moot."

CHAPTER FORTY-SIX

Bellicus stood on top of the shrine to Sulis Minerva, looking out over the assembled members of his Order. Memories of the last time he'd stood there came rushing back and he allowed himself to wallow in them for a moment, reflecting on how things had changed since then. It had been just a short time ago but he'd served as Merlin ever since, fought — and won — a war in Alt Clota, and made decisions that would have far reaching implications not just for him, but for the very future of Britain.

He prayed to Lug that he'd made wise choices and was not about to plunge the island into a maelstrom of chaos and death.

A step behind him, to his right, were Duro and Cai, loyal protectors ready to defend him should Hengist or any other enemy seek to do him harm. Behind and to his left was Qunavo, whom Bellicus had asked to attend him during the ceremony. The druids all knew that Qunavo and Bellicus had been at loggerheads after the previous election, and they would have heard about the war between Picts and Damnonii by now, so it made sense for Qunavo to prove he was supportive of Bellicus. Helping him with this ritual would be the perfect show of solidarity and camaraderie, a public display to symbolise the strength of the druids' bond with one another and acceptance of the High Druid.

He had decided to start things with a poem. Everyone there was familiar with *The Song of Amergin*, which had been written generations ago by one of their predecessors. Designed to capture the essence of what it meant to be a druid, it was very fitting for a Moot such as this. Bellicus had, however, reworked it in his own style and he hoped his audience would appreciate it. Raising his arms, he began.

"I am the wind on the water,

I am the song of the sea," he intoned, and, instantly everyone looked up at him, recognizing the poem and puzzled by the change to the words they were familiar with.

"I am the stag of seven skirmishes,

I am the raven on the rock,

I am a splinter from the sun,

I am the most fragrant of flowers,

I am the brave bloodied boar,
I am the salmon in the sea,
I am the lake in the plain, and the falling rain,
I am the word of wisdom,
I am the stabbing spear in battle,
I am the god that grants glory and grace,
Who shines light on the Moot on the hill?
Who has seen the mountains of the moon?
Who has visited the sun's final resting place?
I have.
And I am."

When he finished the druids stared at him in wonder. Bellicus was not so arrogant to believe his version of the ancient poem was particularly inspired, but he suspected it had been interesting enough, and recited powerfully enough, to intrigue and even move his brothers and sisters. Many were looking up at him in awe, and some were even weeping openly, perhaps remembering Nemias and the others who'd fallen during their previous, ill-fated, gathering.

"My friends," he called, voice booming out over the audience although he did not shout for the builders of the shrine had chosen the place for its acoustical properties as well as its connection to Sulis Minerva. "Brothers and sisters, it is pleasant to see you all again so soon after our last meeting." They were quite a sight, he thought, all clad in their ceremonial white robes, hair and beards neatly washed and combed, staves in hand. Bellicus had seen some of these people literally covered in faeces and filth, hair matted and twisted into bizarre shapes, eyes wild, teeth bared, calling down the fury of the gods before a battle. Bellicus had never been one for such theatrics, but he knew it was a valid way to work magic on both one's own army, and an enemy force. He was glad that the Moot did not call for such *earthy* magic.

"We're always happy to meet our peers," Diseta shouted, hands resting on his round belly. His face was flushed and it was clear he'd enjoyed quite a bit of the ale that had been brought across the river from Caer Legion. "But you've got us all worried, Merlin. What's prompted this second Moot?"

The rest of the druids nodded and murmured at the question. They'd been wondering the same thing, but no one — not even

278

Duro — could give them any hint about Bellicus's reasons for bringing them together once more.

"All shall be revealed," the High Druid called, bowing his shaved head slightly in Diseta's direction. "First, the sacrifice, as we ask for the gods' blessing on this Moot. Qunavo?"

The older druid came forward then, carrying a chicken which was surprisingly calm, ignorant of the fate it was about to meet.

"Lug the Light-Bringer!" Bellicus cried, lifting his arms just as the sun dipped behind the mighty oak tree that had been harvested for its mistletoe bounty at the previous meeting. "Cernunnos, the Horned One! Taranis, God of Thunder! Belenus, Maponos, Brigantia, Dis Pater, Sulis Minerva, and all the other gods that watch over us here in Britain every day — heed our call, and our sacrifice!"

Qunavo brought the chicken to the stone altar that had been erected atop the mound they stood upon and placed it down. It stared at Bellicus but did not struggle, perhaps because its feet had been bound and it sensed the futility in trying to escape.

"Bless this Moot," Bellicus called, lifting the stone knife that lay on the shrine next to the chicken. "And bless the decisions we make here this day."

With that, Qunavo took the chicken by the feet and held it upside down. It did struggle a little now but soon calmed again, disoriented by being placed in such a position. Using his right hand the older druid expertly rendered the bird unconscious so it would not suffer unduly, then he placed it on the altar and Bellicus removed its head using his stone knife. It was all over quickly and with as little fear or pain for the animal as possible — quite a contrast to the methods employed by certain *volur,* such as Yngvildr.

"Accept this offering," Bellicus said, throwing the chicken's head into the bonfire that was blazing on the grass beneath him. It was immediately consumed, the fumes mingling with those of the burning wood, rising into the sky in honour of the gods. Another druid took the body of the chicken to be de-feathered and prepared for the feast that would end the ceremony. There would be more sacrifices later, but this one was enough for now and Bellicus wanted to move on.

"Friends," he called out, spreading his arms wide to encompass everyone who was gathered there, even the guards like Bedwyr and Lancelot who were at the very back of the crowd, constantly alert for threats to their charges. "As you will have heard, Alt Clota was attacked by an army of Picts and Saxons."

Angry muttering at that. Not so much the fact Picts had attacked Dun Breatann for the tribes of Britain were always at one another's throats, and always had been. Drest's decision to hire Horsa and his sea-wolves as mercenaries was what caused such anger amongst the druids.

"You Picts should have known better than that, Qunavo," Diseta called up, standing on his tip-toes to try and see the white-bearded druid who remained silent, allowing the criticism to wash over him even when more in the crowd joined in to decry him. "Especially after the last Moot when we agreed the Saxons were a threat that must be dealt with."

Bellicus held up his left palm for silence and was pleased when it immediately had the desired effect. Being Merlin certainly had some privileges. "Qunavo has come to realise that the Saxons are, indeed, not the kind of allies the Picts need. Gods be praised, Queen Narina and our Damnonii warriors defeated the invaders and Horsa now hangs from the walls of Dun Breatann. He was killed in single combat by my friend, Centurion Duro."

That, predictably enough, brought cheers and an embarrassed frown from Duro. Bellicus smiled at his friend's discomfort and forged on.

"But, like I say, Qunavo has come to understand that the Saxons are, and always will be, our enemies. He is as committed as I am, now, to defeating Hengist's hordes and sending them back across the sea whence they came."

Qunavo nodded solemnly and a few of the druids including Koriosis cheered, for they knew the man and liked him, having studied under him as apprentices or simply come to know him during previous meetings over the decades.

"I called this Moot," Bellicus said, drawing all eyes to him again, "to remind you all of our earlier promise to face this threat head on. To utilise every resource, every wile, every weapon in our physical, magical and spiritual arsenals, to defeat Hengist."

Diseta and the others nodded but eyed one another uncertainly. Bellicus had surely not brought them all there, hundreds of miles in some cases, simply to repeat what had already been agreed? If so, it was an egregious misuse of the High Druid's powers and, as much as the members of the Order enjoyed a good feast and a ritual, they had important work to be doing in the homes they'd only recently returned to.

"Is that all?" Diseta asked in disbelief.

"No," Bellicus replied, shaking his head grimly before more unrest could spread through the mystics' ranks. "I told you all when you arrived that I would not keep you long — no drawn-out ceremonies, no days and nights of feasting. Well," he laughed and spread his hands once more, this time in the direction of the tables that had been setup near the shrine and laden with food. "Maybe one night of feasting."

He stared out at them, feeling terribly nervous for the first time as they all regarded him expectantly. Koriosis was in the middle of the crowd and his former apprentice met his gaze, smiling encouragingly. Then, with a quick look over his shoulder, Bellicus saw Duro and Cai and took strength from their presence. Drawing in a deep, calming breath through his nose, he let it out again through his mouth and stood up straight.

"My friends," he said, voice strong and unwavering, "I brought you here not to feast, nor simply to remind you of the dangers the Saxons pose...I brought you here to tell you I am giving up the title of Merlin. I will no longer serve as High Druid of Britain."

CHAPTER FORTY-SEVEN

For a moment there was silence, and then the Moot erupted as the druids cried out, demanding to know if this was a joke, what was going on, how could Bellicus renounce his title after such a short period in office, and did they need to hold another election already?

Bellicus had expected this reaction and he stood in silence, allowing his fellows to chatter and bicker amongst themselves, trying to make sense of what on earth was happening. All thoughts of feasting had evaporated as some fretted about what would happen to their Order now, and others, more ambitious, saw an opening, a chance to perhaps take the title of Merlin for themselves.

"By Dis, Bel, what are you doing?" Qunavo hissed, coming to stand directly behind him. "Are you trying to destroy us? We've only just elected you, and that was troublesome enough, remember?"

Bellicus turned to him with a small, regretful smile. "I remember," he admitted. "And I would not see a repeat of that, for it just creates tension and bad feeling among our ranks."

"Well, what then?" Qunavo asked, and Duro was there as well now, frowning.

"Why?" the centurion demanded. "I thought we would go to join Arthur together. To take the fight to Hengist like never before. By Mithras's balls, man, what are you doing?"

"Narina," Bellicus replied simply, and Duro took that in, finally nodding in understanding and even bestowing a smile on his friend.

"You would put a woman ahead of your duties as Merlin?" Qunavo asked, shocked. "I must admit, Bel, that I wouldn't have expected that from you. You were always one who fulfilled his duties to the gods, and to the people, with total commitment. Narina is a fine woman, but to give up this…" He gestured at the druids gathered beneath them. "I'm astonished. Could you not remain as Merlin and also be Narina's lover? If the rumours are to be believed you've been bedding her for years anyway." He shook his head, dumbfounded.

"The rumours are wild exaggerations," Bellicus snapped, but decided he did not need to explain the truth there and then, if ever. It did not matter. All that mattered at that moment was finding a suitable replacement to take over as Merlin.

Turning back to face the druids chattering and bickering below the shrine, Bellicus raised his staff in the air and bellowed, "Heed me, friends!"

As was usually the way when the giant warrior-druid gave such a command, people listened and instantly did as they were told. Even druids, trained to use their voices in such a way, were not immune to the effects of a command given by one as powerful as Bellicus, and the gathering fell silent almost immediately.

"I know this is a shock to you all," he said.

"That's an understatement," Diseta rumbled, bringing laughs and murmurs of agreement from those around him.

"I never sought to be Merlin," Bellicus went on. "I only accepted the position because I didn't want Qunavo to be given it. I knew he did not understand the threat the Saxons posed, and I feared being elected to such a lofty position would allow him to attack Alt Clota with more potency than ever before."

"So what's changed?" someone demanded. "Regardless of Qunavo's influence, the Saxons are still a threat. You said so yourself."

"Indeed they are," Bellicus agreed. "They are, in fact, even more of a threat to us, for as soon as Hengist hears about the death of Horsa, and the fact that I, personally, oversaw his execution, well...He already tried to wipe out our Order once. He will most assuredly seek to strike us again in future, and with even more ferocity."

"So why step down?" Diseta asked, more curious than angry now. "Being Merlin will allow you to guide Arthur. To face Hengist head on, no?"

"I don't think so," Bellicus replied. "I fear Hengist will first seek vengeance against Alt Clota — my people, for what we did to Horsa."

"Even though the ugly big prick deserved it," Duro growled behind him.

"I cannot simply abandon Queen Narina and the Damnonii people," Bellicus called, ignoring his friend. "They will need me

283

more than ever now, and I can't just leave them to fend for themselves while I live here in the south beside Arthur and his warriors. My duty has always been, first and foremost, to the people of Alt Clota."

"Then why did you not say all this before?" Diseta asked somewhat testily, and again others in the crowd shared his irritation.

Bellicus sighed and shook his head. "Honestly," he said, "I was proud that you, my friends, my peers, thought me worthy to be your High Druid. I felt it would be churlish to refuse the title. And, on top of that, I feared what Qunavo might do to Alt Clota if he became Merlin. I admit it," he said, "I probably acted selfishly, and it took me some time to realise that. Now, I wish to make things right, and see our Order led by someone who has the experience and skills to do a better job than I could."

His honesty had pacified Diseta and most of the others who'd been angry, and his open, apologetic smile went some way to win over the rest, especially when he added, "Maybe one day, when I've learned more and have more years as a druid under my belt I could be considered for the position of High Druid. It has been an honour. Now, though, our fallen brother Nemias must have a worthy successor, and that is why I called this Moot."

"Another election?" someone shouted resignedly. It was clear the druids had had their fill of posturing and self-aggrandising arguments at the previous meeting.

"I don't think we need bother with all that," Bellicus told them. "We already have the ideal candidate here," and, with that, he turned to Qunavo and drew him forward to stand beside him.

"You didn't want him to be High Druid before," Diseta observed. "What's changed now?"

"I never doubted his qualifications for the position," Bellicus said. "He has spent decades mentoring many of us, and is a seasoned war-druid, as I know from personal experience facing Pictish armies. He also has decades of learning in all our disciplines. Qunavo is one of our finest minds — a healer, a warrior, a politician, a seer, a bard, and a teacher."

"Aye, but he was all that before," Diseta cried. "And still you stood against him, arguing that he wasn't suitable to lead us."

"True," Bellicus conceded. "But I've spent time with him recently. I know he has seen for himself how dangerous the Saxons are, and, to his great credit, he helped the Damnonii defeat Horsa's men, even sacrificing his own king, Drest, and the Pictish army in the process. In short, my friends, Qunavo has shown beyond a doubt that he is the strong leader we need in these dark times. As the current serving High Druid, I recommend that you elect Qunavo as my replacement without further deliberation. You know he is the best candidate we have, and he should take over from me immediately."

Qunavo was staring at him in wonder, as was Duro. Neither man had expected this, although the light of understanding was growing in the centurion's eyes as he absorbed everything that was happening.

"Will you be Merlin?" Bellicus asked his former mentor with a smile. "I'm going to look a fool if you say no."

Qunavo nodded. "Of course. I hope I can prove worthy of your trust, and carry on the good work our friend Nemias started."

"And you *do* recognise the threat of Hengist now?"

Qunavo's nod this time was vigorous. "I do," he said. "Seeing that *volva's* handiwork was enough to show me the danger they pose to our way of life. We will face Hengist's invaders head-on, and, once we deal with them, we can turn our attention to the Christians who seek to steal our sacred groves along with our gods and goddesses."

There was an earnestness in Qunavo's tone convinced Bellicus, not that he really needed convincing, that his decision to give up the position of Merlin and pass it on to this man had been the right one. Now, it was up to the rest of the Moot to accept or deny Qunavo's candidacy.

"What say you, my brothers and sisters?" Bellicus cried, turning to address again the gathered members of their Order. "Will you elect Qunavo as your new High Druid?"

There was silence and the men and women in their white robes gazed at one another, pondering their options. At last, Koriosis called out, "Aye", and Diseta turned to him thoughtfully before he shook his head in amused resignation and added his own resounding, "Aye!"

Their acceptance was enough to inspire the rest and their "aye"s were immediately followed by dozens of similar, positive shouts.

Britain had a new Merlin.

Qunavo was beaming, accepting the approval of his peers with obvious joy. Bellicus wondered how he would get on living and working with Arthur. Hopefully he would do as well as Nemias.

"What will you do now?" Duro asked as the pair climbed down from the mound.

"Return home," Bellicus told him.

"To Narina."

Bellicus smiled. "Yes. Will you travel with me, old friend, or is your heart set on joining Arthur?"

They reached the ground and stopped beside the carved stone shrine to Sulis Minerva.

"I have no home any more," the centurion said with a tinge of sadness. "Not since Alatucca was murdered. Dun Breatann is as much a home to me as anywhere and, if you would lead us back there, Bel, I'll gladly travel with you."

Bellicus was so pleased that he actually reached out and embraced Duro, drawing him into a massive bear hug that left the centurion flushing with embarrassment, especially when Koriosis, Lancelot and Bedwyr appeared behind them, smirking at the show of affection.

"What's to become of me?" Koriosis asked, tugging at his goatee. "I'd been hoping to take your place in Alt Clota again, Bel, but now...? Back to Isca for me, I suppose."

Bellicus nodded slowly. "Sorry, my friend," he said, reaching out to pat the younger man on the shoulder apologetically. "I know you love Alt Clota but Isca needs a druid too. You'll soon make the place your own, I have no doubt of that. Just get those bees of yours producing honey and you'll win the folk over in no time." He smiled, shaking his head at the memory of the golden nectar that Koriosis had supplied them with in Dun Breatann before. "Delicious," he murmured.

"I'll try that," Koriosis agreed happily. "Not had a chance to set up any hives in Isca yet, but I'll get started when I return." His disappointment at not returning north to the Damnonii people was gone as he looked forward with positivity to life in the southwest. Isca might be on the far side of the island, away from the Saxons, but the Christian influence was growing there and Koriosis would do what he could to keep the Old Ways alive, Bellicus knew.

"We'd been looking forward to fighting alongside you again," Lancelot said to the big druid. "We've had some adventures together, and it would have been nice to continue them."

"You really think this Qunavo fellow will do a good job?" Bedwyr asked.

"I do," Bellicus said. "We've had our troubles with him in the past, but that was when he was on the side of the Picts, and we were in the Damnonii camp. Those rivalries, petty in comparison to what we'll face going forward, are no more, I think. Not for at least a generation anyway. No, I think Qunavo will be exactly what Arthur needs to fill the void left by Nemias's death."

"What's he like though?" Lancelot demanded. "I'm sure Duro told us he was an old prick."

"I had my reasons," Duro said a little defensively.

"We were enemies then," Bellicus reiterated. "I'm sure you'll find Qunavo a good companion."

"Just don't beat him at dice," Koriosis put in with a laugh. "He's a sore loser."

Qunavo himself came to join them then, a broad smile on his lined face. "Thank you Bel," he said, eyes dancing with joy. "I will do what I can to prove myself worthy to be Nemias's successor as Merlin. By the Gods, I swear it."

Bellicus nodded, truly hoping he'd made the right decision. "I wish you luck," he told his old mentor. "Britain needs a strong, fully committed High Druid."

Qunavo bowed his head and then held up his hands as he asked, "What will you do now, Bel?"

"We," Bellicus indicated Duro and Cai, "will return to Dun Breatann in the morning. We must prepare for possible retaliation from Hengist. I suggest you, and Arthur, should do the same. The *bretwalda's* fury will be like nothing we've seen from him before, I fear."

"I think you're right," Lancelot scowled. "Britain is in for a long, hard summer."

"What now then?" Bedwyr wondered.

"Now," said Bellicus, grinning and clapping Qunavo on the back. "We must formally introduce our new Merlin to the gods.

And then," he pointed towards the tables laden with food and the barrels of wine and ale sent over from Caer Legion. "Then we feast!"

CHAPTER FORTY-EIGHT

The journey back to Dun Breatann seemed to pass slower than any Bellicus had ever undertaken before. After Qunavo had been named, formally, as the new Merlin and all the rites and feasting was over, Bedwyr and Lancelot had said their farewells and began the ride back to Arthur's army. Then, after a last round of thanks and best wishes to Koriosis and the other members of his Order, Bellicus mounted up and led Duro towards the bustling docks in Twyni Tywod. Cistumucus was still there, of course, with the *Milwr Môr,* ready to sail north for home and it had not been long before the sleek vessel was ploughing through the waves.

At first it had felt like the ship was moving fast but, eventually, the seemingly unchanging coastline on their right began to wear on the druid's nerves and he'd forced himself to meditate, hoping that would make the time pass quicker.

"This is all about Narina, isn't it?" Duro asked him as they finally — finally! — saw the great rock of Dun Breatann looming in the distance and knew they would be home very soon.

Bellicus opened his eyes and noticed that not only was Duro staring at him, but so were Koriosis, and even Cai. He laughed gently, nodding. "Partially," he admitted.

"What about her?" Koriosis said innocently.

Bellicus side-eyed him suspiciously. There was no way a man trained by the druids could possibly have missed the gossip that had circulated around Alt Clota about Bellicus and Narina for years. He did not answer the younger man.

"Does she know?" Duro wondered.

"Know what?"

"That you were going to give up your title, and hand it over to Qunavo?"

"No. Being quite honest, I wasn't entirely sure I would do it myself," Bellicus said. "If the old man had been arrogant, or deceitful, or in any way unpleasant on our journey down to Caer Legion I might well have changed my mind about him. But, as you saw, he was accommodating and respectful and, well, I came to believe that he genuinely would make a good High Druid. Better than I could, since I'd always be pining for Dun Breatann instead of fully focusing on the work with Arthur."

"You really went all that way," Koriosis asked in disbelief, "without knowing what you were going to do until you got there?"

"You're a druid," Bellicus replied with a shrug. "You know it's always best to be guided by the gods. I had faith they would show me the best path by the time I came to stand upon the shrine to Sulis Minerva and address our brothers and sisters. And so they did."

Duro was chuckling and shaking his head. "By Mithras," he said. "There's never a dull moment with you, is there?"

"You must be joking," Bellicus huffed. "This whole voyage has been dull!"

"Thanks very much," Cistumucus called from the prow. "Next time I take you somewhere I'll be sure to hire some dancing girls and a few bards to entertain you, my lord."

"He's just pining for his lady," Duro sniggered, and Bellicus did not chide the centurion for the comment. The time for hiding his feelings for Narina was over, and a bright new dawn beckoned for the Damnonii people.

When the *Milwr Môr* arrived at Dun Breatann it was sunny and fine and, by the time the ship was tethered and being unloaded, a welcoming party was there to greet them.

Catia was first to reach Bellicus and she ran to Cai first, cuddling the big dog who licked her face and almost knocked her over so excited was he to be on firm ground once more. After that, the princess went to Bellicus and threw her arms around him, hugging him fiercely.

Narina followed her daughter at a more sedate pace but, when she came to the druid he drew her in and kissed her passionately on the lips, rather to the amazement of Duro, Cistumucus, and everyone else standing nearby. Even Narina seemed taken aback at first, resisting for just a moment before giving herself fully to the embrace.

"I missed you," the queen said when they finally drew apart and stood gazing into one another's eyes.

Around them, the sailors whistled and some even cheered. Bellicus was pleased to see the guard captain, Gavo, was one of those who was cheering. He knew the grizzled warrior had wanted

Bellicus and Narina to rule Alt Clota together for a while and, if their time had finally come the captain was obviously prepared to support them.

"Is that it?" Catia said, arms folded, eyeing the pair sternly, more like their parent than their child.

"No, of course not," Bellicus laughed, reaching into one of the pockets sewn into his brown, druid's cloak. Normally those little receptacles were used to store herbs, spices and other ingredients either for rituals, poultices, salves, or cooking, but today the druid pulled out a simple iron ring and held it out towards queen. "Will you be my wife, Narina?" he asked simply.

Catia clapped her hands together and she, along with everyone else, including Duro and Gavo, stood in silence, breaths held, as they waited for the answer.

"Of course," Narina replied at last and there were tears in her eyes as she allowed the druid to push the ring onto her finger before they kissed again.

"No wonder you were so desperate to get home, my lord," Cistumucus grinned, leaving the cargo he'd been unloading from his ship and coming to congratulate Bellicus.

"And you got us here in good time," the druid nodded, laughing. "Forgive me for being a terrible passenger."

Cistumucus waved his hand dismissively. "Fear not, lord, I've had much worse over the years." He bowed deeply then to Narina, saying, "May you be very happy together, my queen. I'm sure I speak for everyone when I say it'll be good to have the two of you watching over Alt Clota."

The ship's captain had served the Damnonii royal family for years so it was good to have his blessing, and that of everyone else who joined Cistumucus in offering their best wishes.

"Shall we...?" Bellicus asked, stretching out his hand towards the path that would take them through the gates of Dun Breatann.

Narina nodded and her face was positively radiant in the warm sunshine; Bellicus thought he had never seen her look so beautiful before. The queen hooked her arm through his and, at the other side, Catia took his other arm.

"Does this mean," the princess asked quietly, being careful to make sure only Bellicus and Narina could hear her, "that we can now live as a proper family?"

The druid felt a surge of joy swelling his heart that the girl had asked the question for, ever since he'd discovered that he was Catia's true father he'd wished desperately to let the world know, and treat her openly as his daughter. It was not his place to answer her question however, and he looked hopefully down at Narina. "Can we?" he asked.

The queen hesitated, smiling as they reached the fortress's outer gates and the guards bowed to them, welcoming Bellicus home.

Until now everyone, not just in Alt Clota, but everywhere in Britain, believed that Catia was the daughter of Narina and her former husband, Coroticus. Unfortunately, Coroticus had been unable to plant his seed in his wife's belly and, knowing Alt Clota needed an heir, Narina had gone to Bellicus during the Beltaine celebrations thirteen years ago. As part of the ceremony, Bellicus had downed ale laced with herbs such as henbane and been in a trance when Narina, identity concealed by a mask, had come to him. They had lain together, with Catia being the result of their union. Of course, Coroticus and the Damnonii people had never known about any of this although, now that Catia was growing taller and starting to look more like Bellicus with each passing month, rumours were spreading. Eventually it would be impossible to deny the girl's true heritage, especially now that Bellicus and Narina were betrothed.

"I've always felt it would be disrespectful to Coroticus's memory to make your parentage public," Narina told her daughter as they passed through the inner gates and began the climb up towards the central portion of Dun Breatann.

"It would be disrespectful to the people, Mother, to think they won't all know soon. I mean, just look at us."

Narina did turn and gaze from Bellicus to Catia, smiling lovingly at the obvious familial resemblance. "You have a point," she admitted. "All right. We'll not make any formal announcement that Bel is your father, but we shall live as a family going forward and, if anyone asks, we'll tell them the truth."

Catia shrieked with laughter and jumped up, grabbing the druid around the neck and almost making him fall back down the steps. Steadying himself, he laughed too and, behind them, Duro joined in although Gavo grumpily told them to be careful or they'd all end up with broken necks.

They reached the flat, middle part of the fortress and Duro jerked his chin towards the narrow house that had belonged to Bellicus for years. "I guess you won't be living there much longer," the centurion noted.

Bellicus's eyes lit up at the prospect of moving in with Narina and he nodded. "I suppose," he agreed. "But you can continue to reside there. You'll have the whole place to yourself."

"That's a shame," Duro said, shaking his head sadly, and Bellicus was touched, until his friend finished with, "I'll miss Cai being around the place," and everyone laughed.

The smiles did not fade as they reached the great hall and went inside to celebrate the travellers' return, and the betrothal of druid and queen.

Alt Clota's future looked bright and, as Bellicus sat gazing at his wife-to-be, friends around them, the best food and drink being brought out on heavily laden platters, the druid knew he had made the right choice. Maybe one day in the distant future he'd be Merlin again, and lead his fellow druids but, for now, he would sit beside Narina and guide the Damnonii people to, gods willing, years of peace and prosperity. He thought of Hengist then, and the threat posed by the vicious *bretwalda*, but now was not the time to think of Saxons. Now was a time to celebrate.

Before very long the hall had filled with well-wishers, eager to join in with the feast that had spontaneously begun. The atmosphere grew smoky and stuffy and Bellicus could see Cai wanted to go out for a while so, standing, the druid held out his hand to the queen. "Would you like to get some fresh air?" he asked.

"Of course," she agreed and the trio made their way outside.

The sun was beginning to set and they looked to the west, along the Clota, the sun's red light shimmering on the water as Cai wandered around the grass sniffing and marking his territory.

"I love you," Bellicus said to Narina, holding her close and resting his head on hers.

"I love you too, Bel," she murmured. "And, after all the years of uncertainty and wars, I believe we're now going to be very happy here in Alt Clota."

The druid's eyes were drawn upwards to a single, dark speck soaring overhead on majestic wings and, as Uchaf let out a croak that echoed around the rocky fortress, Bellicus smiled, content in the knowledge that the gods were truly watching over them all.

CHAPTER FORTY-NINE

The Saxon stared at his *bretwalda* warily, swallowing as Hengist, ashen-faced, turned his back and gazed into the flames of the fire that was warming broth on an iron tripod for the night's dinner.

"Are you certain?" Hengist asked, his voice little more than a whisper. "You escaped. Perhaps my brother did too."

The messenger swallowed again. Hengist was not known for his cruelty the way Horsa had been, but bad news could make any man lash out at those who brought the unwanted tidings. "I'm certain, my lord. I saw the jarl with my own eyes."

They were in the single surviving stone building within the old Roman fort at Garrianum. Once it had been used as offices for high-ranking clerks or perhaps to house some powerful legionary, but nowadays it served as a cosy mead hall for Hengist. The Saxon warlord's soldiers lived mostly in tents in Garrianum, blown this way and that in the winter winds, and drenched by the rains that hammered down upon them even in the summer. This stone building meant Hengist was able to live in comparative luxury, but he felt at times those long-departed Romans who'd once lived and worked there still lingered to haunt him.

Shivering, Hengist straightened his shoulders, turning to face the messenger whose cheek bore a long, poorly healed scar from the battle with the Damnonii that had, apparently, led to the death of the *bretwalda's* brother.

"You saw what, exactly?"

"The big druid"—

"Bellicus?"

"Aye, lord, Bellicus. He stood on top of the fortress walls and performed some druid's ritual. I do not speak the Briton's tongue so I know not what was said, but I know what I saw."

"Which was?" Hengist demanded impatiently.

"The big druid performed his ceremony, raising his arms to the sky and all of the things that mystics do, and then two men behind him threw…" The man licked his lips, hesitating before forging on, the words tumbling out in a torrent. "They threw Jarl Horsa's body over the wall. He was attached around the neck by a rope to a long piece of timber that came out from the top of the wall though, so he the body did not fall. It hung there, swinging back and forth."

Hengist's eyes blazed in the firelight as he pictured his young brother's fate. The tall, strong warrior, hanging lifelessly from a rope, spinning silently in the breeze rolling across from the river that flowed beside the Damnonii fortress.

"My brother did not move? He did not fight back, or try to stop his captors from tossing him over the wall?"

"No, my lord. He was already dead."

Hengist nodded, appeased somewhat by that news. Hanging was a horrible way to die — not a warrior's death at all. Knowing his brother had not suffered the indignity of slowly suffocating while his bowels emptied involuntarily was something at least.

"How did he die then?" the *bretwalda* asked, sitting down to take the weight from legs that had become shaky. "Do you know? Or were you too busy running away from the battle to see what had happened to him?"

The messenger bridled at that, finally finding his confidence now that his bravery had been called into question in front of everyone in the mead hall. "I ran because the battle was lost, *my lord*," he spat, hand falling to the handle of his axe that was stuck into his belt. "But, of all those who fled, I was the only one with the balls to return to the fortress, alone, hiding in the undergrowth to see what had become of your brother."

Hengist glared at him for a long, dangerous moment and it seemed like everyone in the hall was waiting for violence to erupt. At last, however, the warlord sighed and bowed his head, waving a hand for the warrior to continue his tale. It was as close to an apology as the man would get, but it was enough for there could only be one winner if it did come to a fight, Hengist being surrounded by his guards as he was.

"The battle was fierce, lord," said the messenger, and he sagged now with exhaustion. Someone handed him a cup filled with mead and he drank it down quickly before continuing. "We were heavily outnumbered, and half the Picts decided not to fight, instead choosing to stand by the river, weapons sheathed, while we and their kinsmen were slaughtered."

"What? Why?" Hengist was intrigued more than angered at that moment.

"I do not properly know," the warrior shrugged. "There was some friction between your brother and the Pictish princess. And Yngvildr, the *volva*. There had been some previous bad blood between them, I think. Needless to say, none of us knew the princess would hold back her warband before the battle started. Without them, we were sorely beset and there was no way we could defeat the Damnonii scum."

Hengist took in this information, finally understanding why Horsa and Drest had not managed to take Dun Breatann as expected. If the Pictish king had been betrayed by his own people — his own daughter! — no wonder the battle ended badly.

"Is this what you feared?" Hengist said, looking at a small man who was seated at the nearest bench.

"Exactly so, my lord." It was Jarl Sigarr, and he got to his feet now. "I warned Horsa repeatedly that his cruelty towards the Damnonii prisoners was turning some of the Picts against him. Eventually he grew so fed up with my warnings that he sent me back here."

Hengist nodded bitterly. "And you've been proved right, it seems." Shaking his head, he glowered at Sigarr. "You were supposed to be the clever one, cousin, that's why I sent you with Horsa! You were meant to advise him." He grunted and waved his hand dismissively, allowing Sigarr to sit down again. The wheezing jarl would always be a bit-part player in the conquest of Britain it seemed. "You did your best, I suppose, but my brother was never one to heed advice." He turned his attention to the messenger again. "Carry on. Tell me everything else that happened."

"As I say, we were sorely beset by the Damnonii warriors," the messenger said, colour returning to his cheeks now that the mead he'd downed had reached his belly and begun its restorative work. "So I could not see everything that was happening around me. But I saw Jarl Horsa calling on the druid, Bellicus, to fight him in single combat as the battle neared its end."

Hengist's eyes blazed. "Bellicus, again!" he hissed. "By Wotan, that bastard has been a thorn in my side for years now. It was he who killed my brother?"

"I think not," the messenger said, and recounted the little he'd seen of the fight between Horsa and Duro. "I did not see the killing blow," he admitted. "But I saw the centurion crowing in triumph, and the jarl lying dead on the grass at his feet."

"Gods, those two have caused me so much trouble," Hengist moaned, turning back to stare balefully into the fire. "First, they thwarted us when we took the Damnonii princess for sacrifice at the Hanging Stones, and then they played a part in Arthur's victory over us at Nant Beac, and now... Now they have butchered my kinsman, and left his body hanging for the crows to make a feast of." He kicked out at the tripod with its bubbling cauldron over the fire, striking one of the legs and knocking the whole lot over. Boiling hot broth spilled everywhere, some of it hitting a slave woman who screamed in pain and ran, sobbing, to hide in the corner.

No one paid her, the wrecked tripod, or the ruined food, any heed. All eyes were fixed on Hengist. Some watched him fearfully, wondering if his temper was spent or if he would do something else even more harmful. Others looked at him with curiosity for this kind of behaviour — unbridled rage — was unusual in the *bretwalda*. Horsa had been the mindless one who acted instinctively, where his brother was more thoughtful and calculating. If ever anyone doubted his love for Horsa — and there had been many over the years, for the brothers had very different temperaments and personalities — this show of naked emotion proved they were wrong.

"What will we do now?" the messenger asked. He'd taken a step back when Horsa lashed out at the tripod but he did not move closer again. It seemed prudent to everyone in the hall to keep their distance, for next time it might be something more than hot broth that struck them.

Hengist's fists were clenching and unclenching and when he turned back to face the messenger his face was scarlet with rage. "If it wasn't for that fucking druid and his Roman friend this island would already be ours! Thorbjorg!"

The *volva* appeared from the shadows, startling the messenger for it seemed as if she materialised from thin air. She walked across to stand directly beside the warlord, the only person in the mead hall, apparently, who was not afraid of him at that moment.

"Lord?" she asked lightly.

"You must curse those two Britons. Do you hear me? Curse them! Call down the fury of the gods so that their cocks swell and turn black, their skin festers with hideous boils, their limbs wither, and all around them suffer as I suffer now!" He stared at the wise-woman, almost pleading as he asked, "Can you do it?"

Thorbjorg thought about it for a moment. "I can," she said at last. "But it will need powerful magic."

"Sacrifice anything, or anyone you like, woman!" Hengist hissed, waving irritably towards the scalded slave woman still hiding in the corner of the room. "We have plenty like her you can make use of. Spill their blood, and call upon Tyr to blast the very flesh from the bones of those named Bellicus and Duro!"

Thorbjorg rolled her eyes. "The blood of such degenerates is worthless for a Working such as this," she told the *bretwalda* scornfully. "Powerful magic requires powerful blood to attract the attention of the gods. One such as Tyr demands more than the sacrifice of serving women."

Hengist glared at her impatiently. "Who, then? Whose blood would be suitable?"

Thorbjorg shrugged. "A powerful warrior."

"Then we must capture such a one," Hengist said, holding out his palms and looking at the woman for confirmation.

"Not just some fool from the next village you plunder, Hengist," she retorted. "It must be one of Arthur's own companions. Lancelot, perhaps."

Hengist frowned. How was he supposed to capture a man like Lancelot? The golden-haired warrior was renowned as the best swordsman in Britain. Still, he had been captured before, and even enslaved by the Jarl Leofdaeg. It *could* be done, if the gods were on the Saxons' side but…

"It does not have to be Lancelot," Thorbjorg said, to Hengist's great relief. "But it must be someone of high standing within Arthur's army. You demand a powerful curse be placed upon two of the Britons most potent warriors, Hengist — such a curse needs similarly potent blood to power it."

"Of course," Hengist muttered. "Nothing can ever be easy, eh? I wonder what kind of prisoners Bellicus sacrifices to his Damnonii gods."

"Weak ones!" Thorbjorg returned venomously, plainly annoyed by the *bretwalda's* tone. "That is why we have been able to cause his people so much bother in recent years. Maybe if they were to sacrifice someone of high standing"—

"Like Horsa?" Hengist growled dangerously.

"Aye, if they'd used him in such a way, rather than simply slaughtering him on the battlefield, perhaps their gods would have expelled us from this shit-heap of an island long ago."

The pair stared at one another for a long time as everyone else in the hall tried their best to remain completely still, terrified of drawing attention to themselves.

"Then let's be thankful they are too stupid to have done so," Hengist murmured, and there was an audible exhalation as the messenger and everyone else let out the breath they'd been holding in.

"So, er, my lord?" the messenger said softly. "What will you do now?"

Hengist's stony gaze turned back to him and his jaw was set firm as he nodded decisively. "Thorbjorg will work her magic using the sacrifice we deliver to her. But, just to make doubly sure that the druid and the Roman will not trouble us again..." He paused and squinted into the shadows, eyes scanning the benches and the warriors who occupied them until, finally, he saw the young man he wanted. "Saksnot!"

The slim warrior got to his feet and walked into the light cast by the fire. Some of the other men in the hall sneered at him, finding his beardless face amusing — what kind of warrior went about with their face shaved like a baby's arse? — but they were careful not to let him see them.

"Bretwalda?"

Hengist stared at the man, sizing him up, head bobbing up and down ever so slightly. In truth, Saksnot was unimpressive to look at, and not just for his hairless chin, but everyone there knew the warrior was as dangerous as any of those who'd sailed there to make war on the Britons.

"You are handy with that axe, eh, Saksnot?" Hengist asked, pointing at the wiry fighter's belt and the iron-headed weapon tucked into it. "And the sword you wear on the baldric there."

"I am, lord," Saksnot said with pride bordering on hubris.

Hengist was still nodding thoughtfully. "Aye, I've seen you fighting," he said. "I have a task for you."

Saksnot smiled. "Of course, lord," he murmured in an oddly soft voice. "Whatever I can do to help."

"You've heard everything we've been saying here today," Hengist said. "Do you remember the druid we've been talking about? Enormous man, taller than anyone that was at that Moot we attacked. Shaven head, big dog at his side."

Saksnot grimaced. "I remember him," he confirmed. "Hard man to forget."

"The Damnonii will be expecting me to attack them," Hengist said, look up to address everyone, not just the slight young warrior standing before him. "And, in all honesty, I would like nothing more than to sail to Dun Breatann to deal with this blood feud. To bring the whole place down about Bellicus's ears. Alas, we do not have the numbers, or the time, for such an undertaking."

Saksnot waited patiently to see where the warlord was going, although others in the hall began muttering, thinking Hengist would do nothing to avenge Horsa's death and subsequent disrespectful treatment.

"I will not waste valuable resources chasing across this flea-infested island," Hengist said, turning back to Saksnot. "It is a matter of family honour that my brother's killers are dealt with, but we have bigger plans for the coming months, as I mean to wipe out all of Arthur's pitiful forces. So…that is where you come in, Saksnot."

The warrior stood motionless, still waiting to be told what he was to do.

"You will make your way to Alt Clota," Hengist told him. "And there you will kill the druid, Bellicus, and his friend, Duro, the centurion. Can you do this for me?"

Saksnot was frowning, and no wonder. Even if he was able to somehow defeat the two enemies in combat — no easy feat — the logistics of getting to Alt Clota and remaining hidden there while he planned and executed his mission must have seemed incredible.

He had not reached his current high rank at such a young age by being hesitant, though. "I can do it," he vowed, with a certainty an older, wiser man would likely not have felt, given the magnitude of the task.

"Alone?" Hengist asked, pleased. "Or would you like to take a warband with you?"

Saksnot thought about it, then shook his head. "I'll go alone. It will be easier to hide — both myself, and my intentions."

"Do not fail me," Hengist warned him. "If you succeed, I will reward you well, and make you one of my senior jarls. But fail and, well…"

Saksnot's lip curled in a malevolent smile. "You can count on me, lord. I will go to Alt Clota and kill Bellicus and Duro," he vowed. "By Tyr, I swear it!"

TO BE CONTINUED

AUTHOR'S NOTE

It's been two years since I last published a Warrior Druid of Britain novel (*Wrath of the Picts*). I signed a deal with a publisher, Canelo, to write a trilogy about Alfred the Great and, rather naively on my part, I agreed to complete all three very quickly, without leaving myself space in between to write another novel about Bellicus. I thoroughly enjoyed the series starring Alfred and it was interesting to tackle a real hero and real events that quite a lot is known about, rather than making up characters and plotting pretty much whatever I want, but, of course, after two years, I had forgotten most of the Warrior Druid timeline. So, when I started this book there was a *lot* of revising, and just reminding myself what the hell had happened in the previous five instalments.

I remembered that I had always wanted Bellicus to eventually become the Merlin but I'd expected it to happen when he was a lot older. When I was trying to think of titles for this novel *The Vengeance of Merlin* popped into my head and I think it was at that point that I knew Bellicus should get that promotion which, of course, meant Nemias would have to die.

It's been interesting that some readers have emailed or messaged me over the years to say they thought it was a really intriguing idea I came up with to have Merlin be a title rather than a name. Of course, we have no way of knowing if this was the case, or if there ever was a *real* Merlin but, as with my Robin Hood stories, it's great to just let your imagination run free and create a living, breathing world that's populated by larger-than-life characters with grand titles. Robin Hood is most likely an amalgamation of a few different people so, I thought, why couldn't Merlin be as well? Julius Caesar tells us in his *Gallic War*, "All druids are under one head, whom they hold in the highest regard. On his death, if any one of the rest is of outstanding merit he succeeds to the vacant place; if several have equal claims, the druids usually decide the election by voting, though sometimes they actually fight it out."

Why shouldn't the elected High Druid be named Merlin?

That passage from Caesar is also interesting for me because I've had a couple of people (on Facebook, naturally) telling me that "the druids weren't warriors" and even demanding proof from me that they were. Well, such proof is out there, but the fact that druids elected their chief by fighting for it should give you some indication that they were not afraid of violence! Funnily enough, whenever I provide the Facebook experts with the proof that they demand I never hear from them again.

Speaking of Facebook, if you follow me on there you'll have noticed me posting photos of the two carrion crows and the jackdaw that come to my garden every day to be fed. My description of Uchaf in this book was based on that jackdaw because it has a malformed leg and gets pushed around by the other birds, so I've made an effort to befriend it and make sure it gets plenty to eat. Unfortunately, I'm not clever enough to teach it to speak, but there's plenty of YouTube videos out there showing corvids talking and acting with great intelligence so I think Uchaf is one of my more realistic characters. I was actually a steward at Dun Breatann (Dumbarton Castle) about twenty years ago and there was a raven that lived there – I remember it soaring over the peaks, croaking loudly, looking enormous compared to the other birds. Perhaps it was a descendant of Uchaf...

So, what next for Bellicus? Well, you'll hopefully be pleased to know that there will not be a long wait to find out as I expect to publish the next book in 2025. I've not planned it out yet, but the seeds have been planted at the end of this novel and I'm looking forward to finding out what Saksnot does, how Arthur and Qunavo deal with Hengist, and how Bel and Narina get along. I hope you are too.

If you're a fan of my Forest Lord winter stories you'll be happy to hear that I'm expecting to publish TWO this December (2024). I'll be writing a brand new one (tentatively titled *The Heretic of Haltemprice Priory*), but I'll probably pair it up on Kindle/paperback with *The Christmas Gift*, the tale I wrote last year and only made available to my email list subscribers. Value for money during the season of goodwill!

Thank you all for sticking with me while Bellicus was on hiatus. I really hope you enjoyed *The Vengeance of Merlin* – if you did, *please leave a review* on Amazon, Goodreads etc as it is a HUGE help and I really appreciate it!

See you soon!

Steven A. McKay,
Old Kilpatrick,
15/8/2024

ALSO BY STEVEN A. MCKAY &

ACKNOWLEDGEMENTS

The Forest Lord Series:
Wolf's Head
The Wolf and the Raven
Rise of the Wolf
Blood of the Wolf

Knight of the Cross*
Friar Tuck and the Christmas Devil*
The Prisoner*
The Escape*
The Abbey of Death*
Faces of Darkness*
Sworn To God
The House In The Marsh*
The Pedlar's Promise*
The Christmas Gift*
The Heretic of Haltemprice Priory*

The Warrior Druid of Britain Chronicles
The Druid
Song of the Centurion
The Northern Throne
The Bear of Britain
Over The Wall*
Wrath of the Picts

LUCIA – A Roman Slave's Tale

Alfred the Great trilogy

The Heathen Horde
Sword of the Saxons
King of Wessex

Titles marked * are spin-off novellas, novelettes, or short stories. All others are full length novels.

Acknowledgements

Huge thanks to my beta readers David Baird and Bernadette McDade.
Thanks also to my editor Richenda Todd, and cover designers More Visual.

Printed in Great Britain
by Amazon

48955203R00179